GW01237064

An Odyssey of Murder

AN ODYSSEY OF MURDER

Frank Binns

iUniverse, Inc.

New York Lincoln Shanghai

An Odyssey of Murder

All Rights Reserved © 2003 by Frank Binns

No part of this book may be reproduced or transmitted in any form or by any means, graphic, electronic, or mechanical, including photocopying, recording, taping, or by any information storage retrieval system, without the written permission of the publisher.

iUniverse, Inc.

For information address:
iUniverse, Inc.
2021 Pine Lake Road, Suite 100
Lincoln, NE 68512
www.iuniverse.com

Published in association with Diadem Books, Spean Bridge PH34 4EA UK
www.diadembooks.com

While the author has used real names and place names, the characters are purely imaginary.
This is a work of fiction.

ISBN: 0-595-27735-7

Printed in the United States of America

CONTENTS

▼

CHAPTER 1

▼

PROLOGUE: FRIDAY 5TH JULY.

The man was walking along the top of the moor—the North Yorkshire moors, to be precise. He had left his car in Middlesbrough near Ayrsome Park, the football ground, walked to the town centre, caught a bus to Broughton and enjoyed "a pint and a ploughman's" in the Jet Miners' Arms.

It was a long time since he had been in this area; boyhood days, climbing the Wainstones, walking up Scugdale and on to the Lyke Wake Walk, forty-four miles from Osmotherley, the village at the junction of the Cleveland and Black Hambleton hills, to Ravenscar on the coast above Whitby. Now every man and his dog was on that path; the path reputed to be the way that the Norsemen carried the dead, from the alien land which they had conquered and settled, back to the sea for their Viking burial.

In these days of hi-tech, people by and large didn't care about the past or any sort of history; but he thrived on it, all of it, French Revolution, Romans, the Protestant martyrs, the Reformation. For him all of it was 'grist to the mill.'

He thought of his wife and his two girls enjoying the beaches somewhere near Marseilles. It was an opportunity for her to be with her elder sister: they would have a lot to talk about, lazing in the sun, the girls enjoying the sea and the sand. He missed them, but he had missed them many times: project after project, to design, commission all points East and West. They were his recent memories, almost thirteen years without spectres of the mind: now they were all rushing back to him. He closed his mind to the earlier past, for he needed some relief from it and the guilt that was ever with him.

It was time to move. It was a stiff climb up to the top of the Wainstones, along Ravenscar, that wonderful tumble of rock, across the Helmsly Road on to Urrah moor, then a gradual climb up to the Viking path.

As he climbed music flooded into his mind, that wonderful introduction from the second to third movement of the fifth piano concerto. Beethoven, with his ear to the floor as he listened to the vibrations of his piano and that triumphal upward cadence of sound that thundered out. He felt like that Emperor, the one-time idol of the composer. Napoleon, the little man with the energy and brains of a hundred men! He remembered a time when he was in the local operatic society. They did the performance of *Bless the Bride,* the comic song of Thomas Trout.

> If I only did the things I thought of doing.
> What a lot to splendid things I should have done,
> Something big is always brewing,
> But it never sees the sun.

That was him to a 'T'! So many grand ideas, never carried through. Okay with the business but not on the education, not on the music; so many first in "Industry," yet never extending them as a commercial enterprise, all in the past! Too many women, too many traumas. He supposed if the truth were known, he was one of many.

But somehow he had the feeling in this desolate place he would pass the Rubicon! A point of no return; from there, onward, forever onward, no matter what the consequences to him and his family would be. With that thought he quickened his step and walked mile after mile, his mind numb, just wanting to be deeper and deeper into the moor, jumping over the peat bogs, the springy heather aiding him. His face wore a constant half-smile, waiting for whatever would be next. He felt twenty years younger.

Chapter 2

Friday 5th July. North Yorkshire Moors.

Jan was with her friends. She had booked in for the night at the B&B in Osmotherley. She met the others at the Queen Catherine Hotel and was drawn into a night of drinking with Maureen, who had successfully paired her off with this new guy Simon, a boring computer type who even had his laptop with him. "A copper working in computer crime," he had said. Sounded very fishy to her! He had a camper van parked up in Scugdale and they ended up in it. There had been a long explanation of how important his job was! She ended up in bed with him, groping, grappling, and her body distant from her. Half way through the night he grunted and flopped over and snored. Waking up from a fretful sleep and feeling cold, she gathered her clothes, opened the camper door and stepped outside; shivering and wincing in the cool summer air as she stood on the sharp stones. A punishment! She put on her jumper, jeans, and anorak. With her boots strung around her neck, she checked her purse and phone and tiptoed away from the camper. Halting only to put on her boots, she then trudged the narrow path leading up the dale. At the top the main path lay before her, a ribbon of grey cutting through the rich purple of the heather. Stopping for breath she gazed at the cold sun as it broke through across the moor, bathing it a golden tinge. The peat pools shimmered like silver. Time to phone, she thought: call the mobile of Bob and Alice, her special friends who were also staying at the B&B. Their phone was on 'message,' so she gave them her position at the start of the Lyke-Wake path top of Scugdale. She would dawdle on it so they could catch her up. The message was long and rambling, a plea for a bacon butty, and a flask of strong coffee, she needed the 'backfill'; and would they also bring her rucksack, which was still in her room?

The man had slept in his anorak, snug in a rocky cleft, deep in Urrah moor. He woke up feeling cold but refreshed. He splashed some water on his face: cold as ice from the little peat pool. He felt hungry, but he had nothing with him that was edible.

When he had arrived in Broughton and after his sojourn in the Jet Miners Inn, he walked across to the little hamlet of Kirkby. An old lady there had a B&B, and was renowned by walkers for her breakfast of bacon and eggs, herby sausages, and toasted crumpets. He rang the bell, no answer; he tried the door, it was not locked; the reservations book lay open on a small table in the hall. There was a vacancy, so he signed the book, found the room, dumped his rucksack, and with his phone, wallet and anorak, left the house. He had only intended to do an evening walk and then return to the house via the "Pub." Instead, he found himself tramping the moor, lost in thought, and eventually dossed down in a sheltered cleft, exhausted. When he came to, his watch told him it was seven o'clock. He thought of that wonderful breakfast being cooked and he used his mobile to ring the lady, Mrs. Allenby, to apologize. She was not annoyed but amused that he had preferred a cold and windy moor to a nice warm bed. Ruefully he agreed with her and asked her to put his unpacked rucksack in the outhouse for him to collect later. The price of the room was very reasonable and he told her he would leave the money in the outhouse, under a pile of empty egg trays.

But, that didn't settle his hunger. He thought what he might do. There was a farm at Chop Yat, on the road to Helmsley. He should be able to walk to it in an hour or so. They did ham and eggs all day! Then, having eaten, he could walk back on the road which led to Broughton, skirt round the bottom of Ravenscar cliffs and then down to Kirkby, collect his rucksack, pay the bill, and walk into Broughton. From there he would eat in the Jet Miners and eventually take the bus back to Middlesbrough.

Sounded good and who knows what might befall him? The excitement and tension was intense. As he walked, he brought the Rigoletto to mind. The music swelled in his brain: the court jester argued with the robber how much money was required to kill the Duke, his voice grim and sombre, whilst the Duke, in glorious voice, was seducing the robber's sister: and they finally tumbled into bed! It felt good to be alive! The music was ecstatic in his brain.

$$*\qquad*\qquad*\qquad*$$

Saturday 6th July

Bob and Alice had not been surprised by Jan's message. They knew how unreliable and messed-up she was: a disastrous marriage with a man who was moody and violent, just when she was picking up the threads of her career again. Finding herself established once more with the 'Mister' who dominated her profession. That was what it was like in Tees-side, Hartlepool, and Middlesbrough. Men dominated everything.

They quickly finished their breakfast and paid up. Bob, a gym instructor, picked up Jan's rucksack. He was over six foot tall, and Alice his wife, tiny in comparison, followed him. They set off from the official start of the walk after recording the date and time and signing the 'record book' kept at the Queen Catherine. They were seasoned walkers and made good time to the top of Scugdale, for Jan was their best friend and they made sure they had that pack of bacon sandwiches for her as well as a flask of coffee.

Jan had been walking for three hours. The track, initially broad, had dwindled to a narrow path. She had seen no signpost or any cairns during her tramp which would have assured her she was on right path. Only moor all around her: A glimpse of the 'early warning arrays' made her think she was in Glaisdale, in which case she was too far north. The moor was covered in mist, the path undulating and the heather quite high. Soon the path disappeared in the mist and she could see nothing. Her phone was almost out of battery, her fault since she had left it on all night! Better keep it for an emergency call; if she did not strike the path soon that would be her only recourse. She turned, and tried to walk in a south-easterly direction in an attempt to join the main path. After an hour, while still plodding the moor, she came to a rocky outcrop which dropped her down to a clear pool with a cave by the side of it. She had had felt 'dirty' for hours. The smell of sex and sweat; it had not left her body! Without more ado she ran down to the pool, stripped off her clothes, and gingerly put her feet in the water: it was freezing! Shivering, her teeth chattering, she splashed the water over her legs, opening them so she could wash in between; then the rest of her body, her breasts tingling and the nipples hardening to the cold water, then squatting to rinse her neck and her face. As she lifted her face to drain off the freezing water, she turned to look at the sky and suddenly saw a man sitting on the top of the outcrop looking at her.

The man was enjoying the moor. His stride was long and regular, the rhythm never breaking irrespective of the terrain. At one time in his youth, he and Barry used to walk together mile after mile, smoking their 'Peterson's'—a moist Irish tobacco, their favourite, the aroma sweet and cloying, and making them both feel content. Now the workings of his mind brought a new contentment.

When he was designing a new project, possibly a feed mill or a food plant, his wife would send him out for three days into Snowdonia. She knew by the time he came back it would be complete in his head, including the costs. He would then work on his computer to finalize the project, for submission to his client. There was his satisfaction, and he had always been successful with his bid.

He had a covered many miles. Soon he had should strike the road leading to ChopYat or Chop Gate, as it was now called. He was amazed, for however bleak the moor seemed to be, the road or a track could suddenly appear like magic. The Rigoletto had finished, and his mind wandered a different way, his thoughts frightening. It was always the same when he considered the past. He felt his penis hardening as his mind plunged deeper. Frightful—all concerning his punishment. Suddenly he heard the sound of splashing and, as he rounded the crest, he looked down from a rocky outcrop onto a girl who was naked and washing herself in a small pool. Quietly he sat down and watched her. She worked the water between her legs into her vagina, the dark pubic hair dank. Then on to her full breasts, massaging them with her fingers: the nipples hard and taught. "She must be frozen," he thought, and he eyed her dispassionately. Like many men he had a great regard for the naked female form, and there seemed to be no one with her. Maybe she had come by car. He knew they were not very far from the road

He was amazed at her hardiness, her stamina that allowed her to enjoy such a cold 'skinny dip.' He looked around and could see no one. His eyes traveled back to her; she had started to wash her face, her legs wide open and her breasts out-thrust.

At that moment she saw him! She gazed at him, nonplussed, as though seeing a dead body.

"Hello," he said. "That water must be very cold. You must be very hardy."

She didn't answer. She gazed at him, making no attempt to cover herself or move.

He felt uncomfortable. "Are you okay? Did you come for a bit of a bathe? Is your car parked by the road?"

With that she came to her senses. "Where is the road?"

"Oh, about two hundred yards that way," he said, pointing. "I was making for it, hoping to find some breakfast at Chop Yat, about five miles away. You can join me if you care to find your clothes!"

She still remained motionless.

Jokingly, he said, "Are you on the game? Is this your new patch? Are you hoping for a bit of business? Is it a case of American Express? That will do nicely."

She smiled, catching on. "My name is Jan," she said. "I have no car on the road, I don't want your business, but yes, I will join you for breakfast."

He smiled and moved to pick his way down through the rocks.

She turned back towards the cave, smiling to herself, wondering what he looked like without his clothes, especially if he were one of her 'patients' stretched, out waiting for her to commence her 'particular examination.' She pulled on her jeans and sweater. Noticing that her phone was on the ground, she picked it up and quickly pressed redial. No answer. She left a text message:

'Lost my way, met another walker on the moor, I am going with him to Chop Yat for breakfast.'

Possibly she could contact them there. For her, the walk was finished. She put her boots on and quickly laced them up, then went back to the pool, bending down to see in the reflection if her hair did not look as if she had been pulled through a hedge backwards! Suddenly she saw a bearded face behind her. Her head seemed to explode into a thousand pieces—then oblivion.

The man's gaze had turned to the girl as she scrambled down to the pool. He walked towards her, the music of Finlandia bursting in his head, "Let me out! Let me out!" He picked up a stone. It had a flat face and fitted comfortably into his hand, the back rounded to his palm. As he came up behind the girl he raised his arm, saw her reflection in the water and the quick flash of panic in those eyes; but the stone had already smashed into the top of her head and she collapsed in the water.

He sat there for five minutes watching the blood discolour the water, her hair flowing round it. She was unconscious and receiving no air. His mind was a vortex. He had done it! No meticulous planning, only careful control, no motive: he had not even touched the body. He had read somewhere that the killer always left something of himself on his victim. Since he had never taken off his gloves, he comforted himself that theory for him would be void.

As the life ebbed out of her, he looked at her and her position in the water. She was under the mouth of the cave, a difficult place to spot from the air, and you'd only stumble on her by accident, as there was no clear path. Perfect! He could see her mobile phone in the cave and her anorak, not that it mattered to him. Off to Chop Yat for that breakfast, he thought. As he left he heard her phone ringing, then it picked up with the message: even more perfect!

Bob and Alice had stopped, threw their sacks on the ground and stretched out. They were partially dozing when the phone rang. By the time Bob got to his rucksack it had stopped.

He read the text she had sent. "Trust Jan," he said, "only out of the sack a few hours, and in the middle of nowhere meets another bloke and goes off to breakfast with him in Chop Yat, of all places."

Alice woke up and laconically remarked: "Jan is one big reaction from Malcolm: you know how he tried to control her, destroy her career, her confidence. Her life at the moment is one big cry for help. And we are her only friends! Ring her back. Don't get annoyed with her since she has abandoned the walk and is with this man; find out where we can meet. Remember we are all booked in at the Ravenscar Hotel. Whenever we get there, maybe he would drive her over to us at Ravenscar."

Bob gave a silent clap to Alice's remarks. "You're definitely the best friend Jan could ever have."

He redialed the number: no reply, message service. He left a message asking her to contact them. He suggested she should drive over with her new friend to Ravenscar. Book in, and wait for them, as with all the delay it would be the early hours of Sunday morning before they got there.

"I assume," he remarked to Alice, "now that she has a new man we have to take 'Pot Luck' as to whether we see her again this weekend."

"Ça en fait rien," said Alice. "On y va."

The man stepped out strongly after leaving the outcrop: he was determined to think about nothing until he found the farmhouse and that breakfast. Then he would plan. He felt no remorse, in his mind; he could hear the bells of Moscow joyful ringing as Napoleon fled with his army, Tchaikovsky's *1812 Overture!* Such a triumphant sound.

As he walked, the clouds overhead began to grow darker and the downpour came suddenly. The storms that these moors were subjected to were notorious. Effectively this would keep the weekend walkers off the moor; perfect!

He arrived at Chop Yat soaked but happy. The farmhouse no longer did food. The sign had disappeared. As he wondered what to do the Helmsly bus came into the village. He saw people waiting at the stop and ran to it, just in time before the bus moved away. He paid to go to Rievaulx, knowing the old ruined Cistercian abbey was popular with tourists and walkers; no one would take any notice of him and he would have his breakfast after all.

Not many were in the cafeteria and he ordered his full breakfast: ham, eggs and thick Yorkshire herby sausages, with tomatoes, two rounds of fried bread and a pint mug of tea. This was the life, none of these continental breakfasts!

The rain was desultory as he gazed on the abbey ruins. There would be no drogues of people on the moors today. What to do? The safest course seemed to be to catch the next bus from Helmsley to Middlesbrough, and then walk back to his car. It would be pretty crowded in Middlesbrough, as the 'Boro' had a friendly home game. Then there was a matter of his rucksack; get off at Broughton, walk to Kirkby, collect his belongings, return to Broughton and bus back to Middlesbrough? No, that was keeping him too long in the area. The rain was heavier now. He could ring her and ask her to send his rucksack by the bus to the 'United parcels office' in Middlesbrough. Whether he collected it or not was not a problem, as there was nothing in it to identify him: The only regret for him was the book that he was reading, *Hitler, A study in Tyranny.* He would have to get another copy.

No sooner said than done. He rang the lady, using his mobile from the lee of the cafeteria, explaining he was drenched and abandoning his weekend. Yes, he would put the money for the room and the approximate cost of having his rucksack sent to Middlesbrough. He went back into the cafeteria, to the shop section, bought a letter card with pictures of the Abbey, stamps and a pack of envelopes, and sat in a quiet corner of the café. He addressed the envelope, put it in the letter card with a twenty and a ten pound note, sealed it, and slipped it into the letter box by the shop.

Mrs. Allenby at the B&B sighed and put down the phone. She was a widow of many years; all she had was this cottage and a little garden. She looked forward to weekends, and the company of younger folk, to be able to cook good breakfasts for them and the occasional afternoon teas.

'Nowt like the present,' she thought. She went upstairs to the cosy little bed-room: his rucksack was there, with a pair of shoes and socks on the floor. She put them all in the rucksack, closed the top with the cord clamp and secured the top flap straps. She took it downstairs, added a tie-on label which she had from the bus company for such purposes, and called Jimmy, the twelve year-old son of her next-door neighbour. She gave him the rucksack and an envelope containing a five-pound note to pay for the carriage. He would cycle down into Broughton and wait at the bus stop for the bus to arrive, and then give the Rucksack to the driver. She pressed a one-pound coin into his hand and said be sure to get there quick so the gentleman can collect his rucksack at the Middlesbrough bus station tonight. She was used to this procedure; many times, people were always leaving something that had to be sent on. Her trust had never been lost, and she was sure that the man who had booked the room would send her the money. Jimmy was off like a shot with his one-pound coin straight to the bus and then on to the sweet shop.

The man took the bus to Middlesbrough. It was the "X "service, limited stop only at Stokesley. Rievaulx was the exception, because of its tourist attraction. The journey was uneventful; rain spattered the windows of the bus and the moors looked desolate and dreary. He passed the spot where they had met the road as it came off the moor without a second glance; his instinct now was to survive and to go on to the next step. Possibly with some interaction! It was just after one o'clock when the bus pulled into Middlesbrough bus station

He walked quickly out of the station, through the town centre along the New-port Road towards Tees-Bridge. He then turned left for the stadium; the football crowds had preceded him, emptying the wastepaper baskets and throwing the lit-ter on the streets. His car was parked in a side street before the stadium. It seemed to be intact, no damage. He unlocked the car and climbed in, and drove off. Goodbye, Middlesbrough, goodbye, Cleveland.

He reflected that there were plenty more places where he had climbed in England, Scotland, Wales and Ireland. Who knows? The Rubicon could be very wide!

Elsie Graham was a thin energetic woman in her late fifties: she was a nice lady to her invalid husband and made sure he had anything he wanted. They had a live-in nurse who looked after him; the benefits of his private pension plan allowed her to take up a late career or, more accurately, a crusade!

Elsie was a traffic warden, known to all and sundry as the 'yellow terror of Middlesbrough.' Her conviction list and the fines accrued to the council put her in the running to be 'Freeman of the Borough,' if she but knew it! She had just turned into the street when the man drove past her. She had a quick glimpse of a bearded face. A nice face, was her thought. Among the litter on the street was the parking ticket, now torn and crumpled that she had left on his windscreen. Pity, if he had seen it, he could have had an on the spot fine which would have been cheaper than one issued by the court when a fine was not voluntarily paid. Not his fault, she thought, he had never been aware that he had a parking ticket: and now it would have to be processed by the court officer along with others, and the clerk would file it for prosecution. She would have to make sure that the filing clerk wrote down the registration number correctly, as it was an unusual number.

CHAPTER 3

▼

SATURDAY 6TH JULY. NORTH YORKSHIRE.

The man drove out of Middlesbrough and direct on to the A19 motorway to Thirsk. Now he needed 'destinations' and a new plan. Clothes were a problem, but he had an idea about that. He decided he would drive to Thirsk on the 'B' road towards Ripon: he would then pass through all the villages, looking for any parish hall or school that had a Saturday afternoon jumble sale.

The drive to Thirsk was uneventful. He passed the turning to Nostell Priory and then drove on to Osmotherley, then further on to Nether Silton; there was a glimpse of the Black Hambleton hills through the drizzle and eventually he drove into the market place at Thirsk. There was nothing to really interest him, so he took the road through the villages and found what he was looking for in Skipton upon Swale.

He had enjoyed the drive; all the places he passed had precious memories for him. He had with him a CD of the highlights of *Fidelio*. He loved the chorus of the prisoners who after years in prison were let out into the sunlight for a short time. The pure ecstasy and joy of the music was wonderful. His version also had the three overtures that Beethoven had rejected for his opera. He loved the *Leonora No. 3* immortalizing the goaler's daughter, friend of the prisoners, and in love with one of them—Fidelio. Pure ecstasy!

He parked his car away from the parish hall and walked back to it. The lady taking his money at the entrance smiled at him as she gave him his ticket. It was early, and there were not many people around. He went to the café counter and bought a cup of tea and a homemade buttered scone. Then he sat down listening to the hustle and bustle of ladies at the stalls as they sorted out the clothes. He looked around him, scanning the variety of goods on offer. Yes! All he wanted was here. On one stall he picked up a couple of polo shirts, three pairs of socks, a pair of shoes and a Blacks khaki anorak, together with a well-used Bergen rucksack. Paying for his purchases he made his way towards the exit. At the back of a hall he found another stall that had a nearly new pair of green cords, a new pair of jeans and a well-worn Harris Tweed jacket.

He went back to his car with his first purchases. Then he returned to the hall. There was a new lady on the door. Repaying his entrance fee he went in to buy the cords, the jeans and the jacket. Going to the toilet, which was empty, he took off his anorak and put the jacket on. Leaving the toilet, he found at the back of a hall a reserve rail complete with hangers. There he left his anorak and wandered back into the main part of the hall. There was a stall selling camping equipment and he bought a second-hand climbing rope, a sheath knife, a torch and some batteries and a set of billy cans complete with a thermos flask. He then left the hall. His transactions had taken under an hour. Driving his car out the village, he took the 'B' road, which would take him to Masham. A thirty-minute drive saw him parking his car in the village square at Masham. He knew the village well. He had been involved in automating some feed mills here; he had always stayed at a friendly and cosy B&B and enjoyed the restaurants the village had to offer, especially the cellar restaurant.

Sitting down in the cafe, by the cobbled square, he had the fish, chips and mushy peas, with a mug of tea; still as good as ever! This was his meal for the day. He intended to have other plans for the evening. Then he went shopping again. First to the men's shop where he bought himself some briefs, then to the chemist for the basic essentials, and lastly to the hardware shop where he bought a role of masking tape, rubber gloves, a pack of strong elastic bands, and a hank of quarter inch nylon cord. This was the rope that the traditional climbers used to make their waist lines. Five times round the waist and completed with a 'Bowline knot.' On the way back to the car he passed the children's shop, 'The Rabbit's Burrow,' where he had bought those beautiful hand-made dresses for the girls when they were small. Nostalgia and memories, it would not do.

The man then drove out of the village to Pately Bridge and took the road to Grassington; a few miles before Grassington he turned off down to Burnsall. This village he also knew, with its fond memories of their holiday here two years ago. He found some small one-bedroom apartments on the village green, which were available on a weekly let: There was no parking with them, so it was necessary to park in the public car park and pay your two pound fifty pence which was for a twenty-four hour period. This suited him ideally; he backed his car into the car park as soon as he arrived, paid the parking meter and then made his way up to the village shop. It had changed hands since his last time in the village; perfect!

They had the information relating to the apartments, and were the letting agents. There was a very small ground floor flat which did not have a view of the famous bridge; it was at the back, but at £120 a week it was a good buy. He paid cash and was given the key. He bought some provisions, plus the local papers for Skipton, Colne, and Bradford along with a couple of bottles of chilled white wine. 'Not intending to have his evening alone,' he turned to go back to his car.

The shopkeeper called after him. "We can trust you, there is no need to bring the key back when you leave! Just post it back through the letterbox of the flat. We have a master key."

Grinning, he said, "Thank you, have a nice evening."

He picked up all of his parcels from the car and then went to the flat laden. The first thing to do was to switch the water heater on, also the kettle, and make a cup of tea. While he was waiting for the tea he put away his purchases and the provisions. There were only two rooms: the small bedroom, and a lounge/kitchenette; very suitable for him. As soon as he had his tea, he sat down in the lounge and scanned the papers. He discarded the Bradford one immediately; too far, and too notorious. In the Colne paper he found just what he was looking for, a lady offering sauna and massage every day up to ten o'clock (Sundays not included). That was all right; it was Saturday. He left the flat and went to the public phone-box to telephone. Yes, she was available; she told him the address, where to park and gave directions from the parking to her home. Her standard charge was £40 but other arrangements could be discussed. All transactions were strictly cash. He checked his watch. It was just after 6:30 p.m., plenty of time as he had arranged for 8:30 up to 10:00 p.m., with a possible extension if the feelings were mutual. His emphasis was to relax from a heavy workload into oblivion; he wanted a passive part. With the transaction agreed, he rang off and went back to his flat. After a long shower, he liberally doused himself in deodorant and after-shave. The second-hand shirt and the cords, with the jacket, looked fairly presentable. Taking the correct amount of cash plus a substantial extra and with his two bottles of wine wrapped in newspaper; he left the flat, locked it, and then set off for Colne. The drive took him down to the Skipton Bypass, passing Bolton

Abbey, and then it was a short ride into Colne. He felt elated, and as he drove he reflected on how he was able to have this holiday of one whole month.

For nearly four years he had been a house-husband, looking after the kids, and in the last year and a half, putting in all the fixtures and fittings in their new house. This had saved a substantial amount of money, and it had kept him fit. People said he looked half his age. But not his soul! For years he had been living in frustration, since he had finished his last project. Now he was regaining his creativity. They had a live-in 'au pair.' He was okay for a month, maybe more, and, with the backlog of an early pension, which had been paid into his U.K. bank, plus the upgrading of his credit cards, there was no lack of cash. He also thought about the lady's last request—for his security, bring a small padlock and only key with him. That was okay. He had the very article in his car. They had used it to lock the toggle chain out of harm's way, when they hitched up the bike carrier to the car.

He switched on his radio for the early news. No mention of any happenings in the North Yorkshire area; perfect!

Mrs. Brown, the caretaker, had nearly finished cleaning up the parish hall at Skipton upon Swale. As she looked round, to check that everything was okay, she noticed that the rail at the back of the hall had a green anorak hanging from it. She recognized it as the same one her son had bought. At the time she had thought it was too much money for her son to pay out. After all, he was only an apprentice, a motor mechanic. Looking in the pockets, she found a couple of United bus tickets and also a foreign exchange currency slip. Euros to Pounds; quite a large sum. She put everything back in the side pocket, folded the anorak, and after putting a donation in the jumble sale box, for she was a very honest woman, she got up and made her way home. "This will be lovely for Joe," she thought. "Just what he wanted for his golf, and for his part-time game keeping on the estate!"

Elsie Graham sighed. It had been a very hard day with the football crowds and the cars that were illegally parked. 'Boro' had lost and the fans' anger had been vented on the cars. The cars had been hemmed in, all were illegally parked, and some were damaged, and fights had broken out. The police had arrived in force and a sort of order was restored. It had taken her a long time to write out the parking tickets. She was glad to get back to the office, record the dockets, and pass them on to the "court clerk" for further action. It was just after seven o'clock. She drove home and let herself in. Her husband was comfortable and the nurse had made a hot supper for them all. She felt very cosy and with her feet up in the armchair next to her husband; she sat back to watch the latest in the 'Dalzell and Pasco' detective series, which promised to be good. She liked Pasco very much: she thought he was 'a bit twee,' and his wife was a bit of a bitch, but 'Fat Andy was the bee's knees.' She could fantasize about him because they were both passionate in their work, strict upholders of the law, and he was a randy bastard to boot. It was something she didn't know anything about anymore, with her husband being an invalid for the past five years! Still! dreams cost nothing, and were private.

When the man arrived in Colne he parked in Tesco's car park, knowing that since the supermarket was open twenty-four hours, people were coming and going all the time. Indeed, he was looking forward to an after midnight breakfast. He went into the Supermarket, selected a box of Belgian chocolates, and with a fresh pack of *hors d'oeuvres* of different fillings, set off for his rendezvous.

The house was at the corner of the street. It was substantial, built in the twenties, with a small front garden. He had been told to go round the back, which bordered the playing fields, and pass through the wicket gate and enter by the back door which was fitted with a special lock. This could be opened with the correct number combination, and could be changed every day; it could be also "master locked" by a key. He had also been given the combination, which he keyed in. The tumblers clicked back and he opened the door, stepped inside and closed the door behind him. He lifted the handle and pulled it sharply down. This had the effect of disabling the combination and locking the door from the inside.

He looked around the room. It was cosy enough, soft chairs with a table that sported some magazines, not a girly one in sight, but some car magazines and some on fashion; clearly the lady had female customers as well as male ones. There was a small refrigerator. He looked in it and found some bottles of beer and also cans of soft drinks. He chose a beer, finding a glass on the shelf above and sat down to enjoy his drink, waiting to see what would happen next. Meanwhile he read through the *Formulae One Magazine*. He had been there about fifteen minutes and was resigned to a long wait when, suddenly, the door into the other part of the house opened and the lady came through. She appeared to be in her early thirties, was slim and pretty with dark hair and a very large bust. Her dress was a "Liberty's" print with a squarish neckline, and she wore black stockings and high heels.

"Good evening," she said. "I saw you arrive on my house TV. You're very prompt and I'm pleased to meet you. My name is Patricia. I have just said goodbye to my last customer. Now I'm all yours, until whatever time. I took a liking to you a soon as I saw you. Obviously though, business is business, and the price has to be right. Sit down and you can tell me your specific requirements." They sat down opposite each other.

He said: "I do not have any specific requirements. All I want to do is to relax in the company of a beautiful woman and take things as they come. I've had a very hard time over the past few weeks on various projects and this is my holiday. I want to make it good. I've brought the money that we agreed on, which I'll give you now; and also, I took the precaution of bringing something extra. We have to see how things go! I've also brought you some gifts, which are for our mutual benefit if you're agreeable? There are two bottles of wine, which were cold when I left my holiday flat; one is a Chablis and the other one a Macon Blanc. From the local supermarket I purchased some Belgian chocolates, Greek delicacies, and a pack of small savoury pastries which only need to be heated up, but not in the microwave."

"You're a man in a million," she smiled. "To do all this for me—so thank you very much. What I suggest is that you have your Sauna now. It's very hot. Go through that door. There's also a shower; go relax yourself. Your clothes and valuables can go in the closet, where you will find a dressing gown. You have your padlock, so you can lock it, and everything will be safe."

"Thank you," he said. "I shall enjoy that."

"Meanwhile I'll go back into the house, to have a bath, relax and put on something more comfortable. Just come through when you're ready."

"Wonderful," he said. "Please make sure the wine is chilled, especially the Chablis." He passed over the money for which she thanked him.

"Don't worry; I will have all the delicacies laid out ready for you, including me! We'll have plenty of time to enjoy each other. Please leave the sauna 'on' at a low setting when you've finished. We may want to use it together; later!"

With that she went upstairs. Within a minute or so he heard the sounds of a bath filling.

Saturday 6th July. 9.00 p.m. North Yorkshire Moors.

Bob and Alice were enjoying a pint in Goathland. They had made good time, having traversed Glaisdale moor, skirted Danby High Moor and now all they had to do was cross over the Whitby to Pickering road to be on the Fylingdale moor. The path would take them to the Flask Inn, on the Scarborough Road, and then it was downhill all the way to Ravenscar. They should be at the hotel between at 12:30 and 1:00 a.m. on Sunday morning. They had rung the hotel to tell them of their estimated time of arrival and also to inquire about Jan, whether she was there?

No, she wasn't there, and she hadn't rung. They could only assume she was with the man she had met and was having a good time. They would not know until Tuesday morning, when they all had to be back at work. Or more correctly, Alice would not know until Tuesday morning, since Jan and Alice worked in the same building and were colleagues, in a manner of speaking.

They finished their pints and picked up the rucksacks. Bob had previously packed Jan's rucksack into his own, they walked out into the evening air. It was only drizzling. The weather wasn't too bad, and even the sunset was trying to break through the mist. They felt sad, for the pleasure they would have by finishing the walk was marred by the fact that Jan wasn't there. She had been a good friend to them. They had encountered a lot of problems over the past two years and she had been there to help them despite her own difficulties. Alice and Jan had become almost like sisters together. The champagne that would be waiting at the Ravenscar Hotel would not be the same without Jan there to help them drink it!

Mrs. Allenby rang Middlesbrough bus station just before it closed at 10:00 p.m. Yes, the rucksack and arrived safely, but no one had collected it. She felt a little worried, wondering whether she had misheard the instructions, but contented herself that she would ring again in the morning.

Elsie Graham stretched and yawned. She'd enjoyed the Dalzell and Pasco, but now she looked forward to an early bed, and thought of the pleasure of one week without parking tickets, dockets, cars, and irate motorists, for she was on holiday. What bliss!

Mrs. Brown, Amy to her friends, was sitting in the pub parlour having a drink with her husband. He was wearing his nearly new green anorak and was very proud of it; so much so, in fact, that he bought his wife a large malt whisky to say thank you. Not that she really liked whisky, but she sipped at it before giving it back to her husband. In the end he had to drink it; all according to his plan!

CHAPTER 4

▼

SATURDAY 6TH JULY. COLNE.

After Patricia had disappeared upstairs, Michael, as he called himself, went to the closet. He opened the door and looked inside. Yes, there was a dressing gown in dark blue paisley: together with a black thong pouch! Very provocative, he thought.

He divested himself of his clothes and took the dressing gown without the thong thing. He put his clothes on the hanger. In the closet there was a waterproof bag into which he could put his valuables. He picked up the bag and the thonged pouch, closed the door and padlocked it; adding the key to the other keys on his ring; he put it all into his bag, then walked through to the sauna.

It was made for two persons, out of real Finnish pine. The light was on inside and the temperature gauge, which was colour coded, was well into the red. The shower and the washbasin were on the opposite side, all very new: the shower was big with double swing doors, certainly good for two people. The room was tiled with mosaics in the rich colours of Provence. The burnt orange and mellow yellows combined with faded Sienna purples and blues, giving welcoming warmth to the room. The towels, stacked in abundance, soft and fluffy, reflected the colours of the tiles. The ambience was scintillating, designed for relaxation. She definitely must be a very artistic person to provide this tapestry of colour, he thought, and wondered what the other rooms were like? It was some classy place!

He hung up his dressing gown with his thong and went into the shower. It was thermostatic, set for comfort: the jet was powerful and he felt a tingling of his body. Not bad, his body! Not an ounce of fat anywhere.

He turned off the shower and stepped out. With one large towel he rubbed himself briskly and then made his way directly to the Sauna. The first ten minutes he just sat there, getting used to the heat and feeling his heartbeat quicken, his pores opening and the sweat pouring out. After a further five minutes he got up, went outside and toweled himself briskly. Then, with an armful of towels, he went back into the sauna, laid them on the bench, padded the backrest and stretched out to think.

For ten minutes or so he dozed. On waking, he found that his mind had cleared. What to do? He wondered when they would discover anything in Cleveland. Could be any time after today! He thought he might have one more escapade before the balloon went up, for he knew he would have to carry on. He felt pragmatic about the whole thing. He realized he could be caught. What would it do to his wife and the girls? Maybe he could kill himself before they had any real evidence. He had faced up to death on two separate occasions: each time he had only felt resignation, not panic.

But if he were caught! Would he be able to stand prison? What if he were put with pedophiles, rapists, or someone like the 'Black Panther,' if he was still in prison? He was a sadist. What if he were found to be mad! Could he live with Sutcliffe and the like in Broadmoor? He shuddered at that: if he wasn't mad he would be 'round the twist' in no time at all. What was it that psychologists had written about? Picking up the pieces of the mind! Well, there would certainly be a lot of pieces in his jigsaw mind. Good thing, he thought, that he had always been a realist. He sat back and relaxed, contemplating!

Now he must make his next set of plans: there were quite a few areas open to him in this part of the country.

The first was Buckden Pike, popular with walkers and campers, with some out of the way campsites.

The second was Malham and Goredale Scar, always very popular with hikers and campers, the water rushing down from the tarn over the rocks and over the base of the scar; plenty of background noise. The tents here were scattered over a wide area. It was not far to take 'carry outs' from a local pub back to the campsite. There were always plenty of parties going on, lots of activities. Thus, the people who wanted to sleep remained quite isolated, pitching their tents far away from the popular areas.

The third was Ingleton and the area surrounding Ingleborough. Many cave entrances and potholes, including Gaping Gill, Disappointment Pot and, further across, near Horton in Ribblesdale, Alum Pot, which was like a giant ice-cream cone: sunk into the ground but 290 feet deep, very exposed. He turned it over in his mind. Tomorrow he would drive to Buckden, enjoy the walk over the escarpment and spend the evening in Burnsall. It seemed he would be in Malham on Monday, especially in the evening.

He got up and went out of the sauna and into the shower. Looking at the clock on the wall, he saw it was ten minutes past ten; not quite the witching hour but time to go to Patricia!

After showering, he dried himself, applying liberally the aftershave she had provided, slipped on the thronged pouch, tucked himself in, put on the dressing gown, conservatively tying it round himself. Then he turned down the Sauna heating control, doused the lights and with his waterproof bag went into the lounge.

The lounge was different: scarlet flock paper, deep red Chesterfield, and a low coffee table in polished walnut. One wall was a complete bookcase unit with shelves and cupboards, and a section for a built-in television, hi-fi, video and DVD recorder. The lighting was indirect and the warm glow filled the room. He sat down on the Chesterfield very primly, knees together. The coffee table was set with glasses, plates and small rosewood-handled bronze knives and forks. She also had the forethought to have made a cafetiere of coffee—the insulated type; the cream jug and sugar bowl were next to it. He pushed the plunger down gently on the cafetiere and then poured the coffee into his cup, adding a little cream. The aroma was warm and pungent. He sipped it appreciatively. The music was playing in the background: 'comfort hearing'—he recognized it: Mozart, Piano Concerto No. 21 in C major. It was a 'Geza Anda' recording that was playing, made famous because of the poignancy of the slow movement and used in a Swedish film called *Elvira Madigan*. The girl was a child in love, her body dying; to this music she danced across a narrow plank bridge, which spanned a stream, to please her first and only boyfriend, the most romantic part of the film.

He smelt her perfume before he was aware she had been in the room. He recognized it! His wife's perfume; the last time he had bought it was in the departure lounge of the airport in Bolivia, Santa Cruz, right by the Chilean border. Patricia entered the room bearing a tray of the hot savouries, then went back into the kitchen bringing in the Greek platter, the bowl of Tacos and the Guacamole dip. One more trip for the wine. He felt the bottles, ice-cold; perfect. She stood looking at him, his beard and hair wild from the shower. Bending over, she smoothed down his hair and stroked his beard. With the remote control she brightened the room and stood back. She was all in red! Stockings, high heeled slippers, red lace waspie with matching briefs, half-cup bra, and a shortie negligee tied with a red ribbon but only at the waist. Her nipples were 'rouged' a cherry red, and her breast burst out of her bra. The perfume was 'heady' and she expressed pleasure that he recognized such a rare perfume.

He moved along to make room for her, or so he thought, but she had returned to the kitchen. He reached out for one of the bottles, a 'Macon Blanc,' good to drink with the savouries and keep the Chablis to drink 'tout seul.' Taking the bottle back to the small kitchen, which was absolutely immaculate, he found she was on her hands and knees using a small hand-held dust-bug to take up flecks of pastry in front of the oven. She looked so incongruous, nearly naked, looking very sexy, 'housekeeping!'

"Excuse me," he said. "I'll put the Chablis back in the fridge; that will be our drink for when we have finished eating."

Smiling at him, she got up and put her dust-bug back on its stand so it kept its charge; then she took his hand and led him back to the lounge, making sure all the lights were switched off and the door closed.

She pushed him onto the Chesterfield and commanded him to pour the wine and begin eating. Crossing over to the hi-fi, she bent over to select a CD, looking very provocative, her legs shapely with the back suspenders under great strain.

"You want to do be seduced," she murmured. "I'm going to put on some music which will blow your head off. It's on repeat so watch out; can you guess what it is?"

Smiling at him she sat beside him, straight and prim with her knees together. The music commenced very quietly, a gondola creeping into a hidden tunnel in the heart of Venice; he could hear the waves splashing against the side and then that demonic laugh as the music beckoned the occupant into the secret chamber. It was the Barcarole from the 'Tales of Hoffman,' an opera full of passion and intrigue. The courtesan Guilietta has been paid by the Doge of Venice to lure Hoffman the writer into this place of love, and then poison him. In her ecstasy and in the midst of passion, creating an aurora of love, she takes the poison herself and expires in a death full of pain. Hoffman is devastated; wherever will he find a true love? The music is full of pathos and remorse as he mourns the beautiful Guilietta. Definitely the singing of Pavarotti and Sutherland.

She came and sat down beside him, then leaned over him and kissed him long and hard. The perfume and aftershave fused together, making the air 'heady.' She loosened the ribbon of her negligee and pulled on the cord of his dressing gown. He felt her breasts pushing into him and he 'stirred' in his pouch.

He playfully pushed her away: "Enough, madwoman, eat drink and be merry, for tomorrow we die!"

She kissed him again and then sat up straight and tried to be prim, not very successful in her state of 'dishabille.' Together they made a toast.

"To you, Michael," she whispered.

He intoned: "Lang may your lum reek."

Being a northerner, she understood! She turned the music back, to Act two, where Hoffman falls in love with a beautiful dancing mechanical doll; her inventor poses as a father and the doll as his daughter. The father has a party for his new creation and no one realizes she is only a doll; the music is that of love and expectancy, and Hoffman is besotted by her beauty. The 'tone' was set for the evening! Contentedly they ate and drank. The savouries were delicious, salmon, prawns, pate-de-foi-gras, plus the Greek feta and the dips. Their talk had to be between mouthfuls; he was not curious and did not ask any glib questions. His praise for the house was enthusiastic; he reiterated that he was on holiday for an indefinite period. The only comment he made was his concern for such a pretty well set-up lady letting men into her house.

"Don't worry, I have set customers. Some of my best are policemen, quite high up. They look after me."

"How did that come about?" he asked.

"Well," she said, "after my husband left me and the divorce went through, I wanted to move out of Leeds to somewhere completely different. Colne suited me and the Dales are magnificent. I bought this house already beautifully decorated and completed, including all the built-in furniture. I added the sauna room; at first for my own use, and if I met a nice man, for him too. Other than the policemen, who only wanted relief, I had met no one at that time. So I decided to set up a business, hairdressing etcetera; boring, so why not a private health club? The sauna and massage with the one advert per week came later." She smiled. "This is the funny bit. I applied for a local government grant for setting up a business. The application was accepted and I went on a business course, which was compulsory for one week. It was held in the local workingmen's club. We had a good free lunch every day. Everyone was friendly. There were ten of us plus the instructor; four of the ten were women. They were fascinated I could be so naive, or so they thought! All nine of them are my friends and come for occasional sauna parties when they can get away from their husbands, or wives. It's all very innocent.

"The instructor put me in touch with a bank, and I had an interview with the bank manager. He came here! He arranged it all, and my £1,000 was safely tucked away in his bank with an overdraft facility also. I was very grateful to him and showed it in the best way I could. He went away groggy! All his middle-class virtues had been swept away; a whole new world opened to him. I see him discreetly about once every two or three months. A letter comes from the bank reading something like this…"

She closed her eyes and quoted from memory:

"Dear Madame; It would be to your advantage if you were to telephone the manager for an appointment to discuss your investments etc'."

She laughed. "I am always the last customer. Sometimes on a Saturday, midday, other times an evening meeting, just after the staff has left; the champagne is chilled and the outcome is very successful as far as he is concerned. But, one thing he did for me for which I am truly grateful; he knew someone on the police committee. I was requested to meet 'the committee member.' He actually was quite high up. This was also at the Bank, and again this man quite willingly ditched his principles. I was assured that I would be well looked after! Hence my policemen friends."

"Fascinating!" he exclaimed, amazed at her 'aplomb.'

She lifted him up by one earlobe and said commandingly, "Two minutes to clear away, then we fly!"

Together they cleared everything into the dishwasher and the 'fridge. The inevitable dust-bug came out to tidy up the lounge and at last they settled back into the Chesterfield with the ice cold Chablis, a glass in each hand.

"Don't forget, after this we have the champagne for 'special actions,' courtesy of the Bank," purred Patricia.

She went to the hi-fi and put on the Max Bruch violin concerto—so incredibly romantic! He was astounded at her taste.

For some time they were immersed in the music. He put his arm round her and she snuggled into him as they sipped their Chablis.

"Oh, Michael" she said, "you're wonderful: sexy, brains and culture: how many women have you had? How many hearts have you broken?"

He didn't answer. The memories were painful and the sins of his life were ever in front of him. Instead, he poured two more glasses of the Chablis and as they drank, they listened, enthralled as the violin blended in perfect harmony with the orchestra. His life was of joy, of pathos, of hate, and of love. Whatever he wanted to make it!

She got up pulled off her negligee: freed her breasts from her bra, and stripping off her panties. She then pulled him up and tore off his dressing gown; quickly, she slipped into the kitchen and came back with the champagne and glasses. She gave him the champagne and while he struggled with the cork she stripped him of his pouch and took hold of his penis with one hand and with the other began to tease his balls! The cork went pop!

"Quickly!" she gasped. "Pour two glasses."

He did so with difficulty as his penis was still imprisoned. With his free hand he handed a glass to her. She took her hand off his penis to take the bubbly, her other hand still imprisoning his balls. He took a long drink of the champagne.

"Quickly, quickly, fill it up!"

She took another long drink and held it in her mouth; then, lowering her head, she took his penis into her mouth. The sensation was ecstatic: the coldness of the champagne as she pumped it round the head with her tongue. She withdrew, and with his penis as hard as iron, she took hold of it, and led him towards the stairs, carrying the Champagne in her other hand. With difficulty they got up the stairs, then into the bedroom. The lighting was soft; the bedroom felt warm and the music was with them too.

"Oh Michael!" she said, "stay with me: have your holiday with me, and then let's take it from there. I can shut up shop: we can go to Spain, Portugal, or Italy. We can use some of the bank manager's money!"

At that moment she did not want an answer. She pushed him onto the bed, forced the champagne bottle to his lips and the froth poured over his face and upper body. She giggled and rubbed it into him, kissing him and forcing her tongue into his mouth. Then, drawing back and drinking from the bottle, she let the froth spill over her, rubbing her breasts with it, then pouring some into the cup of her hand. Opening her legs, she rubbed it into her vagina and into her chestnut brown pubic hair: laughing all the time, and then falling down on top of him, her vagina against his mouth. He caressed her with his tongue and suddenly she exploded, her body arched and trembling, followed by convulsion after convulsion as she went through her climax.

Once more she took him into her mouth and tantalized him, all the time stroking his balls and pulling back the glans. He could feel himself coming and tried to pull away. She resisted him until he was completely spent. He lay back as she went downstairs for a second bottle and some glasses. He just lay there drinking. She kept kissing him and rubbing her breasts all over his body, and there was an unspoken bond that they would not make love. It was too early; this mutual self-satisfaction they had found was enough.

They lay there, arms entwined. "Michael, Michael," she murmured. "You are an angel come to protect me."

With that she dropped off to sleep, dead drunk. He tried to wake her but it was impossible! She was out completely!

He lay there thinking: what had he let himself into! Was she 'entertaining an angel unawares'? Or, vice versa, was it a case of 'beware of the Greeks bearing gifts'? His course was set; he could not entertain happiness again, and as for love, that would flow like a torrent, that would only be putting off the evil day. He must work out his punishment! This lady was too good for him, and too good for this world.

He left her and went downstairs. Rummaging in the kitchen he found rubber gloves, the kitchen spray and a cloth. He went round every surface which he had touched and wiped it clean. Conscientiously he did the same in the sauna after switching it off, and then wiped clean the shower. He found his carrier bag and put the *Formula One* magazine in it. He took the towels, his bathrobe, the pouch, her negligee, and put them all in the washing machine and switched it on. Similarly with the glasses and the bottles; he put all in the dishwasher and pressed the 'start' button. He gathered the wrappings of the savouries and the platter and put them into the carrier bag.

He went back upstairs to the bedroom, still with his rubber gloves on. She was sleeping so peacefully. He took the pillow that would have been his under different circumstances, and gently placed it over her face. Gradually the aroma of her 'Bal de Versailles' was merged with another aroma as the sphincter opened. Gently and peacefully the life drained out of her. Better than Guilietta who took the poison by mistake and died a tortuous death as Hoffmann looked on. Taking the pillow away from her, he went into the bathroom. He came back with a hot soapy sponge and wiped her lips, then her body and between her legs. Having done this, he went back to the bathroom, rinsed the sponge and left everything in place.

Back in the bedroom he pulled the coverlet over her and left her, switching off the lights. He went back to the lounge, checked the answer phone and wiped it clean of all messages. The Belgian chocolates were on a shelf by the hi-fi; he ran his gloved hand over the box; it should be okay.

That seemed to be all. He could not find the money he had given her; he had to take a chance on that. At least he had been careful when handling it. Closing all the doors, he went upstairs and opened the curtains; the same in the lounge. Then with his waterproof bag and the key in his hand he went to the closet, took out his clothes and put them on. Afterwards he wiped everything with his gloves.

He then left the house by the back door, wiping the handles again with his rubber gloves.

Discarding the gloves, he put them in the carrier bag. There was no one around, no movement of any description, and no lights from the surrounding houses. Taking the path through the field, he made his way towards the town. He found a 'ginnel' which took him into the street. Across the road he saw the lights of the supermarket; that was for him, and he put his carrier bag in the first of the skips he came to.

Pausing for a moment, he felt a sadness welling up inside him: he had lost a good friend, a lady who would have given him a lot of pleasure, as he felt sure he would have given her a lot of love and pleasure also. But, that was life, or not life, as the case may be!

Now he was hungry. Breakfast awaited! He was still in the Rubicon. It was certainly very wide.

CHAPTER 5

▼

SUNDAY 7TH JULY. NORTH YORKSHIRE MOORS.

Bob and Alice arrived at the Ravenscar Hotel at 1:30 in the morning after an eighteen hour 'plus a little extra' crossing.

They were the only team making the walk that weekend, and many of the guests who were also enjoying the moors and the sea had stayed up to welcome them. The proprietor and his wife gave them big hugs, and then led them into a champagne reception and a hot meal. It was a walker's dream; a good north country mixed Grill with homemade chips. The people running the hotel knew full well the calibre of walkers for fried foods. After the meal they received their medals and certificates with a commendation for such a fast time.

But, this enjoyment was marred because Jan was not there. They had tried her mobile, her flat, her place of work on the off chance there had been an emergency; but nothing, and nobody had seen or heard from her.

"He must be an outstanding chap to sweep her off her feet like this," Bob remarked to Alice.

Alice deliberated in her reply. "Jan is a professional, a perfectionist. A stickler for discipline; she is so precise in her work. We know she is under strain, but all of this behaviour is foreign to her. I'm beginning to think the worst, possibly an accident of some description."

Bob was nonplussed: he had every respect and love for Alice; he knew how clever and perspicacious she was. Sometimes he wondered how she had ever come to marry him. He was always bluff and hearty, fitness and sport was his profession and life for him was not complicated. Alice and Jan were the 'opposite sides of the coin,' living with crises, many times heart rending traumas, and tragedy.

"Come on, love." Bob grasped her in a bear hug, lifting her off her feet. "Let's take our bottle of bubbly with us and toddle off to bed. We've earned that luxury, and the kisses and cuddles. There's nothing we can do tonight; tomorrow after breakfast my sister and our kids will be here: we have to give them a good two days before they drive us back home."

"Bob, you have the right words and strength to carry a weary girl up to that bed; lead on, McDuff!"

Colne

Michael the man walked across to the supermarket entrance. As he was crossing the feeder road alongside the entrance, the doors opened and two policemen walked out, escorting an unwilling old man. One of the coppers was carrying a couple of bottles of whisky in his hand; they gave him a quick glance, and then walked on with their prisoner.

He went inside; it was quiet but fairly busy. Many people, travelling on holiday, were in for their early-morning shopping before they reached their holiday homes. At the in-store cafeteria the staff were laying out all the fresh cooked foods, eggs, bacon, herby sausages, hash browns, and fried bread with toast. He ordered a full house with extra bacon, hash browns and the fresh fried tatty scones with the inevitable pot of tea. They joked about his appetite: everyone was very friendly; they wanted to know if he were on holiday? Did he have a family? Where were they? He answered all their questions but declined the offer of an escort since they were all over fifty. They thought he looked a bit down and assumed he was missing his family, whereas in fact he was ruminating on his enjoyable evening and its sad end.

"Never mind, love, a 'reet good brekkie' will set thee up." This was the nice plump blonde lady as she handed him one of the early Sunday papers. "If you get a bit lonely, one of us will come and sit with you and keep you company."

He felt warmed by it all. The breakfast was good: he needed the backfill! There was always the fear of being stopped in the early hours of the morning. But this was holiday season: campers, caravans, and cars travelling in all directions. He said goodbye to the ladies. They all insisted on a kiss and wished him a good holiday. Nightshift was boring for them; any diversion was welcome.

The night watchman was standing by the back of his car and called out, "Good morning!" The man was admiring the car. "You can go anywhere in that, to the moon and back; never seen one like that in these parts."

He explained to him that it had just been released in Europe: he had been lucky enough to buy a demonstration model. His drive back to Burnsall was uneventful; the night clouds vanished, to be replaced by a faltering sunset. It looked as though the day may be patchy and misty. The car park was empty; his ticket was valid until mid-afternoon. He parked and went into the apartment, crawled into bed, fully clothed, and slept.

Kirkby

Before going to the morning service, Mrs. Allenby rang the bus station in Middlesbrough. The answer to her query was 'no': the rucksack had still not been collected. She put the phone down, sighing heavily. She was still worried whether she had done the wrong thing. If he had posted the money to her on Saturday together with a note confirming his instructions, it would be Wednesday before the postman would deliver it to her. 'Ah well,' it couldn't be helped. She would wait until Wednesday.

Brompton on Swale

Mrs. Brown was talking to 'the ladies' after the early morning service at the parish church. They all knew of the good anorak she'd been able to acquire and they were trying to remember who might have left it. The consensus of opinion was, 'the nice man who bought the Harris Tweed jacket, the cords, and the jeans'; they recalled that he was wearing a green anorak at the time.

Ravenscar

Bob and Alice woke up at 10 a.m. They felt refreshed and looked forward to a breakfast which they knew would be kept for them. They quickly dressed and went down to the dining room. Surprise, surprise! Bethan and Louise were there, with Moira, Bob's sister, already tucking into a gargantuan breakfast.

"Mummy, Daddy!" they screamed, and launched themselves into mid-air, to be caught by Bob. All five hugged and kissed.

Moira grinned and said, "Congratulations, you idiots!"

She was a computer analyst, amongst other things, and everything for her had to be precise. She could never understand the topsy-turvy life of her Alice and her brother, 'big Bob,' but she loved them all to bits. One day she hoped she would have that kind of marriage. After breakfast they sat outside in a faltering sun to discuss plans. The girls wanted to go to Scarborough, Peaseholme Park, for the boats, then the promenade for fish and chips, and the fairgrounds, and then back to Ravenscar for the evening meal and, later, the singsong at Boggle Hole youth hostel. Monday they would still be on holiday, and they wanted a day in Whitby, naturally to shop with their pocket money for Whitby jet jewelry. Then to climb up the hundred and ninety-nine steps to St. Hilda's Abbey and to have a trip in a fishing boat on the North Sea was also on their want list. After that it would be back to Eaglescliffe and home. Sounded great! Bob agreed to take the girls in Moira's car and give them a good day in Scarborough. Alice warned them to be back for an early dinner which would be waiting for them and then they would not miss the party fun at the nearby youth hostel later.

Moira followed Alice back to their bedroom. Later she would take the things out of the car for the girls and herself—they were to have the adjacent room.

"What is on your mind, Alice?"

"I don't know, Moira. I'm so worried about Jan. It was going to be a wonderful weekend for all of us; but without Jan, Bob and I don't feel like celebrating any more. Bob is unaware of my true feelings, but both you and I know Jan well; you, on the professional front, probably better. For me she is like my sister that I never had. I cannot chase away the forebodings and the sense of disaster that creep into my mind."

"Come on, Alice: just let your mind go and tell me everything."

"Well, Jan, as you know, has left her husband, who is by the way raving mad about it. His pride and masculine charm have been slighted. He's looking for any way he can to exact vengeance; particularly on the money side. But that has never bothered Jan! She has always been independent and for reasons only known to her, has kept her escape money secretly deposited away. I am actually her business manager and executor. Well, as I was saying, when she left her husband she reverted back to her maiden name of Fielding instead of Martin. The marriage had not lasted more than a year and a bit. But she had kept all her private accounts and credit cards without changing names. Strange, as though she had a premonition. She knew he was a bully, from "day one" when she married him, and for some reason she protected herself. So once she was established in her flat in Redcar, we started having more time together; but it's evident that she has suffered some mentally unfathomable damage. Cool as a cucumber at work, as professional as ever. Determined to meet as many men as possible, and as quickly as possible, until she eventually meets 'Mr. Right'.

"As you know, Jan was very fit and enthusiastic about walking. The Lyke-Wake walk was for the three of us. Jan arrived at Osmotherley first. She had a lift with Maureen, one of your lot; then after you came and collected the girls; one of Bob's friends at the college took us to Osmotherley. We were late getting there, and by the time we managed to unpack at the B&B and hasten to the 'Queen Catherine,' Jan was with Maureen and her friends, one of which was Simon Priest who works with you. She ended up in his camper van, bottom of Scugdale. You can imagine how disgusted she would be with herself! Leaves the camper van and walks up to the start of the path. That we know as she left a message for us, asking us to meet her with bacon butties, a flask of coffee, and also to bring her rucksack. Next thing we know, we have a text message: 'Lost on the moor, met a man, we are going to find breakfast somewhere in Chop Yat.' Should not be too difficult; 'spit and you're through it'." She sighed and shook her head.

"In any event, we did not meet up with her on the moors on any of the road intersections, and we have had no word from her."

"Well," remarked Moira. "I can tell you one thing; they would be out of luck for breakfast at Chop Yat. The farm that did it, does it no more. If they were really after breakfast there is nothing until the pubs open in Broughton. Stokesley is too far away from the moors. The only place would be the tourist centre at Rievaulx Abbey, which is only a bus ride from Chop Yat, and there is a regular hourly service. After their breakfast they would probably spend the day and possibly the night in Helmsley. You know how good the hotels are and it has some impressive shops for such a small town. Possibly she would be tempted to shop for some new clothes to please her new beau. Jan can well afford it."

"Never thought of that," mused Alice. "But there's a flaw in your reasoning; if she ended up in Helmsley or some other civilized place, she would ring us. She wouldn't be able to use her mobile; the charger was in her rucksack. But surely, her new friend would have one, or she could call from a telephone box. What if her so-called friend was a hoax? What if she decided she wanted to be alone? Walking in the mist, a peat bog, a rocky outcrop, she could have broken a leg, or anything! You know how treacherous those bogs are. Can we not contact someone?"

Moira hesitated. One phone-call could set a lot of people in motion and it would probably be for nothing.

"Let me make a general inquiry and see if any walking accidents have been reported relating to the Cleveland and Helmsley areas."

The call was quickly made and the answer was negative, no emergencies at all.

"Look, Alice, Jan is on leave until Tuesday, as you and I are; her independence means so much to her, you know that, as her closest friend. Leave it be, enjoy the day with me, all of us out tonight, and in Whitby tomorrow. Look forward to those Dover soles off the fishing boat, and the fresh lobster. We will meet Jan on Tuesday morning when I come to collect the reports, probably a gossip over coffee and have a good laugh about the whole of this long weekend. Forget Jan, and let us enjoy the day."

A very much-relieved Alice heaved a sigh. "You're right, I'm being silly. Forgive me, and let's indeed enjoy the day."

Colne

Patricia's house remained silent on Sunday. The milkman always left double on Saturday. All her friends and clients respected her Sundays; they knew underneath, she was a very private person. Her new friend Sylvia Hall, who had been on the business course with her, related to their other friend Stephanie how Patricia had phoned her about 9:30 on Saturday night very excited, saying a man had rung to make an appointment. He came as arranged, brought wine and savouries, plus some exotic chocolates, lots of foreign things. Apparently he was on holiday, been working very hard and wanted to relax: not strikingly handsome, but with a nice beard, good manners, generous and very polite. She was eager for him to come out of the sauna so they could enjoy the evening together. Patricia never rang back, so it must have been a good evening: obviously he stayed the night and they have gone somewhere today.

"I did try to ring her this morning," she explained to Stephanie, "but there was no answer. Good luck to her; she deserves a good man. We'll see her Wednesday lunchtime. Remember? We are having a meal at that new restaurant in Barnoldswick near the marketplace. She's hoping to have the plans from the architect for the extension of the house at the back, to make the gym, dance area, plus a sunroom and a steam room. You know how bubbly she is over this planning permission? It will be a 'doddle,' as she looks after the men who work in the right places. I bet the builder will do the work at a substantial discount!" She giggled. "To look at her, butter wouldn't melt in her mouth. Still waters certainly run deep!"

Burnsall

The man, Michael, woke up feeling refreshed. It was 11:30 a.m. He looked out of the window and the sun was shining through. It felt good and he laughed. A nice day for walking! Definitely Buckden Pike; no complications today. Drive through Grassington up to Kettlewell; find a cafe for lunch and then to Buckden.

Leave the car in the Yorkshire Dales car park and then walk, taking the path that leads directly to the top of the pike.

Dressed, feeling on top of the world, he left the flat and went over to his car and drove off. What would be on the radio? Ignoring Classic FM he went direct to Radio 4. He was just in time to catch the start of a lunchtime concert. It was Smetana's *Ma Vlast*, my country, Czechoslovakia, the rolling hills and the forests; of Prague and the majestic river personified in *Vltava*. Smetana's music reminded the people of the beautiful country they lived in, and its heritage. He recalled that man of God; Jan Huss, the Rector of the University; he had denied the right of the Pope to forgive sin and the doctrine of transubstantiation. Jan Huss was invited to the Council of Constance in 414 A.D. to take part in the Theological discussions with the Cardinals and Bishops. A promise of safe conduct had been given to him. Notwithstanding he was kidnapped as he walked through the city and imprisoned for a year permanently in cruel restraints. Incarcerated in the prison of the Cardinal on the shores of Lake Constance. Eventually they tried him and burnt him alive in 1415. His followers laboured on. The evangelical awakening of the eighteenth century could be attributed to a legacy of the Hussites, and other persecuted groups, who as the Moravians under Count von Zinzendorf, were responsible under God for the conversion of John Wesley and others which brought about revival in England and averted a repeat of the bloody revolution which was the lot of France.

The music swelled as the river ran into the sea, then the gregarious lilting music in happier times as the people laughed and danced in the woods and fields of Bohemia.

He sighed. This composer, like Beethoven, composed his music out of his head: it was all in the mind; he too was stone deaf, and died in a lunatic asylum in the late eighteen hundreds. He thought, will this be my end?

Banishing any more thoughts, he closed his mind and listened to the concert, savouring only the music. In no time he was in Kettlewell. The cafe was as good as expected, especially since it was serving a fine roast beef with Yorkshire pudding and a pot of tea. Delicious!

Arriving in Buckden, he left his car in the Yorkshire Dales Car Park. The weather was good, and there were quite a few people about. He set off for the Pike keeping himself to himself, arriving at the top a little breathless after an exhilarating walk. Looking around, all he could see was the moors. He decided he would run down to the little road which led to Aysgarth in Wensleydale, famous for its waterfall. Then by Cragdale moor up to Middle Tongue and then down to

Hubberholme, a quick look in the church there and back to the car. About another four hours of easy walking.

As he walked he breathed in the air, the atmosphere, the desolation, the grandeur. Wherever he had been in the world, nothing ever compared to England, Scotland, Wales, or Ireland. In each of these countries he had his favourite spots, unsurpassed scenery. 'One man's meat another man's poison.' It was necessary to be realistic about these things! He crossed the Aysgarth road by the little hamlet of Kidstones, and then over the moor and up to Middle Tongue. At the top he sat down for a rest and enjoyed the view. Straight ahead were Pen y Ghent and the Pennine Way which came up from Edale in Derbyshire, through to Yorkshire, Durham, Northumberland, and ending at Kirk Yetholm on the borders of Scotland.

Further over, Whernside, Ingleborough, the Clint fields the Craven fault through a six hundred foot bed of limestone; creating all the caves, the potholes, and the passages. That was for him, when he was at college making their own rope ladders: buying second hand miners' lamps, some of the acetylene type that gave a vivid bright light that banished the darkness. Cimmerian darkness, since there was no light, therefore no reflection: the darkness was tangible; you could feel it, almost touch it—frightening! He thought of the Jewish prisoners, mostly the rabbis that the SS walled up in cells, no windows, no door, left to die of starvation: what torture, what horror! Why was the human mind so base? What was it the Bible stated? 'Sin entered the world through disobedience to God.' The eating of the apple!

He scrambled down to the village of Hubberholme and walked into the grey stone Parish Church. The Vicar at one time had been John Robinson, the author of a thought provoking and disturbing book with the title of *Honest to God*. Then he became the controversial Bishop of Woolwich, and now he was dead.

'All have to die, and then comes the judgment.' The terror of it struck at him. He ran out of the church and resumed his walk back to Buckden. The afternoon tea at the café and the relaxed atmosphere helped to restore his equanimity.

He bought picture postcards of the area, wrote short notes and posted one each to his wife and his two girls.

Back to Burnsall. Tonight he would walk to the village of Hebden for his evening meal. One of its pubs was renowned for the quality and quantity of its food.

The drive back had been uneventful: a quick shower, a quick snack out of the 'fridge, then the half-hour walk to Hebden; the pub was closed for renovations, so he walked on to Grassington. The town was as noisy as ever. Old cobbled streets and squares housing pubs, cafes, and souvenir shops—all busy and full. He knew a very nice restaurant in Grassington, a bit pricey, but he was on holiday. After negotiating the crowds he eventually arrived at the raised parade of shops where the 'eating house was situated.' They looked askance at him when he went in, the old Harris Tweed jacket, cords, walking boots, but well polished. He explained that he was on his own, roughing it. Yet, in an earlier visit a couple of years ago, with his family, they had eaten many times and enjoyed the food immensely at this restaurant. They were gratified, gave him a seat by the window and brought him the impressive menu.

Selection was quick, the aperitif a Kir Royale, starter Langoustines in garlic, followed by a main course of Chateaubriand with a small selection of vegetables and Pommes Dauphine. For the wine, a bottle of Chablis, preferably very cold for his starter; and a bottle of Margaux with the beef, preferably 96. He assured them he was not driving but only walking back to Burnsall.

The food was delicious. He thought of the girls and his wife who loved the Langoustines, especially in garlic. The Chateaubriand was carved at the table, cooked very rare, perfect with the horseradish sauce and almost raw vegetables. He declined the sweet and liqueurs, paid an exorbitant bill with cash, bade good-bye to the staff, and set off for his walk back to Burnsall.

Lots of people were about, enjoying the walk alongside the river, over the bridge into the Red Lion for few pints of Black Sheep. The new beer brewed in Masham. Then it was bed, tired but happy, his mind dulled by the exquisite wines and the beer: he fell asleep immediately his head touched the pillow. What a grand day—his last waking thought.

Ravenscar

Bob, Bethan and Louise had enjoyed Scarborough. The girls had spent all their pocket money plus a lot of Dad's; he was dizzy from the rides, enjoyed rowing on Peaseholme Lake. All had eaten too much, Scarborough fish and double helpings of chips each, with the malt vinegar, of course.

Alice and Moira enjoyed a quiet day. Certainly a rest well needed for Moira. A few gin-and-tonics on the terrace overlooking the sea, and a couple of good books. That was the day set for them.

All of them sat down for tea and crumpets on the terrace, and then they made their way down and across to Boggle Hole. The youth hostel nestled in a narrow inlet, the sea washing the cobbles on each ebb and flow. It was a good night; some of the lads had brought crates of beer, which had to be left outside the youth hostel. Everybody enjoyed the singing, not to mention the beer, soft drinks, crisps and nuts.

No thought was given to Jan that night. Good luck to her, thought Alice. I hope she's having a nice time. They were now convinced that all was well: they would give the girls a good day in Whitby tomorrow, drive home via Guisborough and then to Redcar to see if she was there.

Colne

Detective Inspector Les Wilkes was having a bad Sunday. He was off duty this weekend. He had been called out three-times already and as compensation had booked Wednesday morning off. Purely for himself and his own pleasure and, he hoped, mutual gratification.

Family life for the Wilkes was gradually becoming unbearable. Row after row, until the air was blue. They had no children—that was one of the problems. Self-guilt on the part of his wife, always overspending and he fed up, with no proper meals. Sympathy had 'gone out the window' a long-time ago. There was the lack of promotion, too; he was probably now a D.I. until retirement. The one bright spot would be Wednesday: she would hear the telephone, ring three times, and then a pause and then another two rings which was the signal to tell her he was coming. He had his own key. If it turned in the lock he could look forward to two hours of pleasure with his ladylove.

CHAPTER 6

▼

MONDAY 8TH JULY.
YORKSHIRE DALES.

The man was awake at five o'clock. He got up, showered and dressed for the mountains. This would be his last day in the flat. After coffee and toast he used the rest of the bread to make sandwiches filled with the leftover ham and cheese and put them into the billycan using what was left of his coffee to fill his flask. He then cleaned the flat, including the 'fridge. The remains of food he gathered together along with the milk cartons and put them up in a carrier bag. He wiped the kitchen surfaces, the washbasin and shower, using the spray cleaner and a cloth he had found in the kitchen cupboard. There were spare hangers in the wardrobe so he kept one of the plastic ones to hang his Harris Tweed jacket on. His dirty clothes he put in another carrier bag; also the rope, the waist-lengths, the tape, and his sheaf knife, in one more bag. These he tucked into his rucksack.

The place looked neat and tidy. Goodbye, Burnsall! He left the flat, posting the key through the letterbox and crossed the road to his car and was off.

His plan was quite clear, the day on Penn y Ghent, ascending from Horton in Ribblesdale, then across to the Hill Inn at Selside for lunch. A brisk climb to the plateau of Ingleborough, and then down the other side to skirt around 'Gaping Gill' and back to his car. At the car he would clean his boots, change his anorak for the tweed jacket, then drive down to Malham via the A65 through Settle, striking off at Hellifield, and by the small roads to the village. He would park his car in the National Park Centre, which was good for long-term parking. Then he would walk to the nearest pub, sit in the garden and enjoy a pint of real ale. His demeanor was calm, one step at a time. First his beloved hills; he needed no companion, only the music in his head. The drive took him through Grassington, Threshfield, round by Arncliffe, and those majestic crags; on to Stainforth and then to Horton in Ribblesdale.

Ravenscar

Bob, Alice, Moira, and the girls were having breakfast: all excited.

"Dad, I hope you can arrange the boat trip," exclaimed Louise.

"I'm going to beat you up the hundred and ninety nine steps!" whooped Bethan.

"Moira and I are going to look at the Whitby shops," said Alice. "Daddy will phone when he has booked the boat, and we'll meet at the cafe by the quayside, or the fish and chip shop next door to it, whatever is your preference. Then, we can sit outside for our lunch."

It was going to be a good day. No more talk of Jan until Tuesday, when the three ladies would meet in their professional capacities.

Colne

The milkman left the usual two pints on Patricia's front doorstep. Most of the people in the street were elderly and kept themselves to themselves. He was disappointed in a way: it was a lonely life as a milkman and he did like a bit of a chat. Saturdays was when he collected his money. He made a second round of all his customers. Other than that, the job was pretty lonely. He liked to see Patricia; such a nice person, always friendly and generous! "Pocket money for the kids," she would say with a smile.

Yorkshire Dales

The man Michael drove without incident to Horton. He was early, only a couple of cars in the car park. He walked to the Post Office, which had opened. The back room was a cafe: he ordered two bacon baps and a pint mug of tea. He turned to the Post Office section and bought a couple of postcards with good views of Penn y Ghent, showing the Pennine Way. While he waited for his breakfast he wrote out the postcards, one for each of his girls, and put the stamps on them. He posted them in the box outside. With sad reflection he thought of the happy times he had enjoyed with his family and friends; yet in the end, and to his shame, he had badly neglected them.

He went back into the café. His breakfast was on the table with his tea. At that moment the door opened. A lady in her early thirties came in, dressed in bright yellow anorak and black ski pants. She had very dark hair.

"They smell good," she said. "I think I'll order the same."

Her English was good but she was definitely French. He greeted her in French.

"But Monsieur," she said, "you're not French, you are English!"

He confessed that he had picked up a little French and German in the course of his travels and where he was living. It transpired that she was a translator for the European Commission in Luxembourg. She was fluent in, German, and English, and had a little Italian as well as Spanish plus a very small amount of Portuguese. But she said with a laugh, "No Luxembourgeshe!"

She came from a small village near Vichy in central France and this was her holiday in England to walk the Pennine Way. Her start had been delayed due to the pressure of work; hopefully she would meet the rest of her party this evening at the next accommodation stop. They were all opting for an easier walk, by having their luggage delivered in advance each day to the next stopping place. The finish of today's walking would be at the Inn, on the road by High Force in Teesdale.

She finished her Baps and tea. "Must be off, why don't you come with me?"

Pondering, he replied, "Okay, I can walk with you over Pen y Ghent and on to Dale Head by the viaduct. Then I must cut over to Selside across Ingleborough top and back here."

"*Tres Bien*," she said, "*On y Va.*"

She had been in training to do the Way and was very fit; even at a fast pace she could keep up a good conversation. He knew that Vichy had been the headquarters of the Petain party, which was the puppet government of Hitler for France. He had recently read the book *Das Reich* which was about the Panzer divisions that carried out such a terrible retribution on the beleaguered French. But that was not for discussion on this walk.

They talked of the escape of Napoleon from Elbe, due to the British officer in charge wanting to see his lady love on the mainland. Napoleon had only waited his chance to escape, a thousand loyal men waiting for him on the shore. They evaded the Dauphine's army sent out to arrest them by taking the precipitous route over the mountains. Marshal Ney was waiting with the 'army of Louis' outside the gates of Paris ready to apprehend Napoleon. But the men would not fire a shot, and The Marshall of France rushed to embrace the exiled Emperor and fell weeping in his arms. Both men were eventually to meet their Waterloo!

Before they knew it, they were on the summit. A quick dance around the triangulation point, and on to Dale head. Now all the talk was of French composers, Saint Saens, his romance with the violin and the piano; Belioz with his visions and nightmares; Dukas the sorcerer, his music made famous by Walt Disney in the film *Fantasia*; then there was the enigmatic figure of a little-known American composer, Gotteschalk, hounded out of France because of his assignations, fleeing to Brazil, loved by the people for his musical pictures of Brazilian life; wonderful, brilliant, flamboyant music. In recent times it had been revived, but only the very gifted had any hope of playing it. The man was surprised at the extent of her knowledge. In no time they were at Dale Head.

"Stay with me," said Valerie, for that was her name. "I have no man. I have rejected many! We must finish the Pennine Way together. *Nous faisons l'armour, n'est pas?*"

"Give me your address. I will come and see you in your village near Vichy. I have things I must do, very important, before I finish this holiday."

She handed him a hastily scribbled card with her address and telephone numbers on. "*Bon Voyage, ma Cherie.* I feel there is something strange that you are needing to do. Please, I want you to know that I live on my own and normally work from home; it is very isolated. Money is no problem, and if you come to my house you will be safe. I promise you that, no questions will be asked. Remember that, when you need 'a haven' in the midst of the storm you are making for yourself!"

He had a sudden urge to give her his mobile number.

"You can reach me anywhere at any time," he said. "Just feel free, but give me more than a week before you do so."

"That's perfect!" she exclaimed. "By that time I will have finished the Pennine Way and will be back in France."

With that she hugged him and kissed him, waving to him as he practically ran away, following the path by the side of the viaduct, across the road and up towards Ingleborough. He tramped up to the flat plateau, which was Ingleborough. The Clint fields, those protruding undulating limestone rock formations, pitted by water channels, stretched as far as the eye could see. This was a place of excitement! Potholes, dropping hundreds of feet into the earth, caves, passages, underground rivers and waterfalls.

'Gaping Gill' was the most magnificent, the main chamber being able to take Saint Paul's Cathedral, a shear drop of three hundred and twenty feet. It was possible to reach it indirectly by 'Disappointment Pot' and 'Hensler's passage,' or one could go down the main shaft by the winch, which was only possible when the Pot-hole club that supplied it was 'in residence.' The direct descent was into the main chamber; it was always a cold and wet experience! Memories of his youth came flooding back, ice cold, and freezing as he finally reached the bottom of the cave. But Hensler's passage had been much more scary, he remembered.

The rest of his walk passed without incident. He walked briskly across Ingleborough, stopped for a moment by the main shaft of Gaping Gill, and then followed the path back to Horton in Ribblesdale. Once more he visited the café for a tea and had his flask refilled, and then drove back to Malham.

North Yorkshire

Bob, Alice, the girls and Moira had enjoyed the day in Whitby. Alice had not spent too much money. The boat trip on the North Sea had been exciting; they saw the cod and haddock catch landed, along with different kinds of flat fish. They had walked along the beach, disappointed that the lobster pots were empty, and then had a good tea, and now, it was time for home.

They drove along the coast road over Burke Brow, through Guisborough and on to Redcar. Jan's flat was in darkness, so they went home to Eaglescliffe, near to Stockton and to Middlesbrough and next to the old coaching village of Yarm. They were very proud of their village, which boasted a large railway station: for this was the original Darlington to Stockton railway of 'Rocket' fame.

Tomorrow would be another day! Yawning, they made their goodbyes with lots of kisses and cuddles.

Malham

The man Michael drove into Malham and parked his car in the Centre as he had planned. He kept his anorak on, put the flask in his side pocket, the tape, and the waist lengths in the other, and made his way down to the inn. It was early; he took his pint from the barman and sat on the benches outside the pub. Thoughts were bursting in his head. He was back in the Rubicon. Tonight would be an eventful night. He finished his pint and went inside, sitting in a nook by the door that gave him a good view of the parlour. The place was filling up. They had a band tonight and Irish music. It was going to be a lively evening.

To stretch his legs he went to the bar to order. The special was a mixed grill with a warning to its size and content, steak, Cumberland sausage, lamb chop, kidneys, tomatoes and mushrooms, with chips and the onion gravy as an extra option. Energy food! That's what the hill-walkers demanded. They took his order but apologized that he would have to wait about half-an-hour as they already had many orders. "No problem for me," he assured them. "I'll have another pint of Black Sheep with a Drambuie chaser while I am waiting."

Two girls came in and sat at the table opposite him. They knew a lot of people and the chat was lively. The musicians came in and warmed up by tinkling on their instruments, whilst everyone else enjoyed their food. Now it was the 'serious' time: drinking and music, dancing to Irish Jigs and Scottish reels. The atmosphere was 'real.'

The two girls had drunk too much and didn't care; they were all over each other and any males that came near them were pushed away. One was tall, blonde with aquiline features, quite beautiful in an esoteric kind of way; the other one was a brunette, short, plump and very rosy. But they gelled! It was obvious they had a relationship.

Eventually came closing time and everyone in good humour migrated out of the pub. The blonde girl had difficulty with her companion who fell down the steps and collapsed in a heap by the road. The man went to help them.

"Thank you so much," puffed the blonde girl. "However am I going to get her back to the tent?"

"Where you are camping?"

"The campsite at Goredale Scar," she muttered through gritted teeth as she tried to lift her companion onto her feet.

He gave a laugh. "So am I. Let me help you. My name's Michael."

"Thanks, Mike," puffed the blonde girl. "I'm Alison, and this is Cathy."

"Okay, good to meet you. I'll take Cathy in a fireman's lift. You lead the way. Stop when you want a rest. I have coffee in a flask."

"Good thinking, Mike," said Alison.

In a fashion they staggered down the road to the campsite. They needed a couple of breaks and enjoyed the coffee. At the site there was a lot of noise and a barbecue was on the go. The fire illuminated the falling water of the scar. It looked like shards of silver as it tumbled down into the bedrock of the stream. Alison turned off to the left, away from the noise. This part of the campsite was quite isolated. Their tent was on its own, its nearest neighbour being a darkened caravan. She opened the tent flaps and between them they pushed and shoved Cathy into her sleeping bag.

"You must go now," said Alison. "I'll see to her."

He smiled and left the flask of coffee for them, and then ducked out of the tent. He went to the barbecue. Someone had a guitar and there was an accordion too. Everyone was singing. He was handed a can of beer and then a plate of bar-becued chicken.

"Where's the kitty?" he shouted.

A man took his fiver and grinned. "What else do you want?"

"A big mug of coffee would do nicely, thank you!"

Tuesday 9th July
Goredale Scar. Early Hours.

For the next two hours he drank nothing but coffee. Eventually everyone stag-gered back to their tents, or collapsed by the fire. But now the night was cold, almost icy. Deafened by the roar of the water, he stood up and made his way along the path to the road. He looked across to the girls' tent, which was in dark-ness. Silently, he made his way to the tent. The flap was open. Taking out the masking tape from his anorak pocket, he cut it into strips, placing each piece across his arm so it stuck to his anorak. Then he ducked and crawled through the flap. Alison was not asleep, she was cuddling Cathy. She saw him and smiled, a little startled.

Quickly, before she could grasp the situation, he was over her and astride her. She was befuddled and didn't utter a sound. Taking the tape off his arm he put it over her mouth; then, pinioning her arms, he bound them with one of the waist lengths which he had in his other pocket. All the time Cathy never moved. He reinforced the tape over Alison's mouth. Her legs, trapped in the sleeping bag, he secured by wrapping the second waist length round the sleeping bag and pulling tight. Two round turns, and a couple of half hitches! Still sitting on Alison, he looked around the tent. There were some plastic carrier bags lying by their provi-sions and he took one, lifted Alison's head and slipped it over, gathering the ends round her neck and holding it until her struggling ceased. Then he secured the ends of the bag with another length of his tape. He sat and watched her as she expired.

With Cathy it was easy, the carrier bag, the tapes, and peace! She never moved. He quietly wiped the bags and the tapes, sat for a few minutes and then silently left.

He secured the tent flaps with the Velcro fasteners. Everywhere was quiet, except for the raging water as it rushed down the scar. The barbecue fire was still flickering.

Meditatively, he walked back to his car, a distance of some three miles. The little road was dark and silent. No one was around. He got in his car and left

Malham. As he left the village he noticed a Panda car parked at the side. He fleetingly caught the glow of cigarettes. Then he was on the road.

Now for action! It was all planned: drive across the lonely moorland roads, onto the M6, into Scotland and then through to Dumfries, taking the road to Newton Stewart and then on to Stranraer in time for the early-morning ferry to Larne in Northern Ireland. From there drive down to Fermanagh and take the little road which fingered its way in and out of the north and south of the country. He knew that the 'garda' patrol was now a thing of the past: he would continue driving until he reached Shannon Airport, near Cork.

When he reached Kirby Malham he cut off across the moorland road direct to Settle and then onto the A65. He drove fast, planning his route as he negotiated the narrow road. Within the hour he was on the M6, at Junction 26. Another twenty minutes saw him at the Kendal Junction stopping at the twenty-four hour transport café. He ordered a full breakfast, ate it quickly and enjoyed it and then he filled up with fuel, paid with cash, and was off again.

He settled down for the long drive all the way up the M6, passing Penrith, Carlisle, and before Gretna Green turned off on the A75 to Dumfries, Newton Stewart and Stranraer, hoping he would be able to catch the early morning Irish ferry.

His music for the journey he had previously selected, and loaded in the discs. It was the full version of Don Carlos. As he drove the music alternately soothed him and excited him. This was a complete tapestry of music, love, hate, violence, terror and loyalty; which Placido Domingo and Nicolai Ghiarov could do justice to and only as Verdi had portrayed. As he passed Penrith he was tempted to turn off and go down Keswick and then to Borrowdale. Probably stay in Hawkshead and have a day on Great Gable. Especially the Napes Ridges! But regrettably it was not for him on this trip. He had to be firm with himself; his plan had to be 'set in stone.'

So he drove on, enjoying the music. It amazed him how fascinated Verdi had been by the historical librettos, which he had used as a basis for his operas.

Phillip II, on the throne of Spain, son of the Holy Roman Emperor Charles V. Phillip's son Don Carlos, in Love with Elizabeth Valois, daughter of the French King, Henry II. Elizabeth promised by the Emperor to Phillip. Thus they had to meet in secret, outside of Spain, the love duet; the beauty of it filling the car. Very appropriate, he thought as he turned off by Gretna Green onto the Dumfries Rd.

Then the loyalty of the Duke of Posa, the friend of Don Carlos; their pact was one of brothers in adversity, undying friendship to the death. The duet being one of the outstanding arias of the opera. A friendship soon to be tested by the personage of the Grand Inquisitor, with all his machinery of terror. That grim bass profunda, the martyrs' song of defiance as they are led out to be burned. The ignominious end of the 'Infante.'

With music like this, no wonder at the funeral of Verdi the cortege was twenty-five kilometers long!

It was amazing how the music made the miles disappear. Now he was in Dumfries, on to Newton Stewart, the road starting to fill as he neared Stranraer. It appeared everyone had the same thought: the early passenger ferry to Larne. He had a better plan: he bypassed Stranraer and drove on to the next bay. This was Cairnryan, where the goods ferry made the same crossing.

No problem: he drove straight on, paid cash on the boat. Here on the heavy goods ferry, the breakfast was always communal, like a floating transport café. Nobody would take any notice of him in boots and anorak. But first he would find the day cabin that had been allocated to him within the price of the ticket. After locking himself in, he cut and shaved off his beard. A shower refreshed him and he used an instant tan lotion to take away the whiteness of his skin where he had shaved away his beard. The effect was okay. He gave it five minutes and then took another shower. Not bad at all: he silently congratulated the makers of the 'instant tan'; now for breakfast.

The ship was ready to get under way; an hour and a half to relax, listen to the drivers' talk, and read the papers. Ideal conditions to prepare for the long drive in Ireland, a lot of it on bad roads.

The crossing was uneventful, the talk desultory, the breakfast excellent, of real 'heart attack' quality with the inevitable fried potato cakes.

The ferry docked at Larne and, his being the only car on board, he was first off the boat and through the gates. There was no security check! He waved his thanks to the custom officer as he passed. Within minutes he was out of Larne and on the Belfast Road. At an isolated lay-by he stopped the car, took out a different set of number plates from the back and quickly unscrewed the ones fitted, replacing them with his reserve set. The old set he put in the hidden compartment underneath the tailgate compartment, eventually to be dumped. Then he was off again.

His plan was to divert to Amagh, then to Monaghan, Cavan, across to Longford in Eire. He knew it quite well, having stayed there when he made an industrial plant in Edgworthtown, a few miles up the Dublin Road. It seemed good to him to stop there for lunch, and have time to think and plan what to do next. In the meantime the countryside was beautiful, with views of Lough Neagh and all the other smaller lakes on the road down southwest to Longford.

CHAPTER 7

▼

TUESDAY 9TH.JULY.
TEES-SIDE.

Detective Superintendent Bob Ferguson was in his office by 7.00 a.m. There was only him and his wife now. They lived out at Great Ayton, famous for Captain Cook's birthplace. There was Roseberry Topping at a thousand feet and the monument to Captain Cook further along the escarpment. A lovely spot; they had been fortunate in buying one of the old Quaker houses. Ten years' hard work to renovate it, his wife Dorothy had done wonders with the garden; the strawberries at the moment were succulent, as were the raspberries, blackcurrants, and soon they would have the Victoria plums.

But not all was rosy with the Ferguson family. Their only son had been killed in a car accident not of his own making shortly after passing his test. A wonderful son and a good copper in the making lost forever. His daughter Jenny, now twenty-two years of age, was working with a Christian organization, 'Operation Mobilization,' somewhere in the nether regions of Turkey on the Iraqi border. She went directly after university, devastated by her baby brother's death. They were proud of her and him, but tears came readily to them when they saw happy group photographs, which filled their home.

Bob tried to live by the standards they both believed in. They were active in the church, which was evangelical; both of them had found their belief in Jesus.

They had met in a youth fellowship in Hartlepool, which was hometown to them.

He could not tolerate bent coppers of any description or rank. He'd been the scourge of the area in cleaning up the force, and for the enthusiasm he had exhibited in eradicating the graft. Junior and senior ranks alike respected him; any difficulty and it was 'Bob' they would seek out. They knew he would fight 'tooth and nail' for them.

With a sigh he put away his thoughts. Good job Dorothy was so hardy keeping faith, running the meals-on-wheels service for all surrounding villagers. They were based in Stokesley and went as far as Chop Yat, Little Ayton, Swainby and Ingleby. She loved all her customers. He thanked God he was in love with her twenty-five years on, just as much as the day they were married.

Now to work; grim reading the crime reports! One day late, that was the trouble of having a Monday off, for whatever reason.

Two bodies washed up near the transporter bridge in Port Clarence, foul play suspected, possibly drug-related. A fire in Acklam; initial investigation pointed to arson, three charred bodies found. One road accident late Saturday night: a driver ran into another car not wearing a seatbelt: the driver died from head injuries. Indications were that he'd been drinking heavily; further investigation to follow.

There followed the usual run of drug busts, burglary, and one suspected rape.

He sighed; it was a miracle that God tolerated man.

Detective Inspector Masters knocked and came into his office.

"Morning, Moira; how was the weekend? Did Dr Jan, Bob and Alice complete the trek?"

"Good Morning, Bob. It's beautiful today, just right for the Greek island holiday which unfortunately was two weeks ago. To answer your question, Bob and Alice made it, big celebrations at Ravenscar. Jan was a non-starter: got herself lost on Urrah Moor, met another walker in the early hours of Saturday morning and has never been seen or heard from since. We should be expecting her any minute to call from the hospital. I will go over for any preliminary forensic findings at 10 o'clock. Quite a workload for the pathologists, Mr. Sinclair Cameron and Jan. They will be in their element."

Moira Masters was twenty-six years of age, going on twenty-seven. She had benefited from the police acceleration promotion programme. Her first degree was in forensic psychology at Aberdeen, and then a Masters in criminal psychiatry at Edinburgh. In addition she had spent time at FBI headquarters in Quantico with visits to secure facilities for violent and perverted criminals, Rampton, Broadmoor, and Ashworth being the ones nearer home. Since the fiasco of

Rachel Nickell and the entrapment of Colin Stagg, the police authorities were gradually steering away from external experts and creating their own. Moira was one of them, taking courses in the profiling of offenders at the University of Surrey, and finally being accredited by the National Crime Facility, part of the police college at Bramshill. She was some impressive lady, unmarried but retaining all the freshness of life; yet remaining dedicated to catching the bad men and women. Here at Tees-side she was chief crime analyst and in charge of all intelligence collated from the police databases. Her department collated D.N.A. information from and to the national database in Birmingham. She monitored and updated the information held on the police programmes; the H.O.L.M.E.S. and C.A.T.C.H.E.M. systems, and was also responsible for the strict implementation of P.A.C.E.

Her chief assistant was Detective Sergeant Simon Priest, totally absorbed with the computers used by him and his team. He updated the 'Home Office Large Major Enquiry System' and the 'Centralized Analytical Team Collating Homicide Expertise and Management' data. The latter was originally set up by the Derbyshire police. She looked after the strict enforcement of the 'Police and Criminal Evidence Act.'

Moira left a summary of the latest information for 'Super. Bob' to assimilate and then went back to her own office. As she collected a cup of coffee she could feel there was an excitement in the air. Something was afoot! Big changes in the hierarchy were rumoured. The Association of Chief Police officers had met for three days and their Chief Constable was to make a statement some time during the latter part of this week. In the meantime the work went on. The team had been busy since six this morning reading reports, feeding and collecting data from the H.O.L.M.E.S. and C.A.T.C.H.E.M. systems, analyzing trends. Simon Priest and his team were now at work monitoring Internet activity, card transaction, the thousands of sites dealing in 'way-out' subjects: Satanism, Pedophilia, and others; monitoring registered users, looking for any pointer of would-be abductors who were about to 'crawl out of the woodwork.' Coupled with the ongoing drug scams, business scams, etcetera, the days were too short, the work infinitely absorbing, new technology bombarding them every day.

For Moira it was a fleeting visit. She was off to the Infirmary to meet the Doctors and Pathologists; almost a daily event. Her car and driver were waiting for her.

"Hello Molly, how are you this morning?"

"Grand, Miss," said the young PC. "Had a lovely weekend celebrating my engagement."

"That's wonderful, Molly. Is Peter just as happy?"

"Over the moon," smiled Molly.

Molly Squires and Peter Brown would be rising stars in the police world. A few months ago they'd been selected for a trip to the States, to Philadelphia. Here the police had for a number of years encouraged the use of a team of one male and one female as murder specialist. It was on the principle that drug related crime had to be solved within seventy-two hours, otherwise the trail and the evidence disappeared. The success rate was remarkable. Many of the teams working in close proximity with each other had fallen in love and married. They had the same amount of time off. On average they could stay together for two years maximum, before the babies came along. It was on the cards to do something similar in England, concentrating on heavy drug-related areas. But other changes were required to be implemented first. Molly and Peter had gained first-hand experience of the scheme: including some very dangerous incidents. The States were so very different with the least and the greatest of the criminal fraternity being armed. For Peter and Molly it had thrown them together and brought love. Hence the engagement; the perks would be good; a new apartment with security, a maid and an 'on line' shopping service.

"Congratulations; I know you will both be very happy," Moira said, giving her a hug. She knew her own hopes and aspirations. It would be lovely, she thought, to have a partner too; but her drive and ambition at this point of time did not allow it. The weekend with Bob and Alice was the first one for over three months, excluding the couple of holiday weeks.

They reached the hospital. After dropping Moira, Molly drove off back to police work. Moira would call her when she was ready to go back to the station. At the hospital reception, messages were waiting for her. The chief medical sister, who was Alice, and also Mr. Sinclair Cameron, the pathologist, wanted to see her urgently. She hurried down to the pathology labs and mortuary and had Alice 'paged' to meet her there. Sinclair Cameron's door was open and Alice was with him.

"Moira, how are you?" Sinclair Cameron's voice boomed out. He was very tall with burnished silver grey hair, pointed beard to match, and immaculately dressed in a worsted grey, complete with a bow-tie.

"Have you brought Jan with you?"

The room suddenly froze.

Alice had lost her composure. She had tears in her eyes. "She's not in her flat, not on her mobile. No one has seen her. Where is she?"

Sinclair tried to bring a note of levity into the occasion. His long tapering fingers waved in the air: "I need her desperately. We're floating in dead bodies."

Moira felt numb. She took out her phone, pressed one button and Bob Ferguson answered immediately. Tersely, she passed on the news.

Bob had no hesitation. "We'll institute a search immediately: I'll speak with the matron to get Alice released. The helicopter will be with you in approximately thirty minutes. In the meantime talk to Simon Priest and get him to put all information you can give him into H.O.L.M.E.S. We'll put out a 'red alert' on all Cleveland, and North Yorkshire police stations. The helicopter pilot will be kept updated on his on-board computer."

The next half hour was a flurry of activity. Priest took all the data into his computer. A doctor from emergency was briefed. Medical supplies, breathing apparatus and a stretcher were all on board the helicopter. Police back-up in the form of a patrol car and 'search and scene-of-crime officers' would be sent out from Tees-side to stand by at Chop Gate. Moira was designated the officer in charge of the operation.

They waited at the landing pad. Sinclair Cameron had to make a start on the post-mortems and was desperately looking for assistance from other areas, so he could not come with them; he wished them 'bon voyage.' He was a bachelor and though there were differences in ages, he had entertained a dream of Jan, that one day there would be more than a mortuary slab as a common bond. But she had always stood in 'awe' of him because of his international reputation; yet underneath it all he was a Yorkshire man born and bred.

They took off across the borough along the coast and then swept into the moors. From the message to the police they knew that the last reported location was Chop Yat for breakfast. So it was possible that, if anything had happened, it would have occurred not far from the main Helmsley road.

The helicopter came down low over the misty moor and throttled back to a minimum speed to commence sweeping. All the 'Ordnance Survey data' was fed into the on-board computer so that the system continually monitored their position.

The powerful close-up lens of the camera, combined with the heat sensors, fed a composite picture onto a separate screen. The alarms of the heat sensors went off more than once, and the ground radar showed objects, which the camera identified as dead sheep trapped in various bogs or holes in the ground. After thirty minutes of continually sweeping the moor, and with no result, they headed across to the village of Chop Gate and then followed the main road until they came to a path which led back into the moor. The helicopter landed; the second pilot left the helicopter complete with his backpack, which contained his ground scan equipment. The man walked at a moderate pace criss-crossing the path, sometimes turning back and making a wide circle around the path, the pilot directing him so the circles were interconnecting. The portable ultrasonic unit threw out a sound beam to impinge on hard objects and to reflect back. It was 'needle in a haystack' work, but the crew was well trained, and accomplished at it. After thirty-five minutes they had a result. The signal altered. It was the hard signal reflected back from a sizeable mass of rock.

The display was fragmented, showing possibly a cave, certainly some sort of cavity and water. The Radar and heat sensors locked on, and started to build a realistic picture. There was a difference in temperature from whatever was in the cavity and two sets of heat patterns in close proximity. The helicopter guidance system gave the co-ordinates and the route. Within minutes the helicopter identified a spot to land while the second pilot made his way to the landing spot. The position of the landing was fed to the Patrol car, the driver reporting that he was twenty minutes from the intersection of the road and the path. It was a Land Rover Discovery: it would get as close as possible to the helicopter. The team met by the helicopter and as they walked slowly forward, they ascended a rocky outcrop. At the top they looked down on a small rock pool in which floated a body. The cave entrance was also visible, and some clothing could be seen inside. Alice and Moira and the second pilot stayed put at the outcrop and Moira telephoned HQ to inform them of the sad news. The pilot had already radioed the position; now the S.O.C.O. team would be there within the hour. In no time the helicopter had returned, and Keith Allen, Detective Sergeant, joined them.

"Stay here, Marm, until the whole area has been photographed. Do not go down the path until we have checked for footprints."

They waited patiently, deep in their own thoughts and grief, with death as a companion until the second helicopter arrived. In the meantime the two uniformed constables from the Patrol car joined them.

"No sense in wasting time," said Moira to the officers. "Dr Janet Fielding's call was early on Saturday morning; they were going to Chop Yat hoping to find breakfast. Have a picture radioed to your 'on-board' computer; show it around the village and start a house check. Ask if anyone remembers any walkers in the village; also check the United Bus Services for that time of the morning, especially the Helmsley one. If the suspect was looking for breakfast he might have gone to Rievaulx or even Helmsley itself. In any case, check the visitors' centre at Rievaulx. I think it's especially important. Try to obtain clear descriptions of any likely suspects." She took a deep breath, thinking. "We will need a local HQ. Use

Broughton village hall; get the Stokesley station to arrange it along with the Broughton Constable. This investigation is going to be very high profile. We must leave no stone unturned. Follow even the slightest lead and keep in touch. Let Detective Sergeant Priest have everything he can feed into police information programmes."

"Yes, Marm," said the officers. They saluted and hurried off.

Moira could not contact Bob Ferguson who was unavailable for the rest of the day. The second helicopter arrived with the rest of the team, including the police surgeon, Dr Frank Hodgson, also a good friend and colleague of Jan's. The team went in with the doctor; all clad in white polyester suits, gloves, and overshoes. They scanned the ground. The rain had been heavy and most of the area had been washed clean of any sort of print. Only at a place where the body lay, half in and half out the water, was a partial set, as though someone had exerted weight and consequently the boots had dug in deeper. They photographed the imprint and also made a cast of it. The body was then gently lifted out of the water so the doctor could examine the wound on the top of the head. The rain had washed the blood clean away. Photographs were taken and the doctor examined the wound. They turned the body over: it was Dr Jan. The S.O.C.O. team went into the cave to check the clothes. Moira, Alice, and the helicopter crews came down to the pool.

The doctor gave a grim smile and murmured, "What a waste, such a fine girl, so dedicated to her profession. The blow to the head did not kill her; it knocked her out. She died of asphyxiation; her face was in the water, unconscious and not able to breathe. He," for that is all they knew about the man she had met, "must have sat here on this rock and watched her die."

The professionalism of all of them was swept away. This was their colleague: the life and soul of many a good party and a friend who had 'stuck closer than a brother or sister.'

The team checked her anorak in the cave. Her purse was intact; also her watch was there and other personal possessions. The mobile telephone was next to the anorak. A record was made of all prints, but it was evident that whoever had murdered her had no interest in her 'goods and chattels'; the opportunity was there to do her harm and he had taken it.

Where was he now? Was this a one off, or did they have a serial killer on their hands? With the permission of the S.O.C.O. team the crew brought the stretcher. Jan was put into a body bag and strapped to it. When loaded the stretcher sat outside of the fuselage. They would airlift the body back to the waiting ambulance on the Helmsley road. From there it would be taken direct to the mortuary.

The second helicopter would stay on at the murder site until the team had completely searched the area around it. The local police would need to arrange a twenty-four hour watch over this desolate spot. It would be some time before the authorities re-opened this part of the moor. The coroner would certainly want see where the murder had taken place. Before she left the site, Moira got on the phone to Simon. She gave him the details, as much as they had, stressing the urgency of having a preliminary report on the police databases.

A short press release was issued, to the effect "that a woman's body had been recovered on the North Yorkshire moors. Police were investigating, and foul play was suspected."

CHAPTER 8

▼

TUESDAY 9TH JULY. GOREDALE SCAR, YORKSHIRE DALES.

Ken and Mabel Seymour had slept well all night, having never heard a thing, oblivious of the barbecue, the muted sounds of which had filled the air.

The actual noise of water down the scar was 'elixir' to them: it was soporific. They loved this place. Even though they could only walk about a mile or so before needing to rest, this was for them. They had spotted a static camper van for sale last time they were here and snapped it up immediately. Ken had some small annuities, which could be taken as lump sums; just enough after the tax-man had his share, to buy the camper. It was a change from Withernsea where he had worked for the council all his life. A sedentary occupation! Always, he had wanted to walk and climb in exotic places. But life is tough, and family came first. Withernsea promenade was the epitome of his expectations. But now, with his camper and the little car, everything changed. Sixty-eight years of age or not, he felt a denizen of his age. Poor Mabel: her arthritis did not get any better! At last he had persuaded her to try a fish diet, so this morning, when the van came from Settle, they would have some freshly caught trout. Mabel had found a recipe in a woman's magazine for something called Ochrid Trout, from Macedonia: the trout were grilled with cherry tomatoes, onions, red peppers and paprika. Well, he shrugged, 'nothing ventured nothing gained.' It was a change from roast beef and Yorkshire pudding, at any rate.

But now at 10.00 on a bright sunny morning he was being a loving husband. He had mashed the tea; the crumpets, grilled and golden with butter, were in the oven; the table was set, and there was a new pot of Mabel's homemade marmalade to boot! What more could one want? Yes! There was one more pleasure! To walk out to the tent nearest to them and shout Good morning to Alison and Cathy.

Two very bonny lasses, always bubbly.

They would spend an hour together. It took Mabel away from her aches and pains He was looking forward to Alison telling them about the good night they would have had at the pub up in Malham. They were cheeky girls: they watched people, especially men; they had Mabel and himself in stitches each morning as they mimicked the men who were so macho, who thought they could pick up any girl. They both exhibited an intense dislike for that sex. "Present company excepted, of course," he said, smiling to himself.

He eased himself down the couple of steps of the camper onto 'terra firma' and walked stiffly along a path to the tent.

Unusual; the flaps were closed. Normally, no matter what the girls had drunk the night before, they were up and about by this time, washing their 'bits and pieces' and hanging them from the guy ropes.

He knelt down with an effort, so he could call through the tent flap.

"Alison, Cathy! Tea and crumpets ready. Come and have breakfast with Mabel and me. Have a go, girls, as Wilfred Pickles used to say!"

No Answer; tentatively he opened the top half of the tent flap and an unpleasant acrid smell hit him. He could not breathe and turned away to get his breath. With his handkerchief over his nose he opened the rest of the fastenings of the flap. The light flooded through and what he saw made his heart lurch. His whole body went weak; he felt he would die on the spot. Blinking back the floods of tears, which were blurring his vision, he closed up the flap and turned away. Staggering back to the caravan, he quietly closed the door and locked it. He did not want Mabel to come looking for him and see what he had seen. Quietly, he walked down to the road, by the side of the camping field. The telephone box was opposite the field entrance. It was empty. He crossed over, pulled open the door and dialed 999 and asked for the police. He told them his name, location, how old he was, and what he had just seen. Then he sat down at the entrance to the camping ground to wait for them, assuming they would come from Settle as it was a small town and would have a police station. It might not be too long, maybe just one 'copper' to authenticate his findings.

Tuesday Morning. Tees-side.

Shortly before midday Bob Ferguson had a call from the Chief Constable's secretary.

"Drop everything, drive to Tees-side airport. I'll be waiting for you there. Please do it now."

He quickly tidied up his desk, put on his jacket and called in at Chief Superintendent Percy Middleton's office.

"Hi Bob," said Percy. He was a very competent, immaculately clad officer, who ruled the uniformed branch with a rod of iron. He was not very flexible, but only ten weeks from his early retirement.

"I'm off, Percy. The 'C.C.' wants to see me at Tees-side Airport, what for, I have no idea. Please inform Moira for me. She's somewhere out on the moors; you must have seen the reports by now; Dr Jan is missing. Whenever are we going to get a replacement D.C.I.? I have no idea." With that he hurried out to his car, taking less than twenty minutes to reach his destination. The C.C.'s secretary Audrey was waiting for him with an airport official.

"Good driving, Bob. He's waiting for you. May I have your keys?"

The airport official took the keys. "I will park your car in the V.I.P. section and leave your keys at airport reception, Sir."

"Come on then," urged Audrey. "The C.C's boarded and the plane is ready to take off." She took him by the arm and hustled him through a door, bypassing the terminal and making straight for the tarmac.

A small twin-engined jet was waiting, its engines roaring. He hurried up the steps and into the plane. A very pretty stewardess met him.

"Please take a seat, Sir, and fasten your seatbelt." No sooner had he done this than the jet was moving to the runway, a short take-off and they were in the air. He looked at the 'Safety Card'; apparently he was in a Cessna Citation, Mark 7 twin-engined executive jet.

The stewardess came back with a tray of savouries, a small bottle of Champagne and a pot of coffee.

"The Chief Constable's compliments, Sir. He's not able to speak with you until you are at your final destination. Transport will be waiting for you at the airport, which will be Belfast, but at the military end of Aldergrove, to take you to your rendezvous."

Feeling very perplexed, he munched on the savouries and enjoyed an ice-cold glass of champagne. The plane was comfortable. He closed his eyes and dozed. Next thing he knew there was a bump and they had landed. He looked out of the window. It was some time since he'd been in Ireland.

He remembered his last assignment! It was undercover detective work in Belfast among British businessmen sympathetic to the loyalists, the secret lodges: lots of hard cash available to fund the terror that they germinated in Northern Ireland without any help from the IRA. He remembered being on the list, and given a dirty nondescript car, with the instructions to hide himself somewhere and not to surface for three weeks. By that time they would have cleared the trouble and would get him out. How would he know? Personal column of the *Belfast Post*.

He had driven aimlessly in and out of Belfast, eventually coming to Donaghadee, and had driven down a road of Edwardian terraced houses and found a vacancy sign. As he went up the steps the door had opened. A very stout lady stood there, dressed in a nurse's uniform.

"Beg your pardon," he had said. "I was looking for a place to stay."

Her first words to him were, "Are you on the list?"

He had been too thunderstruck to answer her. She beckoned him in and explained that the house had been a convalescent home for old people, the last one having just died and she was now turning the house into a guesthouse.

She had asked no more questions. The room was comfortable, a private garden, very good food and the *Belfast Post* every day. He could smile now but not at the time. He had seen the knee capping, the concrete blocks dropped onto a pair of legs, the terrible pain and agony the victims had gone through. He had also been part of the investigation team to investigate the sadism of the Shankhill Butchers and seen them brought to justice.

They were people direct from Hell.

With a bump the aircraft landed and taxied to a halt. A car was waiting for him.

"Good afternoon, Sir." The young lady who spoke was American. "We have a short drive to your rendezvous, which is in Glenveagh National Park. It is very beautiful and the house is lovely. You will wish you could stay forever once you get there." With that she opened the rear door of the car and he sank into the upholstery. The car was air-conditioned, furnished with a mini-bar, but no telephone. He was not a curious man except when detecting; very stoic, in fact. He would enjoy the drive, and the outcome would take its own course.

Late Tuesday morning. Goredale Scar.

The police came in strength; he had waited about 40 minutes. He worried about Mabel; but she should be quite content, to pour herself a cup of tea and placidly wait for him and the girls. She said that in the last few days he had turned into a real ladies' man.

There were two cars and a mini-van, but no one seemed to be in any haste to move. At last two men got out of the front car. He walked over to them and introduced himself.

"I'm the one that telephoned you," he said. "I'm Ken."

No one introduced themselves, but one of the men, not in uniform, said to him: "Before we let troops loose, let's you and me walk over to this tent and take a look."

Ken looked at him. "I don't want to, but I will."

The blessing was that the whole of the scar still seemed to be asleep. Too early for picnickers, and trippers from the buses. A few people were moving about in a desultory fashion.

The man spoke to his uniformed companion. "Keep the lads in the minibus. Take your sergeant and let him stand nonchalantly by the gate. This could be an old man's fancy!"

Without speaking, Ken led the way past his camper. Thank God, no signs of panic. Before they got to the tent, he stopped and turned to face the policeman. "I just wanted you to know I only went to the tent and opened the flaps after I had called and received no answer. I've not been inside. I then re-closed the flaps and went to lock my camper door, so that my wife did not go wandering over there while I waited for you. I did not talk to her, so she has no idea. You will find my fingerprints on the outside fastenings and also on the inside of the flap."

The man's demeanor changed. He now perceived something of the trauma this old man was trying to hold back.

"Thank you, Sir. I am Detective Inspector Patrick Hall. I appreciate what you have said. Please wait here so I can look for myself."

D.I. Hall went to the tent and gently made a gap in the flaps at the top, and with the aid of a torch looked inside. It seemed like an eternity; at last he turned and walked back to Ken.

"The bastard," he said. "I can see how you are suffering."

He took out his phone. "Yes, it's true. Ring 'scenes of crime' immediately, they operate out of Colne. We also need the police surgeon and the ambulance. Get your lads to spread out round the camp. Wake everybody up and gather them in the open field. I want two of your men to guard this tent, not to touch anything and not to go in under any circumstances."

He then rang his station. D S Johnson answered. "Robin, this is for real. Two girls have been murdered." He called to Ken: "What are their names, Ken?"

"We only know them as Alison and Cathy," Ken muttered.

"Did you get that, Robin? Allison and Cathy. When S.O.C.O. have made their examination we will be able to fill in the details. Get a preliminary report out on H.O.L.M.S. immediately."

Patrick Hall waited until the two policemen were in position at the tent and then said to Ken: "It will take at least half an hour to have everyone here. Let's go and enjoy the tea in your camper. Maybe we can break it to your wife gently; I have ordered an ambulance and a doctor. It is too late for the girls, but I don't want you or your wife collapsing on me, you are going to be far too valuable."

Ken unlocked the door of the camper. He just had time to pour the tea when Mabel appeared.

"Who's this?" she said. "Where are the girls?"

The Inspector introduced himself and gently told her that her husband had found the two girls dead, for the moment the cause being unknown. She stared at him, eyes wide open, trying to say something, but no words would come. Then she collapsed on the floor and fainted. The man took out his phone and quickly asked one of the policemen to bring a medical kit.

CHAPTER 9

▼

TUESDAY AFTERNOON. 9TH JULY. NORTHERN IRELAND.

Detective Superintendent Ferguson sat back and enjoyed the ride. The mountains were beautiful—this was a part of Ireland he never knew existed.

Within three-quarters of an hour they pulled in through some wrought iron gates set in a high cobbled wall. The gates opened automatically and they came to another set of gates that did not open until the driver called through. He caught a glimpse of the house as they went down a tunnel through another set of doors that opened remotely to a large underground garage. His driver stopped by a sliding door. She opened his door so he could get out.

"This is the lift," she said. "Press the button and it will automatically take you up to the V.I.P. suite."

He pressed the recessed button. The lift moved upwards, stopped, and the doors opened. A girl in a dark blue costume met him.

"Sir, welcome to Rossapenna. Your party's finishing lunch, but we have set you a buffet in the conference room."

She led the way. The room was comfortable, deep leather chairs arranged in a semi-circle, a small table beside each. One table was arranged with an exquisite buffet, and a chilled bottle of white wine. He never bothered much with wines; as long as they were wet and cold, it was okay with him.

The door opened and he heard voices. His Chief walked in; James Hetherington was an impressive man whose work in policing had set a landmark. He had every faith in his men and encouraged them all the way. "Well, now," he would say. "One day one of them will be in my shoes."

A number of men came into the room, but on seeing Bob they went out again.

One of them said, 'We'll leave you two in private; but not more than half an hour. We have a lot to get through before the day is out."

When they left, the C.C. said to Bob: "That was the Chief Commissioner speaking to us. Sit down. Bob, sorry about all this cloak-and-dagger, but it's taken a lot of effort to arrange this meeting. Here in one building we have nearly all the senior policeman in Europe. This house is known as little Quantico; it is the European arm of the FBI and CIA, originally set up to catch Americans in their funding of the IRA, gun-running and the like. Now it is a centre for anti-terrorism on a global scale."

The C.C. stood up and paced the Room.

"We have had some discussions relating to the formation of a national force of detectives, directly responsible to their own 'Supremo' instead of the local Chief Constable. With European arrest warrant soon to become law, which will be very necessary as crime becomes more global, the investigative and apprehension side of police work has to be much more unfettered and flexible. A survey has been made, and reports compiled, to determine seven top men who could be adaptable enough to use their impressive analytical experience in detection and in leadership to head such a force. That is the reason why you are here! You are the first to be chosen; we are still discussing who will hold the other positions. Your title will be Northern National Commander of Detectives. Tees-side can remain your base; it is an impressive facility with its 'state of-the-art equipment' and its staff.

"The whole of the top floor will be your HQ for the present. The plans have been drawn up and approved. The whole lot can be converted within a weekend; this coming one, in fact. No time like the present! They have to find another office for myself and Audrey. That means you skip Chief Superintendent and any Area Commander position; also, the offices of Deputy, Assistant, and Chief Constable would not be open to you. But that has never been your ambition. You are not a desk man; your formal acceptance will be asked for in the main meeting. Your salary position will change. They now only pay you four times a year in advance. But it will make you very comfortable. An allowance will be given, so you can have the car of your choice. But other forms of transport will be available to you, the Citation jet for U.K. and European travel, and, of course, the helicopter service. Other changes have already been agreed and only require your approval.

"Moira Masters becomes Detective Chief Inspector; Detective Sergeant Priest gets his promotion to Detective Inspector, and oversees the maintenance of all the criminal information programmes. An old friend of yours from Sheffield, Detective Chief Inspector Alan Bridges, becomes your Superintendent at Tees-side."

Bob remembered his Sheffield days very well, the conclusion of the Sutcliffe case and that of Michael Sams, to mention only two; it would be good to have Alan again.

"Sir, you overwhelm me. Of course, I accept, but surely you had thoughts of a younger person?"

"We did, Bob, but you will give us twelve years, which will firmly anchor this revolution in policing; none of us have any doubt about that, so congratulations, Chief Commander. Now, before we join the main meeting, there is an American gentleman waiting to see you."

He picked up a phone and spoke into it. Within a few minutes a much tanned fair-haired man walked into the room.

"This is Morgan Freeman, agent in charge at Rossapenna; but also a member of the joint FBI/CIA Council. He has unrivalled experience investigating serial killers, utilizing profile techniques and, strange to us, enlisting the help of mediums in his quest for catching these animals; but let him speak for himself."

"Good day, Bob. Nice to meet you; it's a pity you're on a flying visit, the golf, sailing and the walking is very good here. Congratulations on your promotion. We hope that we can all celebrate with you in the good old American fashion before you leave. After all, you're not driving." He smiled. "Let me come to the point. Last year a certain American visited your country. He loved the old country, especially the walking and climbing areas. He had four weeks in the U.K. Spent the time in all the favoured areas of outstanding beauty. This man is one of our psychic profilers; don't laugh at me; there are people waiting on 'death row' because of his input. At first we didn't believe him, going back some years now, but something happened which was in accordance with his predictions. We did of course investigate that he had not engineered the outcome to suit his vision, for the want of a better word. So we hired him and he did the various profiling and criminal behaviour courses. In listening to him, and utilizing his uncanny talent we have had some pretty spectacular successes.

"Last year, while he was on holiday in the U.K, he had a premonition. He sensed that you would experience a macabre series of killings. We had a discussion relating to his fears and 'God forbid' that such a series of events could happen. We would be ready to send him over here to help you with the investigation; if you felt you could use his particular expertise. Please feel free to call me. I will arrange to get him here as quickly as possible. His name is Geoff Grenchen; I have put a dossier together for you, which you can read at your leisure. Remember, 'truth is often stranger then fiction,' Bob. I am only a phone call away from you, so call me at any time. We can fly our man over to you within eight hours if necessary!"

"Thanks, Morgan," the C.C. interjected. "We must move on to the main meeting. That's okay, James; thank you for your time, Bob; goodbye and good hunting!"

Midday, Tuesday 9th July. Goredale Scar.

The S.O.C.O. team and the police surgeon arrived at Goredale Scar. They set up their equipment outside the tent. Detective Inspector Hall stayed with Ken and Mabel. The doctor checked out Mabel and gave her a sedative; she was resting peacefully though her eyes were filled with copious tears. Ken was holding up and one of the team had taken his fingerprints so they could start to eliminate whatever they found in the tent. Before going in they checked the prints on the tent flap. Ark lights were set up to illuminate the inside of the tent without having to roll up the sides. They carefully used an ultraviolet light to expose fingerprints and lifted as many as possible around the bodies. A vacuum flask had some good prints on and also a cup. Everything else was smeared. It took another half-hour before the doctor was allowed to examine the bodies.

One girl was lying flat in her sleeping bag. It looked as though her head had been lifted up and a carrier bag slipped over. The ends had been gathered and held until she expired. There was no more interference to her body.

The other girl had been sitting up in her sleeping bag very close to the one that was sleeping. She was tied, her hands behind her back, her legs trapped in the bag. The rope had been tied tightly round the bag, ensuring she could not struggle.

Her head had also been covered by a carrier bag, the ends gathered around her neck and secured with masking tape. Her mouth had also been heavily taped. It looked as though she was awake when her attacker had come into the tent. She must have recognized him, giving him the time to gag and immobilize her.

The carrier bags, tapes and bindings were removed. The doctor examined the girls. No violence had been perpetrated on their bodies. Death was by asphyxiation only. The girls were lifted on to stretchers and taken to the ambulance, to be transported to the mortuary for post mortem examinations.

The S.O.C.O. team continued its work. The tape they examined for fingerprints, also the rope. They kept the knot intact; it was a reef, secured with two half hitches. The rope was quarter inch stranded nylon, at one time used as a waist-length before the advent of climbing harnesses.

The man knew what he was doing when he cut the rope from a longer piece; he had used rubber bands on the cut ends, twisted round the rope to stop it from fraying.

They found the girls' handbags; all was intact; money, credit cards, and cosmetic items, nothing disturbed. The suggestion was that nothing had been taken. Detective Inspector Hall made a mental note: they were dealing with a unusual killer, a gentleman assasin.

Alison was Alison Smith, living in Oak Drive in a village called Marford, between Chester at Wrexham. Cathy was Catherine Roberts, living in Little Acton Lane, Acton, Wrexham. But who was who? Here he needed Ken Seymour to help. He went back to the caravan.

"Alison is the tall one with blonde hair. Cathy is the brunette, cuddly and dumpy." Ken's voice was cracked and broken. He could hardly get the words out, the anguish written all over his face.

So that was that, now he knew. The next thing would be the parents. The station could do that and he phoned them with the details. Detective Sergeant Johnson was already receiving all the information on his computer as the team on the site entered everything into their laptop, and downloaded via the Internet.

Patrick continued to question Ken. Mabel and he had planned to be there for the two weeks, but now?

"Well, Ken," said Patrick, "you'll have to be here for the inquest since you discovered and reported the deaths. I think it's probably upsetting for you to stay here. I would suggest you book into a hotel in Skipton for three nights. The inquest will be after the postmortem, probably Thursday morning. Put a case together for you and Mabel; lock your caravan. No need to worry, it will be well guarded over the next few days. A police car will take you to Skipton. We will organize everything and re-imburse you. It won't cost you a penny. A doctor will visit you this evening and check on Mabel. I will come along and buy you a pint." He shook his head. "I can't remember coming to a scene like this without finding chaos. You behaved very responsibly; the police will be grateful. Now forgive me;

I need to go and see how our uniformed lads are getting on with the questioning of the campers."

Before going on to meet the rest of his colleagues, he used his phone again to speak to Detective Sergeant Johnston.

"Robin, a thought occurs to me; there's been a lot of pilfering and break-ins at these campsites and holiday homes. I know that Skipton, Settle, and Colne have put on extra patrol cars. Find out who was on last night and in the early hours for this area. I want them here within the next hour with their official report. A 'blow-by-blow' account of their shift; this is murder, no holds barred!"

Patrick then went across to the benches where the police were questioning the campers. The Sergeant in charge came up to him. "Nothing yet, Sir; they are all too sleepy to take it in. They had a good night at the pub before coming back and starting a barbecue."

"Have you had anyone up at the pub, and any of the other pubs, questioning the landlords and staff?"

"No Sir," said the Sergeant.

"Well, I suggest you get on with it pronto! We'll meet again here in two hours. I need to go to Skipton and report directly to the Superintendent. Make sure whoever was on patrol last night is here when I get back. Grill them thoroughly. I want to know everything. I will have no mercy on them if I hear a load of lies!"

CHAPTER 10

▼

TUESDAY 9TH JULY.
TEES-SIDE.

The helicopter landed at the Infirmary. Air ambulances had become the norm in Europe. The facilities for landing and taking off were always in place. Moira and Alice jumped out. Bob as yet had no idea what was going on, so Alice hurried to ring him with the details. After that, she checked with the sisters on the ward that all was okay and there were no emergencies. She then went up to Jan's office. Moira was there and also Sinclair, checking on case files.

"Sorry, Moira, what am I to say? I know nothing about her private life. I'm arranging for the Bradford Pathologist to come over to do the post-mortem, which will most probably be on Friday morning. As you're aware, you'll need to have her identified by a close relative. The coroner is a stickler for that."

"Yes," said Alice. "I have the keys to her flat. Moira and I are going there now."

"Pick me up at headquarters, say in twenty minutes. Detective Constable Squires is waiting in the car and will drive me over to my office."

It took no time to get to police headquarters. She went up to her office. There was an urgent handwritten message waiting for her: *'Go to the red phone in the Chief Constable's office. It is a secure line. Pick up the receiver and when asked for the code, give the reference X13.'*

She went immediately to the office, picked up the handset, and gave the code. There was an immediate response.

"Moira, it's Bob speaking. I'm very sorry about Dr Jan. At the moment I am looking at the H.O.L.M.E.S. update. For your information, more murders have taken place at a beauty spot in the Yorkshire Dales. You know it well; it is Goredale Scar, near Malham. Two girls, Alison Smith and Catherine Roberts. We are waiting for more information. I think you and I know there's a link and we can expect more. Please make a note in your diary that I have a meeting tomorrow afternoon with Detective Inspector Priest and Detective Chief Inspector Masters. What you are hearing and other matters are the result of a very special conference, which I am presently attending. I cannot tell you the location. All I can say, the business in here is at a high level and we now have a much wider remit. For your ears only, Moira, you are now speaking to the Northern National Commander of Detectives."

Moira was stunned and feeling very fearful. "I think you have to reconsider concerning Detective Sergeant Priest. From what I understand, Jan would still be alive if she'd not gone off with him to his camper. You know how silver tongued and persuasive he can be."

Goredale Scar. Malham, Yorkshire Dales.

Detective Inspector Patrick Hall was back at the Scar. As a result of the meeting with his Superintendent, he had been authorized to lead the inquiry into the murders of Alison and Cathy and to leave 'no stone unturned,' and be able to avail himself of as much manpower as he needed. Whilst he was at the station the H.O.L.M.E.S. update came up on the Superintendent's computer. A pathologist, Dr Janet Fielding, had been found murdered on Urrah Moor in Cleveland. No other information available at present. Both were shaken by the implication of now three murders.

Sergeant White had two policemen with him and three men from the campsite.

"Good afternoon, Sir. We have completed the questioning at the campsite and also at the pubs. There are some people here waiting to speak to you. Afterwards we will go up to the pub where the staff is waiting for you."

Three men were sitting at one of the campsites picnic tables. Patrick and the sergeant sat down opposite them.

"This is Tim Harrison," said the Sergeant, indicating the man on the left. "He remembers the man helping the girls to walk back to Goredale Scar. The man carried one girl in a fireman's lift fashion. The other girl, tall with blonde hair,

was carrying the handbags and walking along beside him, laughing at the specta-
cle." He paused. "Our next witness is Albert Walker. He remembers the man
being at the barbecue and giving him his first pint. The man on the right is Geoff
Endicott; he took a fiver off the man towards the barbecue and kept topping him
up with coffee for the next two hours. He recollects the man leaving the barbecue
and walking towards the road.

"We can all go up to 'the Arms' now and then they can sign their statements,
which by now will have been typed. I rang the Superintendent in your absence
Sir, to arrange for an artist and identikit team. They are coming from Bradford,
so we expect them within the hour."

"Thank you, Sergeant, and good thinking. You go up to the pub. I will follow
you. By the way, Sergeant, another murder took place on the moors in Cleveland,
a Dr Janet Fielding. She was a pathologist. Not much else is known at present.
Leave me now; I want a private word with the two constables."

Detective Inspector Hall turned to the two PCs.

"I read your incident reports while I was at the station. It was like looking at
blank sheets of bog paper! Then I looked back at your previous ones; nothing to
excite or interest anyone. You certainly live a very serene and seraphic life when
you're on duty. Maybe it's the aura you exude, which unconsciously drives all the
bad people away from your 'serene personages.' I can think of no other suitable
explanation after reading these reports.

"Your desk sergeant, too, must be blessed with the same equanimity, as he has
signed them all without a comment of any description. You are like the two gendarmes in the old song: 'chasing butterflies'; the real world is not for you."

The two PCs looked angry and glowered at him.

"Don't you realize two young girls enjoying their lives, everything to live for,
were callously snuffed out? Someone sat there and watched their life ebb out of
them. He is called a 'Dysfunctional Manipulative Psychopath.' He doesn't care
about the life of others; he takes it as one treads on a spider or swats a fly. You
don't take anything from the spider or the fly; you have killed out of compunc-
tion, without compassion! That is what our killer does.

"Now, let's shed some light on your night's sojourn. Why were you on patrol
and what is its purpose?"

"Sir," said one of the PC's. "We are on a special patrol because at this time of
the year many people like to walk the hills at night. There have been incidences
of cars broken into in the main car parks, people being waylaid, having to give up
their wallets, valuables and car keys in various areas."

"Good! And while you have been on patrol, have these incidences persisted?"

"Yes, Sir"

"And, have you caught any one?"

"No, Sir"

"And why not?'

Both PC's looked down at their boots.

"It's a game to you, is it not? Let us take last night. You have now told the Sergeant you heard and saw a vehicle leave the village at about 2:30 a.m. Think hard and tell me about your last night in Malham. Who was the driver?"

"I was, Sir," said the taller of the two.

"Right Boyo, from the top; a blow-by-blow account."

"Well Sir, we came into Malham. It was quiet and we drove down to the Scar. The fire was still burning; we walked through the field to see that everything was safe like; most people had just collapsed and dropped off. There was evidence of heavy-drinking and still some open cartons of canned beer."

"So you took a couple, and while you were swigging, meandered back to the car."

"Er, yes Sir."

"What next?"

"We drove up to the village and parked in a lay-by, opposite the road which leads to Kirby Malham and Settle. Then we heard this car start up. It flashed by us and disappeared."

"What was the car like?"

"Don't know, Sir, it was too quick, possibly one of these four wheel drive things."

"Let me elucidate for you; both of you were slumped down in the front seats of your patrol car, each with a can of beer and a cigarette, quite content. Don't bother to deny it. I have had your car checked by forensics; definitely the evidence of beer and tobacco, so you don't have a leg to stand on. Let's try it bit by bit. You heard a car start up. Where from?"

"From the Dales' car-park, Sir."

"Well, well! The very place you're supposed to keep an eye on. The driver drove past at speed. Were you parked in the thirty mile per hour speed limit zone?"

"Yes Sir."

"So he broke the speed limit. Do you have a Breathalyzer unit in the car, and have you had training with it?"

"Yes Sir."

"So as bastions of the law, you had every right to go after this car because he was speeding and you could have also breathalyzed him."

"Oh Sir, we try to be a bit more friendly than that. We would be at it all night if we did that."

"Is that so? How many cars passed you last night after 1:0 a.m.?"

"None Sir."

"So don't you think a car at 2:30 a.m. could have a excited your suspicions? At least, if you did not stop it, you might have taken its number and radioed it on to Settle, or the patrols on the A65 East and West."

"Yes Sir."

"Yes Sir," he mimicked. "I'm dammed right; we could have had some clue to who the killer might be if you had followed procedures."

"Yes Sir," they chorused.

"Right," he said. "Go up to the pub, have a look at the Identikit, and see if you can search your memories, to the effect:-

"A: Did you catch a glimpse of the driver, and can you describe him?

"B: Can you describe the car to the artist?

"Make sure that you do not take a drink. When you get back report to the new desk sergeant; the old one has been suspended. Hand in your car keys and warrant cards. You are both suspended from patrol duties. You will be on foot patrol for a year to sharpen up your talents of observation. I am trying to get one of you on the Manningham Lane area in Bradford; and the other for Chapeltown in Leeds. See how you fare with the ladies of the night.

"When you return to car duty, after re-training, you will find yourselves being diligent of even the hedgehog crossing the road."

A press statement was released later on in the day: 'Two girls found murdered at a Beauty Spot in the Yorkshire Dales. No other details available.'

▼

CHAPTER 11

TUESDAY 9TH JULY. LATE AFTERNOON. TEES-SIDE.

Moira left D.S Ferguson's office. Her mobile had a text message: Alice was outside waiting for her. She went into her own office, picked up the phone and dialed a number.

"Martin, Sanderson & Baldwin, Solicitor and Commissioners for oaths," said a disembodied voice.

"Can I speak to Mr. Martin, please? This is the police; Detective Chief Inspector Masters."

"Moira," a voice purred voice over the phone. "So nice of you to call. I expect it's about that invitation I gave you when we met at the Mayor's Ball. Both of us footloose and fancy-free. When would you like to meet for an evening on the town?"

"Never, Mr. Martin; I only rang to inform you that your wife has died. Please attend the station at 10 a.m. tomorrow for further details." With that she put the phone down and ran out to join Alice.

The traffic was heavy. It took forty-five minutes to reach Redcar, where Jan had her flat. The apartment building was new, finished in a grayish white granite. It was located at the end of the promenade, had well-tended gardens and good parking, with uninterrupted sea views. The flats were serviced and very comfortable to live in. They had enjoyed many a night here, girls' talk, professional talk, playing board games, going to the basement for the gymnasium, the sauna and then plunging into the pool.

Now it was different. They were here to go through her papers and find her next of kin. Never had they asked about her private life; she had always kept herself to herself. It was a mystery to them what kind of man she liked. After a disastrous marriage, she had made sure that her friends did not set her up with any blind dates with people she could not tolerate. The Osmotherley incident had been an example. Alice had talked with Maureen; she was also a nurse at the hospital. Maureen said it had all been a bit of a laugh. Jan was upset that Alice and Bob were late, so to cheer her up they had spiked her drink, just a little bit.

The popular drink had been 'Black and Tans' and after the first round, Simon had ordered a second, and altered Jan's drink to a 'Black Velvet' made with a double glass of champagne and topped up with Guinness; after all, none of them were driving that night. Not to make a fuss, Jan had drunk it, with disastrous results!

That made Moira even more determined to block his promotion. Jan was a professional making herself a national reputation under the tutelage of Sinclair Cameron; even at her most vulnerable, she deserved all their respect. If Bob knew Simon had been spiking drinks he would be flying through the air. Alice had loved Jan as a sister and, because Bob loved Alice, he also loved Jan, not to mention his own sister Moira.

They found her 'Deed-box.' The death certificates of her parents were there; also copies of her sister's Diplomas and her brother's Commission, along with her own diplomas and certificates. In a lever arch file they found a recent letter from her sister, who was a couple of years older than Jan. The address was a Canadian one, from a place called Arvida. She was working in a research laboratory.

Now they remembered Jeannine, Jan's sister, had been at Newcastle University on an adult conversion course sponsored by Alcan Aluminum. It had been a success and she had moved over to Canada, temporarily or permanently? Only Jan would have been able to tell them. They made a note of the address detail.

A further rummage found a letter from her brother, including a photograph. It showed a man in his early forties in army uniform with R.E.M.E. on his shoulder flash. His epaulets were adorned with a crown. The letter to his sister was to inform her of his promotion. He was in single officer quarters at a camp near Otterburn in Northumberland. Some sort of development work. Searching through the deed box they found a certificate showing he was a member of the Institute of Electrical Engineers.

Moira picked up Jan's phone and dialed the number of the camp.

"Can I speak to Major Fielding, please;" she said when the connection was made.

"Can you tell me your name?" enquired a voice.

"My name is Moira Masters and I am a friend of his sister."

"Thank you, Madam, I will put you through."

"Hello, Moira," a voice boomed over the phone.

"I have heard all about you and Alice, from Jan, but never had the pleasure of meeting you. What is the problem?"

"Major Fielding…"

"Call me Richard," he interjected.

"I have to speak to you in my capacity as a police officer. We need you to come to our headquarters in Tees-side. There is no easy way of putting this; your sister has died, and we require you to identify her. I will give you details when you are here. Come as soon as possible; tomorrow morning would be okay. When you arrive, ask for Chief Inspector Masters. I'm very sorry to give you this news. We cannot make any press announcement until you have made the identification and are aware of the circumstances of her death."

"Of course." She could hear the tremor in his voice. "I'm stunned; I cannot take it in. I will be with you within the time stipulated."

Alice raised her eyebrows when Moira used her new rank, but she did not say anything. Silently she put everything back in place. They closed the door. As they were locking it, the lift door opened and a uniformed PC came across to the flat.

"Good," said Moira. "I'm DCI Masters. I presume you're going to keep watch on the apartment. Please inform me if anyone comes visiting."

Goredale Scar, Malham, Yorkshire Dales.

Detective Inspector Hall went back to the tent. A single P.C. was there on guard.

"Not long now, son. The S.O.C.O. team will be on their way back in a police van. All the stuff inside will be packed and the tent dismantled. It will be taken to Bradford. The two girls are already there for the post-mortem after formal identification."

With that he left the Scar and walked up the road to Malham. He enjoyed a walk, but for him it was marred. The death of the girls, all their lives to look forward to, hung heavy on his shoulders. His eyes were moist.

"May God have mercy on their souls," he murmured. He felt it must be old age creeping up on him prematurely. It would not do for him to show emotion. He had a reputation of being a hard but fair man. Experience had made him hard. He remembered, as a very young cadet PC, going into a house in Bradford, part of the arrest team for the Black Panther. His blood had curdled when he saw all the instruments of death that man had hidden in his attic. A fitness freak, porn of the worst description, sadism, you name it, the sewers of a man's mind. Even now it made his blood run cold. He had no idea whether that monster was still alive, in or out of prison.

He finally reached the pub. It was like a children's party in the garden for policemen. They were all in shirtsleeves with the witnesses having soft drinks. The artist was there, with the 'Identikit Operator.' One was drawing, and the other 'feeding' his computer. There seemed to be a lot of head scratching.

"When can we have a composite?" he asked.

"Not before tomorrow afternoon I'm afraid."

"Okay," he said. "We know he's long gone from here."

He went back to his car and looked at a map showing the motorways. A thought struck him and he phoned Detective Sergeant Johnson at the station.

"Robin, I'm looking at a map showing the M6. Can you contact the motorway police and see if you can get a list of speeding cars, travelling North and South, approximate time 2:30 to 6 a.m.? The sections to check are as follows. In a northerly direction, from junction 34, that is, Lancaster to the north of Carlisle, say as far as Lockerbie, Junction 17 on the Glasgow motorway, the M74. Then, in a southerly direction from Junction 37, Killington Lake to Junction 28, Leyland.

"That should cover all the intersections where he could join the motorway, North or South. If the cameras are working, get them to transfer pictures to the C.A.T.C.H.E.M. link. So that we are not flooded with photographs, have them transfer a photograph only once, of any car breaking the law, together with a summary of the cameras that tracked it and the speed and time of the offence."

"Thank you, Sir, I will see to it straightaway. By the way, the Superintendent rang. You are to come back to the station at once; go to the Superintendent's office and pick up the red phone; ask for X17. There will be a recorded message for you. That's all, Sir. See you soon."

Perplexed, D.I. Hall drove back to Skipton. He could not think straight; he was anxious to go and see Ken and Mabel. He felt almost a love a son would have for a father, which he himself had never had. He knew nothing about Ken but was very impressed with the demeanor of the man.

At the station he went direct to the Super's office and saw the red phone, which he had wondered about from time to time. He picked it up and asked for X17.

"Good evening, Patrick, this is the Chief Constable recording a message to you. Surprise, surprise! I am at a high-level conference in some place very beautiful. I have authorization by higher authority to personally pass this on to you.

"As from tomorrow you will be working for the 'National force of detectives.' Not under the aegis of the station you are presently attached to. Your new boss is a chap that we all know by his excellent reputation; almost a legend. Detective Superintendent Bob Ferguson. Now re-ranked as Northern National Commander.

"I give you my congratulations and I want you to know I am one hundred per cent behind the reorganization, so don't let me down. Your new rank is Detective Chief Inspector." With that the phone went dead.

Patrick, dazed, slumped into a chair. When he recovered from the shock, he left the office and went across to the little hotel where Mabel and Ken were staying. He knocked on their door.

"Good evening," said Patrick, when Ken opened the door. "Are you settled in? Is Mabel feeling better? The bad news is that there will probably be no inquest until Friday morning. The station's having difficulty in locating the parents; it appears everyone is on holiday. Our pathologist has done a swap: he is doing an autopsy in Tees-side tomorrow morning, and Mr. Sinclair Ferguson is coming over here to do the post-mortem on the girls who are at Bradford. So I have come to take you for a meal."

Ken was moved. "What about your wife and kids, Patrick?"

"Oh, I'm not married. I have a small cottage in Burnsall Bridge and live alone. There are plenty of nice restaurants in Skipton. I would feel very honoured if you would dine with me. It's a bit of a celebration, really, if one can celebrate under such circumstances. Out of the blue, quite unexpectedly, they have made me a Chief Inspector. I thought I was five years away from such promotion, but its official; from the Chief Constable himself."

"Well!" said Mabel. "It's very nice of you, and you were so kind to me during this terrible morning. I know I won't sleep; every time I close my eyes, I see those two lovely girls. They had good careers! Cathy worked in one of those designer salons in Chester. Alison had just finished her degree at Manchester; in Electrical Engineering, would you believe! She was starting her first job after this holiday at British Aerospace near Chester; as a graduate trainee; now it's all gone." With that she began to cry again.

Both men put their arms around her.

"Come on, luv, let's be on our way. We still have to eat. We are not going to be beholden to this young feller; he has already accepted an invitation to a weekend with us in Withernsea. Once he's tried your cooking, Mabel, he'll nobbut want to leave. Mebbe we can find him a nice lass to keep him company. How about Lillian's girl Nancy; she's not walking out with anyone."

"Get on with you man! Let's go. Tak no notice of his blather, Patrick." She smiled. "He really is a good man."

Redcar. Early evening.

Alison and Moira drove back to Tees-side. Moira checked with the station. No further news. Policemen were still out questioning whom they could. There would be a meeting to cover the facts at 10.00 a.m. the following morning.

"Look," said Alice. "Don't be alone tonight in your room; our house is always there for you. The girls will swamp you, but we will be together as a family. Bob will be devastated. He will need his little sister! We are a family? Except, one member is missing; our Jan." Her tears flowed copiously and she stopped the car. Moira drove the rest of the way back to Eaglescliffe.

Moira sighed. Tomorrow was another day, and none of them were going to look forward to it.

CHAPTER 12

▼

TUESDAY EVENING, 9TH JULY. SOUTHERN IRELAND.

The man Michael had changed his mind. He could not run away yet. He was still crossing the Rubicon; so he turned west, round Loch Neagh, onto the M1 motorway and eventually joined the A3 through Amagh, Omagh, Strabane and then into Londonderry.

He drove straight through the city to Derry airport and into the long-term car park. With his rucksack over one shoulder he went to the arrivals hall to look at the flights available on the notice board inside the tourist centre. Nothing tonight, so he booked and paid with cash for an open return to Inverness, flying out at 6.00 p.m. the following morning.

This was one of his advantages, knowing all his favourite areas so well. Leaving the airport, he walked along the feeder road looking for accommodation and finding a Travelodge, which was ideal for him. Furnished with separate entrances to each en suite room, it was only necessary to cross the car park to eat at the restaurant. Just another traveller, completely nondescript.

A very up-to-date Lodge, it was, with no receptionist. Instead, a screen display, showing the layout of the rooms, which were occupied, reserved, or vacant. By touching the screen the details of the room and the cost was displayed. Once room selection was completed, a credit card could be inserted into the reader. The key card was then automatically delivered. Once accepted, the room could only be cancelled by insertion first of the key card, and then the credit card for the final account. Simple, innocuous, and private.

Entering the room after depositing his bag, he immediately left, closing the door after him, making sure he had put the key card into his wallet. Satisfied, he went direct to the restaurant.

The menu looked good, better than the normal fast-food places. He sat down with the papers: no mention of anything germane to himself. He ordered the steak pie with new potatoes, carrots and gravy, and a pot of tea. His food was on the table in a very short time. He ate slowly, for he was tired; it had been a long drive all night and all day. It was something he was used to, but an early night and a good sleep would not come amiss. Tomorrow he would be in Scotland. With that he paid his bill at the cash desk, crossed over to his room, went in and fell on the bed. Sleep was instant!

Wednesday, 10th July

He was awake at 4:30 in the morning; quickly he showered, put his things together and left the room. Depositing the key card and then his credit card, he received his receipt; a brisk walk took him back to the airport. After checking in and leaving his rucksack as baggage for the 'hold,' he went to the cafeteria for coffee and a quick breakfast. The flight was called and it was a direct exit to the aircraft. The plane was a Saab Executive, ideal for quick hops over the water, mainly used by the business fraternity. The flight itself was uneventful. On landing at Inverness he walked through the terminal out of the airport, ignoring the main car rental kiosks. He took the airport bus into Inverness and walked from the centre up and by the side of the prison to a small holiday car hire place he had spotted on a previous visit. He paid in cash for a Nissan Almeira on a three-day hire. To return, he only had to telephone and they would meet him at the airport.

It was to be another long drive for him. The plan was to follow the A82 as it wound its way by the side of Loch Ness, Loch Oich and Loch Lochy and eventually to Fort William. It was there that he planned to pick up extra money from one of his private bank accounts; cash deposited years ago and paybacks from contractors. He had spent nearly two years up here, redesigning industrial plants in the Black Isle, Invergordon, and Inverness itself. From Fort William he planned to drive on to Glencoe. This was one of his favourite walking areas. Two full days of activity and then drive back for the Saturday evening flight.

The music of Mussorsky filled his mind: 'Night on a bare mountain'! The tapestry of evil portrayed in that composition assailed him as he remembered he was still in the Rubicon. His own Odyssey! An odyssey of murder!

Colne. Early morning.

The milkman had been early at Patricia's House. The four pints were still on the doorstep: he sighed, scratched his head, what should he do? Possibly she was late coming back, and had entered her home by the rear door so as not disturb the neighbours. He gathered up the four pints of the 'by-now' sour milk and left two fresh pints, resolving to come back when he had finished his round and see if she had returned. It was a worry to him. He counted this lady as a friend and didn't care a jot about the rumours that floated about concerning the "goings on" in this house.

Les Wilkes left the house at the usual time and sauntered across to Tesco's to have breakfast. Judging the time to be right for Patricia to be up and about, he made his predetermined calls from one of the public phones in the store rather than from his mobile. He would give her another fifteen minutes and then walk slowly across the fields to the back of her house.

The milkman returned after nine o'clock. The milk was still there. He rang the doorbell and walked round the back. No sign, no sound. It was too strange. He felt frightened and resolved to call at the police station on his way home. They would know what to do.

Sergeant Greenwood had just finished viewing the latest C.A.T.C.H.E.M. and H.O.L.M.E.S. information. One murder in Cleveland and the two in Malham, the first, a lady Pathologist and the other, two young girls, left her shaken and with tears in her eyes.

Leaving the computer room, she went to look at the incident reports compiled by the night shift. The pattern had been good over the past few weeks and last night was no exception; pretty quiet for this time of the year. Notwithstanding there was quite a lot of holiday traffic, night and day, and with the new supermarkets open twenty-four hours, the nights were no longer quiet for the budding burglar. It had made a difference!

The phone in the duty room rang. "Sergeant Greenwood, can I help you?"

"Millie, its Sylvia. We are at that new place in Barnoldswick for early morning brunch. Patricia was supposed to meet us here, but she's not turned up. We tried ringing her, but nothing. What do you think?"

"Knowing Patricia, she could have a man friend there for most of the night and is sleeping it off. Possibly the one you were telling me about."

"I don't think so," said Sylvia. "We were to go over the plans for the new extension, and then meet the architect."

"Sylvia, hang on there a bit longer, give it another thirty minutes; as soon as we can, we'll do some checking. Inspector Wilkes is off this morning."

"Wilkes?" said Sylvia. "We know all about him! 'Nod-nod, wink-wink.'"

"You're not telling me that Inspector Wilkes is one of Patricia's special friends?"

Sylvia laughed. "That is for me to know and for you to guess. Stephanie and I will order our brunch and give Patricia a little more time."

Millie put the phone down. "Les Wilkes," she breathed. "I'd never have believed it."

The duty constable on the reception desk put his head round the door. "Have you a moment, please, Sarge, to see Mr. Tom Harris?"

Millie knew Tom. He was her milkman.

"Yes," she said. "Send him in. Morning Tom, how are you? Someone stealing milk off the doorsteps again?"

"No, Mrs. Greenwood, nothing like that. It's Miss Saint; you know her, she lives on the street by the side of the playing fields…"

"You mean Patricia, Patricia Saint!"

"Yes," said Tom.

"What's the problem then, Tom?"

"She's not there, Sergeant. I've left milk on her doorstep each morning since Sunday. After I finished my round this morning I went back to her house and rang the bell a couple of times. No answer. I peered through the letterbox just as the phone was ringing. It rang for a short while and then stopped; then it rang again. Please, Millie, can you do something? I really feel worried about her."

She rang Sylvia on her mobile.

"Sylvia, its Millie. Have you still got a key for Patricia's house? I know she gave you one to let the architect in, when she was about her 'other' business."

"Yes," said Sylvia. "I have it here."

"Good, stay put; I know where you are. We will come and get you."

She called one of the patrol cars and asked their location. They were on the edge of town checking the speed of cars as they came into the thirty-mile an hour limit.

She requested them to pick her up at the station pronto. The car was there in minutes with the blue light flashing. It was a fast drive to Barlick, as it was known to the locals. Sylvia and Stephanie were waiting.

"Come on, you two, a quick ride in a police car; please make sure you don't talk in front of witnesses."

With that they left the café, got into the car and were off. With the flasher continually on, they were soon back into Colne.

Millie nudged the driver. "Right, Geoff, we go quietly and slowly now. You know the house. Pull into the side street next to it."

Sergeant Greenwood, with Stephanie and Sylvia, went up to the front door. Sylvia produced her key and unlocked it, and they went in, Geoff following them. There was a smell permeating the house, nauseating, difficult to understand. They shivered as they went into the parlour. It looked undisturbed, neat and prim, just as Patricia always kept it. They heard a noise, a creek on the stairs, and then a man appeared looking white as a sheet.

"Sir," said Millicent. "What are you doing here?"

There was no answer. He had something in his hand and was trying to hide it against his body.

Sylvia, very sharp eyed, was looking at him. "Les Wilkes," she said, "what are you doing with Sylvia's diary?"

He looked wild-eyed. "She's dead," he said, and went towards the back door. Millicent looked at Wilkes. Although he was her boss, she was wise to all his nasty little scams.

"Inspector Wilkes," she said, "I arrest you on suspicion of illegal entry and tampering with evidence. P.C. Stokes, cuff him and take that notebook off him. Be careful with it! Make sure it's 'bagged'; it's evidence. Call your colleague sitting in the car to take charge of Wilkes, take him back to the station. Once you have him in custody, come straight back here. There's a smell of death in this house. We will all wait outside until the 'Scene of Crimes' team gets here. Make sure you also contact the police surgeon. Call them on your radio as you drive back to the station."

The diary was retrieved and bagged and left on the coffee table until the S.O.C.O. team arrived.

Millicent Greenwood shepherded everybody outside. PC Stokes drove back to the station to hand Inspector Wilkes over to the custody sergeant.

Sergeant Greenwood called the Station Superintendent and explained the situation. He complimented her on her quick appraisal of the situation and the action she had taken. He would talk to Wilkes when he arrived at the station and find out why he was in the house.

"Look Millie," he said, "There is something strange about all of this. I have just been talking to the Chief Constable; he is at a high-level conference at the moment. It appears we now have a force of elite detectives to call on in the future. Rather like the old Scotland Yard image. One of them you know from past experience, D.I. Hall from Skipton, now incidentally Detective Chief Inspector Hall since yesterday. We will get him over immediately. I know he's also busy with enquiries relating to the two girls who were murdered at Goredale Scar."

"Yes, Sir, I saw the computer report this morning."

"Well, my girl, and I think it's about time you got out of uniform. Your inspector examination results have come through and you have excellent grades. I will set up the interview with the Chief Constable as soon as he returns to Lancaster."

"Thank you, Sir; at the moment I am too numb to take anything in. I feel we have a dreadful murder on our hands."

Millie turned to Patricia's friends. "Ladies, we can do nothing here until the investigation teams are in place. I also suspect we will need the Pathologist. So I'll arrange a car and a couple of policemen to guard the front and back of the house, and to receive the experts when they arrive. I suggest we now go back to the station. It will be necessary to get statements from you and that of Inspector Wilkes: then we can have some lunch. I will be required here this afternoon, but I will make sure that you are kept in touch."

At that moment her phone rang.

"Hello Millie, it's Patrick Hall. Congratulations on your forthcoming promotion and on your recent marriage. What is it like having a husband in the air and you on the ground? What are your plans for a family? Tell Alex he pipped me to the post. I know he is quite a bit younger than me, but I did have my little dream that you and I would get together. Husband and wife 'ace' detective team!"

Millie laughed. "On with you, you great oaf, Sir. There's a girl coming for you; I feel it in my water. Yes, Alex is now qualified, flying as a co-pilot with Ryanair to all the holiday spots. Ten years before a family; does that answer all your questions, Sir? On the quiet, I did have a soft spot for you. When are you coming over?"

"Right now; Sinclair Cameron is just finishing the post-mortem on the two girls."

"Seriously, it's very bad here. I'll talk to the police surgeon as soon as he appears. This lady lost her life on Saturday night. The room was left with the heating on and the windows closed, as you well know, the ideal conditions for rapid decomposition. I will talk to the Superintendent. We all know Sinclair Cameron by reputation. I am sure the police surgeon would be very glad to have him here with him."

"Okay. You do your checking and I'll be able to call the Superintendent in about fifteen minutes. Sinclair is here for the day. I am sure he will fall in with our plans."

"Thanks Patrick, see you soon. I wish it was under better circumstances."

She immediately rang the Superintendent, explaining the circumstances, and the probable need for the skills of Sinclair Cameron to help the police surgeon. The Super concurred with her, as did the police surgeon, when he knew the facts. So entry was postponed until the afternoon when all could be present.

On her return to the station Millie spent half-an-hour on her computer, compiling a preliminary report concerning the events of the morning. Sylvia Hall was also sitting at a desk, making a written statement relating to her friendship with Patricia Saint and writing down verbatim as far as she could remember the details of the Saturday night telephone call.

Les Wilkes in the cells was also making a statement relating to his relations with Miss Saint, the reason why he entered the house and had taken the notebook, and more importantly why he had not immediately reported her death.

Millie had glanced at the notebook and photocopied the page for Saturday, including the notes she had written about her visitor, known to her as Michael. The contents of the notebook were dynamite to so many influential people in the town: so she sealed it in a padded envelope and marked it for the Chief Constable's attention, adding a note confirming that a photocopy had been made of the page relating to Saturday the 6th July. She was following the Superintendent's advice; only the Chief Constable could deal with this particular problem.

In Skipton, Patrick Hall was receiving reports from the investigating police constable. There was not much to go on; the man at the pub had been very pleasant and had not spoken very much at all. He had a brown beard flecked with grey; his hair was brown with no grey in it. As far as they could recollect, he was about 45 years of age.

Tim Harrison had watched with amusement when the man had slung the dumpy girl over his shoulder and with seemingly no effort had walked a good half-mile with her. The blonde girl had walked alongside him quite unperturbed.

Albert Walker had also observed him carrying the girl up the path toward what he assumed was their tent: the blonde girl leading the way. He recognized the same man at the barbecue. That's why he had thrust a pint in his hand.

Geoff Endicott had been sitting next to him and had taken his fiver for the kitty. Where that fiver was now, he had no idea. He was the only one that had spoken to the man. He felt he had a North-East accent. He himself came from Sunderland but his accent was not so broad. The Yorkshire influence in the man's accent was noticeable, he thought, possibly south of Durham, but not Tees-side.

They both remembered he wore a one-piece khaki anorak with zip pockets across the chest, very popular at one time, made by 'Blacks' and now superseded by designer mountain ware.

The two policemen in the patrol car could not add very much. It was definitely a bearded face they had seen when he passed them. The car was an off-road type, but they had not taken much notice. Even looking at pictures of off-road vehicles from the database drew a blank.

Checking the roads, no patrol car seemed to have been on the A65 during the small hours of the morning. Motorway camera detection was undergoing radical alterations. Cameras being changed for digital ones, with direct links up to a central computer. Certain ones were operating 'southbound' but there was no record relating to any motoring offence of an off-road vehicle. On the 'northbound' side the system was inoperative up to Carlisle. With regard to the M74, the system was not yet commissioned.

The good news was that they had found fingerprints on the coffee flask and were in the process of eliminating the girls' fingerprints. A good print had been found on the bottom flap fastening of the tent. They would be processed and put on a national database for comparison.

The Identikit pictures would be finalized within the hour. The information would also be on the database, so it could be printed out as required at any police station. The S.O.C.O. team was still examining the nylon cord and the tape.

Sighing, Patrick closed down the screen, picked up his notebook and made his way out of the station and off to find Mr. Sinclair Cameron.

The post-mortem was complete. He saw the girls' bodies lying on the gurneys. All the routines had been completed, the organs examined and weighed, stomach contents analyzed. There had been no violation of their bodies of any kind: the killer had simply watched them suffocate.

Allison had been conscious, and it was possible to see how she wrenched at her wrists, trying to free the rope that bound them. But it was to no avail, for her death had come quickly. Cathy had drunk quite a lot; she had been suffocated while she slept

Patrick knew he had to remain unemotional in all of this, completely dispassionate; but the tears welled in his eyes as he looked at the girls for the last time. The assistant pathologist would return the girls to a 'normal' state so that the sectioning of their bodies was hidden. The girls' bodies would be kept in cold storage until they could be formally identified. The uniformed branch was still busy trying to contact the girls' parents.

He and Mr. Cameron left for Colne. Not an afternoon to look forward too.

CHAPTER 13

▼

WEDNESDAY 10TH JULY. MORNING—NORTH YORKSHIRE.

A sergeant from the Stokesley police station had set up the incident Room in Broughton Village Hall.

The two patrol officers had been very thorough. They had gone directly to Rievaulx Abbey and caught the cafeteria staff before they closed up. Yes, they had remembered the man, mainly because he had such a large breakfast. They did recall him having a beard with a bit of grey in it and brown hair, although they did not really look at faces, but he had seemed to be a very nice man. He had bought postcards and envelopes at the gift counter, and had sat at his breakfast table writing them out; even though it was raining hard, he had then popped outside to post his letters in the box set in the wall of the cafeteria.

The lady at the gift counter had recognized his anorak, a green Berghaus. The officers took statements and asked the ladies to come down to the incident room at Broughton. The Scenes of Crime team would be there with their Identikit operator. They would transport the ladies to Broughton and bring them back again. Possibly only an hour would be needed. They radioed in with news of a possible identification and to confirm that the Identikit team was there.

The two police officers had also checked all houses in the hamlet of Chop Yat and had a confirmation that the man with a green anorak and a beard, just managed to catch the Helmsley bus on Saturday morning and had got off at Rievaulx.

After leaving the ladies with the Identikit team, they commenced to check the pubs and guesthouses. The landlord at the Jet Miners remembered the man with a beard and a green anorak; it was Friday, and he had come in for a ploughman's and a pint. He had quite a large rucksack.

The police officers called back to the incident room; did the ladies remember if the man had a rucksack with him? Apparently not, but he could have left it outside. They rang one of the witnesses who recalled a man getting into the bus.

"Definitely not," said the witness. "He jumped on the bus like a two-year-old, no baggage at all."

The two officers looked at each other, both having the same thought; he had booked in somewhere, but there was not much in Broughton. They went back to the pub.

"If you needed to recommend a place for a walker to stay, where in Broughton would you recommend?"

"Normally no place in Broughton; they are more geared up to families wanting to tour the area. There's only one guest house well known to the walking fraternity; that is Mrs. Allenby's at Kirkby."

They thanked him, got back into the car and drove the three miles to Kirkby.

Mrs. Allenby had collected her post; yes, there it was; the promised letter from the man. She was about to open it when the doorbell rang. There were two policemen at the door and a patrol car standing on the road beyond the front garden.

"Sorry to disturb you, Mrs. Allenby. Have you had any guests staying this weekend?"

"Well, in a manner of speaking, no; and yet, in a manner of speaking, yes."

The officers looked nonplussed.

"A man called in while I was out and booked a room on Friday. But he never took it, though he left his things here. He telephoned me on Saturday morning to apologize and asked me to send his rucksack on to Middlesbrough. As far as I know he never collected it. You will find it at the United Bus parcels office. I was worried whether I carried out his instructions correctly and have been waiting for a letter from him, as he promised to send the money to pay for the room and also for the carriage of the rucksack to Middlesbrough. Here is the letter; I was a just about to open it."

"Don't do that," said one of the patrolmen. "We'll take you to the incident room and have it opened there; then we'll check it for fingerprints."

The envelope was franked for Rievaulx Abbey—so this was the man!

"Mrs. Allenby, have you the time to go with us to the village hall? We have it set up as an incident room. We cannot tell you the reason why; but there we can have your letter photographed and checked for fingerprints."

She was quite excited; this would be an adventure for her!

"A moment," she said. "I will get my coat."

Once at the incident room, the patrol officer telephoned Tees-side headquarters and asked to speak to Detective Chief Inspector Masters. She came on immediately and he recounted their findings relating to the letter posted to Mrs. Allenby and the Rucksack that was at the United parcels office. She promised him it would be collected at once and that she would be with them within the hour.

Moira had arrived at the office early and was there to meet him when Major Richard Fielding arrived. The identification of Jan was completed very quickly. Richard's face was pale and drawn. How could this have happened to his sister? He had arranged to take compassionate leave, and with police permission he intended to take the first flight to Vancouver and find his other sister Janine. He wanted to be with her and tell her before the press broke the news.

Moira hugged him. They were both in tears. He was driving over to Manchester Airport to catch a flight. The army had arranged everything. He would bring Janine back in order that they could make the funeral arrangements after the inquest.

Detective Chief Inspector Moira Masters was perplexed. News was now floating through on the Police network of other murders in Malham, and possibly in Colne. She knew Bob Ferguson would have the same information and would be anxious to be back. A pattern was emerging, but it was too early. They needed the identikit pictures and more information from Colne. Sinclair Cameron was there, so obviously something was very wrong.

As she scanned through the information on the screen, she saw that Detective Inspector Hall was involved. Patrick! She knew him from the profiling courses they both attended at Bramshill, and she quite liked him. But then, as in all police friendships, it was as 'ships passing in the night.'

Simon Priest came into the office.

"Moira, they've had a breakthrough on the Malham case. A good print off the coffee flask and the same print on the tent flap. The Identikit picture from the witness information will be on screen within the hour."

"Good! Thank you, Simon."

She telephoned the incident room to keep them informed. They were busy lifting off the prints on the twenty-pound and ten pound note that they had found in the envelope along with the explanatory note, which, incidentally, showed no sign of a fingerprint. All of them were now waiting in feverish anticipation for the rucksack. The last request was heartbreaking.

"Moira, could you organize us some refreshments, please?"

She thanked them for their diligence and gave assurance that refreshments would be delivered to them very quickly. A call to the local pub resolved the problem. It had always been a favourite venue for her, Bob, Alice and Jan. The landlord assured her that the selection of ploughman's, plus tea and coffee, would be there within thirty minutes.

She then quickly rang Patrick on his mobile.

He was busy with his statements from Patricia's friends and with their renegade Inspector Les Wilkes. Once Sinclair Cameron was available they would be back at Patricia's House. He verbally confirmed that Patricia's night visitor was a bearded man, very nice and pleasant. He felt sure that his and Moira's path were converging and they would meet very soon.

She pondered that the bearded man at Malham was wearing a khaki anorak, whereas in Cleveland he had a green anorak. It was necessary to try and trace the route between Cleveland and Malham. She rang the police at Thirsk and Ripon.

"Make sure when the various Identikit pictures come through, every village constable has copies." She emphasized that they were looking for a man in a green anorak, and then in a khaki one. It was certain that his rucksack would have contained spare clothing and other essentials. Therefore it was reasonable to assume that somewhere along the way he had bought replacements.

The rucksack had arrived at Broughton. It was photographed and carefully opened, the contents all laid out on the table. There was a miscellany of briefs, shirts, one pair of black moccasins of Italian manufacture, a book by Alan Bullock, *A Study in Tyranny*, a toilet bag, toothbrush and toothpaste. Also, there was a Braun electric razor in a case, and, surprise, surprise, a beard dye pack marketed by a national chemist chain, the colour, medium brown! Fingerprints were abundant and the experts were busy logging and photographing them. There was nothing that would give a DNA sample.

The rucksack was a Berghaus, medium price range.

It all came down to the fingerprints to bring some cohesion to the investigation.

Wednesday 10th July. North Scotland. Midday.

Michael had made good time to Fort William. There was no problem with the bank, so he now had an extra thousand pounds sterling in funds. He had formed his plans for selling the car; so simple; he nearly kicked himself as he turned it over his mind. Not the problem he thought it would have been. To dump it, to sell it to a dealer, unthinkable; too many complications; but the real solution was so simple and uncomplicated. He was pleased with his decision, but that was for later.

The excitement was mounting within him; he had his very late breakfast at a small outdoor cafe on the shores of Loch Linnhe, and then did a bit of shopping.

He bought a new anorak, a lightweight dark green Ky-way at designer prices, and a new pair of jeans with zips, so they could be adjusted to half-length or as shorts. Also, extra underwear, a couple of T-shirts and an Icelandic sleeping bag. Rather than staying in a guesthouse or hotel this evening, he intended to bivouac up in the mountains. The outfitters was also the climbing shop, so he bought some cans of self heating soup, a small acetylene lamp, some slabs of Kendal Mint Cake, the brown variety; he did not like the white, which was peppermint.

At the local bakery he bought fresh crusty rolls, and next door at a general dealers, a cucumber and some tomatoes. For drinks, he bought three plastic bottles of the high-energy fizz.

As he wandered through the town he found a bookshop; on the shelves they had a couple of books that were on his reading list, both in paperback. *The last days of Hitler* and *Das Reich*, the latter being the story of the great Panzer division of the SS and the carnage it left as it traversed France to take part in the Battle of Normandy. He was also able to replace his book by Alan Bullock.

Well satisfied with his purchases, he left the bookshop and returned to his car. Detailed plans he could not yet make; for the moment he was content to follow the A82 down the locks and into Glencoe. There, he would turn up to the hidden town of Kinlochleven, not so much a tourist area. That is where he would park his car, sit by the Loch side with a paper of fresh fish and golden chips, plenty of salt and vinegar, and gaze across at the awesome beauty of the glen. He would then take the bus up to the head of Glencoe and spend the evening at the bar of the King's House Hotel, which was always full of climbers and walkers, and go with the 'flow of the Rubicon.'

With that in mind, he took out of his pocket a tape, which he also had purchased; it was Mendelssohn, the *Scottish Symphony*, and *Fingal's Cave*, so germane to his mood and his surroundings. The grandeur of the loch, the mountains, gigantic, sombre, devouring and yet so awe-inspiring. He almost changed his mind; he would have loved to include Ben Nevis. He was only a few miles away! His favourite route would be to take the path from the youth hostel which ostensibly was the old observatory route. Then branch off to the left across the shoulder down into the valley, the north face on his left side black and ominous, famous for the severity of its winter climbs. But for him it would then have to be a stiff climb back to four thousand feet to the summit of Cairn Mor Dearg, passing the Scottish Mountaineering club hut on the way. From there a delightful traverse known as the Devil's Arête to the summit of Nevis. Exhilarating, but not for him; too many people, no easy route of escape.

No, a plan was formulating in his head; it was 'now or never.' Tomorrow the north of the country would be up in arms. He continued down the A82. Glencoe it was.

The tape was running, proclaiming the genius of Mendelssohn, such a poetic musical picture of Scottish beauty, the rush of the waves as they cavorted around Fingals Cave in the Isle of Staffa. He imagined the young Mendelssohn, Felix to his friends and loved ones, performing at Buckingham Palace for the youthful Queen Victoria and her consort Prince Albert. There was so much to life, so many things to live for. Mendelssohn had a full life, a devoted wife and five children, yet he died at the age of thirty-eight.

He dare not dwell on his life, the mistakes, the bad things, and now because of his deeds he would never have any other life.

Wednesday 10th July. Colne. Afternoon.

Cohesion! And it was taking place.

The Identikit pictures from Cleveland and Malham had a similar likeness. The fingerprints found on the letter, and on the articles in the rucksack, matched those lifted off the coffee flask and the tent flap. It was the same man. Now it was suspected that the incident in Colne was also connected. The statement from Sylvia, Patricia's friend, had told them that Miss Saint had described the man to her over the phone. Bearded, nice, but not too handsome; somewhere along the way, Patricia had been able to fill in a better picture in her diary entry; even to describing the delicacies he had bought. She had recognized that they had been purchased from the Tesco supermarket. The police were busy following that line of inquiry.

Les Wilkes' statement and interview with the Superintendent was painful. The Super did not care if he had a hundred girlfriends on the quiet: but to enter the bedroom of a girl, found to be dead and to take the diary in the hope of getting out of that house with incriminating evidence concerning himself and others, was very serious and embarrassing to the police. In discussion with the Chief Constable it had been agreed not to press charges, providing he resigned immediately; his pension could not remain intact, but agreement had been reached with the higher authority that it would be reduced to fifty per cent, payable upon normal retirement age.

The Super warned him not to protest. The alternative was prison. Bent policemen did not fare well in prison, from the screws or from the inmates. His lot would be Parkhurst or possibly Inverness. The publicity of the trial and the relentless hounding of the press would make the lives of his nearest and dearest a nightmare.

Reluctantly he accepted retirement on half pension, and agreed to be bound by the 'Secrecy Act' and not to the divulge any of this.

Patrick was waiting for Millie in the company of a very distinguished man.

"Millie, this is Mr. Sinclair Cameron, chief pathologist at Tees-side and other numerous areas."

"Sinclair, this is Mrs. Graham, once a sergeant, now Detective Inspector, but for her benefit we are not equal in rank; mine is now confirmed as Detective Chief Inspector."

Millie pulled a face at him. The mood changed.

"Let's get to the house; the police surgeon is waiting there."

"Okay, Millie," said Patrick. "Lead the way."

The drive of a few minutes was in silence. A policeman stood guard at the door. He let them in without a word. The scenes of crime officers looked glum; they had completed their investigations, photographed the body and found some prints on a champagne glass in the bedroom, but that was all. It appeared that the killer had been meticulous in cleaning up before he left to the house.

There was an odour in the air. One of the officers gave them masks. The smell of death was all-prevalent. Mr. Cameron suggested that they went out into the back garden while he explained the situation before he commenced the actual examination.

Sinclair cleared his throat.

"Let me outline a few salient facts before we actually go up those stairs. The body has been there from Saturday evening until now, Wednesday afternoon. The windows closed, heating on; decay is exacerbated by such conditions. What you can smell is the aroma of butyric acid, 'the stench of death.' Given the said conditions, the body has been exposed to several events or processes, which have occurred during this period.

"The first is Autolysis—the juices, which digest our food in normal life, reverse their action in death and commence to digest the gastro-internal tract. A few hours after death the acids, which have patiently served us in life, will attack and eat through the esophagus. As one famous forensic pathologist puts it, it's like a minor French Revolution in which the servants become the masters. Simultaneously, in the liver, the protein will break down, forming a crystal-like structure of tyrosine.

"The second is that of Putrefaction. This will take place very quickly as the bacterial action breaks out unchecked within the body. Decomposition due to this is much more evident than autolysis.

"The blood becomes a sea of bacteria, which forms and multiplies; methane gas is released within the blood vessels and the tissues of the body. The body swells and the butyric acids are released. Spontaneous combustion can take place if any source of ignition is available.

"Thirdly, the skin darkens and strips from its moorings. Your scene-of-crime officers will know from experience how difficult it is to take the fingerprints off someone who has been dead for some time. All this is the result of carbon-based compounds turning into other carbon compounds, the elements of life and also of death.

"Please forgive me for the lecture. I wanted you to be aware of what you will see when we mount the stairs. All of us must wear the one-piece suits and keep on the rubber gloves. The doctor and I will go first and give you a call when to come up. We will need one of the crime officers to be with us, complete with a camera and a fingerprint/DNA kit."

Patrick and Millie were called up. It was a sombre time. Patricia had been a very pretty lady. She had on a red lace waspie suspender belt with matching stockings. The doctor and Mr. Cameron had finished their examination and were now waiting for the undertakers to transfer the body to the morgue. The scenes-of-crime officer had, with Sinclair's help, been able to take a set of Patricia's fingerprints; and, also because of the heavy petting which must have taken place, a D.N.A. swab could be very beneficial to them.

Deoxyribonucleic acid, D.N.A. for short, was the breakthrough in police work—the substance which contains the genetic code and which makes every human being unique.

Sinclair elaborated further.

"There are two types of D.N.A in each living cell—nuclear or genomic, and mitochondrial. The first is lost very quickly in decomposition. But it stays longer in dried blood or semen. So we are hopeful, as we found semen present in the mouth. But it is very difficult to isolate when bacteria is present. The latter lies outside of a living cell that is, in this case, the tail of a male sperm. So we are hopeful on two counts for a positive result. As soon as we have them isolated, we will transmit the code to the National D.N.A. base located in Birmingham.

"Another observation. The bruising you see on the buttocks and the back of the legs is not due to a violent action. It is called hypostasis, the name for the settlement of blood. In this case it has congealed in the lower part of the body, the buttocks and the legs. Now we are finished here; I will do the postmortem tomorrow."

Patrick remarked: "It looks as though the 'Coroners Inquest' will have to be on Friday, at the very earliest; if so, contact the next of kin."

Sinclair agreed. "Tentatively, if the one in Tees-side is for 10.00 a.m. on Friday, it will be possible to have the Inquest of the two girls and this lady in the afternoon".

With a heavy heart, Millie and Patrick left the house and went direct to the supermarket. The uniformed police had gathered the night staff in the rest room. They had also checked the records and found an arrest had been made in the early hours of the morning. The two policemen, who had made the arrest, were also present.

The breakfast ladies were quite vociferous. A plump blonde lady had served the man and had taken the early morning newspaper to him. As far a she could recollect he was on the start of his holidays.

"His wife had kicked him out and chased him up into the mountains. Apparently she was quite a bit younger than he. She did this when his business was swamping him. His accent was Yorkshire with something else, a bit of Geordie."

All agreed that he was not forthcoming as to where he lived or where he was staying. The Identikit picture was handed to them, and they all agreed it could be the man. Like all people in shops and cafés, they did not take too much notice of faces.

The night duty officers could only confirm a bearded man had walked into the supermarket as they were going out with their suspected shoplifter. He seemed to be very sprightly and to know what he was about. They had grinned at him and he had reciprocated.

The night watchman had stood close to the back of his car. It was in the waste bin area, which was not illuminated. During the night; only the entrance and the front section of the park were lit. The car, in his words, "was one of those jeep things." It was of a very dark colour. Only two things had stuck in his memory: it was a very nice car, and it had an unusual type of number plate. One of those you buy from a Sunday paper for a ridiculous amount of money. He had no idea of the make. It was definitely not a Land Rover. His brother had one of those up on the farm.

That was it; they realized they could only now try to track his movement. He would be 'well gone' by now. The waste bins had also been checked, but they had been emptied on the Monday. The contents would have been incinerated during the night. Patrick arranged to have the Identikit team within the hour. He courteously asked everyone to stay and help the team to improve the likeness.

Millie, meanwhile, had contacted the station, which now had the address of Patricia's parents in Leeds. Patrick was quite happy to accompany her. They needed the parents to know before the storm broke, and to be able to arrange with them formal identification.

"Sinclair will finish postmortem in the morning, so it would be possible for the parents to confirm the identity early afternoon."

Millie concurred. "I have a telephone number for them, but I have also spoken to the Leeds police who are going to have a couple of policeman standing by discreetly, somewhere near the house. They will wait for us; they have already confirmed there is someone in the house."

Millie sighed. "I hate this part of police work!"

CHAPTER 14

▼

WEDNESDAY 10TH JULY, TEATIME. TEES-SIDE.

Commander Bob Ferguson was back in his office. The Chief Constable would follow later. He had much to do: arranging a weekend of meetings with Detective Superintendents in the North of England; generating a new structure, the improvement of communications and the sharing of information. All outstanding current investigations into major crime had to be reviewed: resources examined with the aim of improving efficiency and capture rate.

But first, the portentous events of the last few days were uppermost in his mind. He summoned Moira.

"Good afternoon, Detective Chief Inspector. I presume by now your new warrant card has been issued, and you have received your letter of appointment. Have you also received a copy of the preliminary circular which has gone out?"

"Yes Sir, I have; and I wish to offer you my congratulations. I know I speak for all your officers here. When the time is right we want to arrange a celebration for you and your wife."

"Thank you, Moira," said Bob, "but it will have to be later, very much later: possibly by Christmas we might be able to recover.

"But first, I have to overrule you regarding Simon Priest, and his promotion. Morals are not police business, and as I have gathered that Jan, God rest her soul, was not coerced to go with him. I can understand your feelings, but I must put the needs of the force first. Here we have an expert on information technology, nearly as good as you: we need the best information officer to co-ordinate a large amount of data. We are drafting other people in. Some will be civilian experts, but our man will be in charge. He is having his promotion perhaps three years earlier than he expected, but we need him and we don't want him head hunted, so will you back me up on this?"

"Yes, Sir; of course, Sir." Moira spoke with a quiver of her lips.

"Good." The Commander leaned back in his chair, put his hands together and contemplated her.

"D.C.I. Masters, you are now released from the information section permanently. Working jointly with D.C.I. Patrick Hall, whom you already know, your job is this current murder trail. We need all your skills as detective's psychologists, profilers, etc., and we need the iron determination of Patrick Hall. You will also have the new Inspector from Colne. Millie Greenwood, she has your calibre and determination for police work. Look after her. I believe her husband is an airline pilot; they are newlyweds! For the present they do not see much of each other; both of them are busy building their careers.

"Your investigation will have no boundaries, even if it leads you into Europe or beyond. One more thing before we get down to brass tacks; your promotion quest and that of Patrick's is far from finished. I stress that you're not in competition with each other. Over a period you will draw in more and more competent officers. Promotion opportunities will be much more realistic and a lot of excess weight, dead wood, will be dropped; there will be no 'jobs for the boys' any more.

"Now to the murders and we hope for a common denominator. We have a press conference directly after this meeting. The following points are pertinent:

"1. Jan murdered early Saturday morning, blow to the head, she then drowned.

"2. We think it was a bearded man. Witnesses in Chop Yat, Rievaulx, and also the recovery of rucksack at Middlesbrough complete with a pack of beard dye.

"3. The letter to Mrs.Allenby; hard to believe, but a man with a conscience.

"4. We have a print match on the murders, but he's not one of ours, no record.

"5. He has a car; he must have been parked in Middlesbrough. We know it is a jeep of some description but no positive identification. We will need to check with the traffic wardens and beat policeman.

"6. The anorak changes colour; did he have two or has he stopped somewhere some way to shop?

"7. We need to know his route from Middlesbrough to Malham; where did he stay? Only the local coppers will find out that sort of information, and the good old British public.

"8. The two girls murdered at the campsite in Goredale Scar in the early hours of Tuesday morning; no evidence of interference or theft, just a plain simple murder.

"9. Patricia Saint in Colne. This murder we believe was not part of his plan; to all intents and purposes he was there for a good Saturday night out. Reading between the lines, it would appear that the night was too good, they had much in common, and she liked him as a man, not as a client. It was a complication he did not want, so he put her to sleep permanently.

"10. Nothing taken, no signs of violence to the body. Where was he staying? We need answers from good citizens

"11. We have a D.N.A. swab, a good sample, but again we have no match. No record of any description.

"12. After the murders of the girls, he disappears; the patrol in Malham missed an opportunity of stopping his car. But for what? The murders were at that time unknown to us.

"We must go through all the motions.

"First, formal identification of Jan. The Major and his sister will be back for the Coroners Court; you, Moira, with the doctor and Pathologist, will have to give direct evidence. Of course it will be adjourned for further inquiries.

"Secondly, Patricia. Similarly the post-mortem, the parents' identification and the Coroner's Court; Patrick will handle that, and D.I. Greenwood will have to give evidence. Again, it will be adjourned murder by persons or person unknown.

"Thirdly, with respect to the murdered girls, the Chester and Wrexham police have been gathering information. It appears that through the friendship of the girls, the parents also became friends, and the two couples are on holiday together. They flew from Manchester to Samos in the Greek Islands. Two officers have now gone out to Samos to locate them; we cannot release identification until we have the parents back here.

"The RAF has come to our rescue and a military passenger aircraft is sitting at Samos airport ready to fly them back as soon as they are located. All, of course, with the permission of the island authorities, but kept at a 'very low key.'

"I think that is a basic summary of your reports, Moira, and information collected by Simon."

Bob Ferguson got out of his chair and went to pour the tea that had just arrived for them. He knew Moira's taste, a little milk only, and the same for him. He handed the cup to her, and with his own cup in his hands he commenced to pace the room.

"We need more, and your profiling skills must come to the fore. There is another aspect to this. I was warned in Ireland that a series of murders would take place. An American medium successfully used by the F.B.I. and had been on holiday here in the UK. He loves all the walking areas and was able to spend time in some of his favourite places. Apparently he felt a general sense of foreboding, a series of premonitions, and he is prepared to explain more to us. The F.B.I. has made arrangements to fly him over to us this weekend. Possibly Sunday, if his health is up to it.

"Transcripts of his investigative work, utilizing psychic phenomena, are 'sub judicaire' and cannot, as yet, be released to us.

"As a Christian man, I cannot visualize this. Saul went to the 'Witch of Endor' to know his end, and he was terrified. My Bible condemns mysticism, necromancy, but in this case we cannot ignore it. He and his colleague will have one of the hospitality suites here at headquarters. We will meet them for supper on Sunday evening. A helicopter will be standing by so we can make visits if necessary. The 'we' is Patrick, yourself and myself at this stage. Good job you are both single. I doubt you will be seeing much of your beds over the next few days.

"Let's keep this in mind. Our man! We do not know where he is, north, south, east, west, but one thing is certain, he is not finished: his sojourn has not yet ended!"

Wednesday afternoon, teatime, mid Yorkshire.

Patrick drove Millie to Leeds. They both knew it well; Roundhay Road was their destination. The house itself was built in Yorkshire stone and looked very comfortable. The front garden was swamped by a multitude of roses in different hues and colours.

The Leeds patrol car was parked discreetly in a side road nearby. They stopped on the main road and went over to it. A uniformed Sergeant stepped out.

"Good evening, Sir. Good evening, mar'm."

Millie could feel herself blushing; she was a very pretty girl, a trim figure, jet-black hair and an engaging smile. Patrick looked at her face which was rosy red, and grinned.

"Take no notice, sergeant; she thinks she's too young to be an Inspector." They all laughed. It broke the tension.

"They are in," said the sergeant. "Mr. Markham was out tending his roses, but has now gone indoors for tea, I suspect. They are both retired; he used to have a fish-and-chip shop in Headingly road, lovely fish and chips too, as I recall. They sold it to a chain that was climbing the Harry Ramsden ladder."

"Okay," Patrick intoned. "Let's go and see them."

The sergeant led the way. He rang the bell; the door was opened by a lady still chewing.

"Good evening, Mrs. Markham. I am Sergeant Thomson of the Leeds police, and these are my colleagues. May we come in?"

Mystified, Sue Markham opened the door. "Please do."

They entered the living room. A small tanned man was sitting at a table set for tea.

"Greg," said his wife. "We have visitors."

"Oh my God, whatever has happened?"

Patrick answered. "Mr. Markham, I am Detective Chief Inspector Hall, and this is Detective Inspector Greenwood. We have to tell you that your daughter Patricia is dead. I suggest you pour yourself some tea and I will try to give you details as concisely as possible."

The man turned to his wife, who stood transfixed.

"Bring some extra cups," he said in a strangled voice. "For our visitors, I expect they will need it as much as we do." He turned to Patrick. "Please sit down, all of you. What's done is done. Have your tea, it must be very difficult for you."

They were very grateful for his understanding. They knew the shock would come later. Patrick leaned forward towards Greg and Sue.

"I am going to let Millie Greenwood give you the details. She has lived with this since the discovery, which was this morning."

Greg was quickly out of his chair. He looked Patrick in the eye.

"Let me say one thing which will avoid embarrassment: we know what Patricia was up to in Colne. One of our mutual acquaintances recognized the telephone number in her regular advertisement, and sent us the cutting. We did not respond. We haven't had any communication with her for years. We did not want her to marry her ex-husband, knowing full well his reputation and after the divorce, she just shut herself away. Building a new life, we heard. Now," he continued with a sob, "she has no life!"

"Thank you," said Millie. "It does save a lot of awkward explanation; we know from the post-mortem that Patricia died early Saturday. Yes, she was with a client. From a telephone conversation she had with one of her friends, we know she liked this man; her diary also relates this, and, in fact, she was looking for a longer association with him. She died without suffering; they had been drinking, and she fell asleep; he smothered her with a pillow. She experienced no other violence. You may read more about this on Friday, and no doubt also it will be on the radio and television. The man who did this murdered a woman in Cleveland, a pathologist, in fact, who was walking on the moors; and also two young girls in Malham; they were camping in Goredale Scar. He seems to be on a pilgrimage, if that is the word."

Patrick murmured: "An odyssey; an odyssey of murder."

Millie continued: "We need you to formally identify your daughter. Can you drive down in the morning, or shall we take you tonight and arrange a hotel?"

Greg looked at his wife. "No, we will drive down tomorrow morning."

"Thank you," said Millie. "Mid-morning will be okay, and the inquest will be on Friday. Would you like us to arrange a hotel for you overnight?"

Mrs. Markham looked at Millie. "No, we would rather come back here tomorrow night and drive down again on Friday morning."

"That's grand," said Millie. "Please understand your daughter Patricia died in the early hours of Sunday morning. We only discovered her body this morning. That has certain implications. You will not see her as...as you remember her.

"In the case of the inquest, which will be at 10:30 a.m. on Friday, you will only have to give evidence of identity."

They looked at each other. The pain that creased their faces was plain to see.

"We understand the implications. Both of us now feel the guilt of ignoring our daughter for so many years. Maybe, if we had supported her, this would never have happened!"

Millie took hold of their hands. "Do not blame yourself too much. All we can do is to offer you our deepest condolences. Until tomorrow, goodbye and God bless."

With that they left, and after thanking the sergeant who was from the Mill Hill station, they set off back to Colne.

Millie murmured: "Drop me off at the airport. Alex is due back. I will wait for him there: I just do not feel like going back to an empty house and certainly, not to cook. He has no idea about my promotion. We will find a nice place to eat in Ilkley."

"Okay," said Patrick.

They were both silent during the drive to the airport.

"See you tomorrow," Patrick called out as Millie got out of the car. She smiled at him and disappeared into the terminal building.

He continued through Otley and eventually to Skipton. Sometimes it was so hard to be dispassionate. The three murders weighed heavily upon him. At Skipton he turned into the hotel where Ken and Mabel were staying. He made a call from the bar. "Come and join me."

Ken came down. "Hello, Patrick, good to see you. Mabel will be down in a minute; any more developments?"

Patrick gave him the bare bones of the day's happenings.

Ken was distraught. "How do you stop him?"

An expressive shrug was the answer. "Come on, Ken, a beer for you and the white wine for Mabel; and then we'll find something to eat. Tell me of your day."

Ken explained that they had been up to the campsite and made arrangements with the manager of the site to sell a caravan. If he were not able to sell it quickly, they would allow him to rent it out as required. In that case he would maintain it and take a percentage of the hiring cost. Mabel was not well enough to go out to a restaurant, so in the end they had bar meals and all opted for an early night. Ken and Mabel confirmed they could stay for a few more days, until such times as the inquest could be arranged.

Patrick went home to a darkened house. He felt extremely lonely. There was a message for him on his answer-phone.

"Hi Patrick, this is Moira speaking. As soon as you finish on Friday, jump in your car and come across to Tees-side. Ring me when you get near to Newport Bridge. I will wait for you as you turn down Newport Road to the centre. You have to be here for Sunday, as you will find out tomorrow, so why not the weekend? Two lonely people; if they want us, they will know where to find us. See you soon, love, Moira."

He quickly scribbled a note to her and faxed it: "Looking forward to seeing you on Friday evening. Love, Patrick."

He refused to think of anything else. A quick shower, and then he collapsed onto his bed. "Sufficient unto the day, is the evil thereof," he intoned as fatigue overtook him.

A short press release had been issued: 'A woman had been found dead in a house in Colne. Police were investigating; no further details were available.'

CHAPTER 15

▼

WEDNESDAY, TEA TIME, 10TH JULY. NORTH SCOTLAND.

Michael had driven in his own aura of music by the shores of Loch Linnhe, and over the bridge which spanned the meeting of Loch Leven and Loch Linnhe, and then into Glencoe. He had diverted this way so he could catch a glimpse of the magnificence and sombre grandeur of the mountains, each side of the glen.

It was breathtaking: his heart raced and his eyes were misty as he remembered the happy times he had spent here. This would be the last, his resolution and the short-term plan firmly fixed in his mind. He drove up the road to Kinlochleven, stopping only to look at the 'Pap of Glencoe' fifteen hundred feet above Glencoe village. This was where the Campbells had descended on the McDonalds and massacred the whole village. They had thrown in their lot with 'Claverhouse', the brutal English officer who had sworn to be the scourge of the Scottish fighting clans. He sighed; so long ago, now that tragedy was the source of a large tourist industry.

Kinlochleven was quiet; the fish and chips were good, plenty of salt and vinegar. He sat on the deserted quayside looking out at the splendour and awesomeness of the mountains. It seemed crazy not to retire to a place like this; the little town was hidden from the tourist, yet it thrived with its own industry.

He looked across towards the way he planned to descend tomorrow, after walking the ridges. The col of Garbh Bheinn was at seventeen hundred feet, a nice run down to the loch, and then the long return drive to Inverness. The intention; to catch the evening flight back to Derry. Finishing his chips, he took his rucksack from the boot of the car; then, making sure everything was secure, he was away to the bus stop.

The tourist service ran up the valley to the place where the lone piper was stationed, at the head of the glen, with Rannoch moor stretching out as far as the eye could see, then on down to Bridge of Orchy, so the tourists could experience the desolation of the moor. As the bus trundled through the glen, his thoughts turned to all the other wonders of Scotland he had enjoyed in the past.

It would be nice if Skye could have been on his itinerary, a short drive over the bridge, which had once been just a ferry crossing, up to Carbost, and into Glen Brittle, and the Cuillins. Those pink-hued mountains of the 'gabbro' rock with its hard pimply texture, skinned the tips of the fingers as one endeavoured to climb its famous faces. The Sron Na Ciche, the face of Scurr Scumain, came to mind, those daunting climbs, the Crack of Doom and the Crack of Dawn, all the time gazing up or down onto the 'A Cioch'; that glorious peace of rock that stuck out like a big nose.

They were happy days, not a care in the world. Only to fight the elements, the nature of the rock and the gravity of his situation if one slipped on 'small holds.' He had always been a 'loner' taking risks on solo climbs, hiding his skill to others. All the trauma and heartache came later.

But, now he was finding his soul again, in a different way; he would have a fame he had always shunned, infamous though it may be.

He left the bus in company with other sightseers and walked up to the head of the glen. The strains of the bagpipe filled the air, haunting, echoing, with its lament of death. He sat down with others and listened to the skirl of the pipes, until the piper was ready for a break and to take his collection. He made his contribution, and then with a spring in his step, walked down the glen to the hotel. Definitely time for a pint of 'heavy'.

Sitting outside in the garden, he gazed up at his favourite mountain: the Buchaille Etive Mor. The strawberry shaped peak of Stob Dearg had a pink haze round it. At scarcely over two thousand feet it was a very pleasant climb.

Other people were drifting into the bar, picking up drinks, and percolating into the garden. It was going to be a balmy evening. This was the place to be; his brain was spinning. He delved into his rucksack and took out his book.

Das Reich Panzer Division had become the subject matter of many authors. The ruthlessness of the Waffen S.S. However, this particular book also emphasized the inter-nicene fights between the various French resistance groups. British agents were parachuted into France, to pull them together, make them strong to fight a common enemy; but amongst the bravery there was a callousness, in picking off their own people, settling old scores and grudges. For them it was legal, justified by one word: Collaborators!

Whilst reading he sipped at his pint. With surprise he found it empty; time for another, he thought. At the bar there was queue. The bar menu looked tempting; he chose a pint of prawns to go with his second pint of heavy. Within a few minutes it was served at his table, the prawns stuffed to the very top of the pint pot, with a platter of brown bread, a small ramekin of butter, and a pot of a spicy dressing.

A young couple occupied the next table; as he munched away with intervals of drinking his beer and dipping back into his book, he listened in to their conversation.

He glanced across. The man was tall with fair hair, a nice face creased with laughter as he remonstrated with his girlfriend. She was a beauty: she could have been Swedish, lithe, blonde, and bronzed. Very fit indeed!

Pouting, she remonstrated with her partner. "Roderick, I have done my apprenticeship with you; we have been together for nearly two years. From being someone you had to pull up on a rope, I am now getting to your standards." She puffed herself out. "Look at my achievements solo on the Ogwen slabs, Faith Hope and Charity. Our joint climbs on the Eagle Nest Ridges on Gable, and our dancing on the face of Gillercombe buttress in Borrowdale. What more could a man want from his future wife? So admit it; I am a tidy climber!"

"Okay, Alicia, we change our plans: instead of the Anoch Eagach ridge tomorrow, and since you are fit, young and beautiful, I will take you up Crowberry ridge, on the mountain which looks like and up-turned strawberry."

She gazed at the Buchaille. "It's glorious," she breathed.

"Yes, I agree. We'll do the ridge on Friday. So tomorrow we will climb on Crowberry, then drop down and up to the Bheig, along by 'The Three Sisters'; and down by Ossian's cave. The views are breathtaking. There is so much more to climbing than swinging on a rope. One day, when we are old and grey, we might not be able to rock-climb any more, but we will still be able to walk the mountains. Wainwright did it into his eighties—so be warned, 'ma Cherie'!"

He smiled and continued: "We need an early start, seven o'clock, and a good breakfast; by midday the mountain will be like Blackpool beach on a bank holiday."

"Okay, Rod. Done! You lead, I will follow. I love to watch you climb; you have such style, like a ballet dancer."

Roderick gazed on this girl he loved. "That's learning the right way, finding a good mountain school. When we are married, but after our honeymoon, we will book into the same school, the one in Snowdonia; get to grips with the Clogwyn du Arddu, Cloggy for short. October is a nice month for climbing. The cold keeps one on one's toes."

The conversation was now interesting to the man. The excitement welled up inside him. His back was half turned to them: they could not see his reaction. It was amazing how everything was going to fall into place. Not quite in line with his original plans, a boy and a girl, instead of two girls; still, he could not look 'a gift horse in the mouth.' He was jolted out of his reverie by the barman collecting the glasses and asking if he wanted anything else.

"Oh, pardon, I was lost in those mountains; but if you twist my arm I will have another pint of heavy with a large Drambuie chaser."

The young couple made their way back to the hotel, presumably to eat; obviously they were staying there. Good, now he could relax, with his own nightcap. He pondered on the situation. He had no news of Cleveland, Malham or Colne. He had made himself the promise that he would not be interested. No newspapers, radio or television.

As he lingered with his drink, he wrote out a couple of lettercards that had very nice views of the glen; the bar had a good selection. He sealed them, added the stamps, and posted them in the hotel letterbox as he went to the toilets. Having paid his bill at the bar, he gathered up his rucksack and was off.

He walked up the road for a bit, and then turned off towards Glen Etive. The route up the mountain was well known to him. He followed the path up through the forest and then a stiff climb up the rocky slopes brought him up to the shoulder of the hill. After a quick rest he was off again, and did not stop until he reached the summit of Stob Dearg. It took him almost an hour to work his way down to the top of Crowberry ridge. Being familiar with the hill, he knew the route up the crag and the best place to make a belay.

He found a place on the lea side of the mountain to bivouac. It was ideal, in hearing distance of anyone climbing the ridge, and yet completely hidden. He looked forward to the morning, and the time when the metallic clink of carabiners would assail the morning air as someone made his belay.

Unpacking his sleeping bag, and the food, he settled down for supper and read by the light of his acetylene lamp. One thought struck him: he should be prepared for the morning. He found an ideal stone, good and heavy, but rounded on one side to give a comfortable grip. He put it by his side.

Most climbers, when they had made their climb and were going to bring up the next person, took off their helmets. They were very constricting and made the head hot. He was banking on this. He had always been at fault, as he found he could not wear one, most probably because he was forced by the regulations to wear a hard hat when working on an industrial site.

He snuggled into his sleeping bag, nibbled a sandwich, taking the odd swig of his energy drink. As he read he felt his eyes closing. After a while he doused his lamp and fell asleep. His last thought was that he would need all his stamina tomorrow if everything went according to his plan.

Thursday 11th July. Early Morning, Glencoe.

Roderick and Alicia woke up just after six o clock. A knock on the door and within minutes they were sitting cross-legged on the floor enjoying a hot Scottish breakfast. Virtually in silence they munched, drank, and then showered together. Their thoughts were not on each other's bodies but the mountain. With the packed lunches in their sack, and with the ropes, helmets and slings from the car, they were off.

Hand in hand they walked up the road and then turned off for a frontal attack of Stob Dearg. They followed the path up the mountain, until they came to the point where the path split. They traversed onto the second path that led to the base of the ridge. A few minute to kit out, and make the base belay and Roderick was off. He danced up the rock, his carabiners, and pitons attached to a ring in his belt and jangling in the morning air.

Alicia watched him, enthralled; he was a big man, but on the rock he was so delicate, each movement thought out, stretching, crouching, as he found his footholds, his hands delicately stroking the rock until he found a place where he could have a good grip. Classic climbing, sticking to the rule of 'three point climbing', only one hand or foot moving at any given time.

In no time he was out of sight. The steady movement of the rope told her he was climbing. Time stood still. It was eerie; a heavy silence, not a soul on the hill. It would be well after ten before the walkers surfaced onto the mountains. The air was crisp and the golden orb of the sun was awakening the sky; the slopes of the mountain were a tapestry of colour, the rock, grey, black and a creamy brown in places, curtained by the white and purple of the heathers. She smiled. She was so happy; it was good to be alive. Finally, she felt the three pulls on the rope. He was at the top.

Quickly, she released the belay, packed up the rucksack, attached the rope to her harness and, with three tugs, the slack on the rope was taken up and she commenced to climb. Roderick was very good in bringing up his second, particularly since he loved this particular one. He felt the rope, and every nuance of her moves. That gave her the confidence. She climbed steadily, amazed at the smallness of the holds. She never ceased to be amazed at the suppleness and dexterity of her body, how it could adjust, to keep her near to the rock as she defied gravity with her contortions. With the deft step of a ballet dancer she crossed out of a fissure onto the face of the rock. She risked a look down; the exposure was terrific. Her eyes and one hand together searched for the next hold. She reached it and took a good grip; one foot went out to tentatively feel for the next foothold, her body now part of this rock. This was the world that Roderick had opened up to her. She loved the man and she loved his mountains.

Michael woke up just after seven, no discomfort at all, as warm as toast. Music flooded his brain. It was the stanza of the seventh symphony, the *Gewanderhous* in Leipzig; as Baronboim brought the orchestra into the third movement, the excitement of the horns as they made their own reply to the rest of the instruments. He could imagine the joy of Beethoven as he heard the music, in his head, never ever able to listen to his compositions, just to be turned round and see the applause of his audience.

His heart was pumping furiously, the adrenalin coursing through his bones: seething inside; was it going to happen? He did not know, but he had to be prepared.

As he considered his options, calmness came over him. He got up and went round the corner of the col to relieve himself. A quick whisk with his electric razor, and a good squirt of the deodorant aftershave over his smooth cheeks, and then breakfast. The rolls were still fresh, his drink invigorating. After eating, he gathered everything together, rolled up his sleeping bag, and packed up his rucksack. From the side pocket he took out his book and settled down to read and wait. He was immersed in the book when he heard the clink of metal upon rock. Quickly, he put his book back into the pocket of the sack, picked up his stone and waited. There was the unmistakeable sound of a boot as it scraped the rock, and then the noise of preparation, more movement; the clink, probably of a carinbiner. He continued to wait. Eventually he heard a shout: "Alicia, it's okay!"

He moved round the side of the col until he saw a figure sitting there, belayed to a rocky outcrop with a rope round his waist, gradually drawing the rope in, keeping it nicely tensioned. Waiting, not daring to breathe, something like fifteen minutes, then he heard a woman's voice calling up to the man. She must be half way. She was on the slab, a shear face. He heard the man's voice as he shouted to her, chiding her.

"Gently, Alicia, not too fast; you're coming to a bit which has a slight overhang. Take it very steady."

This was the time! Heart racing, he moved towards the man. The man saw him, his eyes flickering to the arm that held the stone. There was no way he could rise quickly. The belay and the tension on the rope, his legs dangling over the cliff face precluded any upward movement. The stone descended once and then a second time; he heard the crunching and felt the pain of his skull breaking as he blacked out. Michael was on the man and helped him to fall backwards, one of his hands taking a grip of the rope snaking down the cliff. The man's body was now trapping the rope. Michael pulled the rope out from under the body, keeping a tight grip of it with the other hand. Once free, he took the rope in both hands, and tugged hard on it. He felt a jolt and held on to the rope by twisting it round his elbow. The full weight of the girl hung from it, as she hung in space. He gave a mighty tug and then let go. He felt the burning though his anorak sleeve as the rope tightened round his arm; with a desperate twist of the wrist, he freed it and it went sailing down the cliff face. There were no sounds to be heard. The silence of the mountain was intangible after the screams which had floated up to him only seconds before.

Alicia knew nothing. The climbing was going well. She was exhilarated, thinking of that big first hug from Rod when she popped her head over the ledge and climbed over to join him. Suddenly there was a violent pull on the rope. She scrabbled to keep her handgrip as her feet were swept into space. But the rope suddenly grew taut again, and she felt herself violently swept into space, her hands flailing and finding nothing. For a few seconds she hung there. Then she was falling. Her terror was intense, her scream long and drawn out. Then she met the ground and felt a terrible spasm of pain in her legs and the lower half of her body. Then there was nothing.

Michael took the man's legs and dragged them away from the cliff. He then pulled the body up to the rock where the rope was belayed, and retied his body so that he held tight to the rock. He took out some paper tissues and wiped the rope and the parts of the man's clothing which he had held. He took care not to touch the head, which was bleeding profusely. He wiped the stone he had used round the edges and the face of it, walked round the other side of the col, and hurled it down the cliff-face. The used tissues he wrapped in a clean one and stuffed them back into the plastic wrapping. He would lose those in a waste bin somewhere.

Then he was off, heart racing, the blood pounding in his head. His energy took him to the top of the Stob, then to the right side, racing down the shale of the Buchaille Etive Bheig. The mountain was silent, no noise of any description, only the crunch of his boots on the shale as he leapfrogged from rock to rock, and where the scree was small, letting the mountain take him down in a miniature landslide. He reached the bottom, along the path to the main road to the other side of the glen; still no one in sight. He paused for breath and a quick swig of his energy drink. The next bit would kill him or cure him: the ascent up to the Chancellor, and then the Aonach Egach ridge, the most difficult of the ridge walks on the mainland.

In truth, he enjoyed it. His adrenalin was pumping, the rock was friendly, and there were no early takers for the ridge. He paused at the 'devils staircase,' no use looking at it, just go. He went! The ridge was there reaching out before him, a line of jagged rock, with a knife-edge path, the drop shear on each side. He literally danced along it; this was the first time he had been on the ridge when it was not shrouded in mist. The views were beyond belief. 'Was Scotland part of the green and pleasant land of Cardinal Newman?' Not quite!

The rock was dry. He never missed a step as he literally jogged from peak to peak. The majestic splendour of the mountains filled him with joy. He had no thought for what he had done; it was out of his mind, of no account. That was for later when the spectres came back. For now he was euphoric. He reached the end of the ridge; instead of dropping down to the Pap of Glencoe, he cut across, keeping the loch in view, eventually reaching a path which would take him down near Kinlochleven. It was easy: by the time he had reached the river he had recovered and was able to walk the short stretch of road into the township, as though he were taking a stroll after breakfast. Not many townsfolk about. He strolled down to the quayside. He fancied 'brunch' but it was better to get out of the area as quickly as possible. He quickly walked to his car. To the few people at the quayside he was just another tourist.

There seemed to be no unusual activity in the glen. Nothing in the sky, no out of the way noises. He reached his car, opened the boot and dumped his rucksack into it. After closing it he jumped into his car and was away, driving quickly down to the end of Glencoe, over the bridge which spanned the river Leven, and on to the A82, up to Fort William, and then following the lochs to Inverness. He was determined to have no stops until he reached the Airport at Inverness. The two days in Scotland had been enough for him.

CHAPTER 16

▼

THURSDAY 11TH JULY.
TEES-SIDE.

Bob Ferguson was working in his office. Only a fleeting visit today, for he had a meeting with his new second-in-command stationed for the time being in Sheffield: Detective Superintendent Alan Bridges. There was much to plan and organize. They had to be ready for a final meeting with the civil authorities, the senior police administration officials, who were the people in charge of the 'purse strings'; sometime within the next two weeks.

Moira had his full authority to act in any way she thought fit. Hopefully the inquest in the murder area would take place on Friday. For the present there was still no word from Samos concerning the parents of Cathy and Alison.

The fingerprint evidence was conclusive: they were dealing with the same man. This S.O.C.O. team at Colne had found under Patricia's bed an empty champagne bottle and two glasses. Patricia's prints were on the bottle and one of the glasses. The second glass also revealed another set of prints. This set matched the ones found on the site in Goredale Scar and the North Yorkshire moors. They were dealing with a 'serial killer.' Where was he now? He had been very careful in the cleaning of Patricia's flat. But he had forgotten about the glasses and bottles, which had rolled underneath the bed.

Moira was sickened by the thought of a press conference that they were going to hold in Leeds on Friday evening after the inquests. Would this bring out a wave of copycat killings and abductions?

The outstanding areas of the country popular with walkers and climbers had been identified. All national park wardens had been informed of the danger and extra people had been drafted in from rambling and walking clubs, just to be there in the hills to spot any suspicious activity. Many strange people could be found in such areas, the tramps, the travellers, and others; all just out there itching to be on this particular bandwagon. Police in Scotland had also been warned, but they were so spread out: where would they start looking?

The consensus of opinion was to concentrate on the Lake District and Snowdonia. But, on what basis could they have any confidence in such a decision? Only one person knew where he would strike next, and that was the man himself!

Thursday Morning. Colne.

Patrick and Millie waited outside the police station for the arrival of Greg and Sue Markham. They were on time, and after greetings, they took them to the mortuary. Patricia looked so peaceful and very beautiful. All the ravages to her body by the pathologist were hidden. Mr. and Mrs. Markham took a quick look at her and simultaneously croaked, "Yes, it's Patricia," and then were out of the door within seconds.

Millie had thoughtfully rang Sylvia Hall. She and Stephanie were waiting outside the mortuary. Millie introduced the two girls as Patricia's friends. Sylvia took charge at once. "We have made lunch at my house, not that you will want to eat much. Why not stay with us tonight? I have my own flat; I can put you up so you are not alone. We will both come with you to the inquest tomorrow. But for the moment we have so much to talk about."

Greg and Sue looked at each other. They could not trust themselves to speak and just nodded. That was their flesh and blood lying lifeless on the slab. What had happened for it to come to this? Where had they gone wrong? Too much time building up the business? These questions lay unanswered in their minds.

Thursday, late Morning. Samos.

Inspector Demetrios Gyros was driving a hired Suzuki jeep round the island. His passengers were Detective Sergeant Bill Pryde and Constable Andrew Phillips from the Wrexham police. They were looking for the parents of Alison Smith and Cathy Roberts. The British policemen were armed with blown up passport photographs of the parents from the Liverpool Office.

Samos town had yielded no results, nor any of the popular spots on the east side of the island. They were packed with tourists. Bill Pryde shivered: this was not a place he would like to spend his holidays.

Now it was different and the heat-soaked rocks of the mountains towered above them. The area was stark and arid. Demetrios pointed to the steps cut in the face of the mountain. This was the way to the Cave of Pythagoras, the place where the ancient mathematician had hid as others sought to take his life. It was difficult to believe an ancient mathematician being under such a threat. There were only a few tourists, their cars parked on the dusty track; not so many people wanted to brave the climb to the cave with the sun beating down on them. Strictly speaking, they were off route, a little diversion, and the sun beat down mercilessly on them out of an azure blue sky. Ruefully, they thought of the two R.A.F. pilots lodged in one of the best hotels on the island, sunning themselves and dipping into the pool whenever they felt like it.

They were on their way to Maremboulos. Dimitrios's brother lived there. It was a fishing port, very small, the square built round the harbour within the bay. This was the place where most of the island's boats were built.

Mika, the brother, had a boat, and every Wednesday and Friday he took about sixty tourists across to Patmos, famous as the place where the apostle John was imprisoned by the Roman garrison in A.D.90. From his visions the last book in the Bible, Revelation, was written.

But they were not going for the boat, but for lunch. Mika's wife Sophia ran the restaurant, the specialty being the fish her husband caught. They drove into the square that was full of open-air restaurants, all busy. Sophia's place was in the middle of the square, directly in front of the harbour. There was much embracing and handshaking, and then they sat down to eat. Mika took the orders and Sophia went off to prepare a dish of Red Mullet, Whitebait and Scampi.

Mika opened some bottles of the Samos wine, ice-cold, syrupy with a good alcohol content, very refreshing. After lunch they would inquire around the small town for any sighting of the parents. Sophia came back with a large dish of salad topped high with sliced tomatoes. Within minutes the fish arrived, and there was silence as they enjoyed such wonderfully fresh fish and the seafood.

Sophia called out, asking if they would like coffee. They had spread out the photographs, which they intended to show around the apartments, with the hope of someone recognizing the missing parents. Sophia came back with a tray full of coffee cups which she set down on the table. As she did so she glanced at the pictures they had laid out.

"But I know these people!" she exclaimed. "They were here last night. It was a good evening. Greek dancing, lots of food, they left at midnight. And, I know where you can find them."

Dimitrios stood up. "Well done, Sophia," he said, giving her a big hug. "Please put us out of our agony."

"Kyracklia," she said. "Five kilometres up the coast; they have rented an apartment there, but every day they eat at Chester's restaurant. As you come into the village, there is a small food store on the right-hand side, about 200 metres further; on the opposite side you have Chester's. If you have breakfast there in the morning, they offer you the beach beds and parasols free for the day on their private section of the sands. They serve good food and there are snacks and drinks all day. If you hurry you'll catch them as they finish their lunch."

"My Aphrodite," Demetrios beamed at her. "You have saved us days of searching. Thank you for everything."

With that they were off, and ten minutes later parked outside Chester's bar restaurant. Dimitrios knew the family; they had emigrated to Canada, changed their name and then had come back after five years to build this restaurant.

The elder brother was behind the bar.

"Hi Tom," he called. "Have you seen these people?"

Tom looked at the photograph. "Yes," he nodded. "They are over there."

"Tom," said Dimitrios. "These two gentlemen are policeman from England. Something very serious has happened. Do you know where their apartment is?"

"Yes, it is not so far up the mountain road."

"Tom, you and your wife go up there now. Get the spare key off the Patron; pack everything as quick as you can and bring it back here. I'm going to telephone for the helicopter and it will be here in about thirty minutes. Now, could we use your back room?"

Tom nodded, pointing the way.

"Thank you, Tom. Will you ask your sister to bring the people to us? Forgive this imposition."

"Demetrios, once I was in your hands when I was arrested after that car crash. You were good to me. My house is yours. Obviously this is serious. Luki will put out a pot of coffee and a bottle of brandy in the back room for you all."

"Thanks, Tom. Tell Luki not to alarm them. Invite them in for a drink, and while they are with us, gather up all their baggage from the beach."

Luki had brought in the coffee and brandy. Dimitrios rang his headquarters. A police car would be dispatched to the hotel to collect the pilots, and the Air

Traffic Controller would plot a route so they could land at Leeds and Bradford airport. A helicopter would pick them up and take them direct to Colne.

The parents walked in mystified. The Smiths were reasonably tall, well tanned and the hair bleached by the sun. The Roberts had suffered by having too much sun, were smaller and with fuller figures. Their faces and bodies were an angry red.

"Mr. and Mrs. Smith, Mr. and Mrs. Roberts, my name is Detective Sergeant Bill Pryde, and this is Constable Andrew Phillips. My Greek colleague is Inspector Demetrios Gyros. I wish we could meet under different circumstances. What we have to tell you is very serious. We are your friends and we will do everything we can to help. Your daughter Alison and your daughter Cathy, camping in Goredale Scar, are both dead. They were murdered. We do not know as yet who the perpetrator is."

The family sat down. "You're serious?" asked Mr Smith, bewildered. "This is not a joke?"

"No, Sir, it is not. We need you for formal identification of the girls and to attend the inquest. The helicopter will be here in a few minutes. Mr. Chester and his wife have gone to pack your bags. An R.A.F. passenger aircraft is standing by at the airport. It has clearance for immediate take-off and it will take you to Leeds and Bradford airport; a helicopter will then take you on to Skipton. The handling of your baggage and all the necessary details will be handled by the police. Please take some coffee and brandy and just relax for a few minutes. The helicopter will not be that long."

They sat in silence, lost in their own thoughts. It seemed a long time before the roar of the rotor announced the helicopter's arrival. Within minutes the Smiths and the Roberts were on board and they were off.

At the airport the RAF plane was going through its flight checks. It was one of the larger twin-engined Cessna's. The Smiths and the Roberts were ushered into the plane and settled back in the comfortable seats, declining any food or drink. They were lost in their own grief.

At a hotel near Skipton reservations had been made for them, and Detective Inspector Mollie Greenwood would be waiting at the designated place where the Helicopter would land. She would pick them up in the morning for formal identification of their daughters. For the moment they had no idea when the inquest would be.

Thursday, early afternoon. Tees-side.

Moira checked her computer,

Jan's brother and sister were at Manchester Airport. A helicopter would bring them across to Tees-side. They would not have to leave the tarmac, as reservations had been made at the Airport Hotel. They would stay for the inquest on Friday.

The Markham's had identified Patricia's Saints body. The inquest would also be on Friday morning in Colne.

The Smiths and the Roberts would confirm the bodies were of Alison and Cathy, and the inquest would most probably be on the Friday afternoon at Skipton.

Next on the agenda would be the press conference, which would be held in the early part of the evening at the Yorkshire Post Office in Leeds.

Moira rang Patrick Hall. She was going to drive across to Skipton to meet him and visit the two murder sites, and also have a look at the bodies in the mortuary.

CHAPTER 17

▼

THURSDAY 11TH JULY.
MIDDAY, GLENCOE.

It was nearly the end of the week. Many walkers were taking it easy for the day. This was true in the gardens of the hotel where holidaymakers were relaxing, having a beer or a coffee with the hot bridies and tatty scones.

The two men were enjoying their pints, very refreshing. They got up reluctantly, picked up their rucksacks and a coil of nylon rope and said goodbye to no one in particular, and trudged off to the mountains. They were going to try a new route up the crags of the Buchaille Etive Bearg.

Mike Styles and Andrew Briggs were seasoned climbers. They had decided to have a couple of days in Glencoe after spending nearly a fortnight in the Cuillins of Skye. Now they were relaxing; they had terrified themselves too many times on some of the severe climbs that Skye was famous for.

From the climber's diary in the hotel, they knew at least two other people were on the crag, but it seemed pretty deserted. They went up the frontal path and then crossed to the cliff. Both were equally matched in ability so they would climb up each pitch, alternately leading and following. Mike identified a good place to start the climb. It was easy, fifty feet up; he found a place to belay and brought up his companion. Andrew effortlessly climbed past him and picked his way up the next section of the cliff. He was heaving himself onto a wide ledge when he spotted a man tied to a rock. Moving very carefully, he sat on the edge of the ledge and tugged on a rope to call up Andrew. They were together within minutes and Mike wordlessly pointed to the man, silent and still.

Together they went over to the man who was tied to a large finger of rock, which obviously had been used as a belay. They could see he had suffered a heavy blow to his head; blood was everywhere, matted and caked into his hair. They dared not touch him; he was in a very bad way, but they did not think he was dead. Where was his partner? They had seen no one. Mike took out his phone but he was already aware that he would have no signal. The mountains overshadowed them.

"Andrew, you are the runner, off you go down to the hotel: call the 'Mountain Rescue' and tell them what you have seen, and that there's a possibility that there's another casualty or worse. Impress upon them that they will need also to call the police. In the meantime I will climb down the ridge and see what happened."

They both knew the ridge climb. They had been on it many times, but the descent was more difficult. Andrew was soon away up to the col and down to the scree path and 'en route' to the hotel, sprinting all the way. Mike walked across towards the ridge, and carefully lowered himself off the edge of the cliff and found his first foothold. The top was the trickiest part, as it was completely exposed. He felt his way down carefully until he came to the fissure. Then he eased himself down the crack and into the chimney. With body braced between two rock faces, he shuffled down to a ledge. One more exposed section and then a climb down the inner corner, and he was at the mid-point of the ridge. It had taken him forty-five minutes. Now there was a sheer drop, which he would abseil. He took a coil of thin rope from his belt and, after driving a piton into the rock, he looped the rope through the hole in the piton and let the equal lengths of rope hang down the cliff. After clipping the hanging ropes through his waist belt carabiner, he gripped the rope above him with his right hand; and, with the rope across his shoulder, his left hand held the rope low behind his back, allowing him to control the speed of his one hundred and fifty foot abseil. He leaned back on the rope and allowed it to slip in his grasp until he was horizontal to the cliff. Then, with a rope lightly held in his hands, he was off jumping backwards, allowing the rope to let him drop, hitting the cliff again with his feet and springing off and down again. Within no time he was at the bottom of the cliff. He scrambled down the slope until the rock met grass. He stopped. A loose white climbing rope snaked through the grass. Without touching the rope he followed it down the grass and there, jammed between a jumble of rocks, was the body of a woman.

Mike could see that she was dead. He drove another piton into the rock and pulled down his abseil rope. He secured one end to the piton, took off his yellow anorak and rolled it into a bundle. He wrapped and tied the other end of the rope round it, and then threw it down the incline. It would serve as a marker. With that he was off, running and jumping down the slope, and within thirty minutes he was at the hotel. Andrew and the hotel's staff had watched him as he came down.

"I found the body," he puffed. "It's a woman! I've secured our abseil rope to a piton and tied my anorak to the other end so we have a marker to climb up to her."

"It must be that couple who stayed here last night." The manager looked in the diary. "Yes, here we are; Roderick Kent and Alicia Hamilton, climbing Strawberry Buttress, B.E.More. We have already telephoned the police, and mountain rescue, with Andrew's news. I will update them at once. They'll be busy organizing their teams, I expect.

"The best thing now would be for you two young men to go back up the mountain and stand by your marker. Then you'll be able to stop anyone from using the path or the climbs. We will tell the police and the mountain rescue where to find you. We have made a rucksack up for you both, with signal flares, vittals, and a spare anorak."

Mike and Andrew made their way back to the mountain while the manager went to his office to call the police again. They had news for him.

The mountain rescue team had assembled and was waiting for the RAF helicopter from Kinloss. A police mountain team on duty in the Ben Nevis area was transferring to Glencoe my means of a second helicopter. They would be picked up outside the Glen Nevis youth hostel. The manager passed on the details relating to the two climbers, stressing they had touched nothing. They were equipped with flares, enabling them to guide in the helicopters. He also rang the police at Fort William and suggested that they would need more men to cordon off the area.

Detective Inspector Stuart Mackenzie was aware of the happenings in England; he looked over the shoulder of the duty computer operator with a sinking feeling in his heart. The update on the murders showed they had no more knowledge of the whereabouts of the killer. But his gut feel was that he was here, and had been in Glencoe. He said to the sergeant operating the computer: "Send a preliminary report on H.O.L.M.E.S. concerning our suspected murders in Glencoe. Inform the Crianlarich station; advise them to cordon off the south-easterly approaches from Rannoch Moor. We must do the same at the

Loch Leven Bridge. Arrange also for a police team to be at the Visitors' centre, and to visit the hotels in the glen. Check everyone, inform the Super. I am going with a helicopter into the glen. We will use the hotel as our headquarters.

Thursday, mid-afternoon. Tee-side.

Detective Chief Inspector Moira Masters was on her way to Colne, seated in the back of the car with her laptop. Detective Constable Mollie Squires was driving for her.

Now was the time to reflect on the killer, to start and build up a picture against the known facts. Moira regularly had updates from her universities, Aberdeen and Edinburgh, relating to profiling techniques, Quantico also was not 'fussed' about the mass of information they downloaded to her. Ruefully she admitted that without Simon Priest, now confirmed as a Detective Inspector, she would never plough her way through the morass of data. He was marvelous: it was uncanny how quickly and easily he could sort the data and rearrange it for easy access to all the salient points.

Her phone rang. Talk of the devil; it was Simon!

"Hello Simon. I was just having a good thought about you for a change. You will be pleased to know I have forgiven you; but you must find yourself a nice girl and stick with her. It will make life so much easier."

"Yes Ma'm," he mocked. "Find me a slim, lithe, stunning blonde as my secretary, which I am now entitled to, and I will be in your debt forever. But first, I have some news; not very good, I'm afraid. Information from Fort William; there is a mountain rescue team and also a police team on their way to Glencoe, where there has been an incident. Detective Inspector Stuart Mackenzie wants to speak to you; he says he knows you from Bramshill. I gave him your mobile number and also the station numbers at Colne and Skipton. He suspects the worst. They are setting up a headquarters at the hotel, which is at the top end of Glencoe, and they have sealed off the glen."

Thursday afternoon, Inverness-shire

The man Michael was making good time. He was at the far end of Loch Ness and would be at the airport in time for the early plane. He was confident there would be a vacant seat. Previously he had telephoned the garage and confirmed the car would be returned with a full fuel tank. He did not expect a refund on the three-day hire. All he had to do now was to park in one of the reserved bays and post the key in their box, which he would find inside the airport building by the cafeteria. No problem at all. Possibly there would be a passport check, but that also was of no consequence.

The British government had been very kind to him. He carried two passports, one with a photograph of himself complete with beard, and one without. His original passport had been with a visa for working in Iraq. He had been part of the design team to provide a potable water treatment plant with a pipeline from the Shat Al Arab waterway to Basra. The Iraq-Iranian war had made it a non-event! They turned the plant into a forward military establishment. So his second passport was required for working in Israel. At the time of applying for this second passport, he was clean-shaven.

The drive had been enjoyable, thanks to a programme on the radio which was a tribute to a singer, the coloratura Eda Grubarova; her range of the octaves from low to high was amazing. He felt ecstatic as the operatic arias of Verdi and Strauss, particularly written for the coloratura, floated across the air.

He knew he should feel remorse, but could not. Should he walk into the nearest police station and give himself up? What would his life be like then? Dull, grim, his crime enormous in people's eyes. All those young lives lost, so much promise removed from the world. Maybe there was some mechanism to bring back hanging, or import a special injection from America. He did not know, and the thought of capital punishment sent shivers down his spine. The garrote, the electric chair, the guillotine; now all in the past except for the chair. He had to face it; he was a murderer, a serial killer, cut off from his wife, children, and family.

Yet the world had been and still was full of killers, mass murderers. The soldiers of the Third Reich, the armies of all those decorated in every war, every skirmish. The revenge of the military forces in Afghanistan, mass bombings, awesome firepower; women and children killed. So many people lived with death on their consciences. Why not he?

He remembered his days in Cyprus. He was a technician. No commission at that time, for he had not passed his Institute exams, no university background, only a one day release, and four nights a week slog to gain a Higher National Certificate. But Cyprus had been good. He ran a transmitter station with a few auxiliaries and guards. Sometimes it was possible to have 'a pass out' and spend some time in Nicosia. A taxi down Ledra Street; a walk, if you had the nerve, always with a Colt 45, or a Sterling sub-machine gun fully loaded and cocked. You had 'carte blanche' to fire if attacked. This was terrorist country. Some of the photographs of what Grivas and E.O.K.A. had done to their own countrymen, women and children included, were horrific. So, even as a humble technician, for a time he had been a potential legalized killer.

The world was a peculiar place: his faith was in ruins, a life hereafter! He dare not even think about it.

His ruminations had taken him through Inverness and into the airport. To the people he would meet as he went through the terminal and took his seat on the plane; he would be a nondescript being; completely invisible to those who were taken up with their own problems. Tomorrow, he thought, would be different. They would have heard on Radio, TV, or by reading newspapers; maybe there would even be an Identikit photo of him. One in a crowd, he was amazed at his iron will, no TV, no radio, no papers. He had his books. He did not want to know, there was no hiding for him. With that he locked his car, took out his rucksack from the boot, changed anorak for jacket and then made his way into the terminal. His ticket was validated. He popped the car keys into the box. Security was no problem. Time for a cup of coffee in the departure lounge, then out to the plane to take the seat allocated to him.

A lady came and sat next to him. She was wearing a smart grey worsted costume with a short skirt; possibly in her mid thirties, she was absorbed in the paperwork which spilled out of her black leather briefcase, the flap of which was embossed in gold with a portcullis. He leaned back in his seat, patiently waiting for take-off. Only a short flight to Derry and for the moment his life was open, no plans! He wondered how Julius felt with only a few men as he looked on the river, which was the frontier between Gaul and Italy. It was the Rubicon. Where was his giant apparition playing the pipes, and to what purpose? For Caesar it was to lead his men through the waters, and fight battle after bloody battle, with an aftermath of cold-blooded murder.

His life had always been a battle, but now he was enjoying it in a strange sort of way, the aftermath. His reverie died as the engines roared. Within seconds it was goodbye Scotland.

CHAPTER 18

▼

THURSDAY AFTERNOON, 11TH JULY. YORKSHIRE DALES.

Molly and D.C.I. Masters had arrived at Skipton police station. Patrick Hall was there to meet her. A message awaited her, to ring a hotel in Glencoe. She dialled the number and Stuart Mackenzie answered.

"Hello Moira, Stuart speaking. Congratulations on your promotion. Before you ask, my wife and bairns are fine, but we seem to have inherited your man."

"Thank you, Stuart, for pre-empting my questions. Will you hold on a moment until I make this a conference call? D.C.I. Patrick Hall is also involved."

They heard Stuart shouting at someone at the other end, enquiring if the team was on its way to the hotel.

"Ten minutes," someone else shouted.

"Sorry about that," said Stuart. "We're waiting for the medical team. The helicopter should be here very soon. Two people, one badly injured, and one dead, were found by two climbers on the face of a mountain called the Buchaille Etive Mor, at the top end of Glencoe. Both are experienced climbers; they touched nothing; one ran down the mountain and across the glen to this hotel, in order to alert mountain rescue. The other made a perilous descent down the crag from the place where they had found the injured climber; it was a man, until he found his companion, which was a woman, definitely dead. He had the foresight to mark the spot by driving in a piton and tying a rope to it; weighting the rope with his rolled up bright yellow anorak so that the 'mountain rescue' would have a marker. Those two climbers have now returned to the mountain, with flares to signal in the mountain rescue and police teams. The priority is to reach the injured man as soon as possible."

Moira agreed. "Stuart, make sure you go in with the S.O.C.O team. Remember the 'Locard Principal.' Take photographs and examine under UV light. The 'modus operandi' is similar to the killing of Dr Jan in Tees-side. The rope tied to the woman; make sure nobody touches it until your team has examined it. It will be very difficult for you; the mountain rescue team will most probably want to take charge: but remember this is possibly his fifth and sixth victim. You have the Identikit picture? Rely on the one where the man is beardless. That is the one to distribute. We know it's not very good: it fits many people, but it's all we've got. The glen I know well. Have your men visit all the hotels, the B&Bs, the cafés, etcetera. Don't forget Kinlochleven. Also around the Fort William area. See if you can improve on the Identikit picture, and learn something of his movements. He must be about six hours ahead of us. He could be anywhere!"

"Thanks, Moira, we'll take on board all you have said. The Super and the Provost want to know when you and Patrick will be here. They are formally requesting your help, and at the moment talking to the 'National Commander'."

With that the phone went dead. It rang again: this time it was the Commander.

"Hello Moira, I've heard all the news. You and Patrick work together on this. Whatever it takes? That's an order! Co-opt your team, D.I. Simon Priest, D.S. Molly Maguire, her promotion is now confirmed, and that of her future husband. D.I. Millie Greenwood, and of course D.C.I. Patrick Hall, your associate. Please note Patrick's comrade in arms, D.S. Robin Johnson, also now has promotion to Detective Inspector.

"You have a powerful team there. Put your mind to it. You have to take on the mind of the killer! Your ability to do this is uncanny. After tomorrow you will be through with procedures, victims' relatives, coroner's courts.

"You have to find him, no matter how long it takes; you will feel discouraged and frustrated, but stick at it. He cannot be allowed to roam the country with such impunity."

"Thank you, commander, for your confidence. You have given us a great team."

"Yes, I think so. We have a special bus for you, too, but at the moment the delivery is not confirmed. They are still commissioning it. I first saw this type of bus at a Christian camp. An evangelist named Bob Gordon had a vision of taking the gospel round the world. He raised the money to buy and equip three double length single deck buses. They have a concertina section in the middle, which makes them very maneuverable. Very common in Europe; I remember riding in one on our last visit to Luxembourg. Like Bob's, it will be full of 'state of the art' computer equipment; there will be two drivers and also a lady steward. Between them they will look after all your material needs, including servicing of the equipment and catering. Their quarters will be completely separate from yours. It will accommodate an investigating team of up to six people, enabling them to work in comfort anywhere in the UK and the rest of Europe. But, unfortunately, we did not anticipate it would be required so quickly; so I suggest you and Patrick fly up to Inverness on Friday evening. The Scottish police will look after all your needs."

Late Thursday Afternoon. 11th July. Glencoe.

Andrew was back at the top of the crag leaning over the injured climber, whom they now knew to be Roderick Kent. He appeared to be in a coma. Andrew detected shallow breathing, but dared not touch him, although he was an intern at Manchester Infirmary and in his first year after qualifying, working in the emergency ward. He felt under the circumstances it was not wise not to reveal his own profession. The doctor who was on his way was most probably very experienced in dealing with climbing accidents. No room for 'rookie interns', this was definitely out of his league.

He heard the roar of the helicopter and, moving away from the injured man; he breasted the rise and found a spot suitable for the helicopter to land. The flare from his gun illuminated the area with an intense white light. He also ignited a yellow marker flare, which he had set in the ground. The helicopter swooped down and landed.

Men tumbled out, all with rucksacks and wearing one-piece white suits. One man came over to him.

"You must be Andrew. I'm Dr Malcolm Fraser; the man in charge of the police team is Detective Sergeant Hamish Ogilvy. Can you take us to the injured man?"

Andrew pointed the way and led them down to the top of the cliff. The S.O.C.O. team immediately took photographs, and checked with an ultraviolet light around the man, taking more pictures while the doctor unloaded his kit.

"Stand back, everyone. Before any physical examination I want to take an 'X ray' of his head, so we have a better idea of the extent of his injuries. If we try moving him without some prior knowledge of his condition, we will most certainly lose him!"

The portable unit was quick to set up, and with everyone away from the site, the doctor gently placed a protective sheet over the man's face and body and then took the X-rays he required. Within minutes he had a result; definitely a compound fracture of the skull. Without hospitalization, it was not possible to ascertain the state of the brain.

The doctor gave an injection to relax the muscles and combat the shock if he did recover consciousness. He dare not do any more until he had more data; gingerly he continued his examination, finding the heart rate to be slow and irregular, the blood pressure virtually zero.

The doctor groaned, and muttered to himself. "I am too late; he needed treatment hours ago."

The heart rate monitor he had set up faltered and the alarm, when it went off, was shrill and piercing. Then, there was nothing!

The Doctor stood up. "He's gone. There was nothing I could do. He's been in shock for so many hours, and lost such a lot of blood, his body just gave up the ghost. I will go with Andrew to investigate what happened down there. Take Roderick back to the ambulance when you are ready; it will be waiting in the hotel grounds. Then come back to the other site. We will set up some flares. Come, Andrew, take me down to the girl."

"Okay," Andrew said as he straightened. "It's only a scramble down the scree; Mike, my climbing partner and friend, will set off a flare when he hears us. Then we can cut across the slope."

Andrew guided the doctor down the path to the right of the cliff face.

"Be careful," he said. "The rock is loose; we call it scree. Stay behind me. On the initial jump, the scree will start to move with you. Keep your eyes skinned for any boulders, so you have time to jump over them; the scree will be moving quite quickly; after a hundred metres or so you will find that the movement is rhythmic."

With that he gave a leap and landed on the scree. The doctor followed and together they slid down the mountain, leaping over rocks and across small fissures. Under any other circumstances it would have been quite exhilarating. After about twenty minutes of running and jumping, they saw smoke far down the mountain and to their right; they continued and reached a point parallel to the smoke. They traversed a steep slope of loose rocks. The smoke turned into amber light and then Mike's voice filtered up to them.

"You need to come further down. Traverse at sixty degrees. I will guide you."

It had taken nearly an hour. By the time they reached Mike, the helicopter had returned. The S.O.C.O. team was examining the site, testing the end of the rope for fingerprints; they knew the 'perpetrator' must have gripped it. But the nylon strands yielded nothing. They grimaced at each other; the prints they had lifted from the reinforced parts of Roderick's anorak were blurred. It would be difficult to make a positive comparison.

The doctor knelt by the body; the girl's cap had come off and her long blonde hair fluttered in the wind.

"I need to turn her over but I am afraid that she might fall again."

Mike drove a couple of pitons into the cracks of the rock, and attached harnesses to the waist belt of the girl and also to the doctor.

"Don't worry, Doc. She won't fall now. I'm afraid she's fallen enough in this life!"

The examination was difficult. Her pelvis had been broken on impact. It appeared that her body had violently twisted. Her face had smashed into the rocks, resulting in a neck fracture, and death had been instantaneous.

A man came up to them with the Detective Sergeant.

"I am Detective Inspector Mackenzie. I came up with the second helicopter. There is nothing here for us! All the criminal work is now elsewhere." He looked at the girl, who looked so beautiful. "What a waste," he muttered in a voice barely audible. He turned his attention to the two young men. "Mike and Andrew, get yourselves back to the hotel; have a soak and a few Drambuie chasers. The hotel has prepared everything for you. When the shock sets in, it will hit you hard. The helicopter will pick up the girl first. I am going up to where the man is belayed, so I can see for myself the carnage. After that I will come back with the helicopter, so we can have a chat and take statements. At present we are combing Glencoe for anyone who might have seen or heard something. We have also effectively sealed off the glen." He shook his head. "But, I fear, we are too late."

Late Afternoon, 11th July. Skipton.

Patrick had joined Moira in the incident room.

"Two more murdered in Glencoe. We have no further details, and it could be anyone. Certainly not a copycat as we have released no details."

Patrick put an arm round her shoulder. "Come, lass, our job is to catch the beggar; we have witnesses at the Malham Arms who will tell you what they know. Then a quick visit to Goredale Scar, to show you the site; after that to Colne, a visit to Patricia's House, and then to the station to talk to her two friends; and don't breathe a sigh of relief, because I then have other plans." He gave a wry grin. "Then we'll have dinner with Ken and Mabel; Molly is invited too. Ken was the one who reported the deaths of the two girls. We both have Coroner's Courts tomorrow; after that we will meet on the evening at Leeds and Bradford airport, so we can fly up to Inverness together."

Moira groaned. She felt very scruffy under his gaze. Everything about self had gone out of her mind after Jan's death.

"Okay, Patrick, you're the boss. Let's go, but first what about the parents of the girls?"

"They are here, just outside of Colne. Millie Greenwood is with them. She is staying at their hotel tonight to be on hand, and to look after them. She'll also take them to the inquest tomorrow."

It was a 'whistle-stop' tour! The reasons lay heavy on them; they could not appreciate the beauty of their surroundings; the Scar was grim and foreboding. The witnesses gathered at the inn, ashen and ashamed that they had enjoyed such a good night and a cracking barbecue. The horrific epilogue of it all was the death of these two dear girls. There was Patricia's house, too, empty and carrying the scent of death, her two friends dismayed at losing someone they cared for very much.

"See you tomorrow night, Patrick," said Moira. "Take care of yourself and thank you for everything. Say hello to Millie for me." With that she and Molly were gone.

Tomorrow was just another day of sadness and tears. The grim truth would be spoken in court; well-nourished modulated voices, dry, devoid of any passion, they did not have to live so close to reality as she and other people like her experienced almost every day, in one form or another

She had enjoyed the meal with Ken and Mabel. She reflected on it as she was driven home. Traditional Yorkshire food had been chosen, but Ken and Mabel very frail and careworn and had no appetite. Big black rings circled their eyes. Patrick was concerned, almost acting as a son to them at the table. She recalled their words.

"Thanks, Patrick," said Mabel as he escorted her to her chair and helped her to be comfortable.

"Maybe I'll swap Ken for you. I need a strong man about the place. Ken could do with one too."

They had all relaxed. Ken talked about Cathy and Alison, his eyes glistening with tears. He thanked Patrick for the way he had looked after them, and the care he had lavished on poor Mabel.

Mabel had kissed her husband and reached across to take Patrick's hand. She looked at Ken.

"Don't worry, husband of mine. Patrick will have his reward. God will take care of him."

Patrick and Moira had sat together opposite Ken and Mabel, and Molly at the far end.

"I hear you are all to be congratulated," said Ken. "Lot's of promotion! Eh bah gum! Ye'll certainly earn yer brass, catching yon bastard."

"Now then," said Mabel. "Let them relax."

She turned to Molly. "I hear you've just got engaged."

Molly blushed. "Yes," she breathed.

Ken joined in. "Yes, and both with promotion for such young folk. When is the happy day then?"

"Three months' time," answered Molly. "When we have our transfer and our new apartment."

Ken turned to Moira, and then looked at Patrick. "This is a good man, kind, honest, considerate, and very lonely. I do not know how we would have got through these last few days without him. And we did not ask! I've always been a man to stand on my own two feet. Always he has been there for us; he's like family. Mabel's already matchmaking him in her mind to a lass in Withernsea; but I reckon he should look no further than this table. You are a bonny lass, and well educated, I'll be bound, just like Alison was."

With that he burst into tears. Mabel stretched out her arms to cuddle him. It was with a great effort, and her arthritis was not very friendly to her.

"There there, don't take on so." She turned to Moira. "He loved those girls, and they loved him. It took twenty years off him. A proper ladies' man, but he's been the best. He also had plans, inviting them to stay with us, and maybe for Christmas or New Year. Now he has a big black hole.

"Patrick can come anytime. But, my dears, you have all this responsibility; how on earth are you going to catch this terrible man?"

Moira and Patrick looked at each other. There was no answer. Moira reflected on the last thing Mabel had said to them: "I say this to you, my dear friends; whatever happens, never lose your faith. God is good. There's naught else I can say. I wish you every blessing. God bless you both together!" Mabel smiled. "Come on, Ken, time for bed. Busy day tomorrow for us old folk."

Moira gazed vacantly out of the window as a car hummed along. Her eyes misted up; that old lady, in so much pain, was nevertheless a pillar of strength to her husband. Patrick had been mesmerized; he did know what to say to Moira. He fled, needing time to think.

"See you at the airport," he called back

She was jolted out of her reminiscences as Molly pulled into her drive.

"Thanks Mollie, please forgive me. I am going to crash out. Pick me up in the morning at seven o'clock. I need to think and use my brain; or what's left of it, before the inquest and the press." With that she opened the car door, found her keys and rushed into the house.

Mollie waited a few minutes, and then was off. It would be good to see Peter. It seemed an age since they had been together.

CHAPTER 19

▼

THURSDAY 11TH JULY. GLENCOE. EARLY EVENING.

The glen was a hive of police activity. They had checkpoints on the bridges at Kinlochleven and at South Ballachulish. The police on duty had copies of the 'identikit' picture compiled by Tees-side and Skipton stations. A checkpoint had been set up at the head of the glen to cover the main road out to Rannoch Moor, and for the two minor roads to Glen Etive and the Bridge of Orchy.

Teams of police were engaged in visiting the hotels, guesthouses and the cafes in the Glencoe area. An interview team had been installed in the visitors' center. They had drawn a complete blank!

At the hotel the management and bar staff were being questioned. The police had taken charge of the luggage and personal effects of Roderick Kent and Alicia Hamilton who had been sharing a room. At the Fort William station they were actively tracing the next of kin. The bodies had been taken to the mortuary at Inverness. A request had been made for the services of Sinclair Cameron, who was now on his way in the 'Citation' to perform the autopsies.

The bar staff had seen the identikit photos of the suspect, but any recognition was vague. There had been many people in the bar, and in the gardens, with only one barman on duty. One waiter remembered serving a man sitting by himself with a pint pot of prawns and a pint of beer during the evening. The man was friendly, and had given a good tip. The thing that stuck in his mind was the books he was reading. Two books had been lying on the table and he had glanced at the covers while he served the man his food. They were both about Hitler's Germany: *Das Reich* and *A Study in Tyranny*. If he had not been so busy, he would have enjoyed discussing them with the man, for he himself was a university student reading modern history, and in the course of his studies he had read both books. The policeman interviewing him wrote everything down with dour efficiency.

The co-coordinating officer of the detectives was Sergeant Robert Corrie; he had a corner of the visitors' centre, and was transcribing the reports as he received them into his laptop, sectioning them into areas of the search and time, together with any relevant witness information. He took the report sheets of the constables who had completed the interviews at the hotel, along with any data relating to Alicia and Roderick.

As soon as all the reports were compiled, he closed up his laptop; a patrol car was waiting for him; and then they were away back to Fort William. Detective Inspector Mackenzie was also back at the station.

"How did you make out, Robert?"

"Not much information. Give me a moment to download into the mainframe and then you can pick it up on your office computer."

"Thanks, Robert. While you're doing that, I'll make the coffee with a 'not so wee' dram! To warm the cockles of your heart."

He was as good as his word, and when Sergeant Corrie came into the office it was waiting for him.

"There you are, Robert, you deserve it after traipsing round the glen. Now then, let's see what we've got."

Stuart scrolled through the headings and listings.

"Very well put together, Robert. It's very easy to assimilate. This is interesting, our student of modern history noticing the books. I suppose it's not relevant. Wait a minute! Robert, activate the secure computer whilst I ring Glasgow for the password of the day."

He took the direct line, identifying himself, and immediately received a recorded message. One word was spelt out, letter-by-letter. He gave a grim chuckle and went over to the secure computer.

The H.O.L.M.E.S. programme was displayed. He entered the password, HYKER, and selected the section relating to the Tees-side murder. He quietly murmured to Robert that there was something in one of the reports concerning a book. Absorbed, he scrawled through the report until he came to the heading entitled, 'Contents of the rucksack.' A Mrs. Allenby, in accordance with the man's instructions, had forwarded the sack on to the United Bus depot in Middlesbrough.

"Shoes, underwear, a toilet bag and a book! *Hitler: A Study in Tyranny.* It's him, it's the same man, all right: he must have re-bought the book!"

Robert quickly updated the H.O.L.M.E.S. and gave it five-star urgency. Within seconds all Northern police stations, including Tees-side, Skipton and Colne, were aware that the serial killer had struck again.

"Where did he buy it? It could be anywhere. Wait a minute, just an idea; I am going to ring the booksellers in the centre of town. They live above the shop. I would like a copy of it myself, and the *Das Reich.* Moira will be interested too."

The local paper had an advert for the bookshop, but he needed the unlisted number; once again the computer coughed up the information. He dialed, and listened to the ringing tone for some time. Eventually a man's voice answered.

"Mr. Whitaker, is it? I'm sorry to bother you. I hope you can help us. This is Detective Inspector Stuart Mackenzie speaking—your good customer: all those orders for criminal psychology books!"

"Och aye, I ken ye! But what would it ye be wanting at this time of the night, Stuart Mackenzie, on a private number?"

"Two books, Sir, *Das Reich* by Max Hastings, and Alan Bullocks on Hitler."

"Well! It must be a strange coincidence, I sold copies of both books on Wednesday morning; I now only have a last copy of the Hitler book. I ken well the gentleman who bought them. He was very pleased to have them. Apparently he had lost his copy of the Hitler book before he could finish it. We all know how aggravating that can be."

"Sir, I must warn you that, inadvertently, you are now in the middle of an official police inquiry. I am sending Sergeant Robert Corrie to get the copy of the book you have and to take a statement from you. A special team of police will need to examine your shop. They will be with you in thirty minutes. Please make it available to them and do not touch anything. You are plum in the middle of a murder inquiry."

"Okay, Inspector. I do not know what to say. You have interrupted our dinner-party, but I do understand. I will make my apologies without giving a reason. I am told that I'm not the easiest person to get along with, so the guests will put it down to my idiosyncrasies."

The sergeant and a fingerprint team were at the shop within half an hour. The doors were unlocked and the lights were on.

"Mr. Whitaker, was this the man you sold the books to?"

Sergeant Corrie passed over a copy of the Identikit photo to him.

"Wait till I find my glasses. I have a pair here; good heavens, it is not the best of pictures? But it could be the man. So you think he could have been murdered? Such a nice man, we could have talked for hours."

Robert did not enlighten him at this stage.

"Please," he said. "Show me the shelves where he would have found the two books, but be careful. Do not touch anything."

"It's over here; he had a good browse. There was also an interest shown in a novel about Goring, too."

"Okay, thank you, Mr. Whitaker. The fingerprint team will check everything on those shelves. I cannot see a copy of the Hitler book. Do you have a copy in the stockroom?"

"Yes, I do. I will get it for you. Inspector Mackenzie asked for a copy."

"I will give you a receipt, Sir."

Mr. Whittaker came back with the paperback.

"Thank you, Sir; go back to your dinner now, and enjoy it. We won't make any noise; once we are finished we will call you. Take this alarm unit; put it in your trouser pocket. We will test it, to make sure it is working."

The Sergeant dialled a number on his mobile.

"I can feel it vibrating," said Mr. Whitaker.

"Good," said Robert. "When you feel the vibrations, just excuse yourself and come back down to the shop. Don't discuss this with anyone, will you?"

It was an hour before they called Mr. Whitaker down.

"Sir," said Robert. "We have a match; please telephone your staff now. Give the patrol car driver names and addresses. We will pick them up, and all of us will rendezvous at the station conference room. I will make sure that drinks and snacks are available; this may take some time. I'm afraid you must curtail your dinner party. We need your wife too, as she helps you in the shop. By the way, are any of your guests fellow tradesmen?"

"Yes, as a matter fact they are."

"Good, so a Constable will go with you, and show copies of the photograph to your guests. It would be good to find out what else he purchased and anything about him they may remember."

Inspector Mackenzie received the latest information and put it directly on to H.O.M.E.S., along with the fingerprint data. The match was confirmed. It was the same man.

Far into the night the statements were taken, until they had an inventory. Other shop and café owners had been brought in. Eventually they had a complete picture of his purchases. But to no one had he talked about where he was from, or where he was going.

"It's obvious from his purchases," said Stuart. "He has set himself up to bivouac on the mountain: no hotels or guesthouses for him. Completely anonymous!"

By the early hours of Friday morning, a full description of his movements in Fort William, and the sketchy information they had of his sojourn in Glencoe, were being read off computer screens in every police station north and south of the border. But for the present, his whereabouts remained a mystery.

CHAPTER 20

▼

THURSDAY EVENING. 11TH JULY. INVERNESS AIRPORT.

The plane eventually took off. Michael the man had been dozing and at the same time trying to read his book. Every time he nodded off, the book slipped and he had to catch it. The woman looked up at him.

"Tired, are we?" she said.

Surprised, he looked at her "I've had a couple of good days on the mountains. Not so used to it these days. Age catches up on one. Still, I enjoyed it. Now it's back to the grindstone." He smiled. "Since you've spoken to me, I'll introduce myself. My name is Michael, and I'm about to make my way down to Belfast to look at some new projects. But I intend to take it easy and stay somewhere tonight."

She smiled at him. "My name is Moragh, and I am a Ms., not a Mrs."

"Pleased to meet you! Obviously you have been here on business in that outfit, nice as it is."

"Cheeky monkey," she smiled.

Her speech was very precise and she spoke with little mouth movement. It was an educated voice with only a faint trace of an accent.

"I have a good idea of your profession. You must be a solicitor or similar."

"Well done," she said. "I didn't realize it was that obvious. For my sins I'm a barrister, and I have been to prison. Two of them actually; Aberdeen and Inverness, a good guy checking the bad guys."

"I'm intrigued, tell me more."

"It's quite simple, really. Here in Scotland, there are many people in prison who funded the Loyalists, and in some cases the IRA. They have information and we want names of contacts in Ireland; this is a joint venture if we can gain enough information for a conviction. Then the promise is that the informant's case will be reviewed in relation to an earlier release. If you are facing twenty years in jail, the reality of it is grim and foreboding, especially if you are used to the good life outside. I shouldn't be talking to you like this, it's meant to be all very secret."

"Why are you?"

"I was watching you in the lounge. You seemed to be very courteous and caring. I thought it would be nice to sit next to you. It's very stressful after dealing with scum during the last few days; one yearns to meet a nice man again."

She smiled at him; he turned away, embarrassed.

"I'm not the best dressed, I'm afraid."

"I shouldn't worry about that. As soon as I find a hotel, this lot's coming off, probably to be replaced with jeans and a sweater. I have tomorrow free; no family to worry about, and a divorced husband somewhere, but of no consequence. What about you?"

"Oh, I'm on a long holiday, with a bit of business thrown in; a consulting engineer; not civil; electrical; power-generation and control systems, etcetera."

"Sounds intriguing," she said.

"Yes, I enjoy it, but sometimes it entails long periods in other countries, coupled with long hours on site. You certainly 'earn yer brass,' so to speak."

She smiled again. "Come now, you're having me on with your vernacular."

"I apologize," he said. "I'm not good at first conversations."

At that moment their talk was interrupted by the stewardess announcing that "they were ready to land, and to ensure their seatbelts were fastened." The landing was smooth and in no time they were through the arrivals, with no luggage to bother about, and out of the terminal.

Michael turned to Moragh who was following him.

"Shall we share a taxi into Londonderry?"

"Why not?" she said.

They walked to the taxi rank and climbed into a waiting taxi.

"Where to, Moragh?"

"I need a hotel."

"So do I," he said.

She smiled at him. "Looks like the die is cast." She turned to the driver. "Can you take us to a reasonable hotel, please? Not too ostentatious but near to the restaurants." She whispered to Michael: "I'm game to share if you are."

"What? He smiled. "The taxi fare or a room?"

"The room, you idiot," she said, blushing to her roots.

He looked at her. She was quite pretty with a good figure. She must exercise a lot.

"Okay, in for a penny, in for a pound, Ms…?"

"Denver-Marshall," she said.

"It's on the condition that I pay. I'll be off early in the morning, 'the milk train' to Belfast, most probably. I won't wake you and I will not steal your handbag, even though I feel like a 'down-and-out'!"

"Don't worry," she said. "I trust you. A good shower will put you right and we can slum it tonight."

"Fine by me."

The taxi drew up at a medium-size hotel. "Very reasonable, Sir, and comfortable," said the driver. "It has a restaurant, but you also have many restaurants in the centre to choose from."

"Is there a Greek?" asked Michael.

"Yes Sir, about ten minutes away. From the hotel, take the first turning on your left. It's quite a long street, but eventually you come to a square. The Greek restaurant is at the far end. They have a bonny garden, and tonight they'll have a barbecue. It's a set price including wine. I can book for you now if you fancy— they give me a bit of commission."

"Fine by me," said Michael. "How about you, Ms. Denver-Marshall?"

"Sounds great!" she said.

The driver phoned through. After a few minutes he gave the thumbs-up. "You have the number-one table on the veranda overlooking the garden."

"Thank you very much." Michael paid with a substantial tip and helped Moragh out of the taxi.

"Enjoy your stay, good night." The taxi driver waved as he drove away.

The hotel reception was very efficient. They had an en-suite double; would that be acceptable? Michael glanced across at Moragh, who raised an eyebrow.

"Fine," he said, and signed the register under the name of Denver-Marshal, omitting any address. The receptionist did not seem bothered.

"I will pay in advance, as Mrs. Denver-Marshal will be staying for breakfast; but I have a very early morning meeting so I want to be out by six in the morning."

"Thank you Sir."

"Whilst you are making up the bill, include for a room order of a bottle of Bollinger, ice-cold; can we have frosted glasses? Also a platter of oysters, as soon as you like. Oh, and since we are celebrating, add a dish of caviar and some crackers. The Beluga, if possible."

"No problem, Sir, it will be with you within the half hour."

Michael paid with cash and they went to their room. It was fine, light and airy, well appointed and the divan very springy. The bath was huge; a family could get into it, and there was also a double shower cubicle. The closet had two fluffy white dressing gowns hanging there.

"Perfect," he said.

"Yes, I agree."

"Well, it's no use saying 'I'll bath first' when it's big enough for both of us!"

"One thing I must say, let me go half on the room. I didn't expect you to pay for all of it."

"Don't worry about it. I'll give you the bill so you can claim it back on your expenses."

"Thank you," she said, "but the meal is my treat. You can buy the wine when we run out."

"That's settled. Now, what I suggest is we both have a quick shower to freshen up and then put on our dressing gowns. By then our champagne and victuals will be here. After that we can have a bath, get dressed, and have plenty of time to stroll down for our meal."

"Michael, you're certainly an organizer. I can see how you make your money; I concur!"

They stripped off without any more words. Michael was pleased he was tanned, lean and fit. He looked at her. She was not shy; her breasts were large but firm, her waist supple and her legs very shapely. Certainly she exercised. She was a brunette, but was completely shaved down there and had no underarm hair.

She saw him looking!

"I do it on purpose! The prison visits are not to be recommended. There is always a smell and the heat is oppressive. I try to eliminate the body sweating and the resultant odours."

He gazed critically at her. "You do have a good figure. You must work out very regularly."

"Yes, I do. I play tennis when I can, and I walk a lot. I try not to always jump into the car but I wish I could keep my face as young as my body."

He smiled. "You have a nice face."

"You're not so bad yourself. A good body, all the right bits, but a beard would suit you. Your face is right for it; besides, I like beards."

"Did your husband have a beard?"

"No comment and all talk of husbands and wives is banned, or I shall not go out with you; instead I will go to bed!"

Michael held up his hands. "You will have no argument from me. Race you to the shower!"

She won, and turned the shower on. It was freezing. He joined her and gradually the water turned warm. She passed over the shower gel. He had cranberry, she had mango. They rubbed it into each other's bodies; as she washed him down there he felt himself harden.

"Down, boy," she said and slapped him. "Later."

He worked the gel between her breasts and down her body, his fingers entering her crevice. He could feel the juices oozing out of her between his fingers.

She shivered. "That's nice."

Bending down, she gave him a kiss, and then abruptly stood up and turned the shower to cold; with a yelp, they both rushed out for towels.

Just in time; there was a knock on the door. Grabbing dressing gowns, they quickly wrapped themselves up and she went to the door. A white-coated waiter came in with the champagne, oysters and caviar; the repast was complete with fresh toast, lemons, olives, and small cherry tomatoes.

"Shall I pour, Sir?" he said.

"Yes please, perfect."

He expertly popped the cork, without it rocketing off to the ceiling, and poured directly into the frosted glasses. Michael went to his wallet and gave the waiter a fiver.

"Thank you, Sir, I hope you have a nice evening."

They raised their glasses. "Santé!" he said.

"To you, Michael. You're a kind and generous person." She sipped her drink, smiling at him. "Michael, I must say one thing. This is a one off evening! I'm not in the habit of talking to men, unless I have to, never mind picking them up! I have had a marriage, a disaster! Now I am consolidating my career. If we bump into each other again, in the course of our travels that's okay, but not any prior arrangements."

"Fine by me, Moragh; 'ships passing in the night', eh?"

"Thanks Michael. There was just something about you. The little boy lost syndrome. My attraction to you was instant."

"Let's not make it a fatal attraction!" he intoned, his voice grim.

She gave a weak laugh. "Come on, top up. Have some of this Beluga, it's delicious."

The atmosphere was comfortable. It was a long time since he had celebrated with caviar and champagne; not to mention the oysters, what a combination. They finished every drop and scrap. She dressed in washed-out jeans with a peasant blouse, the pattern picked out in red cotton. He put on his new dark green slacks, and tee shirt. But he only had his climbing boots for his feet. Not a problem; he thought they looked quite reasonable.

"Come on, Moragh, let's go."

The restaurant was buzzing. The barbecue was in full swing and there was a combined outdoor cast-iron stove and oven, fed by pine logs. The cook was in the process of withdrawing a large meat dish from the oven in which legs of lamb had been roasting, simmering in garlic and rosemary with the potatoes and onions stewing in the juices.

"Kleftico," he breathed. "My favourite."

"It looks good," agreed Moragh. "Let's go and find our table".

They went up a few steps to the veranda. The table was at the front. The ensemble was just warming up.

"Bet we have to get up for Zorba's dance."

She grimaced. "Better keep some puff for that!"

They sat down, and a Mezé had been laid out for them. Dolmades, Feta cheese, Whitebait, prawns in garlic with Taramasalata and Tarziki side dishes The pita bread was left to keep warm under a cloth. A bottle of Keo Brandy with a set of small barrel shaped glasses sat on a serving trolley at the end of the table.

"Reminds me of my Cyprus days," he said.

The waiter smiled at them.

"You have the special Greek barbecue menu, but we serve French wines; you will have the Burgoyne Aligoté served ice cold as a starter, is that okay?"

"Great," said Michael.

Moragh broke in: "Can we also have a bottle of champagne? I'll pay for that separately."

The drinks came and it was time to relax. The square was lovely with some lime trees and lots of magnolia bushes. It was cobbled with a raised platform for the group, a dancing area, and a place to cook. Very soon every table was taken, and the chatter from each rose into the air. The Square was full of laughter and the strains of the music.

"This is fantastic," said Moragh. She reached out to a hold his hand, and then dropped it down on his lap to hold him.

"Let's not get too drunk, or we'll miss our night together!"

The food came, a complete Kleftico with the potatoes, spinach and broccoli. For good measure there was also a plate of kebabs garnished with peppers, and if that wasn't enough, Greek salad decorated with thin slices of beef tomatoes, feta cheese, and green and black olives with chopped red chili on the top of it. For the next half-hour it was eating time, not to mention drinking. Now it was the Retsina, but also there was a bottle of the Samos wine, syrupy but very good. Quite replete, they sat back finishing the wine with a pot of Greek coffee, watching the dancing.

"Let's go," whispered Moragh. "We only have tonight. We can have a bath together and then jump into bed."

"Be careful," he said. "Our stomachs must be pretty full."

They lay in the bath, replete, caressing each other, as they finished off the rest of the champagne.

"A Sauna would be nice too," she said. "Pity the hotel has not yet finished its health centre. I saw a notice; it opens in August. Maybe we can both come back."

He murmured as he climbed out of the bath: "I think we can create our own body heat, especially with a randy barrister."

"Be careful." Moragh's hands were like paddles. "I can do a pretty good job of soaking you from here."

She too climbed out. They towelled each other and fell onto the bed and their bodies intertwined. Most of the night was spent chewing each other, caressing nipples and breasts. His penis felt sore and continually throbbed. She became dry, completely spent. At last they just fell asleep in one another's arms. Her last words were: "Pity you can't stay in the morning. I'll be 'champing at the bit' again; please don't wake me up when you go out."

His alarm went of at five o'clock. He could feel the vibrations! A quick wash and he packed, dressed, and was out of the door. The night receptionist was 'out to the wide,' snoring. He quickly walked to the station and picked up a taxi to take him to the airport. Once in his car he paid at the auto-toll and was on the road, out of Londonderry. His plan was straightforward; drive down to Wexford. He hoped to be there for about eleven. His phone was on charge. He had an important call to make at nine o'clock.

The route was fixed in his mind, and mostly on quiet country roads. Down to Sligo, then to Roscommon, cutting across to Porteloise where most of the prisoners of the troubles were incarcerated. Then through to Carlow, and on to Wexford.

Hopefully his business there would be successful. By three p.m., four at the latest, he wanted to be on the train to Cork, and then in a taxi to Cobh.

It had been a good night, taking away any of the spectres of Urrah Moor, Goredale, Colne and Glencoe. He thought he deserved a treat. Flicking through his CD collection he found the boxed set of Beethoven symphonies, which did not include the ninth, the Choral. These were the piano transcriptions written by Liszt. He listened to many of the modern virtuosos playing some of them; they never seemed to get it quite right.

He had one of the all-time greats to listen to; Wilhelm Kempf! Truly he understood Beethoven, and the love and perfection that Liszt had created.

With the music on high volume, he drove fast and carefree; he knew his time was running out, but he thought he still had a chance. He was determined not look at any newspapers, TV, or listen to the radio. This way he would remain completely ignorant of the furore he had created.

CHAPTER 21

▼

FRIDAY 12TH JULY. EARLY MORNING. FORT WILLIAM.

Detective Inspector Stuart Mackenzie woke up with a jolt. Detective Sergeant Robert Currie, looking as fresh as a daisy, grinned down at him.

"Here you are, Sir, a big mug of black coffee with plenty of sugar and some hot bridies with bacon. That should help you wake up! You dropped off to sleep over your computer; we substituted a cushion for your keyboard. I rang your wife before she went to bed, not having the heart to wake you; she sends you her love."

"Thanks Robert, you are a good friend as well as being a colleague. I'll have a quick shower and a shave. Good job I keep an electric razor here. There's something niggling me about our inquiries last night. Maybe after coffee and a shower it will come to me. Check the latest reports please, I will be back in about five-minute or so."

With coffee in one hand and his bridie in the other, he went off to shower. He came hurrying back, buttoning up his shirt.

"I know what it is! We've checked the shops, pubs and cafés: but we have not as yet tried the garages and banks. Let's you and I do the banks; we will have Sergeant Hamish with one of his constable's check the garages. Come on, there are only five Banks and seven Building Societies; we can catch them before they open. Please ask the duty sergeant to ring round the managers, so they know we are coming. Meanwhile, I'll finish this wonderful cup of coffee. It's not necessary for us to take a car; we can walk round the lot of them."

It took time. People were already queuing outside various establishments, waiting for them to open. They drew a blank at the Building Societies and at the Banks, with one exception.

One of the lesser-known English Banks had a small branch, simply a manager and a cashier. They took turns in keeping the customers happy. The cashier could not help; he was a relief from the Inverness Branch. Their permanent cashier was on holiday somewhere in the Caribbean, possibly St Lucia, and had been for nearly two weeks. The manager was at a golf tournament, but he was only out for the day, of this he was sure. During the holiday season they opened on Saturday mornings so he had to be back for that duty.

"If he telephones in, have him ring the station. Ask for Sergeant Corrie or myself any time of the day or night. Please check with your Inverness Branch and see if he's discussed his plans with anyone. Now if you can give me the manager's address, we will check with neighbours; also, we will obtain details from vehicle registration; that way we may be able to stop him 'en route.' Unknowingly he could have valuable information concerning a case we are working on."

It was frustrating: his house was quite isolated, no near-neighbours. They tried the golf course and drew a blank. The manager was new, recently transferred from Stirling. Their inquiries with the Stirling police had not produced any results. He was certainly not playing golf at any of the city courses, or in the surrounding area. No one had seen his car. They would have to wait, and it could be 'something or nothing.'

Stuart Mackenzie drove back to Glencoe. He wanted to check the postboxes in the glen and the one in the hotel. All had been emptied, and the mail had disappeared to points north, south, east and west. There was a call on his mobile informing him of Alicia's and Roderick's parents' itinerary. A Dr Mark Kent, who was a heart specialist from Southampton Infirmary, would be flying up to Inverness with his wife, Margaret, on the first available flight. The police at Inverness would meet them at the Airport.

Similarly Mr. Oliver Hamilton, a lecturer in biochemistry at Liverpool University, and his wife Sara, would fly from Liverpool to Inverness. The police would also be there to meet them. A quiet room in the Post House at Inverness had been arranged for their reception. The Superintendent would attend, to explain the circumstances of the deaths.

The mortuary staff needed more time to complete the examinations. They would telephone when the bodies were presentable for identification. Once the formalities were concluded, they would be able to set a date for the inquest. Stuart gave a sigh of relief. He wanted to be in Fort William to meet the bank manager when they had located him. The trail was rapidly drawing cold.

Friday morning, 12th July. Northern England.

The day dawned early for Moira as it did for Patrick in Colne. She was at headquarters by six thirty in the morning. D.I. Priest had beaten her to it, and had a printout ready for her.

"Simon!" she exclaimed. "I have to say this, you are unbeatable where computers and informatics are concerned. Have you chosen your assistant yet?"

"Yes, Mar'm."

"Moira, please."

"Okay, Moira, yes, I have. It is Detective Constable Roy Green. He has good skills, not too young, but bright and he has passed his Sergeant Exams. He is very streetwise, but also quite an intellectual when it comes to informatics. He writes his programmes in JavaScript as well as C++and Visual Basic."

"I believe you, Simon. Make out the appointment sheet with the job description, recommended rank, etc. I'll sign it and take it to the National Commander."

"It's already done, Moira, one second." A flurry of keys and the printer whirred, and the document was handed to her.

She signed it. "Be back in a moment."

Bob's office was empty and she left the document in his 'in box' and then made her way to the canteen, to collect a tray of coffee's and some bacon butties. The canteen staff made up the tray without a word. They knew Moira and the way she took care of her people. Back in the computer room the staff had assembled. Moira cleared a place and put the tray down on the conference table.

"Help yourselves; take a few minutes to relax before we get down to business."

Five minutes of bliss ensued. She had even remembered to bring down the brown sauce!

"I congratulate you, Roy, on your promotion. The National Commander will sign it when he gets back and you'll be able to draw your new warrant card tomorrow. Possibly next week, when the furore is over, we may all be able to get together and consolidate our modus operandi. The events of this week, even excluding our killer, are incredible! Accelerated promotions, enough clout and facilities to tackle anything, with a man at the top who is approachable to all of us. Alternately, one of the best and worst weeks I have known in policing!" She picked up the printout. "Let's check the latest from Glencoe." She studied the information. "Well, the identification is positive enough from his taste in reading: let's hope this bank manager comes up trumps when they find him. For the moment we still have no clue to his whereabouts."

The phone rang. It was Patrick.

"You okay?" she asked. "Did you get some rest? Listen, I've booked the flight for Saturday morning, destination Inverness. When you are finished at Colne and Skipton, come directly to the *Yorkshire Post* office in Leeds."

"That's fine, Moira. One of the patrol cars will drive me over."

"That's good. Molly will come with me, so she will drive us back to Tees-side. Surprise; we are flying in Bob's jet!" She adjusted her tone, becoming serious. "Look, Patrick, this is a bit awkward for me, please don't think I'm pushing myself on you. The lady who looks after my house has a home party business. She does dinner-parties and her specialty is French, and would you believe, Belgian dishes. So tonight she is making us a finger buffet. I have invited Molly and Peter, who are very excited over their promotion and their new apartment, to join us. The invitation is also for Millie and Alex, if they are available. They would not have to rush back. Molly and Peter have a guest room."

"A nice idea," said Patrick. "Millie is here. I'll ask her." There was silence before Patrick came back to the phone. "Yes, fine, can you e-mail your address and a map?"

"Simon will do it now." He nodded.

"I will tell my lady to cater for six; we need some sort of break. Your accommodation is okay, Patrick, I have a spare room."

With that she rang off, blushing.

She ran up the stairs and onto the flat roof of the building. Bob and Alice were already there, at the small reception enclosure by the side of the helipad.

"Hello Moira, beat you to it," smiled Alice. "Both of us have taken the day off. We will ask Richard and Janine to stay with us until they have to go back. We hope the Coroner will rule that Jan can be interred. They will need time in the flat sorting documents and other things. Not to mention organizing the selling of it, and the disposal of the goods and chattels. We will do everything we can to help." Alice was close to tears. "They want to donate all the proceeds to improve the sports facilities used by the various orphanages in the north-east."

The helicopter landed. Someone who could only be Jan's sister stepped out, followed by Richard. The greetings were subdued. They could not imagine the rest of their lives without their impetuous Jan! Alice and Bob, without a word, took them down to the car and then drove them over to the mortuary so they could see their sister for the last time. All of them were in tears as they left the mortuary and drove over to the court buildings for the Coroner's hearing.

There were not many people there. Moira joined them and apologized for the National Commander's absence. He had to be at a meeting in Sheffield, but he would join them later after the press conference.

Moira gave evidence relating to the finding of the body, requesting an adjournment on the verdict, as police inquiries were ongoing.

Richard Fielding formally confirmed that the murdered woman was his sister.

Dr Frank Hodgson gave his evidence relating to the examination of Jan's body, and the Bradford Pathologist concurred with him. The blow to the top of the head had badly fractured her skull, but death had been due to drowning whilst in an unconscious state.

The coroner asked the police if they required the body to stay in the mortuary until their inquiries were completed.

Moira, on behalf the police, stated they had no objection to an order being given allowing release of the body for burial. The coroner consented to this and made the order, allowing the undertaker to have charge of the body. The clerk of the court produced the document, which the coroner signed. This was handed to the next of kin. Nobody could speak.

Moira hugged Richard and Janine. "Alice, Bob, please forgive me; I must prepare for the press releases."

It took two hours. She and Molly would eat on the way. Her mind was spinning: still no time to sit down and try to analyze this man. Events were happening too fast. Where was he? She believed this man had no fixed plan, but worked on contrived opportunity.

Colne. Friday Morning. 12th July.

Millie brought Greg and Sue Markham to the Coroner's Court where Patrick Hall was waiting for them. The courtroom was packed. Sylvia and Stephanie were also waiting for them. Other friends from the business course were there too.

Patrick Hall gave evidence on behalf of the police relating to the discovery of the murder.

Gregory Markham confirmed the body was that of his daughter Patricia.

The police surgeon Dr Henry Roberts, and the Pathologist Mr. Sinclair Cameron, gave evidence on the state of the body and the cause of death. Most people were weeping during the twenty minutes, as the pathologist gave his carefully phrased medical evidence.

The coroner sympathized, but called for order. Again the police had no objection to the release of the body. The coroner observed that the police investigation was centred in three locations and possibly a fourth.

The verdict was murder by person or persons unknown.

As they filed out of the court, Patrick shook hands with Greg and Susan Markham and gave them a hug. They were staying the weekend. Sylvia and Stephanie would help them with the funeral arrangements and also with the disposal of the assets. With respect to the house the proceeds would go to help Sylvia build a small fitness center, utilizing an established franchise.

"Patricia would like that," remarked Sylvia. "She only did what she did, to raise capital."

Patrick departed for Skipton. He had lunch with Ken and Mable and together they went to the Coroner's Court.

Millie went off to fetch the parents of Alison and Cathy. She would have a quick lunch with them and ensure they were in good time for the Coroner's hearing.

Skipton. Friday Afternoon. 12th July.

The court convened precisely at two o'clock.

Ken Seymour gave evidence of discovering the bodies of the two girls.

Mr. Smith and Mr. Roberts formally identified the girls as their respective daughters.

Patrick Hall confirmed the discovery of the murders and asked the court's commendation of Mr. Seymour; relating to the orderly way he had summoned the police without any panic at the campsite. He further added that due to Mr. Seymour, the crime scene had been free of any tampering or unauthorized interference. The coroner concurred and agreed a formal commendation would be awarded.

The police surgeon Dr John Mills gave his evidence of the initial examination of the girls. Mr. Sinclair Ferguson, the pathologist, agreed the deaths were by asphyxiation. No other abasement of the bodies had occurred.

Patrick Hall further confirmed whoever killed them took nothing from their persons, or anything from the tent. He made a statement that the police had no objection to the body being released for burial. The coroner made the order and gave the verdict. Murder by persons or persons unknown, the police to continue their investigation. Patrick and Molly said goodbye to the Smiths and the Roberts. Arrangements had been made for them to be driven home. They were going to have a Wrexham undertaker bring the girls back home for burial. Sorrowfully, they departed.

A patrol car drove Patrick down to Leeds. Moira was waiting for him at the Yorkshire Post office. She was dressed in a grey worsted suit with a white blouse and black bow tie; black stockings and high heels completed the ensemble.

"Hmm, quite the business lady."

"Only for show," blushed Moira. "Don't worry, Bob has arranged for the Leeds police press officer to conduct the proceedings. She has all the facts: CD discs are available to all the papers and TV companies with complete statements. We hope to issue a final identikit photograph tomorrow morning, if Stuart can find his missing bank manager in time."

The meeting was short and to the point. The officer knew her job. She had handled the Ripper press releases and the others.

Moira and Patrick settled down in the rear of the police car for the drive back to Tees-side. She put her hand in his, not a word was said. Her head lolled against his shoulder and she just gave up to the tiredness, which overtook her. Patrick, also lulled by the smoothness of the car, found himself dozing. Molly had a quick glance at them whilst at a road junction. Two sleeping beauties: maybe they could find the same happiness as she had with Peter; they certainly deserved it.

Chapter 22

▼

Friday 12th July. Eire. Late Morning.

Michael the man was making good time. He had stopped only twice. Once between Sligo and Roscommon where he had seen a refuse lorry parked in a lay-by, emptying the waste bins. He drove on, passing the next lay-by, stopping at the third. Yes, the bins there had not been emptied. He dumped the false number plates in one of them, and in the other he discarded his spare walking clothes. For his final journey he needed to travel light. At Roscommon he made his second stop and went into a chemist to buy a 'brush-in hair dye.' As he drove out of the town he noticed a shop selling broad-brimmed leather hats.

It was worth a quick stop. The one he selected had a nice warm look, and the leather was old and soft. Trying it on, the shopkeeper looked across, remarking that it looked well on him and he could have it at a discount. Just the job, he thought, paying for it, and was off again. He drove into Wexford; unerringly he turned off the main road into a side street, missing the town-centre, and eventually arriving at the docks. He stopped by a large car park next to an enclosure. There was a barrier at the entrance of the enclosure, and a notice above which read 'Cars for auction only.' Stopping at the barrier, he went into the office adjacent to it.

"Now, Sir, what can I do for you?" said the man sitting behind a desk.

"I want to sell my car."

"Can I look at the registration documents, please, and take a copy? Also, the certificate of conformity; we are in the E.E.C., you know."

"Certainly," said Michael as he proffered the papers.

The man glanced at the documents and then nearly fell backwards off his chair, his eyes wide open.

"Are you sure about this?" he said.

"Yes."

"But the car's only six-month old and left-hand-drive. Would you not be better selling it in Europe?"

"Problem is, we have moved from Europe. I've taken a job as a consultant engineer, and a house and a car is part of the perks. I tried to get them to buy my car and then give it back to me, but being left-hand-drive they wouldn't entertain it. I told them it would be no problem for me, but apparently there would be insurance complications." The lies came glibly to him.

"I suppose you've been headhunted by one of these Japanese companies that offer such very attractive packages; good on you. Do they want any good mechanics? Never mind, let us go and look at this dream machine."

They went outside to the car.

"It's beautiful, man; dark-green, matching leather upholstery, stereo, and CD. Automatic, tow bar attached and absolutely pristine. Can I look under the bonnet?"

Michael operated the bonnet lock.

"Fantastic engine with turbo, huge air-conditioner. What is it, 2.6 litre? Something like eighty kilowatt? Exhaust, good, tyres, all-weather; is it auto into four-wheel drive?"

"No, my other car was, but after a hundred thousand kilometres there was a difficulty with the clutch and differential. The manual change gives no such problems."

"They certainly know how to make a car, so we'll put you up first."

'Volvo SC90,' he wrote on a placard in large black letters. "I will set a reasonable reserve price against it and see how the bidding goes. We have people coming over from France looking for left-hand-drive cars. I think it will sell; you know it is cash sales only. The bank on the site is open all afternoon; they will take your money anytime."

"Thank you for your cooperation. If it sells I can confirm to my company and I will have the new car by Monday morning. That's when I start my new job."

"It's lunchtime now. The auction starts one p.m. sharp."

"Let me buy you a couple of pints of Guinness. I appreciate the consideration you've given me. My name is Michael, by the way."

"Very nice, thanks, Michael; never say no to a pint. My name is Seamus, by the way."

"Good to meet you," said Michael as they shook hands.

They sat outskde the caravan, which sold Guinness and a selection of Irish beers. The smell was tantalizing. They had hot pies and colcannon, fresh out of the oven, made for the expectant sellers and buyers. Michael purchased two plates along with the Guinness, which was ice cold.

"There you go, Seamus. That first pint will go down great, as we say, without 'touching the sides'!"

The auction did not start until 1:30 p.m. This was due to a mini-car transporter arriving unexpectedly with six extra cars that had to be processed. Michael scanned the 'show' area. His car had attracted a lot of attention. He picked up his bag and rucksack and went to find a seat in the auction hall. Seamus had made a promise, that if it sold; they would process the transaction immediately. Normally no payouts were made until the auction was finished and all proceeds had been collected.

Michael could not bear the waiting. He hurried out of the auction and walked along the quayside. He found a pub with chairs and tables outside and had another pint. He would give it half an hour and then go back. The bidding did not interest him; only the result.

He watched the seagulls landing on the cobbles, snatching any scraps that had fallen from the tables. There was a cormorant sitting on the rudder of a trawler, quite unconcerned. The Atlantic Ocean was a greenish colour, the waves rolling quite peacefully and lapping against the quayside. Time passed slowly. He gave it over the half-hour and then went back to the auction.

"Thought we had lost you, Michael!"

"Couldn't bear the suspense, Seamus."

"Ach! Only an excuse for another pint! Anyway, we sold it! I reckon all you have lost is thirty percent of the purchase price including our commission; and, now knowing you for the last few hours, I reckon you already recovered the T.V.A."

Michael grinned. Apparently a Frenchman had bought it. He had travelled by train and ferry especially to be at this auction, and he was ecstatic! Because it had taken so little time to find the right car, he now planned to spend a few days in Killarney before travelling back home.

"Thank-you," said Michael as he passed over a hundred Euro note. "Here, Seamus, get yourself a few vintage bottles of the 'Bushmills.' You deserve it."

"Thanks, Chief. Here's your cash in Euros. Sign a receipt slip—and this is your copy of the transaction. The bank's down there to your left; eighteen thousand Euros is a lot of 'geld'."

At the bank he deposited half of the money direct into his wife's account. The other went into his float. He would probably have to exist a year on that at least. He was pleased he had other accounts open to him anywhere in Europe, but only for emergencies.

He felt a new contentment; wonderful, he thought, the way his mind could blot out the immediate past. Yet it was a disaster he could not blot out the distant past; those failed marriages, the affairs, the hurt and the turmoil that went with them. He found a café by the station and sat there with a pot of tea and a plate of sandwiches. All his worldly possessions were now with him, a large bag on wheels, and his rucksack. He took out his phone and rang Valerie Charlier.

"Hello, hello," came her voice. "It must be you, Michael; no one else has this number. I wanted to call you, but I know you haven't finished your work. *N'est pas?*"

"Yes, you're right."

"I think it's a very bad work. I feel it even on the Pennine Way. We have heard rumours."

"Valerie, I'm going to try and book the ferry to Roscoff and then I will make my way down to Vichy and find a guesthouse."

"Good, but forget it about the guest house. Go direct to the mountains, to my retreat. I assume you will still have a car. I will text you with directions and where the key is kept. There's a barn where you can hide the car. Food will not be a problem. The freezers are full. Arrive early dawn and do not leave the house. I'll be with you by Wednesday evening next week. Keep the bed warm for me; that bit I'm looking forward to."

"*Bon Voyage Ma Cherie. Tout l'heure.*" He disconnected the phone. "Now for the ferry," he said to himself and dialled the Cobh terminal number. "Hello, do you have room for a foot passenger on tonight's ferry?"

"Yes Sir, we sail at five. Can you make it?"

"I am speaking from Wexford."

"Take the train. It's every half-hour; get off at the station before Cork. It is only a short taxi ride down to the ferry port. Shall I make the booking for you?"

"Yes please. Have you a cabin? It's a fifteen hour crossing, is it not?"

"A little less than that. We have a sea view cabin available. The cost includes your evening meal and breakfast; with the repast; you have a house bottle of red or white wine. There is an in-ship TV with a selection of pay programmes, which are added to your bill. The same for extra drinks, etcetera. The welcome tray, of tea and coffee and hot savouries is complementary. Is that satisfactory to you, Sir?"

"It is indeed. Thank you very much."

"I'll book you directly. I need your name, and the credit cards details. Visa or Master, the number, and expiry date please."

He gave the details.

"Thank you, Sir. Your reference is ROF 637. Your cabin is upper deck 45. If you take the 3:30 train from Wexford, we'll arrange for the taxi to be at the station to meet you. Don't pay him; all expenditures will be itemized in the final bill. Any gratuities are at your discretion."

"Thank you very much."

"My pleasure, Sir. Have a good voyage. Do you need a hotel at Roscoff?"

"No, I want to travel north as soon as possible."

"Okay Sir, goodbye."

Everything went well; the train, taxi, all on time. He gave his reference number at the terminal. After they took an imprint of his card and checked his passport, he went straight out to the boat.

He stopped at the ship's shop to buy a road map of France, and then went to the purser's office to collect the cabin key. From a menu he selected his dinner, with an extra bottle of wine; a Frascati, very cold. He then ordered the full Irish breakfast for seven a.m. the following morning.

Well content, he went to the cabin, deposited his bag and rucksack, and then stripped off. The shower was hot and the force of it stung him. Feeling invigorated, he combed the dye into his hair until it was jet-black. He waited the requisite time and then showered again; the surplus dye ran-off into the drain.

A dressing gown was supplied. Feeling comfortable, he answered the knock on the door.

"Good evening, Sir, I'm your steward. I have brought you a pot of French coffee and a complimentary tot of Irish Mist. Your wine will come with the dinner in about two hours. In the interim, we provide a tray of hot savouries." With that he deposited the tray on the pullout table and left.

He was always amazed at the tradition of hospitality at sea; remembering as a young engineer going to sea on the first generation of the hundred-thousand tonne tankers. For him it was to sort out problems on the bridge control of the engines, and the temperature monitoring systems of the turbines. But he was always given a first class officer's cabin, and dined at the captain's table; at twenty-six years of age he had revelled in it.

This was going to be a good voyage. The vessel was French owned and controlled. He knew he was 'skirting against the wind'; they must be near to him! He would know soon enough. If he disembarked and managed to get through customs unscathed, he thought he would still have a chance. He felt it would have been much more dangerous if he had kept the car.

Six a.m. was docking time, but the passengers who had cabins were allowed to sleep until later, have breakfast and then disembark. He did not intend to be in the later contingent. After an early breakfast he'd be off. For the moment there was the prospect of a quiet dinner, reading his book, no T.V. It would be a long day tomorrow and as yet he had no idea how we would travel.

Midnight. Friday, 12th July. Tees-side.

Moira was asleep, as was Patrick. Molly and Peter had gone. The evening had been subdued. The food had been well prepared, but they had no enjoyment in it and perfunctorily sipped at their wine, lost in their own thoughts. Moira stirred in her chair and smiled as she looked across at Patrick slumped over the table. She gently shook him.

"Come on, Patrick—wake up. Time to go to sleep, in a bed; we are on the early morning plane this morning, remember? Leave everything, my lady is coming in tomorrow morning. She's a good-natured soul. Tumble into my bed; at least we can have a cuddle. That's all we'll be able to manage tonight!"

CHAPTER 23

▼

FRIDAY EARLY EVENING.
12TH JULY. ISLE OF ISLAY.

The bank manger, Martin Haldane, had enjoyed his day irrespective of a very long early morning drive through Glencoe to Crianlarick, down to Tarbet, Lochgilphead and on to West Tarbuck in the Mull of Kintyre.

The first ferry of the morning to the Isle of Islay was waiting. The coxswain had remarked that it would be a fast crossing, only three cars; they would be docked by nine o' clock. With a grin, he had assured him of a good day's golf.

As he drove off the ferry after a calm crossing the coxswain stopped him again to remind him that the last sailing was seven o'clock in the evening, and not to have too many tipples in the McCrae lodge. He drove out of Port Ellen and up to Bowmore. It was only a half-hour drive, but very enjoyable. The air seemed to be permanently infused with the smoky peat aroma of the distilleries. McCrae lodge was easy to find. The golf course lay open to the eye, right to the very edge of the ocean. He booked in at the reception, buying a day ticket which included lunch and evening dinner.

The course was an undulating one; one of the holes required a long drive to reach the crest of a hill, and then a nice six iron shot to lob the ball onto the green below.

His favourite of the day was the drive later on in the course, which hopefully took the ball across the bay, from cliff to cliff. Incredible, the sea roaring in one's ears as the breakers crashed against the cliff, completely masking the sound of the impact as the driver lifted the ball into a long sweeping ark. His companions were as bad as he was, but he rationalised that it was due to tiredness after the long drive; he did not have the energy in his arms and shoulders for the drives the course demanded. He was determined that there would be many more times, but for the future, he would arrange to stay at the lodge possibly for two nights.

They were back to the lodge for the nineteenth! He had elected to have a dram of the 'The Paps' and with a bowl of homemade soup, and some good black bread, he felt ready for the second round.

They fared no better, but the adrenalin was pumping and the gust of icy air sweeping in from the sea kept his head clear. All the same, he had been glad when once more they all retired to the clubhouse, changed and made their way to the dining room at the lodge.

The tables were laden with haggis, neaps and tatties; loins of lamb were on another platter just waiting to be carved. He had eaten his fill, and washed it down with quite a few drams of the smoky Bowmore. Ruefully he reflected he had sampled more of the island's whiskies before leaving. Now he was on the ferry making his way back to the mainland. The coxswain had passed him a huge mug of black coffee with a dour shake of his head.

They landed at Tarbet without incident and he was away up the Mull, the windows open to allow the rushing wind to clear his head.

The police stopped him at Arrochar. 'That's it,' he thought, knowing he was well over the limit; probably a night in the cells and his licence gone. Not a good advert for a bank manager!

A Sergeant came over to the car. "Mr. Martin Haldane?"

"Yes, Officer."

"Step out of the car, please, Sir. We have been searching for you. You must be back in Fort William as quickly as possible. Can I see your licence to check identity?"

The card was produced and the Sergeant checked it off against a paper on his clipboard.

He went over to the police radio.

"We have him, let D.I.Mckenzie know. Radio for the police helicopter; tell the pilot to land in the big car park, where the portable highland cinema is set up. In addition, they need to send a car transporter; for Mr. Haldane's car!"

The Sergeant beckoned across to Haldane.

"We have a helicopter coming for you; we will see that your car is taken care of and delivered back to you. We will need your car keys. In the normal course of the events we would have stopped you anyway and asked you to take a test. I think you realize you've had too much of the golden stuff. This time we will take no action. Your car will be waiting for you at the Fort William police station. In the interim, we will look after you. The helicopter will be here within the hour; in the meantime we have coffee and sandwiches in the car. You're welcome to them; I think you're in for a long night!"

Mystified, he settled back in the police car, accepting the coffee and sandwiches.

No one was talking to him; obviously he would have to wait until he was back in Fort William for any kind of explanation. He felt himself dozing in the warmth of the car, when suddenly the air was shattered by the noise of the helicopter. The park was bathed in light from its quartz halogen floodlight. The flight was very brief; within thirty minute he was sitting with more coffee in the police station at Fort William.

A tall spare man came in. His hair was dark brown, very thick. He swept it back with one hand; his face was etched with the deep lines of fatigue.

"I'm Detective Inspector Stuart McKenzie. Nice to meet you, Mr. Haldane. You should be grateful to the Hellensburgh police; they treated you with considerable kindness, and you may not know but those patrolmen can sense how many milligrams of alcohol you have in your body without the use of a meter. Its instinct to them! Alco tests only confirms it legally. I think you've learnt a valuable lesson this night. Not to drink and drive, eh? Your fine would be a heavy one with that sort of consumption, and a year's ban. No more trips down to Isle of Islay and the McCrae lodge. I know it well, and the quality of the malts!" He sat back, looking serious. "Now to business; can you look at this composite picture and an artist's impression, and tell me if you recognize the man; take your time."

"No need, I do know him. He was in my bank, Wednesday morning. However, it's not a great deal like him. I recognize the likeness because I spent some time with him. He drew out a reasonable sum of money, which required authentication, and whilst we were waiting we talked of mountains and golf. In fact, he was the one who told me of the special golf days in Islay. He was very keen to revisit Skye, walk the Cuillin ridge and bivouac overnight and then drop down into Glenbrittle. From there he hoped to get a boat over to Culnamean in Isle of Rhum, walk the high peaks on the south side of the island, stay the night at Kinloch and then take a boat back to Skye. He would then go by bus back to Sligachan where he would have left his car. He seemed to have a very flexible itinerary; able to go wherever the fancy took him."

"Could you describe him, and do you remember his name?"

"Off the cuff, not very well. I can't remember his name. But the video will help, and I can look up the transaction records at the bank."

"Let's go," said Stuart, turning towards the door.

"There is a problem; the time locks do not operate until eight o'clock."

"But surely you can override it?"

"Yes, it can be overridden, but it needs a second key, and a second electronic identity, a palm print."

"Whose?" demanded D.I. McKenzie.

"The manager at the Inverness Office."

Mc Kenzie pressed a digit on his phone.

"Get me the duty Inspector at Inverness, please."

After a moment his phone rang. He picked it up and identified himself to the officer at Inverness Police Headquarters. They were all good friends. The duty man already knew the strain he was under with a double murder on his hands. Stuart explained the need to find the manager of the bank, and the urgency of getting him across to Fort William.

The Inspector promised it would have top priority, and they would ring as soon as they contacted him.

"Good." Stuart inwardly breathed a sigh of relief. "The helicopter has just left here. We'll call their control and have it diverted to Inverness, and they will bring the manager back here."

Martin Haldane yawned. "I've been up over eighteen hours. Can't it wait until morning?"

Stuart turned to him. "Mr Haldane, this is a murder inquiry. A serial killer is on the loose and every second counts in my book. You are the first tangible lead we've got. I've been on the go for almost thirty-six hours. I dare not sleep, I cannot face the nightmares if I try to sleep, and I may be stealing time of someone's natural life. How about that on your conscience? I sympathize with you. I'm trained to understand, and accept long hours with very little sleep."

They waited, dozing a little. Robert Corrie came in.

"Chief, I can't stay at home whilst you are slogging away here. I have to do something."

"Robert, you're a gift from God. I have been trying to psyche myself to updating the information programmes. Here it is, all written down. A good job you can read my scrawl. Would you be kind enough to input it for me? The sooner we have the voice recognition systems installed the better; but your keyboard skills are second to none. It's very important, especially for Tees-side, Skipton and Colne, that they are updated. Make sure you send it to the Skye police with a

Red Alert. It's all down there; his possible itinerary. It could well be his next escapade!"

"No problem." Robert sat down at the computer and began sorting out the sheets of scribbled notes. "This is okay. About an hour and it will be available to every police station in the country."

The phone rang; it was Inverness.

"We have him, Stuart. He will be with you in about twenty minutes."

"That's great; can you make sure he has his bank keys for the Fort William Branch? Oh, and one more thing, will you organize the artist and Identikit operator to be here by seven? Tell them to bring the photo imagining equipment. We will have the tape from the Bank's Video."

"Okay. See you in the morning. Get some sleep."

"Chance would be a fine thing," sighed Stewart.

The banging of doors interrupted his reverie. The police inspector from Inverness was there. His companion was short, fat and balding. Martin Haldane stirred and then went to the man and clapped him on the shoulder.

"Good of you to come, Sir. Our apologies for such an early morning trip." Stuart had risen from his chair, hand outstretched.

"I can only hope this will not take too long. We have our holiday flight in the morning. The family's packed and ready for the first plane down to Heathrow."

"About fifteen minutes, if you're able to release the Bank doors and the Video lock. However, please do not worry over your flight; my colleague will arrange everything. A car will pick you up at your home; it will be there for you on your return also. You will have special clearance to the plane, no waiting; all your baggage will go direct to the hold. Similarly, when you return."

"The Inverness police will confirm this?"

"Yes, I will authorize it immediately."

Mr Ridley was mollified. "That is very kind of you. My wife is up for the night. I will ring her and tell her the good news."

Within a few minutes on arrival at the bank, the locks were neutralized both for the door and the video. The Inverness manager turned to go.

"Goodbye," said Stuart. "Have a good holiday, you and your family."

He called back, "I'm going on a fitness regime: hope to lose some weight!"

"Nice man," Stewart remarked to Martin Haldane.

"Yes, a stalwart Presbyterian. He has refused promotion a couple of times. He enjoys being in the North of Scotland."

The transaction for Wednesday was on the screen. A man going by the name of Michael Brown had drawn a thousand pounds. The account was a savings account with card access. A memo relating to the account stated that the customer was a worldwide traveller, and correspondence was to a 'poste restante' address located in Hull. Prior to Wednesday's withdrawal, none had been made during the last five years. Statements had been sent on an annual basis along with a certificate relating to tax deductions. Each year they had received an acknowledgement of receipt, signed and dated. His card had been renewed every two years.

The video picture of the man was blurred and grainy. The man's face was partly obscured by other customers.

Stuart took the reel and gave a receipt; it was up to the experts to extract a better image for them.

"You need to install new surveillance equipment. If you did have a raid, we would have very little chance of identifying any villains. Must be ten years old at least."

"Yes, I think that the bank over the last two years has been negotiating with companies to replace the security systems in all the branches. But with threatened takeovers it has never happened."

"The story of my life," Stuart intoned. "Get some sleep, Mr. Haldane. See you at eight o'clock. By then we'll have the experts here. The patrol car will take you home and collect you at eight o'clock. You'll be able to drive home in your own car when we finish the business of the morning. Now I'm going to crash out for a short time."

Before dropping off to sleep in one of the spare hospitality suites, the cells, in common parlance, he left a memo for Robert to have the Hull police check the poste restante address.

"Obviously," he remarked sleepily to himself, "it was a false name. And at the time when the account was opened a name and normally an address was sufficient. Identity checks were not considered necessary."

How long, he mused, had this man been concocting this? He obviously had a plan of some description. Had something like this occurred elsewhere in the world? It was something else to check, to talk to his American F.B.I friends about who had been on the profiling conferences at Bramshill.

CHAPTER 24

▼

SATURDAY MORNING. 13TH JULY. FORT WILLIAM.

Stuart stirred. He heard the metallic chink as the cell door opened. He closed his eyes again and then he felt someone pushing his hair and then a light kiss on his cheek. He looked up and saw his wife smiling at him.

"Good morning, darling. You have to thank Robert for this. He told me how hard you were working, and that a reward was in order, so he telephoned me. They are making breakfast for us. Isn't that nice?"

"But what about the bairns?"

"Don't worry about the children. My sister turned up last late last night. Apparently Geoffrey had to go off to London for an urgent weekend meeting with his directors. Kate felt lonely and wanted the company of her twin sister. We're going to take the children to the theme park near Oban today. I've been warned that I'll not see much of you this weekend!"

Breakfast was ready. They sat down and Robert joined them with a sheepish grin on his face. Fiona leaned over and gave him a big kiss.

"You know Robert, I still have a wee sister, nearly finished university, and looking for the right man. She's quite keen on you, almost one of the family! I don't know what Stuart would do without you. Why not make it legal?"

Robert turned a bright red and Stuart laughed. They sat back and relaxed. Breakfast was served; herb sausages, bacon and eggs, and the inevitable fried slices of haggis.

The cook came in with a steaming pot of coffee. She looked and saw they still had plenty left to eat.

"Eat up now," she said. "We were up early catching the haggis on the slopes of Ben Nevis."

Everyone laughed. Stuart said, "I agree, we don't know when we'll have the next meal."

Martin Haldane joined them. "Very kind of you," he said as he produced a bottle of Bowmore and commenced to unscrew the cap.

The aroma of the rich blend of fermented barley and smoky peat filled the room. He waved aside their protest as he topped up each steaming mug of black coffee with a liberal dose of the whisky.

'It's my thank-you to you. During these past hours I've learnt some valuable lessons; what is it Paul the Apostle writes? 'Examine yourself to see if you be in the faith.' Well, I have done that, and found that I'm in the faith of the living. So my toast to you is: 'I hope you cast catch this bastard and break him on the wheel,' which was an old Scottish custom and would be too good for him."

Stuart turned to his wife. "Fiona my darling, it was lovely to see you. But now we have to get back to work. Give my love to the kids and have a good day. God bless you. For the rest of us, we must now go to the conference room. Everything is set out there, including more coffee; so take your Bowmore with you, Martin."

Once settled and replete, with more coffee, Stewart spoke to them.

"Gentlemen, I have promised we will have on the C.A.T.C.H.E.M. network, a refined identikit photograph and a composite from the artist by ten o'clock this morning. The powers that be feel it's important to be able to give midday TV coverage and possibly photographs for the evening editions of the papers. We can only but try."

The two experts set up their large screens and displayed the Identikit and Composites derived from Tees-side, Colne and Malham. They then merged the constituent images to display a single Identikit picture, and similarly for the composite.

Stuart turned to Martin. "I would like you to work first from the Identikit screen. Try to visualize the man, and then look at the picture. All you have to do is to make comments; for instance, is the jaw line too weak? Is the nose too small? Perhaps the ears don't stick out that much, etcetera. Then focus on the composite. Let your mind reflect back on the conversations. Close your eyes if you want to. It doesn't matter if you're wrong and correct yourself; the operator will follow up on your every remark relating to a description. He's trained to do that. Once you've closed your eyes, try not to look at the screen until you've exhausted your memory. The artist will have the same composite on his screen. He will put the flesh onto the identikit."

Martin closed his eyes and tried to visualize the man. He had enjoyed the conversations with him. The man was very knowledgeable, and he knew his mountains and his golf, staying from time to time at the McCrae Lodge.

He had described the course, and the panorama one met as one reached the top of the hill and gazed down at the Island of Jura with its twin peaks, commonly known as the Paps of Jura. To visit it was only a short walk down the hill over the little bridge, the distillery in front of one, and after a wee dram, a very pleasant circular walk over the Paps and then back to the bridge. Yes, it was coming back; he reflected on their time together, the earnestness of the man's face, as if he were on some sort of crusade. Martin knew he had to forget about the conversations and concentrate on the physical appearance of the man. He wrestled with his mind, trying to visualize that face again.

The identikit operator and the artist were very patient. They picked up every nuance, altering, correcting, virtually losing most of the original image; eventually Martin slumped in his chair.

"That's it, my mind is drained. Can I see the result?"

The operator beckoned Martin over and also the artist.

"That's him!" said Martin. "I would know that face anywhere."

The artist did not say a word but continued to study the picture. At last he turned to the operator.

"Time for you and Martin to have a cup of coffee. Bring me one back, but give me fifteen minutes before you do so."

They sat with their coffee. Jim Pearson, who had produced the Identikit image, remarked, "This is the time when I wish I smoked." Martin grinned.

"The detectives are desperate for this. They have no idea where he might strike next. You are the only man who has seen him, who was sober at the time and had some extended conversation with him."

With a cup coffee in his hand for the artist, Jim led the way back to the conference room.

The artist had erected his easel, pinned up his drawing, and then covered it with a blank sheet of paper. Robert Corrie was busy setting up a digital camera, which he had connected to a computer.

"The moment of truth! I hope I have it right for you." The artist turned as people walked in.

"Let me introduce our colleagues," said Stewart as he followed them in. "This is Detective Chief Inspectors Moira Masters, and Patrick Hall. They are concerned with the murders in England and are in overall charge of the investigation." He beamed at the new arrivals. "Good to meet you! You're here at the right time." He unpinned the black paper and exposed the drawing.

Martin went up to the picture and gazed at it, and then closed he his eyes, once again recollecting the time he had spent with this man. He turned to them.

"It's identical!" he enthused. "In every detail. I hope you pay these men well, when they conjure up a face almost out of thin air. There are no 'ifs or buts', please remember, I'm a bank manager. I have trained myself to look at people and beyond them. This is your man; I have no apprehension at all."

Moira stood up. "This is excellent work. It's good we have a result. Now Stuart, please arrange to have the picture downloaded to every police station in the country, including Ireland, and to all the news agencies. D.I. Priest at Tees-side will follow up with the facts; all borders, airports etc will be watched. The picture will be circulated also on the police European network. The press officer in Leeds will handle the television interviews." She turned to her companion. "Now Stuart, it's back to Inverness for us collectively. The Hamilton's and Kent's have arrived and Sinclair has confirmed he will finish the post-mortems before midday. We need to be there. Oh, and we must include the Garda in Southern Ireland. Can Robert see to that? I'm sure you have good contacts. We must all stay mobile. Once this breaks there are going to many, many sightings. The majority are going to be false, but we cannot afford to be lax or blasé. Every report must be followed up, no matter how frustrated we become. Remember the next one might be genuine and real for us."

With that they departed and the helicopter had them in Inverness in no time. The bereaved parents had been collected by the police at the airport and were waiting with the Superintendent in the reception room at the Mortuary.

"Please forgive us," said Stewart McKenzie as he went up to greet the parents. "These are my colleagues, D.C.I. Masters and Hall. But you must know them as Moira and Patrick. We think we have a breakthrough, but its early days yet. Hotels have been arranged for you, and whilst you are here the Superintendent has kindly offered to be available for you. The inquest is scheduled for Monday, but the coroner has been apprised of all the facts, and we have requested an interim hearing for Sunday. If this is confirmed, please advise the Superintendent when you feel able to travel. In the event of any change in travel plans with regard to yourselves returning home, the police will arrange and confirm all the details. We all want to express our sympathy and condolences. Those two young people; good careers ahead of them, wonderful lives snuffed out. All we can say is that we are dedicated and determined to hunt down the killer. We will leave you now with the Superintendent. After midday you will be asked to formally identify your son and daughter. We have to be in attendance at the post-mortem also."

Saturday Morning. 13th July. Roscoff.

Passports had been checked on the boat, and by eight o' clock he was through the custom hall and outside the harbour gates. He walked slowly along the shops of the main street, enjoying the aroma of the freshly baked baguettes, but decided at this stage to resist the temptation. Eventually he reached the town square. Recollecting the map he had looked at earlier, he knew the route he would take; but by what means was still an open question.

He sat down on a bench near a bus stop. Within minutes a single deck bus pulled up. Its destination was Brest. Perfect!

The ride was uneventful and within half an hour the bus had pulled into the square adjacent to the railway station. He decided he would risk one rail journey. This would be to Quimper. The old city he loved so much. Not so far down the line and still in Brittany. However, there was an added bonus. A couple of years ago, whilst holidaying in Concarneau with the family, his car had developed a fault and he had taken it to a garage in Quimper for repair. The head gasket had gone, and the garage breakdown truck had come out to collect the car. He had ridden with the driver, who was also the owner manager of the garage. From that incident, he knew they kept a good range of cheap cars for quick cash sales. To kill time whilst they changed the gasket he had wondered round, looking at every car, prices and condition. They offered instant registration and insurance. He knew the cars for sale were all mechanically sound, and he had been very impressed by the efficient way they had repaired his. The garage was completely underground, only a large lifting steel door at the end of a drive below street level. Would it still be the same? He could only but try.

The train travelling east was waiting at the station. Within an hour he was at Quimper. He left his luggage at the station in one of the innocuous storage lockers, pocketed the key card and walked out into the square. Whilst he was waiting for his car on the last occasion he had walked the streets of the old city, found a place to eat, and then made his way back to the garage. Unerringly he walked the narrow streets with the towering dark grey old buildings on each side of him, and came to the garage. There now was a small showroom set back with a couple of

new cars in. He entered; no one was about. There was a lift with a sign by it identifying the used car showroom. The lift took him down to the huge cavernous
hall. The lighting was dim and the air smelt of exhaust fumes.

He gazed round. He judged that there were about seventy cars as he counted
the rows. A man came up to him and then gazed hard at him. "Monsieur!" he
exclaimed. "Two years ago, was it not, when we met?" His English was very good.
They shook hands.

Martin explained he was unexpectedly in France. Having finished business
with a client, he had a few days spare. He was thinking about opening a French
office for his business, and needed to buy a car that he could keep at his new
office. It was to be a runabout, to look up old clients and follow new leads.

"Have a good look round. If you see anything you fancy, come to the office.
Be sure I will make you a good price."

Michael accepted a coffee and then slowly walked the lines of cars. He had no
idea what he was looking for. After the sale of his car money was no problem, but
he knew he must be frugal in all things

A cabriolet caught his eye, a Peugeot 306. It was seven years old but in very
good condition, the tyres and exhaust were good, and the seating did not look
too worn. He opened the bonnet and the engine gleamed up at him. He checked
the oil, which was at the correct level, and virtually colourless. The water in the
overfill chamber showed that the all-the-year-round antifreeze was a clear pinkish
colour, a good sign. He could see no evidence of deposits or sediments. The manger had evidently kept an eye on him, for he came over with the key. The engine
fired first time with a full throaty roar. There was no play on the clutch; brakes
okay, and the gears gave a good sound as they meshed. He drove it round the
perimeter of the garage: the steering was positive, and there was good road holding on the bumpy cobbles of the garage floor. He tested the brakes, stopping in
the well-lit area of the garage; no problem. The bodywork was in his favourite
green, dark but lustrous, and only a few scratches. The hood was okay and folded
down nicely. Opening the boot, he found that the tyre on the spare wheel was
new. He drove back to where the manager was waiting.

"You have a six month no quibble guarantee, valid at any garage within the
trading syndicate which covers all of France. There is a book in the car with maps
and a directory of supporting members."

"Fine, I want to take it if we can agree on a cash price, including insurance,
registration and number plates fitted. How soon would I be able to drive it
away?"

"Thirty minutes, less if you are paying with cash rather than credit cards, or bankers checks."

"Good, I'll be paying in Euro."

"Fine. The cash price includes insurance and tax. All documents are ready. You have a full tank of petrol; the number plate will be fitted immediately. You can drive straight out of here onto the open road. For you I make a five per cent reduction on the cost."

"Still a little more than I wanted to pay!"

"No problem; for a valued customer I will go to seven and one half per cent! That is it, I'm afraid; take it or leave it!"

"I will take it."

"Good. Come to the office. A couple of signatures and the money and the car will be waiting at the door for you to drive away. I think an excellent cup of coffee with a glass of Cognac will seal the bargain."

The manager was as good as his word. Michael handed over the cash, which still left him with a sizeable sum; he leaned back in his chair, sipped the coffee and the cognac, and puffed at one of the dark French cheroots he had been given.

The car was ready on time. He thanked the mechanic and after shaking hands with the manger he was off.

The roads of Brittany he knew well. He stopped at the station to collect his luggage and spent five minutes checking the map for the best route to Limoges and beyond. It was going to be a comfortable run, Nantes, Niort, Limoges, through to Tulle, up into the mountains of the 'massif centrale' and following the Dordogne towards its source.

He knew a very nice restaurant in the village of Charroux, midway between Niort and Limoges. It would be just right for a late lunch; he would sit by the river, almost a narrow lake at that point. Perfect!

With his leather hat jammed firmly on his head and the hood down, he was off.

Pity no C.D. However, there was a radio, and France five was a good classical station.

Late Saturday Morning, 13th July. Inverness.

The post-mortem had been completed. The injuries were as expected.

Roderick had died due to a massive implosion of the skull. Alicia had died by the impact of the fall. Mercifully, her lungs had been crushed and death was instantaneous.

Moira, Patrick and Stewart thanked Sinclair Cameron, who promised the bodies would be made presentable for the forenoon so the parents could formally make identification and say their last farewells. D.I. McKenzie would stay in Inverness for the afternoon to confirm the application to the coroner for the inquest to be on Sunday Morning, if possible.

He also needed to contact the two climbers, Mike Styles and Andrew Biggs, both staying in Inverness courtesy of the police authority. They would be required to attend the inquest, as they had discovered the bodies. The admiration for them was mutual among his colleagues, and he intended to see the 'procurator fiscal' with regard to their receiving civil recognition, certainly a commendation and possibly a decoration.

Moira pulled Stuart to one side. "If you do not mind, we will skip lunch; it has no appeal for us at the moment. Would you be good enough to ring your office and book the conference room for us? Please have Martin Haldane to come in, and also Mr Whittaker, the owner of the bookshop. They are the only two men we know who have had any extended conversations with this man. With their contribution it may be possible to make a profile."

"Yes Mar'm, of course."

"Shut up, you great oaf," she said, tongue in cheek. "I happen to know your promotion's not far away."

"I'll believe it when I see it!" replied Stuart. "I've lived in hope since we went on that course together, over two years. The wheels certainly grind slowly. I'll get Robert to arrange it, and let him know what you want in the way of hotel arrangements." The last said with a twinkle in his eye.

"Thank you, Stuart. I don't think any of us will be able to make plans for tonight. Hopefully we are going to be busy with any genuine replies we have. The local stations will sift calls. D.I. Priest and his team will analyse them and look after any preliminary work before passing them on to us. He will be our collator. I think it will be a very long night for all of us."

CHAPTER 25

▼

SATURDAY 13TH JULY. AFTERNOON. NORTHUMBERLAND.

Valerie Charlier was footsore and ready to drop. They had walked over from the Twice Brewed Inn located on the high road to Hexham, crossed over the ruins of the Roman wall, skirting Crag Lough and were now approaching the village of Bellingham. She could see the hotel where they would stay the night. As she and her companions trudged up the high street she was already visualizing that long soak in a hot bath.

Tomorrow would be a rest day: possibly a picnic by the upper reaches of the Tyne, gaze across at the spectacular waterfall Horeshaw Linn. The next stop would be Byrness and its friendly hotel. It was the last outpost before the border, and the penultimate night before the end of the walk. The Border Hotel at Kirk Yetholm was the official finish. Here they would sign the register, confirming they had completed the Pennine Way and would stay the night. A bus would take them the following morning to Newcastle Airport. Her flight was to be to Limoges, and then she would drive up to her retreat.

She felt exhilarated as well as tired. This was an achievement for her. She hoped after the rest day that they would be fit enough to crest the "Cheviot" as they plodded onwards to Kirk Yetholm. But tonight she was looking forward to a pub lunch, the Northumbrian hospitality and hopefully some of the singing and the skirl of the Border Pipes. But once home, as she called her hide-a-way, there were other things to look forward to, maybe a greater achievement than the Walk. She sat down and sent a long text message to Michael with directions to her retreat and the hiding place of the emergency key.

Normally she lived in her apartment at Toulouse. Her job was arduous, and she valued the privacy of her small mountain cottage. She had not been truthful to Michael when they had discussed jobs, but she was just as sure that he had not been truthful to her regarding his own occupation. What he did not know was that for many years she had been a professional student of human nature. In her own right she had the respect of many. From that meeting in the café, she had known something in the man did not gel. It excited her. Were they the same? Was this the end of her quest? She looked forward to seeing him again, but it would be on her territory.

Saturday afternoon, 13th July. Fort William.

D.C.I. Hall and Masters were back at in the Conference room. A late buffet had been provided. They sat at a table with a telephone, pens and paper. The duty Sergeant, Mary Graham, announced the arrival of Martin Haldane and Mr. Whittaker.

"Thank you for coming again, Martin, and thank you too, Mr. Whittaker."

"Just call me Bill. I think we are both intrigued to be here."

"Let me explain." Moira Leaned forward. "Patrick and I have no first-hand knowledge of this man. We are endeavouring to formulate a profile, so we can anticipate what this man will do next. We have talked to people who had some sort of conversation with him, cafeteria staff, and drunken revelry at a barbeque, nothing tangible, until today when at last we have a reasonable idea of what he looks like, thanks to the sterling work of Martin here.

"We are dealing with a 'Dysfunctional Manipulative Psychopath'; thank God they are a pretty rare animal. To date he has killed six people in the space of a week. To do so he has travelled across the North of England and now into the Highlands. He is a man of resource; money is no object. It would appear that women are attracted to him. We know this from the evidence of the first two murders. He comes across as a friendly and a helpful man; this is evident from the third and fourth murders. Nothing is too much trouble. He is a man of energy, but now he is a killer. A man with this type of character can change in an instant, one moment kind and helpful, the next, dispassionate and able to kill as though he was swotting a fly.

"Normally such people are manic-depressives, and the abnormality is detected fairly quickly; they have a serious mental disability and normally find themselves quickly incarcerated in a secure hospital.

"But our man is the opposite. We do not know any history of him as yet, but our gut feel is that he is as normal on the surface as you or I. Before I go further I would like to hear your impressions of our friend. Bill, start the ball rolling, if you please!"

"Well, obviously, when he came to my shop I could see he was well pleased with himself. He remarked that he had visited the bank down the road, and was now in funds. He looked forward to a browse and the books he would buy. Then he hoped for a few days in the mountains surrounding Glencoe.

"I was interested. The shop was not busy. He was well read, and passionately fond of history. I took him to the relevant sections and he found a book on Hitler by Allan Bullock; he also wanted Thomas Carlyle's book on the French Revolution. I told him it was out of print, but he corrected me and found it in one of the catalogues. Sure enough, it had been reprinted by an American company. Regrettably he would not be round long enough for me to order it. He was a man of information. He found a copy of *Das Reich* on the shelves, and that was a find for him. Apparently he had ordered a copy from an English bookshop in Luxembourg, but as yet had not received it."

"Luxembourg?"

"That's what he said; he also knew most of Europe. Well read and well travelled."

"Luxembourg is interesting, that is the first time we have any mention of a possible place where he might live."

She turned to Patrick. "I will carry on here, Patrick. Could you put the wheels in motion? Can you organize D.I. Priest to send a basic précis, and photographs to the Police Grande Ducal in Luxembourg? You will need also to extend this procedure to France, Belgium and Germany, for there are many people living in other countries who work in the Duchy. They are called 'Frontallieres.' I know Luxembourg. The police have good computerized systems and they will be able to check if he lives or works in Luxembourg.

"Check with Bob first; but I believe we should raise a 'European Arrest Warrant.' Ensure everything is kept confidential and on a low key. Also, get our 'National Commander' to have clearance for the Citation to fly anytime this weekend. We will have to file a flight plan when we know a little more.

"I was in Luxembourg, some consultation work with disturbed patients in a hospital in the north, and some general observations in their central prison,

Schrassig. The village of the same name, where I stayed, was hidden away in the folds of the forest. It was beautiful.

"Tell Bob that D.I. Greenwood would be useful over there. She speaks fluent French. Part of her studies was at the University of Montpelier."

"Okay, Moira, I will get to it pronto! Give a shout when you've finished here."

Moira turned and shook Bill's hand. "Thank you very much for all your help. Enjoy a good weekend. Our regards to your wife."

"Glad to be of help. I hope the investigation goes well for you. One more thing, though. He asked if we had a book called *Spiritual Depression* by a Doctor Martyn Lloyd Jones. Being a good Calvinist I recognized the title. I told him the Christian book shop in Inverness quite near to the prison would have it or order it for him."

"Thank you again." Moira was thoughtful. Possibly a religious freak; that may be something to follow up. She turned to Martin.

"Now Martin, after listening to Bill, have you any other reflections that may help?"

"It's my job to try to understand the motives of people who come in the bank. One after all could be a potential mugger or worse; one never really knows, until it happens. Many of my colleagues have ruefully repeated those words to me. I did have a discussion with him after checking the computer records and finding that there had been no withdrawals for some years. Nevertheless, he knew the details of his account and had his cash card, so there was nothing more to say. He could have withdrawn a substantial amount of cash with his card direct out of the any of the cash machines; I had no reason to withhold the money."

"Of course, that is quite right; but is there anything else you can recollect, possibly an idle piece of conversation which could be another piece in the jigsaw?"

"You know of the golf, and of Islay. He told me a little of the places he had been to, and the reason for a 'Poste Restante' address. He was periodically in other lands. His favourite place was Bolivia, a mountainous country. It was evident he was a man who read a lot; he also knew his music; by that I mean classical. There was something compelling about him; haunting, his eyes looked directly through you. He was a man who would grow on you. Definitely a man alone! He was eager to be away to the glen, as though he was on a mission."

"Thank you, Martin."

"I'm sorry I've taken up so much of your time."

"No rush, I have to wait here. Stuart McKenzie is on his way back from Inverness. I had invited him and his family to dine with Patrick and myself. But his wife's sister is there. They do not see each other very often, so they are going out 'en famille.' He is a very good man and we have promised to keep him informed of any developments."

Patrick came back into the conference room as Martin was leaving.

"Good to meet you, Martin. Enjoy your night. I have heard all about it. By the way, when this is all over I would like you to come down to Yorkshire for a weekend. We have a very nice Golf course at Woodhead near Bradford; the number eight hole is similar to one on the island. One drives from the top of the hill with a six iron; if you're on form the ball drops directly into the hole! It's the only time I have had a 'birdie'." Patrick slumped down into the chair next to Moira. "Right, my luv, listen to words of wisdom! Firstly, I've booked us in at the Nevis Hotel; we have a suite with a lounge. We take the portable computers with us, plug into the telephone lines they are installing, and we can monitor everything from there. I took the liberty of informing them we will eat in our suite. Here are the menus; choose what you like and the time we want to eat, they are waiting for our order."

"You're a man in a million, Patrick, so thoughtful."

"Don't you believe it! But I think it's important to take care of the 'inner man'." He cleared his throat. "Now to business; I spoke to an Inspector Hans Jaeger, who works out of the criminal police headquarters in Rue Glaesner, in Luxembourg City. I believe you know him. He certainly recollects meeting you. He will clear the 'Citation' with the airport authorities, so we will be able to fly in and out at any time. I have asked Simon Priest to take care of the specifics and the official paperwork."

Bob wanted a chat. He had cancelled the mobile bus for this exercise; apparently the contractors were having teething problems and needed another couple of weeks.

"Les Wilkes has been re-instated, on a probationary period, so that D.I. Millie Greenwood can be seconded to us. Robin Johnson will now be promoted, so he can look after current cases in the Skipton area; and another inspector has been transferred to Tees-side from Hartlepool, a man that you know, Tim Scott; he transfers from uniform to detective status. He will take over your ongoing workload at Tees-side. Of course, he will rely heavily on D.I.Priest."

"This I find amazing!"

"That's the wonder of having a national detective force."

He gave Moira a hug. "You and I are released to follow this investigation through wherever it takes us. D.I. McKenzie's promotion is confirmed, but he cannot be released from his present station until a suitable replacement is available. Robert Currie has been recommended for promotion, and once they find a

Detective Sergeant to replace him, the police authority in Scotland will sanction his promotion. He himself is keen to be here, single, no family, and a real challenge for him.

"Priority now is for Bob to talk to Stuart! A meeting has been arranged for next week. The problem is moving his wife and the bairns. They would not want to be parted for very long; and Bob is a great believer in keeping families together.

"Now, you are up to date!"

"Thank you, Patrick and now back to our killer. Your thoughts first, Patrick."

"An open man; we know he can be charming. An engineer working all over the world, but also a man of letters, and of music and definitely a lapsed Christian."

"Why do you say that?"

"*Spiritual Depression* is a very famous book, written by a Harley Street Doctor, turned Preacher. He must have reshaped the lives of thousands of people; more than that, he was a Calvinist, a believer of the acronym T.U.L.I.P. relating to the state of man.—

"Total depravity.

"Limited atonement

"Irresistible grace.

"In other words, he's gone from the saint status back to sinner; total depravity."

"My, Patrick, what knowledge! Tell a poor unlearned Tees-side girl some more."

"My Grandfather used to go to a charismatic church in Bradford. There was an old man there called Smith-Wrigglesworth, born in the late eighteen hundreds, who travelled all over the world preaching the gospel of Jesus Christ; he also had the gift of healing. He was born in a tin hut at Menston near Ilkly; his wife was one of the first Salvation Army officers in the north. He was an optimist and he recognized the good Welsh doctor as a great man of God.

"Often the man in Bradford used to discuss the differences in their faith, but the Love of God afforded a bridgeable gap between them.

"Our man Michael is always under guilt. We need to investigate his personal life if we get the chance, marriage breakdowns, repeated failures, unachieved ambitions, kind and generous on the outside, but not particularly noticeable to other people. Inside he has been churning for years. His real self is hidden away, for underneath, he is completely selfish, impervious to others, or to their pain. His outward emotions are a total sham."

"Yes, I understand what you're saying. We have categorized him as a Dysfunctional Manipulative Psychopath. What you believe fits in; totally selfish on the outside, appeasing his own guilt, his earlier life a turmoil of compound emotions. Outwardly a serene personage, knowledgeable, generous to a fault, as our witnesses have observed. Loved by certain ladies, as one of his victims enthused to her friend.

"Now I am certain he is a recidivist; he has gone over the brink, a death wish, as all the doors are closing against him. What will he do, kill again, or kill himself? We cannot rule out the possibility that someone close to him could also be the cause of his eventual death."

"Right Patrick, I vote we take up your suggestion and move to the Nevis, lock, stock, and barrel!"

"Excuse me, Moira; before we go any further; what is our situation? As Ken and Mabel would say, 'Is tha walkin oot wi me?' Mabel whispered to me after you went out to the car, 'Yon lass is fair looking, tha wants to catch her afore some other bugga does. Tha know alls about her education, but remember lad, she's a woman at heart, and a goodun to boot, if she's not stepping out with anyone, catch her now!' Excuse my French and my blushes, but I know nowt about thee. I have always been attracted to you, but in our careers it is always 'ships passing in the night.' I am no oil painting and a rough copper to boot, but I need to know something. Obviously, from the dinner last night, you seem to live alone, so you could be single or divorced; you do not wear any rings, and you have never spoken of your private life, so where does this guy stand?"

Moira came over to him, put her arms around him, and gave him a long and lingering kiss.

"Patrick, you great oaf, you lovely man, I have thought about you a lot. I do not care about looks, and to be kind to you, I could say you look ruggedly handsome. I want a nice man, honest and true. Up to a couple of months ago I have never found one. My runt of a sister, that is how I think of her, older than me but tiny, has a giant of a husband, and two lovely girls. They adore each other. Remember, they had finished the Lyke Wake Walk, which poor Jan should also have been enjoying instead of lying dead in a cold rocky pool on Urrah moor. My sister, actually, an in-law, small she might be, is exquisite, like a china doll. I feel awkward and gawky when I am with her, but I love her and Bob to bits." She smiled. "Patrick, I am very ordinary, the wrong side of thirty, too many universities, conferences and the like; soon I will be an old maid. Rescue me! I want the man who will stand up to me, understand me, my career and drive, and love me without reservation."

"Phew!" Patrick gasped. "It's like standing in front of a tornado. I am blown away and completely captivated. Yes, I'll walk out with thee and after we have caught this madman I will ask you to marry me. I also would like to see some kids of my own!"

Moira beamed. "Let's away to that hotel. Friday we both needed to sleep, but it would be interesting to see what tonight brings. I am psyched up to working all night, but at least we can be comfortable. Come on, the car is waiting, I will race you to the shower or the bath, whatever is your fancy! 'Nookies' possibly before dinner."

Saturday Evening, 13th July. Mid-France.

Michael was tired. His drive down to Charroux had been great, a warm day, almost without wind, but no sun, the sky overcast. The Peugeot performed well and he felt exhilarated, driving with the wind sweeping round him.

He had sat at a table in the garden of the restaurant, looking down on the River Charente. It moved slowly and purposely to lose itself in the Atlantic, at Rochefort, south of La Rochelle, that great Napoleonic seaport. He had travelled about three hundred kilometres, spending an hour idling over his lunch; a steak cooked rare, with a bottle of well-chilled Rosé of Provence origin. Everything was so peaceful. He looked forward to his first glimpse of the Massif Centrale and now he had passed through Limoges and was fast approaching Tulle. The majestic shadows of the mountains were appearing in the distance. He envied Valerie her retreat, but he looked forward to sharing it with her. His soul felt purged, realizing he would not see his wife and girls again. He would live virtually as a prisoner in one place. To go out would be difficult. Maybe he'd have to dye his hair nearly white, possibly grow his beard again and dye that. How much could he trust Valerie? He was cognizant of the fact that he had made mistakes. No matter how careful he had tried to be, he had also had his moments of madness. The police were not stupid; they would have a good dossier on him by now.

That lady Barrister, certainly that was part of his madness! Would she keep mum? If she went to the police, possibly her job would be on the line; yet she would have sworn to uphold the law, and most probably had influential friends to protect her.

He wondered why he hadn't killed her! But to be honest with himself, the thought had never entered his head. There would have been complications; as it was, it had kept his escape route clear. No dead body in a hotel room! He had been free to drive the length of Ireland without incident, sell his car, and find himself relatively safe in France. The fifteen-hour crossing had been the test.

Valerie; she was the conundrum, trusting him with access to her home. By the time she arrived the news would be out. She would be well aware that he was a killer. Possibly she wished to enter into some sort of partnership in murder, not an unknown syndrome. What was her real profession? It was evident she was extremely well educated, more so than the lady Barrister, certainly not as a translator. Why him?

A short conversation in a café! She would have quickly spotted that he was not anywhere near the academic level she had; but, he certainly was not 'a bit of rough!' Self taught, maybe, but he had enjoyed the Open University courses and the summer schools they held in various universities.

He stopped the car and closed the hood. It was time for the concert on France Five. He switched on the radio. They were announcing the programme, from Leipzig, the Gewanderhous. A Beethoven night, the seventh symphony and the fifth piano concerto; the Emperor. That sent his spirits soaring. It would take him very near to his journey's end; he intended to dawdle a little, knowing it would be safer to arrive at the cottage in the early hours of the morning. Her directions were very clear. There should be no problem.

Saturday Evening, 13th July. Northumberland.

Valerie Chalier had a good evening with her friends. They were tired and weary; the bar and lounge was packed and it was difficult to talk. This was Saturday night; almost all the village was there.

The food and the beer had been consumed in large quantities. Now they were ready to 'crash out.' Picnic lunches had been ordered for the morrow and the best treat would be breakfast in bed. It would be a day of leisure, poodling about, a stroll up to the waterfall; she had her book, and her friends. It would be good to be alone. Within the party she was the only one who spoke English; sometimes it was very exhausting, translating back to her friends and being on call for their every need.

She was enjoying the peace and her own solitude; no television, no newspapers.

Monday would be a hard day, as would possibly Tuesday, as they made the final push to the border and Kirk Yetholm. Then the flight home to Limoges. A few days with Michael and back to work. Her base was located in Toulouse. They maintained an apartment for her there; it was one of the 'perks.' She shuddered at the workload that would be waiting for her.

Saturday Evening, 14th July. England, Scotland and Ireland.

The Evening papers, the television and radio news bulletins, gave full coverage to the spate of killings. Pictures of the man were on every front page, and on the television channels. The police statement defined each of the killings and confirmed that their evidence linked all of them to one man. No other persons were involved.

Saturday Evening. Belfast, Northern Ireland.

Moragh Denver-Marshall was relaxing in her bedroom before going to a dinner party, which would be hosted by her boss. She turned on the television, idly wondering what was happening in the world this fine Saturday evening. The newscaster was giving an account of some murders that had taken place. She went over to her wardrobe and slid the doors open, the thought uppermost in her mind being what she would wear.

She heard the words; "Have you seen this man? If so, telephone, or report immediately to your local police station. The importance cannot be stressed enough; your information could possibly avert another murder." The urgency of the tone made her turns and look. She froze. It was Michael, without a doubt.

Shivering with shock, she rang her boss.

"Sir, forgive me for bothering you when I hope to see you later this evening, but have you seen the latest news broadcast?"

Her boss was the head of the Judiciary in Eire and lived outside of Dublin in the small town of Bray, by the sea and nestling under the Wicklow Mountains. He and his wife were just about to drive up to Dublin for a dinner he was giving his senior staff.

"Moragh, what's bothering you; are you in trouble? I can hear a note of hysteria in your voice."

"Please, Shaughan, switch on your television and turn to B.B.C. Northern Island."

"Okay, one minute. I'll take the portable phone with me; it must be serious for you of all people to be in such a panic. Right, it's on; hello, what's this? A murder hunt? Nothing unusual in that, especially in our line of business. What's so terrifying, Moragh?"

"Sir, officially I have to inform you I spent the Friday evening and the night with this man."

"Good God, Moragh, what are you saying? When did you decide to do one-night stands? You're a senior Barrister, a highly placed government official. The reporters will make mincemeat of you!"

"Sir, it wasn't like that. We were on the plane together; we just gelled! I was hoping that when he finished his business in Belfast we would meet again."

"Stay put, Moragh! I will ring the Chief Constable; he will know what to do, how to handle this. It's Clintonville you live?"

"Yes, the Belfast police have my details. As you know I was on the Loyalists hit list for some time."

"Yes, of course, don't worry. I can see it was a genuine, even if it was a pretty quick association on your part. Now be calm and wait for developments. I will ring round and cancel the dinner, guests and restaurant. My wife and I will be with you in about forty minutes. By that time you will have the police for company."

Moragh stayed by the phone, wondering how she would face her boss and his wife who had supported her throughout her own troubles. All hopes of a good evening were gone.

CHAPTER 26

▼

SATURDAY 14TH JULY.
EARLY EVENING. NORTH
WEST SCOTLAND.

Moira and Patrick had moved to their suite in the hotel in the Nevis. Patrick had disappeared into the shower, leaving Moira ensconced in front of the two portable computers, which had been set up on a dining table for them. The police technician had connected the Internet links. Moira was now downloading on one computer the latest information from the police systems; this they would keep permanently connected, and on line for receipt of secure information. The other they would use as their working machine.

Moira called out to Patrick.

"You've done us proud, my man, better than the hospitality suite at the station. My God," she breathed, "I have just thought of something. "Please, please pray that I am not too late."

Her hands were shaking as she opened up her explorer programme and dialled a number.

"*Bonjour Monsieur, Chief Inspector Masters dit, jai besoin parlé Inspector Hans Jaeger, si'l vous plait.*"

"*Merci Madame, une moment.*"

"Hello Moira," said a voice. "You are back to me so soon."

"Hans, I have only just realized, Satellite T.V. I am having a nightmare of all the Brits' in your Duchy tuning in for Saturday night programmes. BBC, ITV, World News, and others will be transmitting our appeal and the artist's impression of our man. It's going to be very possible that the wife, friends, or, God forbid, the children will see it on Television."

"You're right. I will check if we yet have an address and a name. Possibly someone will ring here, as you are asking them to contact local police stations. I will inform the desk immediately."

Luxembourg

Josie had escaped from her husband and her boys, who were having a wonderful time in the new Olympic swimming pool in Kirchberg. She was enjoying a walk through the leafy paths of the village, now very exclusive, as it was adjacent to the European Courts of Justice and other parts of the Commission. This was her way by the back routes to the Auchan shopping plaza. Later her husband and the boys would meet her for a quick snack in the fish bar before going on to her friend Barbara's for a barbecue. It was amazing how they had all settled in Luxembourg, coping with multi languages and enjoying so much of what this small country offered. So many walks through the hills and forest, and the Luxemburger penchant for cycling and gripped them all. Everyone enjoyed being on bikes. For Josie now it was a quick peek at the boutiques, a chance to pick up something special, and maybe a surprise gift for Barbara too.

It was fairly quiet in the centre. She went first to the computer shop; a new cartridge for the printer was a must. The displayed T.V. sets were all switched on, showing a multiplicity of stations: French, German, English and Portuguese. She was startled when suddenly the screens went blank and the music emanating from the speakers ceased. The screens came on again showing the message 'News Flash.'

She stopped to watch and listen.

"We interrupt your programme for a police message. British Television has asked for this broadcast to be repeated over the European networks. A series of murders have taken place over the last ten days in various popular tourist areas of the U.K. They are believed to be the work of one man. It is now possible that this man is in Europe. The police have issued an artist's impression of him. If you know this man or have seen him, contact your local police station immediately."

Josie stared at the picture which had flashed onto the screens. "I don't believe it! It's Barbara's husband; Jonathan!" she gasped. Thank God he never managed to get their satellite working before he went off on holiday. She rang her husband,

and left a message on his mobile: "Scrub meeting at the Plaza, hold on the BBQ; pick up a Chinese takeaway for you and the boys. That will keep them going; something urgent has cropped up; see you later, then I will explain."

A taxi took her into the city, to Rue Glaesner. The Police Station located there dealt with criminal affairs. She had phoned the police from the taxi to warn them that she was coming to see them, in response to the police message. After paying the driver she hurried into the station. At the reception area a man stood waiting.

He came towards her. "Good Evening, I am Inspector Hans Jaeger. I believe you have some information for us?"

"Hello, I am Josie Alderson. I recognized the man; it is my best friend's husband and he is at present on holiday in the U.K."

"You are sure of this?'

"Quite certain!"

"Come up to my office. We need to take down details, and at the moment the technicians are establishing a video link with the British police. You will be able to talk to them face to face in our conference room."

Once seated, he said, "Take your time and tell me all you can."

"His name is Jonathan Kearny, and his wife is called Barbara. I am Mrs Alderson, and we live in Eischen; the Kearny's live in Koerich."

Hans Jaeger had opened up his computer. "Right, Madam, your address, their address, telephone numbers, and do you know any of their bank details?"

"Yes, they bank with the same bank as us, the Luxembourg National Banque."

"Madam, for the moment I will leave you. I must have the phones blocked and arrange for discreet road checks near their house; also, I need to freeze any withdrawals from cash machines etcetera. The link is now established. If you come this way you will be able to talk with the British officers in charge of the inquiry."

The face of a woman filled the screen of a large monitor.

"Hello Moira," said Hans Jaeger. "We seem to be getting somewhere; now we have the name and address. I have made arrangements for blocking the road to their house, one entrance in, and out. As you know, Luxemburgers are very used to barred roads, nothing unusual. A patrol car will stop every one approaching the house. The phones are blocked for normal calls, and a code number will be required to ring into the house. Same applies for the computer I.S.D.N. link. All the necessary information is being downloaded to you. Here is Mrs Josie Alderson to talk too you."

"Hello Josie," said Moira. "You know something of the seriousness of the situation. First I must set your mind at rest. The husband has disappeared. We do not know where he is and we are expecting many calls tonight.

"We belong to a squad of detectives working under a National Commander. A 'European Arrest Warrant' has been raised, and my partner D.C.I. Patrick Hall is at this moment arranging for D.I. Millie Greenwood to fly to Luxembourg. We have a private jet on its way to collect her at Leeds Airport. Inspector Jaeger will arrange clearance and pick up for her. She will be with you about two in the morning. Her French is fluent; she actually studied at a French University. In the meantime, go to the Barbeque. The Luxembourg police will stop any visitors before they get there, and will turn them back. Can you arrange for the two girls to sleep at one of their friends? Would that be possible at short notice?"

"Yes, our mutual friends live in the same road. They have two girls and two boys. With your permission I will ring them before they go to the Barbeque and arrange for the girls to have sleepovers. They are very discreet, and I will take the girls across to them. Now I must go to her, I need to be with her."

"Okay, you must be there. What about your own family?"

"My husband will take care of the boys."

"Okay, I believe the helicopter is waiting for you. It will take you and Hans near to the house. Once you're in the house, we will be in constant touch through an open link. We need to know more about him! Our big problem is to catch him before he kills again."

"Moira," said Inspector Jaeger, "all the bank details will be with you within the half hour. We are now checking car details of the family. Mrs Alderson tells us that he was picking up a new car a few weeks ago, but did not know the details; the husband tends to be away from home a lot. Our crime analyst is now checking for all unsolved murders throughout Europe."

He turned to Josie. "Come, the helicopter is waiting for us."

"Thank you, Inspector. I will ring my husband now."

She explained to him the circumstance, in succinct terms. He was a man who was very stoic; he quickly grasped the seriousness of the situation.

"Don't worry, darling. I will look after the boys for as long as it takes. You must be with Barbara."

Saturday evening, 14th July. Mid Yorkshire.

Millie Greenwood was packing. It was good that Alex would not be back until mid-week. She rang her Mum to tell her she would be out of the country. Her Mum was used to this, ever since she had joined the police force.

"Don't worry, luv," she said, "we'll take care of the cat, the house and Alex."

The car was waiting for her. As she sat in the back she mused on the turn of events. Les Wilks re-instated; although she had been angry with him, in a way she was glad. He had experienced a sharp short shock. Probably learned his lesson, especially retrieving his full pension rights; it was a second chance for him.

Saturday evening, 14th July. Fort William.

Moira leaned back in her chair. She called out to Patrick: "Hurry up, my York-shire Tyke. I'd like a shower before the food arrives. You're needed to man the computers." At that moment the phone rang. She picked it up. "D.C.I. Masters."

"I don't know where you are, lass, but I got summit which may be important to you. Harry Hobson, the desk Sergeant, put me through to you. It's Elsie; Elsie Graham."

"Hello Elsie. I'm up in Scotland. What have you got for me?"

"Before I went on holiday I was duty warden on the Saturday afternoon, in the Ayrsome Park area. I put a ticket on a man's car; I only caught a glimpse of him as he drove away. It was a nice face; he had a beard, but it's definitely the same face as the man on the telly."

"Elsie, you mean our killer?"

"Yes."

"You left a ticket on his car?'

"Yes, but there was a lot of rumpus with the football yobs. They were rampag-ing; I found the ticket in the gutter and stuck it back on his car. I hung around the area for some time, ticketing all those cars parked for the match. On the way back I saw him get into his car. He drove away without noticing his ticket. I ran after the car, thinking I could give him an on-the-spot fine, as that would have been cheaper for him. But he was in his own world. He never noticed me."

"The car, Elsie, tell me about it. Can you remember?"

"Of course, it is all in my little black book. It was a big 'un like a jeep, but more posh. A Volvo SC90, it said on the back. The number plate was yellow, and a strange registration number FF 112."

Patrick came out at that moment and heard part of the conversation.

"That's Merionethshire. I know it because as a cadet I had a spell at Traw-sfynnedd nuclear power station on security. I actually bought a car whilst down there, a new one, in Blynwdd Festiniog; the number was prefixed by FF for Meri-onethshire."

At that moment one of the other phones rang. Patrick picked it up.

"Hello Sir," said a harsh Irish accent. "I am D.I. Edwin Curran of the Belfast Police, Antrim Road Station. I am with a lady Barrister who works out of the 'Doyle' in Dublin. Her name is Moragh Denver-Marshall; she was in Inverness on Thursday visiting the prison there. She met a man on the plane, as she travelled back to Derry; they booked in at a hotel and spent the night together. It was the man you are looking for."

"Good grief!" said Patrick, "and she's alive to tell the tale?"

"Funny enough, yes; in addition, she really liked him. He left early Friday morning without waking her. He had remarked the night before that he had an early meeting in Belfast. To tell you the truth, they had talked about no commitment, but she secretly hoped he would contact her again. She is making a full report at the Station. It's in concise legal language, no holds barred, a complete 'blow by blow' account. It will be on your screens within the hour."

Bob rang, and Moira updated him on the events and actions.

"Yes, stick at it. A Mrs Jenkins has rung in; she is the caretaker of the village church and hall at Brompton upon Swale. They had a jumble sale last Saturday. She and her other ladies recognized the man. He bought clothes there, including a Blacks khaki anorak, leaving a brand new green Berghaus on their reserve rail. Mrs Jenkins bought it for her husband. It has not been washed, so we will borrow it for tests."

Patrick was checking car registration numbers.

"It's false, not registered here. However, it could be Luxembourg; you can choose your own letters and three numbers there. I've sent it through to Hans. Another piece of the jigsaw falls into place."

Within the half hour another call was routed through. This was from the Garda in Wexford.

"Hello, Sir. I am the duty Sergeant at the station in Wexford. I have a fella here, who knows yer man. I'll put him through to you; his name is Seamus Donnelly and he is the manager of a car auction centre here in the town. Seamus, all yours boyo."

"How do you do, Sir; I know yer man. I sold his car for him on Friday afternoon. We had a few pints together. I could not understand him wishing to sell such a cracking vehicle. He told me he had to have a company car."

"Do you have the details of the sale?"

"Yes, Sir, right here. Before the Garda rang you I went to the office to pick up the papers. It was a Volvo SC90, left-hand drive, registration number FG919. Certificate of Conformity okay, purchased in Brussels, but registered in Luxembourg. I have his signature as Jonathan Kearny. It was sold to a Frenchman who came on a vacation with the express purpose of buying a car here. Mr Kearny did not lose much on the sale, less than thirty per cent. He went to the bank which we have in the auction grounds with a sizeable sum of money."

"Did he discuss any of his future journeys with you?"

"No Sir. As far as I know he was settling down somewhere in Ireland to a new job."

"Thanks. Please ask the Garda to obtain the bank's details whilst you are there? The sort-code, name of bank and address will do. Ask the Sergeant to send it on the police network to me; I assume he has the details of the branch and the manager."

The details of bank transactions came through quite quickly. There were periodic deposits into Barbara Kearny's personal account over the past two months, including one from the Wexford bank dated Thursday 11th July, a Euro transaction of nine thousand.

He checked that D.I. Priest was receiving all the information to put together the business life of a Jonathan Kearny. Priest confirmed he would need three days to present a complete dossier.

It was all good stuff for later, but where was the man now? They seemed to be no further forwards

He rang D.I. Curran at Belfast. Tersely, he explained the situation. It was necessary to find the Volvo and run it through the standard forensic tests. Curran agreed he would liase with the Garda to have the car stopped at any entry or exit point between the two parts of Ireland, and keep a watch in the border towns. A colleague in the Garda would check the ferries, especially the ones that only ran during the Holiday season.

"Good work," said Patrick. "Come back to me as soon as you can."

"It will be tomorrow Sir. We will check all the airports and the ferries when their offices open at six o'clock in the morning."

Patrick relaxed a few minutes and lay back in his chair. Moira was still in the shower. Idly, he wondered what time the food would come. The phone rang again.

"Hello, Sir, are you D.C. I. Hall?"

"Yes."

"I am Mr Stott. I live in a village called Burnsall. The man you are looking for, I have met him! He rented a small holiday apartment from me; a week's let."

"Jim, it's Patrick, you know me! I virtually live out of your shop, no time for supermarkets. You're telling me this man rented one of your flats?"

"Yes, Patrick; I never knew you were a copper! It was the little flat, opposite the green, the car park end. He took it for the week. I told him not to bother to return the key, just to post it back in the letterbox of the flat. Tomorrow we will go in and clean. The people who will take it for the next two weeks are not due until the afternoon."

"Stay put, Jim, I'll contact Skipton. They will have officers with you before the hour is out. You know Robin Johnson? He scuttled you at the last cricket match, the fast bowler for Settle. He is now a Detective Inspector. I will ring him also; he should be at home. Whatever you do, stay in the house; don't go anywhere near the flat until Robin is there."

"Okay, Patrick. I'll wait; take care of yourself."

Robin was in. Patrick gave him the details; he would call out the forensic team and be at the flat within the hour.

For the next fifteen minute Patrick busied himself updating the police information systems. The dinner arrived unnoticed.

Moira returned and sniffed at the food. "Smells good, we will have to eat it before it dries up completely. Your Champagne is okay. Someone remembered to put the handle of the spoon into the neck of the bottle. I don't know what it does, but it certainly keeps in the bubbles."

They looked at each other, dishevelled, clothes crumpled and awry.

"We must look the un-sexiest pair ever," sighed Moira.

"So much for our romantic evening."

Saturday evening. 14th July. Mid-France.

Unaware of the events in the U.K. and Luxembourg, Michael was negotiating the steep narrow roads out of Tulle. He had driven through to Neuvic without any problem, but now he was tired. It was difficult to concentrate. The mountains towered above him, black and sombre, and the bends were getting steeper and narrower. He had to stop, otherwise he would find himself crashing down into the ravine. He spotted a clearing and drove into it. After cutting the engine, he locked the doors, leaned over and adjusted the backrest of the passenger seat as far as it would go. He doused the lights, slid over to the other seat, and dropped off to sleep.

Saturday evening. Luxembourg.

Josie had talked to Sonia who lived down the road from Barbara. It was arranged that her two girls would make the suggestion to Barbara's girls that after the barbeque they would have a midnight party over at their house, complete with the latest music and disco lights.

The helicopter landed and a car was waiting to take them into the village where Barbara lived. They stopped at the roadblock; everything was low-key. The police would ensure that the family remained in ignorance of the true facts until after the barbeque when everyone had left. Hans checked with his office; Millie Greenwood would be with them sometime after midnight. He would drive her himself up to Barbara's house.

The police had complied with Josie's suggestion that she needed time with Barbara. Forgetting the clearing up, they would crack open a bottle and just talk. Nothing unusual about that! They had spent many nights in each other's company, sometimes up to the early hours, much to the consternation of respective husbands. Josie's husband Ken had already agreed to take the boys home as soon as they had finished their barbeque food. It would not be a problem as they were already tired from their exertions in the swimming pool.

Barbara had welcomed the suggestion when Josie had proffered it over the phone. In her heart of hearts, she was worried about Jonathan. She missed him; he had been so strange these last twelve months. It was difficult to understand why he had 'upped sticks and gone' whilst she and the girls were on holiday. They had wanted him to be with them, but he had pleaded pressure of work. Now they were alone, no phone calls from him, no letters, and the postcards had been only to the girls. His mobile was cut off; she did not know the reason; it was as if their marriage was on hold for a year or more. It would be good to talk to Josie. A quiet bottle of ice cold Cremant would fit the bill nicely. But now it was time for the Barbeque. She greeted Josie and Sonia and the girls as they arrived together. The steaks were sizzling on the coals. The girls had set up their disco, and the food was ready to be consumed in vast quantities. Ken and the boys arrived and, after their fill of Thuringers and Baguettes, the boys had amused themselves by chasing the girls, dog and cat round and round the garden. The air was sultry, tinged with the smell of charcoal and various aromas of cooked meats. Many people were eating outside that evening. Barbara sighed happily as she placed some black plastic bags in strategic places on the lawn. Everything went into bin bags, plastic plates, knives, forks, spoons and glasses. Wonderful!

She looked at her friends. There seemed to be something wrong. Already they were preparing to go, though the night was still young. What was the matter with Josie? 'Like a cat on hot bricks,' she thought. Her movements were jerky and she was urging everyone to clear up quickly. A right 'bossy boots' tonight. She giggled. Josie was really upset about something. Her speech, normally quiet and well modulated, was raucous and Lancastrian as she berated Ken to get the boys home, reminding him they were all singing in the family service tomorrow.

Saturday. 14th July. Evening. Burnsall.

Robin Johnson was at the apartment. Disconsolately, he looked around; 'as clean as a whistle.' Forensics would still go through the motions, but everywhere the flat sparkled. The waste bins, had been emptied, scrubbed and left upside down on the draining board. He reported back to Patrick.

The Hotel in Glen Nevis.

Patrick put down the phone. "Poor Robin," he remarked. "A wasted exercise, nothing. The apartment is immaculate. So what have we achieved, Moira? If and when we catch him, we can with confidence take him through his itinerary."

Moira knitted her brows and frowned.

"We certainly know his movements up to a point. We know a lot about him and will know more when Millie Greenwood is with his wife. We know of his faults; garrulous, wanting to talk, air his knowledge, looking for some recognition; that most probably is the biggest flaw of his life; unachieved ambition.

"He likes the ladies; the ladies like him, and more's the pity. Patricia would still be alive if she could have handled him differently. It all points to a massive and obsessive inferiority complex and it is all going to be up to Millie now: she will be on the spot; but we still have no idea where he is. Let us hope we have some news when the ferry ports open in the morning. That's my gut-feel; he is out of the country."

There was a knock on the door and two waiters came in. They took one look at the food, hardly touched; they looked very miserable and groaned. One of them picked up the phone and in a low voice spoke into it. After a few moments he replaced the receiver. He turned to them. "Sir, Madam, we will clear all of this mess out of the way." As he spoke he glanced dispassionately at the table. "I have ordered you a large platter of hot savouries, a pot of coffee and some cognac. That will keep you going for the night."

"Thanks, Hamish. Sorry about the wasted food."

There was another knock on the door and D.I. McKenzie walked in.

"Stuart, you should be curled up in bed with your wife and kids. You have to take over tomorrow."

"You're right, Moira. I only called over for a minute or two. See if you are both okay. I do know of all the latest developments."

"Good on you," Patrick grinned at him. "Stay now and have the coffee and a wee dram of brandy with us. I believe we are also having the Scottish savouries."

The waiter was as good as his word. Very quickly the table was re-set for them, and the food and drinks brought in. They sat there munching and discussing the day's events. Stuart rose, brushed the crumbs off his suit, hugged them both and returned to his family. What tomorrow would bring was anyone's guess.

Moira and Patrick curled up on the divan, knowing that the night would be one of high activity for them as the reports came flooding through. Each one had to be analysed. They would dose, with one eye on the screens, an ear anticipating the next call. Millie would be tired, but they knew she was as dedicated as they were. They could only be patient and wait.

CHAPTER 27

▼

SUNDAY 14TH JULY. EARLY HOURS, LUXEMBOURG.

D.I. Millie Greenwood woke up with a start as the aircraft bumped into its landing. The plane had been so comfortable she had not bothered with the drinks and snacks the steward had offered her. She had relaxed and thought of her new husband, probably asleep in some hotel room down on the Adriatic. The stewardess opened the door. A car with blue flashing lights had drawn up beside the plane and a man stood up by the car. He was tall with good strong features.

"Bonsoir," she said.

"I know you speak good French, but I also speak good English: is that okay with you?"

She nodded, smiling.

"Come," he said. "We go to the customs lounge. We shall have coffee and some brandy while we quickly go through the formalities. I have talked to the British Embassy; but to all intents and purposes we must look after Mrs. Kearney as we would look after any Luxembourgeshe family. The husband is out of our hands; as far as we know he has committed no crimes during the seven years he has been here. No serious driving offences, no parking offences, nothing. In fact, he was highly commended by the industrial organization that employed him as a specialized projects manager,

"After three years when their production plants had been constructed and commissioned, they dismissed him. Later they recognized their mistake, but it was too late; he took them to tribunal and won his case. I have the dossier here. For a short time the family lived in Belgium, then they bought the land in Luxembourg and had their house built; that is all I can tell you."

The car arrived at the customs lounge. The officer took an imprint of her warrant card and passport, and they were directed to the lounge. Hans poured the coffee and two balloons of brandy.

"We need to set up some lines of demarcation. I understand you are drawing up a European arrest warrant and the husband will be your business; we have informed the Belgian, French and German police. Wherever he is, we will have full co-operation. Our concern is for the family. The news is contained for the moment, but satellite TV is the norm; and in a few hours the English newspapers will be out; normally here at the airport, the station and in the hotels. We know the girls go to Belgium schools. We are thankful for the next five weeks they are on holiday. The family employs an au pair so we can contain the situation, but the long-term is a different matter. I do not know the length of your stay? We will discreetly guard the house. Do you want me with you tonight?"

"No, if it's okay with you, I want to talk with them. Tomorrow we will need forensics. If we can get a DNA sample and a good set of fingerprints, the case is complete. We have samples from the second murder and fingerprint evidence from the third incident which was the killing of the two girls."

"Very well, I will have forensic there in the morning; it will be one small car, nothing obtrusive."

"Thank you. I appreciate your help."

"Come now; Mrs. Alderton is keeping Barbara company. She told me, until the inspector came they would chill out. They are very good friends, apparently; all belong to an English church here in Luxembourg, one of six as far as can I gather."

Twenty minutes later she rang the bell at a house in a quiet village. Barbara heard it.

"Who can it be at this time? It's nearly one in the morning! It cannot be Jonathan, the dog doesn't bark when he comes in, even though he might have forgotten his keys."

"No," said Josie. "It's a friend of mine. She needs to talk to you. Forgive me for not telling you."

"That's okay," Barbara laughed. "You're like a sister to me. There must be a reason even at this time of night. Where does she live? Do I know her?"

"She comes from England," said Josie, as she opened the door. "Hello, good to see you, Millie." She turned to Barbara. "Barbara, this is Millie Greenwood from England, and we all need to talk together."

"Hello Millie, I'm very pleased to meet you, but I am at a complete loss as to the reason. You've come a long way, so let me see to your needs first. Leave your case in the hall and we will all go into the lounge. Josie had the forethought of getting the coffee ready and making you a plate of sandwiches."

She led the way to the lounge. The house was very airy and all the floors tiled, the furniture minimal. On a pine dresser there were some photographs of the girls and Barbara, but none of the husband. There were some postcards propped up on the second shelf. She looked closer. One of them was of Rievaulx Abbey, the next the Pennine Way over Pen y Ghent, and the last, the Buchaille Etive Mor in Glencoe. There was no mistake, this was the man.

Barbara came in. "They are from my husband. Now we have an au pair he has taken it into his head to spend a few weeks in England climbing mountains."

"Do you know where he is now?" asked Millie

"No idea, I don't even warrant a card, or a phone call!"

"That's funny," said Millie. "What are these unopened letters?"

"From the bank, I don't bother with them. When he gets back he will check the letters and bills and file them; he has a study and keeps everything in some sort of order; his own sort," she added darkly.

"Could I see a photograph of your husband?"

"Yes, of course." She took one from the drawer of the dresser. "This was taken a couple of years ago when we all tramped the Yorkshire Dales. That's the famous bridge at Burnsall. We both look fit in that picture, but he's older then me by quite a bit."

Millie looked closely at Barbara. She was beautiful, good bone structure; it looked as though she exercised quite a lot, and her demeanour showed she had nothing to hide. No way was she in with the machinations of her husband! An Irish lilt could be detected in her voice. Josie was different, cultured but home-spun. They gelled together.

Barbara turned towards the door. "Let's go into the lounge; we can talk there. Josie has said nothing to me, we just flaked out after the Barbecue; my girls are with their friends down the road for the night. I'm pleased in a way as Jeanette, our au pair, isn't back until Monday evening."

They settled down in the comfortable lounge chairs, Millie facing Barbara and Josie.

"I am Detective Inspector Millie Greenwood. I have to thank Mrs. Alderton for looking after you. There were certain disclosures on satellite television this evening, which would not be good for you to have seen or heard. That is the reason for my being here, so I can personally acquaint you with some of the events that have taken place in the U.K. over the past two weeks."

"But no one has bothered me. All my friends have satellite, except us. Jonathan, my husband, put the dish up, and at one time it worked; but not for English programmes, now it's 'kaput'."

"You have to thank Josie for that; she saw a TV picture in a shop window as she was walking through one of the shopping arcades. She went direct to the police, and we in the U.K. were already talking to them. Nobody has called, because in order to save you from distress, your phones are blocked to incoming calls, including your mobile. What about your husband's phone?"

She looked alarmed. "He didn't take it with him, it's here. Please, please, tell me what this is all about."

"Barbara: there is no easy way of putting this. Your husband has caused a furore in England. First he went to the North Yorkshire Moors. Is it true women are attracted to him?"

"Oh yes, I am not his first wife; he has a way with women. They like him and trust him."

"On the Lyke Wake Walk."

Barbara interjected: "He actually did it, did he?"

"No." Millie paused. "He met a lady doctor, a police pathologist. Her name was Janet Fielding: he killed her."

"My God!" gasped Barbara, wide eyed. "An accident?"

"No, it was murder, plain and simple; and that, unfortunately, is not the end of the matter. He then went to Burnsall Bridge which you know very well, stayed at a flat opposite the green, then went on to have a night in Malham which included a barbecue at Goredale scar. There he murdered two young girls in their tent, Cathy and Alison." She paused, seeing Barbara's look of horror. "You must let me continue. He also went up to Glencoe, and on the Buchaille Etive Mor he killed two climbers, Alicia and Roderick. I have purposely left out one other murder. It did happen, but we have to discuss it later."

Barbara was shivering; Josie put her arms around her.

"Get the brandy, quick, Millie; it's in the middle bottom section of the dresser."

Millie rose quickly. She found the brandy and the glasses and poured three full measures. After a sip or two to bolster her resolve, she carried on relentlessly.

"I will tell you about the second murder. It's better that I get it off my chest sooner than later. There was a lady called Patricia Saint. She ran a sauna and massage service in Colne. He made an appointment with her and went 'like a Greek bearing gifts.' This we know from independent sources. We think she had a crush on him, according to the telephone call she made to a friend. It would seem that Michael, or Jonathan, as we now know him, enjoyed his evening very much; but any association of this nature was an inconvenience to his plans, so he killed her.

"He also met a lady barrister on the plane from Inverness to Derry. They had a night in a hotel and enjoyed a very good Greek meal together. For some reason he did not kill her, mainly because she knew so many influential people. We know she was not interested in any affair, but she had enjoyed her night with this man, and she did hope that he might contact her again. I am sorry to be so brutal."

Barbara and Josie were too stunned to say anything. They all sat in silence for a long time, sipping their drinks and lost in thought. Barbara could not hold back the tears. Josie went to comfort her, but Millie motioned her back. It was best that Barbara had time to cry it out, inwardly. This was something that was never going to go away. The horror of it was appalling.

Millie continued. "The most urgent task for us is to track him down. He may kill again. Can you tell me anything, Mrs. Kearney? Have you any ideas where he might be?"

"He will go where there are mountains. If he stays in Ireland it would most probably be Killarney, the Ring of Kerry or the Dingle Peninsula. In the north of Ireland, the Mountains of Mourne. If he goes back to Britain you can be sure of North Wales. It would be Snowdonia or the Ogwen valley. But, of course, you also have the Lake District, so you need to think of Borrowdale, Gillercombe Buttress, the Kearn Knots and the Napes ridge. The latter is on Great Gable. I know; I have had to be very enthusiastic in all these places."

Millie sighed. "No, we think he is out of the country. He sold his car in Wexford at a motor auction. If you look at your bank statement, you'll see some surprises. He has banked a lot of Euros for you. I think, honestly, that he is now on a death wish and could probably be in France. Have you any idea where he might go to in France?"

"Well, we have walked the Pyrenees, but from Andorra. We stayed in a small town called Encamp, and tramped along the high ridges. I do know he was set on spending some time in the Grand Central Massif. When we came back from the South of France last year, we made a detour after Vienne into the mountains. He was enthralled by the grandeur of the distant peaks." She paused, thinking, the tears glistening in her eyes. "You would not need to consider Switzerland. He's too old for those peaks. But what am I going to do? He's had his fun and now he must pay for it. What about me and the girls? We have to live here, with all of the people who know him, our friends; and what about reporters and the ghouls who will want to see where this, the real killer, lived? The girls at school, so-called friends. The press and TV will get hold of us, offering big bucks for articles." She gave a bitter laugh as she imagined the headlines. "'My days of friendship with the serial killer!' The thoughts of it all are terrifying. Even when shopping, some-one taking photographs; and my job, it's our livelihood and my sanity."

Millie fought the panic rising up inside her. "My God," she gasped, "I really feel for you. For the moment your girls are not in school. The Luxembourg police are going to do everything to protect you, but nothing's going to be easy. You will find yourself propositioned by newspaper conglomerates and TV com-panies to make interviews and a series. The money offered could be astronomical; you would never have to work again. You would then need new identities and a house far away.

"In some respect, although it's too early and possibly remiss of me to say it, good may come out of bad; you have to think of all the suffering wives who would watch such a programme and possibly identify the hidden demonic depths of their husbands. It is not far-fetched; history invariably repeats itself." She stood up. "Excuse me; I must contact D.C.I. Masters and Hall. Can I use your phone? All the costs will be reimbursed."

"Of course," said Barbara. "I will get the spare room ready for you. Please stay as long as you are able. The girls will be fascinated. But, what do I tell them? They love their daddy." With that she burst into tears.

Josie hugged her. "Come on, love. I'll help you, and then both of us can crash out together."

Barbara gripped Josie tightly. "How do we pray for him? He had such a strong faith. So much knowledge and now he is dammed forever! I blame myself, we have just not communicated or had the fellowship we used to over the past two years."

Sunday 14th July. Early hours. Fort William.

Moira and Patrick had finished their savouries; also the coffee and a few wee drams. They lay together in one room, both in dressing gowns, but it was too hot in the room and they had thrown off the gowns. In the glow of the bedside lamp he looked at her body, lean, supple, very athletic, not an ounce of fat, slender long legs, a flat stomach and very shapely breasts. He knew that she and Alice, her sister in law, and Janet Fielding, used to work out regularly and kept an all-year-round tan. Her face was elfin with a cupid bow of a mouth, and high cheekbones. The limpid brown eyes were so deceptive of her profession, as was her chestnut coloured hair, long and flowing.

He felt ashamed. He was white and flabby round the stomach, nowhere near fit; how could a creature like this see anything in him?

She read his thoughts. "Yes, Patrick, my boy, you might well look ashamed if we are walking out! There's some training to be done. We'll soon have your body tanned and glowing." She lifted his penis with her little finger. "And that's not going to do anything tonight or any night until we have a commitment! 'All work and no play makes Jack a dull boy'."

Patrick mumbled: "It's been out of use for as long as I care to remember."

"Never mind, baby boy, it's taken some time for us to get together. Over two years and now we are the high-ranking duo. This will be all of Bob's doing; he knows I have been sweet on you since the last case we were both on. I'll let you into a secret! I have had no interest in any other man since that time. So, fatso, you'll just have to work to keep me, won't you? But now, as our joint effort, let's nail this bastard!"

He nodded. "We have to hope for some sort of breakthrough within the next few hours."

At that moment the phone rang. Both picked up the extensions.

"Hi you, I bet romance is blossoming! Patrick always had a yen for you, going right back to the time when I was a lowly D.C."

"Millie!"

"Of course! You want a report? Here goes. Barbara is a lovely lady, very pretty and hardworking, and she has two girls. Her friend Josie is the salt of the earth; she has two boys. Forensics are due in a few hours' time; they will make a thorough check and transmit the results over to you. Nothing in his study has been touched, so it should be relatively easy. He has been planning his furlough for some time; transferring large deposits into his wife's account over a protracted period. So in the medium term she has no money worries.

"Our discussions confirm what you already know. He is probably in France, and there are two likely places, one he knows well, and one which he aspires to. The first is Andorra, in the Pyrenees, but it is possible he could be on the French side, somewhere close to Lourdes. The other is the Central Massif, possibly between Vichy and Limoges.

"That's about the sum total; the Luxembourg police are very competent and co-operative, and certainly concerned and sympathetic regarding the welfare and privacy of the family.

"Barbara has an elder sister in Taunton. Can you have her contacted? Her name is Selina, and I will download all the details to you as soon as I have a computer connection. She needs to be here; can you arrange for her to have some time off and have her flown over as quickly as possible?

"Possibly Commander Ferguson will allow the use of the Citation. A suggestion, for a few days, it would be advisable to have a senior officer here. May I suggest Stuart McKenzie? I hear through the grapevine he's the next D.C.I."

"You hear too much, young Millie," Patrick interjected. "But 'I luv yer for it'! Now be off with you. We will arrange everything just as you say. Moira will ring Bob now. We don't expect him to be asleep."

Bob answered the phone immediately. Moira gave a concise report.

"Thank you, Moira, the computer is on. Download to Simon and ask him to forward all the reports and actions to me after he has logged the receipts and acknowledgments. Don't worry, I concur and will make the necessary authorizations."

Moira replaced the receiver and looked at Patrick with dreamy eyes.

"I do not believe what I hear; all the red tape is gone, no-one is pulling rank, no snide action; common sense at last! Now let's pull in all the reports. We have to find him before he strikes again!"

CHAPTER 28

▼

EARLY HOURS OF SUNDAY MORNING, 14TH JULY. MID-FRANCE.

Michael was almost there. The old Peugeot had travelled well. The car lurched along a stony track out of the village of Neuvic. It was very difficult to miss the potholes. All around him were the ghostly silhouettes of the mountains. He could make out groups of sheep and some ponies as the sky lightened and the grey mist rolled over the grassy slopes.

Suddenly! Turning a corner he was there; a low building, with a slate grey roof, glistening with the recent rain. He stopped the car and gently eased himself out of the seat; he was so stiff. Everything was still. He looked around, and there it was; a dovecote set in the high walls of a barn. Some steps led to a platform, presumably to feed the doves; it was here he would find the keys for the cottage. The steps were old, worn and slippery. With care he reached the platform and felt around inside. The straw was moist and sticky; he groped around, until he felt something lying on the base of the dovecote. He withdrew his hand, clutching a packet; it was a stiff polythene bag with a bunch of keys inside.

Gingerly he descended the steps and commenced to examine the buildings in the half-light. Eventually he came to a double door which was locked. The largest of the keys fitted the lock. He turned the key and then pulled open the doors. It was a large barn; empty, but space for two cars. He drove in. He left the keys in the car. After opening the boot, he took out his bag, closed the lid, exited the garage and locked it. The key he replaced in the dovecote, knowing he would not be requiring it again.

The cottage was next to the barn, one story, low and sprawling, it was tightly shuttered. He was resigned to the prospect of living in Cimmerian darkness for some time. No way would he be able to open the shutters. He opened the door and went in, feeling around the walls, hopefully for a switch; surprise, surprise, the area was lit by a dim glow. The lamp, which provided the illumination, was of low voltage. She must have a generator system with a battery back up, he thought.

He was in a small hall boarded out in pine. In reality it was a corridor. He tried the door at the end. It was locked; three more doors to try. The first was a bathroom and a toilet, and the second opened into the living area cum kitchen. The third led to a flight of stairs. Again there was a switch. He descended into a cellar; dimly, he made out the wine racks that covered one wall. There seemed to be a surfeit of dusty bottles. A stack of stone blocks and bags of ready mix plaster occupied one corner; obviously a 'do it yourself' enthusiast. A door let into the cellar walls gave way to a bedroom. The space was taken up by a large king-size bed, with tables each side. There was a small hand basin, and the wall facing the bed was covered with shelves and hanging spaces for clothes.

Well, at least it appeared he would not be sleeping on his own too long. He dropped onto the bed. He was too tired even to think and was asleep in an instant.

Sunday Morning. Bellingham, Northumberland.

Valerie woke up feeling refreshed. It was good that they had taken it easy yesterday. Today would also be a fairly relaxed day in preparation for the final section.

She wondered about Michael. Would he be at the cottage? She assumed so. The text message she had sent to his mobile; he must have received it, providing he had kept his battery charged. He was a responsible person, so she assumed that by now he was safely installed in the cottage.

They had ordered an early breakfast, so after a shower and the luxury of clean shorts and shirt, all her dirty items she dumped into a carrier bag, knowing that they would be laundered and sent on to the Border Hotel in Kirk Yetholm. Today the party would travel light with only their night things and clean underwear for their stay in Byrness Hotel.

Now for the trek of the day! Only eleven miles; tomorrow would be twenty-nine miles. That was the killer, no place to stop; all eating would be done 'on the hoof.' If they decided to make the ascent of 'The Cheviot' they would add on another four miles. A daunting thought.

Breakfast was good; plenty of bacon, Cumberland sausage, with fried eggs and toast. Feeling bloated, they staggered out into a misty morning. The same mist hugged the hills. It was ethereal, so calm and peaceful. They had seen no one at breakfast, it had all been laid out for them buffet style. Similarly at the bar, no one, their packed lunches prepared for them. All cost had been paid in advance, so there was no need to disturb the peace of the innkeeper or his staff.

Once out of the village they followed the track to the long disused colliery. There was not a soul about; it was hard going up and over the rolling hills, until they reached the monument. This she had read about it.

It was where the Scottish covenanters met for worship. Each had to collect a stone on the way, and eventually there was enough to build this monument.

The book had been published a few years ago. It told of the awful torture they endured, from the army of the English crown under Clavering. Women and girls, entering into womanhood, tied to stakes in the River Tweed, at low tide left to drown as the river unrelentingly reached its high water mark, the troopers oblivious to the demented cries of the doomed. Their loved ones, all condemned prisoners, were forced to watch the agonies of wives and daughters before going to their own cruel deaths.

Valerie fought back the tears as she visualized the scene and resolutely commenced to walk north again. She needed to catch up with the others.

Sunday morning, 14th July. Fort William.

Moira and Patrick woke up to banging on the outer door. Quickly, Moira disappeared into the bathroom. Patrick put on a dressing gown and opened the door. It was the police; three of them, Stuart grinning like a Cheshire cat.

"Come on, lazybones, its after six. Breakfast is here." He indicated the trolley behind them. "Hurry up, I shall join you. The 'boys in blue' will pack up the computers and transfer them back to the station conference room. Bob, our national commander, has called for a video meeting at nine o'clock sharp. D.I. Priest is co-ordinating all the calls which we will undoubtedly have when the papers hit the British breakfast table."

"Right Sir." Patrick grinned back at him. "Take that grin off your face and remember, for the present I am your senior officer; and just to satisfy your curiosity, nothing happened, but we like each other!"

"That's good Pat; Fiona and I were having a private bet on the two of you. She's looking forward to having lunch with us. You remember her, my wife, to be obeyed, but beautiful with it. She came down to Bramshill, when we had the endorsements for the profiling course."

Moira bounced out of the bathroom, vigorously towelling her hair; she saw Stewart and with a start, pulled the loose flaps of her dressing gown across her body.

"Away ye go, Patrick; five minutes maximum, and then breakfast. Remember, we still have our serial killer on the loose."

Back at the Station, the Sunday papers were spread out on the conference table.

A lot of imagination had been used, for they covered in great detail the murders in Tees-side, Colne and Malham, with some sketchy notes relating to Glencoe. No names had been used.

The first call patched through to them was from the Post Office in 'Horton in Ribblesdale'. Yes, the owner had recognized the man. He remembered that he had bought postcards and stamps whilst waiting for the bacon butties he had ordered; later he dashed outside to put them in the Pillow-box. This had seemed a bit strange to the proprietor, as normally the walkers put their letters or cards direct into an open box that sat on the counter.

He remembered it was early last Monday morning. A lady came in after him, in her early thirties. They had struck up a conversation. He had thought she must be French, as the man answered her haltingly in French. She had ordered the same as he, and was interested in the books that were for sale on the Pennine Way. Apparently she was doing it, but was late in starting. She was hoping to make up enough ground to catch up with her friends.

A car had brought her up to Horton, one of the Settle taxis. They had left together, both in high spirits, looking forward to tackling Pen-y-Ghent, which was a section of 'The Way'.

Patrick picked up the phone and dialled a number.

"Robin, its Patrick. Are you okay? Good, listen, our man met a French girl in the Post-Office café at Horton. They went off together up the hill; the café owner reckoned she came by taxi from Settle. Can you check the hotels and B&B's; it's worth following up, seeing as they were so friendly.

"I have a copy of Wainright's book on the Pennine Way. There's a spare key to my cottage in my desk. Have a P.C. pick up the book; it gives all the recommended accommodation en route. Ring round; see if a French party booked in at any of them. Normally if a party is tackling 'The Way,' they book in advance and there exists an arrangement for the luggage to be transported from place to place; all they require for the day is a small rucksack for food, drink and other essential items.

"I suggest you start at Kirk Yetholm, which is the final destination of the walk. Consider it top priority and come back to me as soon as you can."

Belfast. Sunday morning.

Moragh Denver-Marshall shivered in her bed. She had not been able to sleep. A policeman was on guard in front of her house and a patrol car was in the vicinity, but it brought no comfort. The police were concerned that he may have rifled her handbag and had her address. She got up and dressed without any of her normal rituals. The Garda were on their way to collect her. The Head of the Judiciary in Eire had almost commanded her to move out and stay with them. She had agreed readily and had booked for a two-week stay.

Ruefully, she recollected his words. "Be warned, Moragh, not a word must leak out about your association with this man. The police in Derry have warned the hotel and the Greek restaurant. They have been given an understanding of the 'Official Secrets Act' and its consequences. Your work is too important; if anything does come out, you would be disbarred for life."

As she waited in the hall with her case, she mentally kicked herself; how could she, normally such a reserved person, have been such a fool, especially discussing her work with that man; not to mention the carnal lust bit!

Sunday morning. The Garda Headquarters, Dublin.

Alistair Brady put down the phone with a self-satisfied smile. He turned to his computer and rapidly compiled his report. He sent it as a Red Flash, 'Top Priority':

> *A man named Jonathan Kearny travelled as a foot passenger, on the Cobh to Roscoff Ferry on Friday Evening; the boat had docked in France and was ready for offloading by 7.30 a.m.*

The Gendarme Liaison Officer for the area was an Inspecteur Duval. He had been furnished with all the details of the case as well as the Identikit with the artist's drawing. It was hoped he would be able to have the passport details, including the photograph, downloaded to him as soon as the Authorities would release them.

Sunday morning, Settle.

Robin Johnson had a quick result. A Miss Valerie Charlier had stayed the night at a hotel on the outskirts of the town. The taxi had taken her from the hotel to Horton in Ribblesdale.

The hotel register showed an address in Toulouse, and a passport number. Now he was checking with the French Police for further details.

Patrick and Moira in Fort William digested the information.

"There's something odd about that passport number. It's bugging me! Let me make a phone call."

She dialled a number and spoke in French to someone called Pierre. Patrick muttered, "Sounds like an old boyfriend."

She glared at him and continued with her phone call. It was a long one and seemed to be very serious.

"That was Capitaine Pierre Balmain. We were at the Locard Institute together; D.N.A. analysis and blood spatter theory amongst many other things. A very dishy man, but not for me," she added as she ruffled Patrick's hair. "Our Lady, Valerie Charlier, is a very special person. She has diplomatic immunity, a 'Magistraat de Investigation Judicaire.' Something indigenous to France. Pierre checked the records; she is based in Toulouse and is due back in her office next Monday, but they believe she is having a few days in the mountains first, possibly leaving the U.K. Wednesday and flying out of Newcastle airport."

Robin Johnson came back on the phone. "Valerie Charlier is booked in at the Byrness Hotel for tonight, along with five other French ladies. I am going up to be there when she arrives. Don't worry, I will keep it cool."

Patrick informed Robin of her status.

"Be very careful. Most probably the others in the party don't know her true vocation. We have also found out that their walking tour was organized by a French 'Trekking Organization'."

"Okay, Patrick. See you soon."

Luxembourg. Sunday morning.

Millie woke up to brilliant sunlight. She looked out of the window. The garden was of medium size, with ponds and a waterfall arranged at the bottom of the garden. A lawn that had at one time been well kept, but which was now badly in need of cutting and rolling, dominated the view. The whole of the garden was surrounded by a variety of trees.

How could anyone, she thought, want to turn their back on this? So idyllic; she could imagine the happy times they had enjoyed. Had this man always been like he was now, a Jeckyl and Hyde? Charming and deadly! Most of the European police were now checking their files, since 1994, when this man had entered the country. They were also checking through a passport trail over those years too.

With the information she hoped to obtain today, the team would soon be busy tracing him back to his adolescent years, and checking against murders unsolved, and serious attacks that happened during his lifespan.

She showered and dressed. Josie was busy making breakfast for everyone. The doorbell rang, and Hans Jaeger entered, along with two men in white overalls.

"This is one of our forensic teams, Fernand and Carlo; they will take samples throughout the house. They will be very quick, but they must have access to his clothes and all of his personal things. I will stay and have coffee with you; that way I can ensure and assure the family of their privacy, and their protection as inhabitants of the Duchy. We will have surveillance on the house at all times until he is caught, just in case he does come back here."

Millie quickly reported back to Moira. "Hans has told me he will have the DNA results through to you this morning; also fingerprints and hair sample data. He was a good D.I.Y. man; his tools have given some good prints. The DNA hair results are from the follicles, and also from a dental prosthesis, which he normally wears but forgot to take with him. It was also good for us that he forgot to sterilize it.

"With respect to the family, we are trying to ensure that they have the chance of living a normal life. Today we are going for a picnic in the north, a place called Vianden. Very beautiful, apparently, with a restored castle set high on the cliffs overlooking the town. This way we can leave the house to the technicians and search team. Barbara's numb at the moment. The reactions will come later."

Moira listened, and understood. She could imagine the trauma the woman was going through. She would have to talk to Hans about counselling. Possibly she could find the time after they had caught him to go over there and help.

"Millie, you're doing a wonderful job. I am so grateful that you could be there for them. Please check with the search people regarding private papers. We need to have all relevant documentation. Have Hans confirm to me that from the documentation he will be able to freeze all credit transactions throughout Europe. This, of course, also has to include his English accounts.

"An appalling business! Normally chasing villains is cut and dried; plenty of action, lots of criminal activity involved. But, here we have an enigma! From the discussions that we have had with various people, I'm convinced he has been nothing but a loving husband until now. No secret murders, he has never been under any sort of suspicion; what was the trigger?

"Keep close to Barbara. Eventually she will want to talk, unburden herself; you must be there for her.

"By the way, Alex will join you next weekend; we have been able to re-arrange his flight schedule. We have booked you all into a hotel near Maastricht, which has a range of fitness and game activities. The costs will be covered under the 'witness protection programme.'

"But, I cannot stress too much to you; spend plenty of time with Barbara. We must know every last detail of his life and their life together. There are a lot of unfilled gaps; we have contacted various companies he has been involved with; everyone speaks highly of him. The key has got to be in his frustrations, his dark side. I assume that the search-team will interrogate his computer for all the deleted files. In addition ensure they look for any ghost images on his hard discs.

"Now I leave it to you, take care; we are with you all the way."

Sunday morning, Brest.

Inspector Duval was frustrated. The man had left the boat on foot. Unless he had an accomplice, he must have taken a train or bus. The gendarmes were questioning people at this moment, but for the present no luck. He was hoping "the tide would turn" after midday. By that time the newsflash would have been transmitted over the airwaves. He sighed and turned to his computer. With a password he keyed into the U.K. police information systems. He gave a gasp. Apparently a French Lady only known for the time being as 'X' had made his acquaintance; it was believed she lived in Toulouse, and there was a possibility that this man might try to contact her.

He looked at the area map on his wall. Reflectively he mentally conjured up the route. Make for Quimper, on to Limoges, and then to Toulouse. If his deduction was correct, he had to be by car, not by public transport; but he could possibly be hitchhiking. Alternatively, had this lady arranged for someone to pick him up? It was all guesswork. He would have to investigate every avenue.

Sunday morning, Inverness.

The coroner had consented to a preliminary hearing when he had heard the facts of the case. He appreciated the pressure the parents were under. The police also raised no objection to it being on a Sunday morning.

Mr. and Mrs. Hamilton, and Mr. and Mrs. Kent sat facing the Coroner as he opened the inquest. Previous to this, they had been taken to the mortuary, where the bodies of their kin were now presentable for an identification to be made. They sat numb and unbelieving that this was happening to them. To see those two young lives snuffed out, finished, the end of two beautiful people; always they had been happy and so deeply in love, and now nothing.

The pathologist had been invited to rise and give his report relating to the cause of death. They were brought back to reality as his grim words hung in the air of a hushed courtroom. They heard of the quick death of Alicia as her fall ended in a violent collision with rock, and that of Roderick's slow death as the blood had ebbed out of him. The doctor also gave evidence and it was his opinion that Roderick had been unconscious because of the violent blows to his head. Mercifully his life had flowed from him in that unconscious state.

The Coroner gave his Verdict.

"Murder by persons or person unknown!!" It was his understanding, he explained to the court, that the police now had positive leads in this case.

He then adjourned the court, giving permission for the bodies to be buried.

The parents had agreed that the bodies would be cremated in Inverness; then, together, they would walk the path up the Buchaille Etive Mor and have the ashes scattered from the top of Crowberry ridge. Mike Styles and Andrew Biggs were to accompany the parents and then take charge of the urns for the final ceremony.

The Coroner had commended both Mike and Andrew. In due course they would receive an award in recognition of their services. They simultaneously stated to the court that they would not accept any reward or commendation. Any climber or walker worthy of his salt would have done the same. The cremation had been set for Friday of that week.

Sadly, the parents departed; they would meet up with Mike and Andrew later on in the week, when they brought the rest of their families up for the funeral. The police had offered to make all the necessary arrangements for them, and they too would be in attendance at the cremation.

Later Sunday morning. North West France.

Henri Duval had picked up a lead. A call from the owner of a restaurant in Charroux, a small village on the road to Limoges, had been patched through to him; yes, he had seen this man. That was enough for Duval. With siren flashing, he took the 'route nationale' towards Limoges. It was a two hours' drive to the village and the restaurant. A man waved to him from the entrance as he drove up. It was the owner; they shook hands.

"An aperitif, Inspecteur, after that drive? We will sit outside by the river and talk."

Henri was grateful for the respite. He was not of the build for rushing around places. He closed his eyes and heard the rushing waters of the Charente. Looking across, he could see the white breakers as the fast waters broke against the stones.

The owner with his wife came out with a tray. He poured the wine and passed a glass over to Duval.

"The chef is making a plate of appetizers for you. My wife will collect it in a few minutes. I hope it is not too cold for you out here. There are still some late diners in the restaurant, and here it is private.

"Your man was actually sitting by the river. He moved his chair up there when his food arrived. He ate with the tray balanced on the stones. At that time we had a few diners eating outside, but in the lea of the restaurant, he actually remarked to me that he was very tired and did not want to be involved in long drawn out conversations. His need was to relax and then be on his way. I assured him he would give no offence by wanting to be alone. A very nice gentleman, he spoke of dining here in the past; probably before we bought the place. His French was difficult to understand. The restaurant was very busy and the car park was full. I suppose we assumed he had arrived by car, but we had no reason to ask him. He came in and paid his bill, waved goodbye and he was out of the door. Which way he went I cannot tell!"

Henri Duval walked the length of the village. He knew this road could be very busy; possibly the man was hitchhiking. It was good to stretch his legs and think; he continued to stroll along out of the village in the direction of Limoges. Eventually he came to a lay-by and picnic area; comprised of a few wooden tables with fixed benches, waste paper bins and a nice grassy area for the children to play, safely away from the road.

He was clever, this man, if he came by car. He most probably parked here. Nice and quiet and quite anonymous. He sighed. It was conjecture, not one single fact to know whether he was motorist, or a hitchhiker. The gendarmes were already checking the bus routes for the area, and also the taxis; though, for the sort of distance involved it would be prohibitively expensive by taxi; so he was inclined to rule out that area of investigation.

Chapter 29

▼

Sunday evening. 14th July. North Tyne.

Valerie Charlier and her friends walked into Byrnes. It had been a reasonable day. She stopped at the village store. The bell on the door jangled as she went in. A little old lady came out of the living room to serve her.

"Yes dear, can I help you?"

She selected her purchases and put them on the counter, toothpaste, shower gel, and a couple of bars of Kendal Mint cake, the brown variety. The television was on in the lounge. She saw a picture, an artist's impression, it could only be Michael! She felt numb and closed her ears to the appeal of the uniformed police officer who was describing what they wanted him for.

Her heart was racing. Her instincts had been right! Her training had confirmed it, that this man was different. How many years had she waited? She had been qualified for thirteen, plus the seven for her studies in colleges and universities. At last she had found her man.

The old lady glanced back into the room.

"It's terrible what some people get up to! Not safe to walk the hills anymore. The local bobby called in not so long ago. He said there is a big investigation. This man seems to be everywhere! They are setting up volunteer teams and co-opting from the army also, to patrol the holiday areas; apparently they are now worried about having copycat incidents. It could happen anywhere, from Land's End to John O'Groats."

Valerie paid for her goods and said goodbye to the lady.

"You'll be staying in the hotel. Mildred told me they had a French Party staying tonight. You're having roast turkey for dinner. Frank, my husband, killed it and plucked it this morning. You have to eat well. It's a tidy stretch for you to tomorrow; all the way to Kirk Yetholm. Goodbye dear."

The hotel was built in the grey stone of the Cheviot. It nestled under the foot of the hill. The church and the graveyard were below it. She went in, the door opening directly onto the bar. At the end, there was a section with a display of brochures, and the hotel register lay on the bar top. A lady appeared on the other side of the bar.

"You must be Valerie; your party said that you had popped into the shop. There is your room key! You have an 'en suite'; dinner will be served at seven. Also, you have a visitor; a young man; he's over there, in the corner. I took the liberty of making you both a pot of tea, and there is a plate of hot scones too. I think your gentleman friend has already poured two cups in readiness; you'd best get yourself over there before it goes cold."

Mystified but with an inkling of the truth, she went into the lounge. The man was fresh faced, fair hair, lithe in his build and wearing a well cut tweed jacket. He looked up as she came in and rose to meet her. He was quite tall and ramrod straight. With an easy smile, he held out his hand.

"Mademoiselle Charlier, I believe you are in the same business as me. I am Detective Inspector Robin Johnson, based at Skipton and Settle in the Yorkshire Dales. Forgive me, I need to ask you some questions and hopefully enlist your help."

"Enchanted, Monsieur; let's have some tea and ask your questions. My name is Valerie. As you possibly know, I am a '*Magistraat de Cours de Assizes*' attached to the Toulouse Arrondisment. As you have managed to find me, you obviously know I am attempting to complete the walk of the Pennine Way. I am incognito to my companions; this is my vacation.

"If the British police, probably special branch, have spoken to our Ministry of Justice, you will also know that I have very wide powers of investigation, and follow the path of law and order most assiduously. There are many guests in the Santé prison and other penal settlements that can testify to my poor efforts. Sometimes I wish that the Guillotine was still in use; it would considerably reduce the prison population."

The diatribe left Robin shocked. He was surprised by her veracity; he had not expected it. He felt he had lost the initiative.

"Mademoiselle, thank you for telling me something about yourself. Now I must ask you to look at this photograph, made up from an identikit exercise, from which the police artist produced this impression."

She nodded, examining the drawing. "It is a very good impression. You have an excellent artist; and yes, I know him. We spent about three hours together."

"When and where was that?"

"Obviously you know of my introduction to him. It was in the small café in Horton in Ribblesdale. I was not able to join my friends at the start of the way in Derbyshire. I travelled with some other friends, who were holidaying in England, touring the North and Scotland. They were able to drop me at Settle. I stayed the night there and then the following morning I was taken to Horton, by taxi. It was early. I did not bother to wait for breakfast at the hotel. The taxi driver knew the café would be open, 'voila' door-to-door service.

"The café had only one customer, a man; he was ordering bacon butties. The smell was delicious, so enthusiastically I also ordered the same; it was natural to sit together, even if it was only to share the sauce bottle. He was an affable man, kind eyes and with a very easy manner. Obviously he loved his wife and family: he was finishing off his postcards when I joined him.

"We left the café together, and climbed the stairs up to the summit of Penygh-ent. Our endomorphines had certainly been stirred; we were exhilarated and actually ran all the way down the hill to the viaduct at the crossroads for Hawes, Ingelton, and Horton. I continued by the moorland path to meet the rest of my party at Hawes. He set off towards the Hill Inn, and then he intended to climb up Ingleborough. The top, as you know, is a plateau; his intention was to drop down to Gaping Gill, see if the winch had been set up, watch the trippers descending and returning soaking wet. After his entertainment was over he was walking back to Horton for his car.

"My party is here, you are welcome to join us for dinner. Apparently Roast Turkey with all the trimmings! A summer Christmas repast."

"Thanks, but no thanks; I have to be back in Settle. It's a fair old drive; so, this would be when?"

"Last Monday morning, very early. We walked at a very fast pace; he spoke very little French. We talked of the Nazi occupation. He had read a lot of books on the subject. The conversation then switched to French composers; that was because we had discussed the Wagnerian influence on Hitler and Himmler. Again he was very knowledgeable. One thing that impressed me was that he knew their lives almost intimately, particularly their mental states. He made a valid point that without this aspect there was no way of understanding Berlioz, Dukas, Ravel, etcetera. I did not know of Gottschalk, an American composer adopted by the French, a friend and contemporary of Berlioz; he fled France after some disastrous assignations, and settled in Brazil where he became their living patron saint of Brazilian music.

"I tell you this to give some idea of the breadth of this man's knowledge and his unbounded enthusiasm for all that he did. It felt good to be with him. He was extremely fit, and very difficult to determine his age; he never spoke of why he was there, or of his family. It was a case of 'ships passing in the night', to borrow an English expression. He was relaxed, apparently harmless, as if 'butter wouldn't melt in his mouth'."

"Madame Charlier, you may not know this, but by then he had already committed two murders, and would commit another two in the early hours of Tuesday morning."

"Then I must thank God that I was not his third, and hope I never meet him again." She was vehement in her denunciation of him. "I tried to persuade him to come as far as Hawes with me, but he wasn't having any! His mind was set to the route he had planned. So we said our goodbyes."

Robin probed further, but she could not or would not elaborate further. He felt overwhelmed by her, and wished Patrick or Moira were with him. She exerted such an authority; her English was impeccable and he felt that he was still a Sergeant in the guise of an Inspector; it was too early for him, the transition was not yet complete.

Bidding her goodnight, he climbed into his car to take the long drive back to Settle through the upper reaches of Tyneside and Teesdale and back into the dales. He lived with his widowed mother; they enjoyed each other's company, but conversation was sparse. That introspectiveness was with him now. He needed to think through his meeting with Mademoiselle Charlier; the expressions, the body movements; something was not quite right. "The lady protesteth too much," he thought.

He rang Patrick, still in Fort William.

"Hello, Robin. We will be flying back tonight. I will be in the Skipton office tomorrow morning. I will be driving back from Moira's. We meet very early in the morning to exchange notes; but I would appreciate a preview from you."

Robin recounted the interview and added his own impressions to it.

"She knows something, Patrick! There is a sort of satisfaction in her manner; nothing tangible, just a gut feeling."

"Well, Robin, you are the one to follow it through. Say goodbye to your Mum for a week or so. First thing tomorrow we will arrange your new itinerary. I have spoken to Inspector Duval. You are to join him; I will arrange a midday flight for you, to Toulouse; he will meet you at the airport. He speaks very good English and normally works out of Roscoff, but his superiors have instructed him to follow this case to the bitter end, along with an English colleague; which is you. The European arrest warrant has been raised in your joint names. Possibly you will be able to see Millie also, over in Luxembourg.

"I suggest that you go direct to the station tonight. Make out your report on Mademoiselle Charlier, and have it transcribed onto the police network with a note for Inspector Duval. I will have a car ready to take you to the airport. Remember your passport. Bypass the check-in, and report only to the security office, and then straight on the plane. Take care though, Robin; I do not want to lose my new Inspector. Oh, by the way, you will draw a side-arm from the Gendarme office in Toulouse."

Robin drove back feeling exhilarated. It was all happening; all the years of slog and routine had come to an end. He rang his girlfriend: "Meet me at the Peregrine, pick up Mum; we will have dinner there tonight. I think it's time to give you that ring I bought a few months ago."

Valerie was in a state of euphoria. The policeman seemed satisfied. Now Michael was hers for life, however long that was! She was content. It had been a long time to find a man such as this! She tucked into the turkey, oblivious of the conversation around her. A few glasses of some unknown white wine, and then bed. Now she was anxious to finish the walk and be back in France.

Neuvic, Massif Centrale, France. Early hours, Monday morning, 15th July.

Michael woke up. He had slept many hours. The room was so silent, the bed so comfortable. He went to the living room, turned on the heating, selected some music from the C.D. collection, and then went foraging for food. He was hungry.

The Slavonic dances broke the silence and he felt himself relax. Bread, bacon to defrost, eggs to scramble, tinned tomatoes to open. In no time at all he was sitting down to breakfast. He thought he would sleep most of the days—that would shorten the time until Valerie arrived. Plenty of reading: the Rougon Marquet novels by Zola, copies of the full series in French and English. *La Bette Humaine*, the beast in man, was his choice.

He thought about his family, his wife and girls. He had 'burned his boats' there; he would never see them again. At least Barbara had the extra cash; it was all above board and they could not take it off her.

He felt impervious to his life before. His mind had shut the door, cleansed in the blood of those he had murdered. All the frustrations, the horrific thoughts, living in a world of his own, were of the past. He would be infamous; same difference, really, no longer a programmed robot. Now it was over he felt cleansed, beyond forgiveness from a merciful God; he was now branded forever as a serial killer, snuffing out life like swatting a fly, not belonging to the scene but moving on, away from the carnage, away from the investigations. He felt proud of himself, for having the willpower to shun any of the media, knowing full well had he succumbed, self-consciousness would have set in, hiding in corners and drawing attention to himself, causing him to make mistakes and lose his self confidence. He would have been caught under those circumstances quite quickly.

There was another side to it as well. He was impervious to parental grief, husbands, wives, whatever; he wondered whether he and Valerie would continue to make another odyssey, possibly even make Taussauds eventually. What an epitaph to their lives.

He felt a bit strange over Colne. He had liked Patricia. She had a good body with a certain refinement. It was a pity; the right woman at the wrong time. He comforted himself with the thought he would soon be experiencing Valerie's body.

The woman on the moor, he did not know who she was. She had a good body, what he had seen of it. The lady herself had been very refined and well educated. He had sensed that in the few words they had spoken together.

The two girls, lovely girls, he had enjoyed the walk down to the scar, carrying a ton weight, Alison reeling a bit and bubbling over with laughter. They had accepted him and trusted him, spurning the advances of the drunken yobo's. But by then the compulsion had gripped him; the barbeque was a cooling off period, a time of reflection, sobering him up with all that coffee, a time of clear-headed resolve, not only for the murders, but to ensure a clear escape. His identity was quite undetected as far as he was aware. It was a case of being over the Rubicon. Murder was so easy!

Glencoe was different; just opportunity and a chance of 'a night on a bare mountain.' He must find the Mussorsky in Valerie's collection. That would be his music for the evening. He could not believe the fast traverse of the Anoch Egach ridge. That had allowed him to escape out of Glencoe with impunity.

The epitome must have been the lady barrister; a tigress in bed! That was another chance he had thrown away, a new life with her, as it could have been with Patricia. It could only always have been a sole encounter with Moragh; anything else and he would have been apprehended pretty quickly.

The murders, his marriage, the lady loves were now all in the past. The present and the future solely hung on a friendship of a few hours; he was in her house and her hands. He knew they had a rapport, but on what basis? A few hours on the mountain; judging by her library she was more than a translator; international law books, studies of the criminal mind, psychology, psychiatry, forensics, profiling, it almost mirrored his library. What was missing? No religious books, plenty of history, especially Roman and the French Revolution.

He found a hidden door, possibly her study. It was double locked; otherwise everything was free to him. The next two days would pass very slowly. He would just have to be patient. He felt whatever was happening in the outside world, he was very safe.

Sunday, late evening. 15th July. Tees-side.

Moira and Patrick were with the National Commander. Bob was summing up the investigation.

"Everything is finished here. We have the coroner's verdicts, full witness statements, forensic results; we know his identity, have access to his accounts; we have a protection and resettlement programme for the family; his wife is an outstanding lady; we have full co-operation; similarly with the Luxembourg and French Police. The only outstanding item is the matter of catching him! So what are our options?

"We can sum it up in a very few words; Inspector Duval and his insatiable desire to be in at the kill, Inspector Jenkins, who will be there to help him. They will definitely follow up on Mademoiselle Charlier. Millie may yet turn up other possible leads from his files. We need to explore every avenue, no matter how remote it may seem.

"So I suggest you each return to your respective stations. You will find a heavy workload. We have a snippet of information which could lead to a very large investigation, but it is early days yet. It's not going to go away. Next week, I will require you both for a three-day conference. D.S. Bridges will be there and so will D.C.I. McKenzie. Yes, he has accepted, and we have the procurator's fiscal blessing.

"We are looking for a house for him; somewhere around Stokesly. For the time being he will have a furnished police apartment and we will use the Citation to fly his family down every other weekend, depending on the workload. I'm glad that you are pleased. That completes our team for the moment. We will co-opt if we need to. In the case of Patrick! I have not considered anything with regard to his accommodation. Something tells me that others have that in mind.

"Nice to see you in a freshly ironed shirt, Patrick; and take that silly grin off your face, Moira!

"Now to our two European detectives! Millie Greenwood will stay in Luxembourg at Barbara's invitation, until the end of the month. To all intents and purposes she is a friend. No one other than her best friend Josephine will know any different. She is to have some time with the Ducal police, and will write a report; similarly, with the German police. One day in Frankfurt, and one day in Metz with the French police. The Belgian police are a different matter. She is only three kilometres from the border. The Arlon police are arranging a seminar in Neufchateau in conjunction with Charleroi; this is an exchange of views in relation to Paedophile investigations. We are compiling a dossier for her to make a presentation at the seminar. Millie will compile her own reports relating to all meetings.

"Robin Greenwood; he is our lynchpin. Tomorrow he is off to France. As you know, Inspector Duval will meet him at Limoges Airport. This Duval has really got the bit between his teeth. He is convinced that somewhere along the way our man procured a car. Nothing has turned up relating to stolen cars, or hire cars. He is most probably right; we know our killer has plenty Euros about his person. It is reasonable to assume he found a garage with a cheap runabout already taxed and insured, ready to drive away. In Brest, nothing has come to light; the next town is Quimper, actually a city.

"Tomorrow Henri Duval will check the banks in the city for any reasonable deposits of cash that have been made relating only to the small garages. This is most probably faster than trawling from garage to garage. It is hoped the car can be tracked down once the registration details are available. France also has video cameras on its motorways; we should be able to establish his route.

"Once Henri has his answers, he and Robin will make their way to Toulouse to meet up with the Police Judicaire, and hopefully fill in the gaps on Valerie Charlier. Robin, as you know, has a gut feel about this lady. He feels she is going to be the key to finding our killer. He will learn more in Toulouse. Mademoiselle Charlier will be in her office a week tomorrow, but we have to find our man as soon as possible. Robin and Henri will talk to her colleagues; possibly they will know a little more of her private life. Robin will keep the European arrest warrant on his person; we cannot ignore the possibility that Valerie may be his next victim.

"So, good night to you both! I shall be down in Sheffield for the next few days. D.I. Priest will keep me informed of any developments."

Moira and Patrick left together.

"We just go home, Patrick," Moira said. "Mine is yours, and the weekends we spend in your cottage if we have any free ones."

"That's fine with me," Patrick smiled. "I need more than one suit and shirt. I will make time whilst at Skipton tomorrow. There will be some handing over to do at that station, and we need to prepare a place for Robin; it will take most of the day. But I do have a condition. As soon as I am back we go late night shopping for the ring. I want that commitment!"

"And so do I, Patrick. It's a deal. Now home for a nightcap and a cuddle; there is no way we will be able settle down until this case is over."

"Just how I feel, Moira; I can wait, we have to soldier on, because you can be sure the villains will give us no respite."

Bob watched them go, sighing. He felt their frustration; he picked up the red receiver and dialled a two-digit number. It was answered instantly.

"Morgan Freeman."

"Morgan, its Bob Ferguson. I expect you have seen the papers. Our killer is now in France. It looks as though the predictions of your psychic profiler were correct. Geoff. Grenchen, was it not? Maybe we could have him over for a seminar, once we have apprehended the killer."

"I'm afraid not," said Morgan. "He died a few days ago, a massive coronary; death was instant. I think it was due to all the nervous energy he exuded. We shall miss his peculiar talents."

"I'm very sorry, Morgan. See you in the near future. Goodbye and God bless."

CHAPTER 30

▼

MONDAY EVENING, 16TH JULY. SOUTH SCOTLAND. KIRK YETHOLM.

They were at the Border Hotel. At last it was finished. It was a hard day's slog. The most adventurous of the party had detoured to take in the peak of the Cheviot. Valerie had contented herself with keeping her eyes on the well-worn track and striding out. There was little conversation. The girls with her were strangers. The common bond had been to complete this walk through the magnificent scenery of Northern England.

The hotel was quiet. There was hardly anyone in the village. She made a quick decision. Arranging with the management for a taxi, she jumped into the shower and, after brisk towelling, changed into clean clothes and went down to reception. The receptionist told her not to worry about her clothes; they would all be laundered and sent back to her in France. With that assurance she paid her bill and climbed into the waiting taxi.

Her walking friends had understood her dilemma. They were looking forward to the evening celebrations and receiving their certificates for completion of 'The Way' which the French trekking company had arranged for them. Valerie was not eligible, as she had joined the group in Yorkshire, thereby missing out the

Derbyshire section. Her mind was elsewhere; the three-hour taxi ride was a blur. She dozed most of the way, missing the scenery of the Northumbrian coast.

At the airport she changed her flight. There was a Paris flight with a direct connection to Toulouse. Using her special status, there was no problem in transferring her ticket. It was the early hours when the plane landed. Her car was in the privileged car park, no checkout required. Driving out of the airport she took the bypass towards Limoges. The city was quiet. Her favourite hotel had a room vacant and she was asleep as soon as her head touched the pillow.

Monday evening. Toulouse.

For Robin Johnson and Henri Duval the day had been frustrating; true, a garage in Quimper had sold the car, a cash deal, all above board, to a man who was touring France for an indefinite period. He had bought it to continue his holiday, and then he was hoping to open a French office for his business and keep the car as a runabout for whoever ran his business in Europe. A Peugeot Cabriolet in a nondescript green had been his choice. The name on the receipt was a Michael Anstruther. The man had been very pleasant, paid cash, and driven away with only a rucksack for luggage. With that knowledge they had travelled the route; but other than the restaurant at Charroux, nobody could help. Henry had the satisfaction of knowing that he had been right in his deductions.

They spent the evening at a hotel in Toulouse, hardly tasting the food laid before them, lost in their own thoughts.

"Tomorrow we visit the 'Police Judicaire' and find out some more about Madam Charlier. My friend, remember, every policeman in France is now looking for that Peugeot. Certainly they will check every place where he could buy essence and possibly change number plates. It is common in Europe when a transfer of ownership takes place."

Robin telephoned D.C.I. Hall to give a brief report, and then he spent two hours on his laptop making an update for H.O.L.M.E.S. and downloading it via his GSM; then it was bed. Police work could be so frustrating and tiring!

Tuesday 17th July. Limoges.

It was late morning before Valerie managed to push herself out of bed, feeling refreshed. The aches and pains had gone. She spent an hour in the bath luxuriating and looking down on her lithe body, breasts a bit too large but good legs, no surplus fat, not bad for mid-thirties. Sometimes she felt she'd been alive for ever. She stroked herself between her legs and felt a tingling. A cold glow of excitement of what was to come came over her.

Reluctantly she climbed out of the bath, dried herself and put on the fluffy white dressing gown that the hotel thoughtfully supplied. Ringing reception, she ordered coffee and hot croissants. The hotel provided notepaper and envelopes. She sat down to write just as her food arrived. Thoughtfully nibbling at the hot pastries and enjoying the coffee, she composed in her mind what she wanted to put on paper.

It took a long time. By mid-afternoon it was finished. She stuffed the bulk of the papers into one envelope. A further short note and the envelope then went into a larger one.

Quickly dressing and gathering up her belongings, she went to the reception and checked out. Leaving her car at the hotel, she walked to the main post office to have her letter sent 'special delivery'.

She felt a degree of satisfaction in wandering round the city, looking for a negligee that would suit her for the evening; it had to be something black and sexy. Having found it, she went in search of food.

The selection was good; truffles and langoustines in a savoury jelly, a complete Beef Wellington, only to heat and serve. There were also Potatoes Lyonnais, and an Italian Salad plus two fresh baguettes. The sweet was more of a problem. In the end she settled for a Raspberry Pavlova. Wine was never a problem in France, but something different was called for. The wine shop had a large selection of vintages. The choice was difficult. She eventually settled for two bottles of white wine from the high Pyrenees; the area Juraçon, such an exquisite aftertaste. For the red wine she chose her own favourite, a couple of bottles of the Hospice de Beaune, a good vintage, incredibly expensive, but this was going to be a meal to remember, very similar to a 'last Supper'.

Then it was back to the car, dumping her purchases in the boot, and making her way up to the mountains. Her heart was free. She was looking forward to meeting the man Michael again.

Tuesday morning. Toulouse.

Inspector Henry Duval and D. I. Robin Johnson were in the Gendarmerie.

Robin rang Newcastle airport police and asked them to ascertain when a Madam Charlier would be flying from there to Toulouse. Whilst they waited they drank coffee and looked at the Computer Reports for any sightings of the Peugeot or Jonathan Kearney. There was no news of any description. At last the airport called with some information. Madam Charlier had cancelled her flight and rebooked for Monday Evening on the late Paris flight with the connection from Orly airport to Toulouse. With her V.I.P. status there had been no problem. Further checking revealed she had landed in Toulouse without incident and driven off in her car, which was a dark green Saab turbo diesel saloon with diplomatic plates.

Robin turned to Henry Duval. "I'm sure I'm right, she knows where he is; that is her destination."

"Come, Robin, we go to the Police Judicaire."

The building was remarkable for its architecture; they were expected and shown into a dark panelled oak conference room. Coffee had been prepared and two men joined them.

"*Bonjour Monsieurs.* I am Pierre de Grune, Chief of the Bureau, and this is Roger Desormiére, Madam Charlier's chief assistant. We know the background of your mission and the effort of the Inspector with whom we want to talk to later. We have the full history relating to the macabre exploits of Jonathan Kearny and we are as anxious to catch him as you are. We agree with you that Madam Charlier has an interest, but we differ with you in the way you think she is involved.

"This we will go into in some detail. We have checked her apartment. She is not there; nor is there any answer when we call her mobile. We have a recorded message promising that she will be able to contact us tomorrow morning. At present the investigation is her own, something personal to her; we know not what! As you are aware, she is on leave and not due back to the bureau until next Monday. So, unless we believe and know there is some criminal activity involved, our hands are tied.

"The mountains are her love, and we believe her retreat is somewhere in the central massif. We know it's completely isolated. Often we have joked with her, that such an attractive lady should keep herself to herself resisting any attempts of having any social intercourse. We know if there was a difficult case she would disappear to this retreat of hers and then eventually re-appear with a complete prosecution brief. Always we have respected her privacy. A charming person in her mid-thirties, immaculately dressed, and the scourge to the underworld. To our belief, she has never married.

"As far as we know, there was some accident with her family and her mother, father and sister. An elderly aunt brought her up who has since died. Her studies were at the Sorbonne, the Locard Institute, together with a period of study in the universities of Montpelier, Berlin and Moscow. She also had some of her apprenticeship in the London Inns of Court, and the Brunel in Bristol. A qualified electrical engineer, would you believe, before she became an advocate!

"We cannot go into detail over her cases. Roger Desormiére has been her chief assistant for the last five years; he knows her better than most; also her secretary and the investigators working under Roger can give you their impressions. We are arranging for lunch and suggest you both stay another night. Her word is her bond, so we shall know by the morning the full details of any investigation. We are used to this. Her talent is an individual one, and we have to respect it."

"I sincerely hope you are not clutching at straws!" Robin exclaimed.

"Reading the reports, you have not a great deal of reason to suspect that Valerie is involved with this man. The only sighting you have of him is in the small village of Charroux between Niort and Limoges. He could be anywhere!"

"Apparently from the information given by his wife he is in love with the high Pyrenees; therefore he may be making for Andorra; if he knows the area, he could travel the small roads, without having to see an auto-route."

Robin seethed with frustration. There was nothing else they could do. Lunch was a communal affair with the director and Valerie's staff. In the afternoon they were privileged to go through some of her outstanding cases and understand more of her methods and her reputation.

Tuesday evening. Massif Centrale.

Valerie had driven fast, keeping to the small streets of Limoges and out into the country, crossing the main Tulle-Clement Ferand road, at the outskirts of Ussel and through to Neuvic. Leaving the village, she took the unmarked road that ran by the side of the Dordogne Gorges and into the mountains. The air was still; the clouds were turning a misty grey and the mountains loomed up black and sombre. This was her country, her little bit of heaven, shortly to turn into a hell.

Her driving was too fast for the bends. She felt the stones hitting the underside of her car while negotiating the steep curves of the unmetalled road; it would never do to crash into the gorge below. Her foot eased off the accelerator; yes, it would be nice to be in one piece to meet Michael; in less than an hour she would be at the cottage. Eventually and without incident, the grey stone walls which surrounded her retreat came into view. At one time it had been a shelter for the shepherds sojourning the hills during winter. The walls were what were left of the sheepfolds.

All was still, shutters closed, no noise. She knew the generator would be working. It was an expensive model with a good silencer; with her own hands she had dug a trench to the stream that ran into the Dordogne. By this means she had extended the exhaust pipe of the generator so that the outlet was far away from the cottage. It had been successful: her retreat had never been discovered.

Quietly, she opened the barn door and parked next to the Peugeot. Removing her purchases from the car, she laid them by the front door, and then went back to lock up the barn. He was inside her cottage. Her heart was beating. She gently turned the key in the lock and pushed open the door; there was still no sound. It took a long time to transfer her purchases into the corridor. At last it was done and the door was secured with the heavy-duty lock and bolts top and bottom.

"Michael, it's me; Valerie!"

He came to her and hugged her. She disengaged herself.

"Please run me a bath; I need to change into things more comfortable. I would welcome a glass or two of champagne, if you would be so kind. Whilst you're doing that I will prepare the food I have bought. After my bath we can eat and relax. Please be my friend and lay the table while I am in the bath. In addition to plates and cutlery you will need glasses for white and red wine, and also small cut glasses for the liqueur we will have with the coffee; it will be an Armagnac."

Preparation was fast, the truffles and langoustines came ready prepared on a stainless-steel platter. They went into the 'fridge along with the white wine. The Wellington *en croute* required a half hour in the oven. Potatoes Lyonnais and the bread could stay in the warming compartment of the oven. Carefully she opened the red wine, and put it on the hearth so it would settle and gently mellow in the warmth to bring out the bouquet.

"All is prepared *ma Cherie*."

With that she went down to the bedroom, stripped off and laid out her negligee with the black stockings, suspender belt and the high-heeled pumps. With a dressing gown over her arm, she entered the bathroom. It was full of aromas; it seemed as though Michael had been very liberal with her expensive perfumes. Sinking into the water was luxurious. A fifteen-minute soak relaxed her. Regretfully she climbed out and towelled herself dry. Emulating Michael, she liberally sprayed herself with what was left of her precious perfumes; rouged her nipples, applied her lipstick and brushed her long hair which now hung free down over her shoulders. Then it was back to the bedroom to dress in her dishabille, covering all, in her fluffy white dressing gown. Pressing a button in one of the floorboards, a small section slid inwards; she took out a sachet of white powder and slipped it into the pocket of her gown; leaning over; her fingers encountered another object, but this one was for later in the heat of passion. The board slid back with a satisfactory click. She called to Michael to have a quick bath and come to the table in his dressing gown.

"Comfort is the order of the day," she called." I am going to put on the music of Berlioz; Harold in Italy. I have the Berlin Philharmonic playing it and the solo playing of the viola is incredibly romantic."

The music suffused her. She sipped at her champagne while she completed the final preparations. An evening of passion was alien to her; tonight she would be naked with a man! All those years of chastity coming to culmination with an amazing and lasting conclusion. She could not afford to be gauche; sophistication had always been the key to her life, the glittering society, presidential banquets which she had attended but had never been part of. Considered the equal of the best minds in France, but nobody had ever really known her. Her secrets and ambitions were her own, to share with no one. That would have always been the case, as she had almost given up hopes of meeting the right man.

Back in the kitchen, the air was filled with the smells of cooking. It was warm and cosy. From the cupboard she took out two china coffee cups and saucers. They were exquisite. One was etched in red, depicting a fiery dragon, the other etched with a petite lady in a blue kimono. From her dressing-gown pocket she took the white sachet and opened it, pouring the fine white powder into the cup with the fiery dragon.

"There, Michael," she murmured. "There is my aphrodisiac, so I can perform on you!"

With that, picking up two glasses and the champagne bottle, she went to the bathroom. He was lying in the bath, eyes closed; she watched him for a moment and then put the champagne bottle down on the floor with the glasses. Shrugging off her dressing gown and the negligee, she bent down and filled the two glasses with champagne. Standing and dipping her finger in one of the champagne glasses, she shook the drops over his face. He opened his eyes and saw her standing there; black stockings and suspender belt, her legs slightly open, her pubic hair damp and dark round her sex. Handing a glass to Michael, again with her fingers dipping into his Champagne, she allowed the drops to dribble over her nipples; then she leaned over and shook her breast so that the surplus fell on him. Putting her hand in the water she closed it around his penis and felt the blood throbbing as he became excited.

The strains of the viola wafted through from the lounge. She held him for a minute and smiled at him.

"That's your five-minutes of passion, Michael my man; you have only a few minutes to be ready before I serve."

Topping up his glass, again she shook her breasts at him and then put on the negligee, leaving the dressing gown on the floor.

Back in the kitchen the jellied dish of truffles and langoustines sat, ready to be served. He came in and she refilled his glass and drew close to him.

"The dressing gown suits you; you should have been a girl! We can sit down now and enjoy the food; let's eat."

He felt relaxed but overwhelmed. Never had he imagined a reception like this.

Such a beautiful lady, evidently ready to make love but with her own particular sophistication.

"Now, eat!" she commanded. "Truffles and langoustines with a special wine from the high Pyrenees."

The wine was incredible. It was ice cold, but in the mouth it mellowed with a marvellous fruity aftertaste. They took a long time over the starter and contemplated each other as they finished the wine.

"Now for the *pierce de résistance*, the Beef Wellington *en-croute* with a dressing made of crushed walnuts."

The meat was rare, the pastry crusty; the potatoes providing a perfect complement. The side salad with a cool lemon dressing was there to refresh the palate.

"Wellington's favourite meal whilst in Brussels, as he contemplated his Waterloo. You know they lived like kings right up to the start of the battle, which lasted only a day. The carnage was dreadful; only he could have defeated Napoleon. He was all over the field of battle, bullets all around him, flashing sabres, encouraging his Horse Guards, the Grenadiers, his foot soldiers, and coming out completely unscathed as others of high rank fell about him."

Valerie poured the Hospice de Beaune. They raised their glasses. He knew it must have cost a fortune. They sipped together, rolling the liquid round their tongues, masticating it with the blood of the beef and having that terrific aftertaste left in their mouths. He had not noticed that her intake was smaller than his. Finally the beef was finished, and she brought in the Pavlova.

"You will only need a little of this, just to sweeten the palate to enjoy the second bottle of the Beaune."

Her words were true. She leaned over and poured another glass of wine for him. Her negligee gaped open and her breasts hung down. He took them in his hands and kissed each nipple.

"*Ma Cherie, plus tard*, now you must talk to me while the coffee percolates and we have the Armagnac. Obviously I know about you and you realize that here you are safe from anyone, providing you do not leave the cottage. I know what you have gone through, shall we say, some sort of development; you must be a very clever man."

Then he recounted to her, how it happened, the opportunity with Jan, and no second thoughts, he had just struck at her. He told her how he knew nothing, not listening to news, or reading a newspaper, completely ignorant of where the authorities were in the hunt for him.

"I am not going to enlighten you," she said. "It is immaterial."

Continuing with his narrative he told her of his journey, the opportunities, and the assignations. She listened without a word, drawing her chair alongside and lightly holding him as he grew hard in her hand. The negligee had fallen away and she was exposed. He gently caressed her pubic hair. She took out of the cupboard two squat glasses of unusual design and poured the Armagnac.

"To us, Michael. Let this night be special to both of us! If we ever manage to wake up, we will talk about our future plans tomorrow."

Together they raised their glasses and toasted each other. She rose and poured the coffee, passing the cup with the dragon on it over to him. The coffee was Colombian, dark and mellow. It finished the evening; for a few moments, with solemn eyes, they looked at each other.

"Come, leave everything; we will clear up it in the morning. Enough dallying, take the champagne glasses and another of the cold bottles in the 'fridge. Hurry up; I am burning for you; you are my first and last man."

He could not believe what he was hearing! Was it true? He felt heady; he looked at her, smiling; she dropped her negligee and was looking at him, her breasts heaving, her legs apart, one hand stroking the moist lips.

"Come," she said. "You should be doing this."

With that she went down the stairs to the cellar bedroom. He followed, precariously balancing the bottle of champagne and the glasses. He looked at her on the bed, her legs stretched out, her sex moist and open, the pubic hair glistening. She was trembling and feverishly stroking a breast with one hand, the other held out for a glass of champagne.

"Quick, put on the Berlioz. The Symphony Fantastique. It is by the side of the stereo. I have a special surprise for you when we get to a certain part of the Symphony; as the English say, it will blow your head off."

The soothing music of the strings filled the bedroom, the Adagio depicting the idyllic scenes of the French countryside. He stripped off the dressing gown and lay beside her. She was relaxed, not touching him, her legs open, a half smile on her face.

"You have fifteen minutes to arouse me as the Adagio plays; then you get your special surprise, but first pour the rest of the champagne."

He did so and she raised her shoulders to take the glass. Her hair hung across her eyes, her demeanour now of a wanton and voluptuous nature; she dipped her fingers in the champagne and then stroked her body, her breasts and the lower regions of her stomach.

"Now kiss it off me," she commanded.

He did so as the music swelled. It was idyllic. Making no move to touch him, intent on the music, her body was firm and pulsing, her breasts heavy, the nipples engorged, beads of perspiration covering the sensuous skin. His heart was beating rapidly as her body arched against him. He felt the change of the music as the 'March to the Scaffold' brought grimness to the room.

Without any warning, his body went into a spasm! He felt disembowelled, and with an effort he eased himself on top of her. It was too much for him. His legs felt leaden, his arms heavy. It must be retarded exhaustion, he thought. For the first time his brain was allowing the body to relax on top of this beautiful woman; he felt her caressing his back. Suddenly he stiffened. He could not move his legs. His arms were numb and his head was heavy.

He tried to move but it was impossible. Yet he was fully conscious. He was paralysed! It must be a stroke, he thought, or something to do with a delayed reaction that was affecting his body but not his mind. All he could do was to lie heavily on top of her. The music was now strident. It terrified him. The Cornet, the Trumpet and a French horn, and the booming of the Bass Trombones over-whelming the Strings, were sending out a message of doom.

She, with an effort, sidled out from underneath him and knelt on the bed, her body glistening. He smelt the perfume as she sprayed herself with more perfume and deodorant. He heard the hiss of the bottles.

She caressed his back and stroked his hair.

"Michael, you are temporary paralysed, it's the effect of Curare distillation you had in your coffee. You can see and hear but you cannot move. Now you are mine! I can do what I like with you."

His mind was working overtime. What would he feel like when he regained his limbs? Maybe she was a sado-masochistic and this is how she got her kicks.

"No Michael, I can read your thoughts; this is not for me; your turpitude is unbelievable, base and arrogant."

He heard a click; her voice came again.

"I have in my hand a small automatic pistol. For your technical mind, it is loaded with six millimetre soft point bullets. They tend to make a mess of carti-lage and bone. You will feel the effects of all six. That is the number of people you murdered."

She paused for a moment.

"I am stroking your back with the barrel of my pistol. If I had you arrested, you would be tried, found guilty, and then they would find you a comfortable cell, or a hospital bed. You would not suffer anything. This way, after fifteen minutes, you will feel pain, terrible pain; it will last until you bleed to death. I will not be able to help. I will be dead, also; my life has been lived only for this; to meet a murderer under the right circumstances and to be able to execute him."

With that she stopped speaking. The music had gone into a dirge as the victim mounted the scaffold.

"Ah, the right time. The first is for Dr Jan! The pistol is at the base of your spine; the bullet will paralyze you permanently."

He heard the crack. The force of the bullet jolted his body. He felt nothing; the tears welled up in his eyes.

Her voice came to him again.

"The second and third will be in the back of your knees. Your kneecaps will shatter. This is for Alison and Cathy."

Placing the gun at the back of his left kneecap, she pulled the trigger. The gun had little recoil. He heard only the sharp crack. Impassively, she placed the pistol at the back of his right kneecap and fired. Once more he heard the detonation, but his mind could not focus any more. Again she spoke.

"The two climbers that you killed were Roderick and Alicia. The poor girl died of dreadful injuries due to the fall. Roderick suffered in a part coma, for long hours; no one knows how much he suffered. Their two bullets will smash and dislocate your shoulder blades."

Again he heard the two reports.

"I have one bullet left! This is not for me; it is for Patricia. You went to her for sex, violating her trust and taking her life. It is only fitting that you should be rewarded in a special way. One up the arse, to use a vulgar expression."

She gently parted the cheeks of his cleft and inserted the gun. He heard the report and the clatter on the tiles as she threw the gun away.

"There Michael, it is done! My twenty-eight years of agony and waiting is over. Yours is about to begin! I have no idea what damage I have done or how long it will take you to die. Your agony will be intense, that I know. You will scream for hours and no one will hear you. The body fluids will give way and that wonderful dinner will congeal around you. If Doctor Jan could have been here she would be able to tell you exactly; but I can't. But I can say goodbye to you now."

With a grimace of distaste, she picked up the negligee and tore it into pieces and stuffed it round his body; similarly with the stockings and suspender belt. After locking her door top and bottom, sadly she climbed the stairs and went into the bathroom. She turned the hot tap full on and emptied all her special shampoos into the water; the bathroom was heady with the heavy smell of perfume.

While the bath was filling she went down into the cellar again and buried the bedroom keys in one of the open bags of cement. A quick look in her toolbox, and she found what she was looking for; then back to the bathroom. She went in and locked the door behind her. The water was very hot; she waited a few minutes with the cold tap running to cool it a little, and then climbed into the bath. The packet from the toolbox she had balanced on the rim of the bath. It took ten-minutes of rubbing and scrubbing with a loofah before she was satisfied that all traces of the man had been washed off her body. Her skin was beetroot red and she felt exhausted and languorous. Taking the packet from the rim, she opened it. The knife was a retractable one with a gleaming blade and a half triangular point. She pushed it out to half its extent, and then gingerly sinking down into the bath, she waited until she felt relaxed and lethargic. Stretching out her left hand, palm upwards, she drew the knife across her wrist, severing the artery; quickly transferring the knife to her bloodied hand, then stretching out her right hand, she repeated the procedure; again the artery was severed. Dropping the knife on the floor, she sank down into the bath and watched the water run red before losing consciousness. The blood continued to pump out of her wrists until there was no more and she was no more.

Down in the cellar bedroom, Michael's screams were demonic. They rang hollowly around the room as the drug wore off and the pain came. He could not move. He was in unspeakable agony. But there was no one to hear him or help him.

CHAPTER 31

▼

EPILOGUE: WEDNESDAY 18TH JULY. TOULOUSE.

Robin and Henri had spent a quiet night in the hotel lounge, swapping stories and generally feeling frustrated.

The next morning found them in the conference room at the Police Judicaire. Pierre de Grun and Roger Desormiére were there.

A registered envelope lay on the table; de Grune picked it up and carefully slit it open with his pocket knife.

"It's okay," he murmured. "It has been scanned."

He withdrew another envelope and a sheet of folded paper. It was a map; hand drawn, showing her retreat up in the mountains.

"Obviously, we are meant to go there."

He opened the other envelope.

"It is French. I will translate as I read."

His eyes quickly perused the note. His eyes widened and the colour drained out of his face. When he spoke, he choked on the words.

"*My dear colleague; when you read this letter, I will be no more. Unlike Seneca's wife there will be no one to bind up my wounds.*"

"My God!" said the Director. "She's cut her wrists."

He continued: "*For twenty odd years, I have wanted to write this letter. As a little girl of eight, I was in a boarding school, a convent near Paris. My parents lived near*

Lyon, in a small village called St Jean de Bourne. One night two men broke into the house; they raped and killed my mother, father and big sister. They were never caught; the pathologist determined it was two men by the semen liberally sprayed on the bodies.

"I lived with my aunt in the city of Limoges and was formally adopted. I learnt to live with my hatred of men, to mask it. It was only revenge that led me to be a brilliant scholar of Jurisprudence. It was the same motive which made me implacable in hunting down villains. You always remarked on my ability to be dispassionate about my work, but all the time under my calmness and serenity lurked an obsession to exact revenge. Understand me, not to manufacture it or search for it, but for the opportunity to be presented naturally. I had studied men for a long time, and I always knew one day the right man would come along. Time meant nothing; the hatred within me would keep me going for the rest of my life.

"The revenge had to be a retribution for the murder of women; the killer I knew as Michael fitted the criteria. I did not know he was a killer, I just felt something; most probably the attraction was for him at first, but there was a flaw. As we walked together up the hill, my inner being knew he was not what he seemed to be. A Jekyll and Hyde split personality. As you are aware, the English Inspector met me before we had finished 'the way' and confirmed my suspicions. It gave me a thrill; I knew I had my man.

"A place of retreat had long been prepared; ultimately, for this very purpose; this was to be his escape. I had his confidence, and I would entertain him; the best wines, food of the Gods, Coffee with cream, and flaunt my body before him in the perverted language that he would understand. 'Butter in a Lordly Dish.' But no mallet and tent peg. I would have to content myself with six millimetre soft point bullets. Six of them, one for each murder; with an unusual gun for an execution.

"He would still be in pain long after I had peacefully expired. Valerie."

"Get the helicopter, quick!" Roger Desormiére rushed out. He heard the director shout, "Do not say a word to anybody."

Turning to Valerie's staff who had quietly entered the room, he embraced them, tears in is eyes.

"Go home, quietly and silently. We will come and see you after we have found this cottage. Please remember, you are bound to secrecy; not a word to anyone."

Roger came back, remarking the helicopter was on its way.

"Come Roger, Robin, and Henri, my good friends; the sooner we are with her the better."

Within minutes they were in the air. The navigator took the map and plotted the co-ordinates on his screen.

"Twenty minutes, Sir."

"Good; have you got a compressed air ram on board?"

"Yes, Sir"

"Good. We will need that to break down the door."

The mountains loomed before them. The helicopter dropped height and followed the course of the Dordogne River up towards its source. After circling, the pilot spotted the grey-slated roof of a building hidden in the fold of the mountain.

"There it is, Sir. I will land in the yard."

The pilot put the helicopter down in one fluid movement.

The first door they smashed open was the barn. Two cars were there, drawn up side by side.

"Right," said the director, "that one is Valerie's and the other is no doubt the Peugeot you have been looking for. Inspector Duval, this is now a police matter. Call your colleagues in Limoges. They already know the circumstances. The helicopter will be there in ten minutes. We need a forensic team here and the pathologist."

They waited in the yard, sombre and not speaking as the pilot called up a second helicopter. The navigator distributed cups of black coffee which they sipped at, until the second craft arrived.

"Okay, we go in."

It took three operations of the ram to break the locks and the bolts on the door. They went in through a corridor and into the lounge. The remains of a meal lay congealing on the table, the empty bottles on the worktop.

"A cosy meal for two," murmured Robin.

The director looked at him, grim faced, and shook his head.

"There is nothing facetious here, Inspector. It appears I have lost a brilliant colleague and a very dear friend."

Robin followed the director down to the other rooms, feeling chastened. They broke into the bathroom. A Stanley knife lay on the floor. They could see the bloodstains around it. Valerie lay in the bath; the water was opaque with a reddish brownish hue. Her head was back and her eyes were closed. The bathroom was cold. Her face was white as the blood had drained away in the hot water; but her face gave a comfort that she had passed away peacefully.

They went down a flight of stairs and came to a locked door. Henri retrieved the ram and used it once more. The door flew open and the smell of death permeated the room. Henri took one look and gulped. He hurriedly blocked the shattered door with his body.

"Steel yourself to look," he said, "but do not enter." He stumbled over his words to the director: "It's…its…horror incarnate."

The director and Robin, with hands in their coat pocket, took a step forward so they had a view of the bedroom. The forensic team, now in full sterilized kit, stood by. They looked at a naked body. The blood had mixed with other body fluids and waste. The smell was appalling, the air pungent.

The director gazed on this thing that was once a man.

"Never have I seen anything like this before. The poor devil died in agony, I wonder how many hours? Eventually we shall know. It was a cold-blooded execution! What a hate Valerie must have been hiding in her heart. Completely implacable in her resolve to exact her revenge on a man. One could never imagine that lady could be so merciless. The gun is on the floor! It looks like a Biretta."

Barbara went with Millie to see the body before it was cremated. She identified it as that of her husband. It was agreed that the ashes would be dumped at sea, no ceremony. She said goodbye to Millie, and a month later moved back to Ireland, a little house in Connemara.

Robin was at the cremation too, with Henri Duval. Afterwards they met in the Director's room. They discussed the case and its outcome, and then the director thanked them both for their dedication. He then turned to Henri.

"Inspector Duval, Roger has now taken over Valerie's position, and we have the vacancy for a Magistrat Judicaire. I want you to take the post. You have all the qualifications."

Henri Duval was overwhelmed. He could only grasp the director's hand and nod his acquiescence.

They made their farewells at the airport before boarding the Citation. Bob himself had flown out to take them home. Pierre de Grune put an arm round Bob's shoulder.

"Well, we never used the European arrest warrant, but what an exercise in European cooperation. The sadness and waste of good lives we will never get over. All we can do as an epithet to the lovely people who have died is to continue, body and soul, to catch villains. No doubt we will meet again. *Au Revoir.*"

Inspector Jaeger reflected over the past few weeks as he made out his final report. His protection of the family, and the way everyone had rallied round to look after Barbara. But now she was off to Ireland, a new life for her and the girls. He envied her; his mother was also Irish, and his father a Luxembourger Judge, now retired. He had taken them over to Koerich to see Josie, by invitation of course. His mother kept dropping hints for him to look after her; remarking she had not deserved to find herself under such trauma. It was his mother, still a practicing advocate, who had taken on board all of Barbara's legal affairs, including the eventual house sale in Luxembourg.

Together she, Barbara and the girls had flown to Shannon. They had taken a week to explore the western areas of Ireland, settling eventually for the area of Connemara, his mother's childhood home. They had found a house nestling between the sea and the mountains; all of them had fallen in love with it immediately. He had taken a week's leave to 'house-sit' the cat and the dog. It disturbed him, staying in that house with memories which had once been happy ones, and now were an anathema. He had something more than a regard for her, and his mother was always telling him that Irish girls made the best wives.

He sighed. It would take a long time for Barbara to recover from this saga of nightmare events. All he could do was to be there for her. He knew that he and his mother and father would be travelling across that sea quite frequently. Only time would heal and rekindle the trust for another man.

He would wait. There was the wedding of Robin to look forward to, and that of Moira and Patrick. Hopefully she would be there.

His heart warmed to the camaraderie which he now had with the British detectives. The ongoing fight against those who would wreck society could not be in better hands. He felt sure their association and friendship was going to be a long and fruitful one.

About the Author

The writer is an Electrical engineer, who came to Luxembourg to commission a major Industrial project in the South. For the past four years he has been a house husband, looking after wife and two girls, very busy on projects for the new house. Interests include Travel, Music, History, D.I.Y., and Writing. He is an inveterate walker and a one-time climber, potholer and caver.

A new interest—writing—has opened and *An Odyssey of Murder* is a first book, with three more in the pipeline.

0-595-27735-7

Printed in the United Kingdom
by Lightning Source UK Ltd.
107388UKS00003B/163-168